Memory of Memories

Serenity McLean

DOME TREE
Publishing

Published by Dome Tree Publishing (http://www.dometree.com)
ISBN 978-0-9937314-1-9

Author's Note

For now we see through a glass, darkly,
But then face to face.
Now I know in part,
But then shall I know even as also I am known.
No eye has seen, no ear has heard,
And no mind has imagined
What God has prepared
For those who love him.

1 Corinthians 13:12 (KJV), 2:9

Memory of Memories is a fictional view of the future of the reclaimed people – what life might be like in heaven. Although fictional, I used the Bible as the foundation, but there are many things we are not told. Since we do know it will be bigger and better than anything we see or imagine, we have permission to dream. Colossians 3:1–4 says, "Since you have been raised to new life with Christ, set your sights on the realities of heaven, where Christ sits in the place of honour at God's right hand. *Think about the things of heaven, not the things of earth.* For you died to this life, and your real life is hidden with Christ in God. And when Christ, who is your life, is revealed to the whole world, you will share in all His glory," (emphasis is mine).

It is the first book in a series called A Glass Darkly, focused on life during the different ages to come. There are three timelines in the book:

It's about a main character Lani, living over a thousand years into the future.

In a reminiscent mood, she thinks back to her first anniversary after arrival in heaven. The day before her first anniversary is the second timeline.

While preparing to deliver an honour story at her anniversary celebration, Lani searches for inspiration. She seeks out her favourite creative place and

3

spends much of the day reading the poems she wrote over the first year after arrival, remembering the events leading to the poem.

The third predominant timeline shares the significant events of her first year. Because Lani's memories wander as memories tend to do, each chapter opens with a timeline bar. This shows the first year memory timeline and highlights the time covered in the chapter.

Each chapter opens with a timeline to provide information on the date and time span of the chapter. It will look like this.

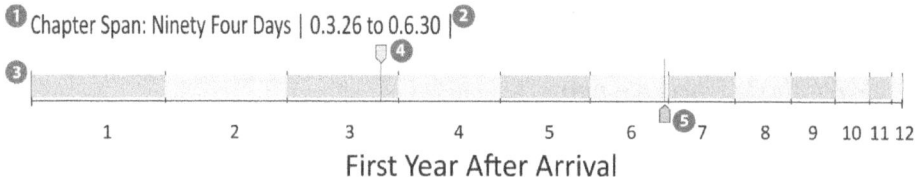

1 – This tells how many days pass over the chapter

2 – This is the range of dates. The first number indicates the year number since arrival. The second number indicates the month. And the third number indicates the day of the month.

3 – This blue banded bar is the first year after arrival. Twelve bands represent the twelve months on the timeline.

4 – This green marker shows the start of the time span on the timeline.

5 – This red marker shows the end of the time span on the timeline. If the span is quite short, the green start marker and the red end marker will be aligned on the day.

6 – If the chapter takes place either before or after the first year, you will see an arrow indicating the extension (see example below).

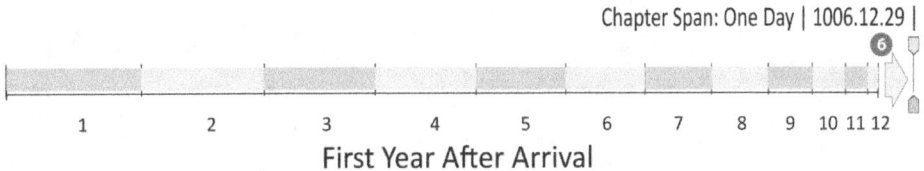

Chapter Span: One Day | 1006.12.29 |

1 2 3 4 5 6 7 8 9 10 11 12

First Year After Arrival

I've included a glossary of words and profiles of the main characters I used during my writing. If you like to read ahead, this might be an interesting section.

To paraphrase Oliver Wendell Holmes, a mind once stretched by thoughts of heaven will never be bound by earth again.

I hope you enjoy the read and dream big!

Credits

Thanks to the many who encouraged me along the way. I so appreciate my mom who puts up with the many hours of dreaming, imagining and writing. Thanks to Kelly Grant who graciously gave the first draft a read and provided great feedback and encouragement. Thanks to my Hawaiian pastor JD Farag, for being my online pastor, graciously consenting to being a character in the story and contributing a message to the readers. My great thanks to my editor Janet Dimond who both passed along improvement ideas and painstakingly pointed out all my errors. Biggest thanks to my Lord who gave wisdom and creativity.

Contents

1 | Memories

Chapter Span: One Day | 1006.12.29 |

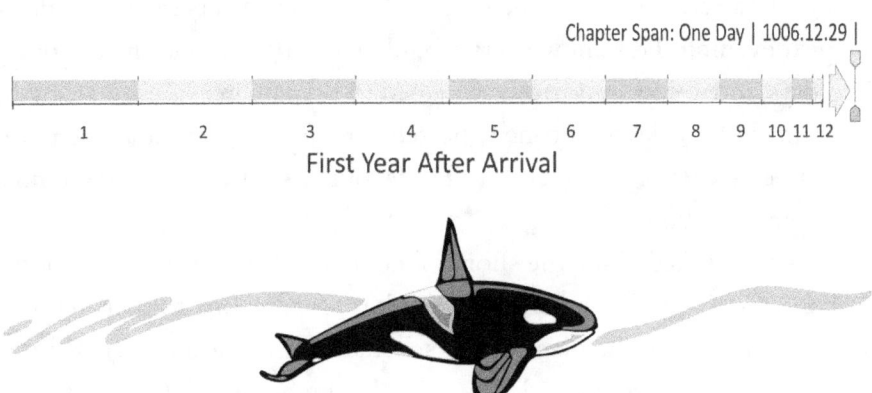

1   2   3   4   5   6   7   8   9   10 11 12

First Year After Arrival

The weaver's poem: Mental Life Inside

Body still and relaxed,
Mind wanders,

Disengaged from the now,
Lost in the past,
Dreams of the future.

Play in the warm waves of memories washing through the mind.
Caress the tumbling pebbles of thoughts, rounding them to smooth.
Ponder the ideas like clouds forming imagined shapes.

Source of future planning,
Vehicle for creativity,
Fountain of inspiration.

The Story Behind the Poem

With a contented sigh Lani wandered down to her beach. She looked forward to a relaxing day as she prepared for her anniversary celebrations the next evening. This anniversary would be the 1007th one since arriving. Two days, today and tomorrow, remained to prepare her honour story. As the weaver of stories, everyone expected something special and she never failed to deliver. She headed out to her favourite spot to spend some time in private reflection.

As she walked along the shore of her ocean bay, her mind wandered back in time to her first anniversary and her preparations for her first honour story. This time she planned her schedule to include a buffer of time to finalize her story and decided to relax, letting her mind dance with her memories.

She rounded a grove of palms and came to her favourite spot. After settling into the warm pink sand, she looked out over the quiet waters of her bay. This was her spot. Her inspiration point. She came to this place many, many times over the past thousand years when she wanted to think.

In the long past, before arriving here, she sought inspiration by retreating alone into nature. She always loved being outdoors and once arriving here, she found this spot. It became her private place where she slipped into her mind and sought innovative and creative ideas.

Today promised to be another beautiful day. The morning mist burned off and the sun provided a comfortable warmth. Lani closed her eyes, listening to the soft, rhythmic wash of the waves tumbling to the shore and the gentle breeze rustling the palm leaves behind her. Soon the waves, wind, and warmth receded into the silence of thought. Unaware of her present she became immersed in the past. In a reflective mood, she smiled. Today, she would play in her warm memories.

As one of the reclaimed, Lani arrived here a little over a thousand years ago. In preparing her first honour story, she thought about all the firsts. Her first year was filled with so much new. Upon arrival Lani received her inheritance, an oceanfront property where she regularly played with Celebration, a young orca who regularly visited. She stepped into leadership on an enormous scale with hundreds of unearthly beings who now worked for her. She learned the purpose for the creation of time and space and the cosmic love story threaded throughout. Inspired, she created a memorial to the love that reached back beyond time and space. And she turned her spectacular property into a mayan, a spring of refreshing. She lived in a new body that did not age. She carried her new name Lani, weaver of stories of what was, is and is yet to come, on extravagant identification made from the rarest, most precious gem in the universe, her thronestone.

It had been a whirlwind of experience. At the end of her first year here, she sat in this very spot seeking inspiration. All the Ahuvati, the reclaimed people, were preparing for their Haga'at feast, the anniversary of their arrival here and their spiritual marriage. Rather than a dignified, quiet, private event, she expected an enthusiastic, jubilant party. To toast their spiritual mate, the Ahuvati decided to talk about the great things that occurred in that first year. They wanted to honour their Beloved. They planned a days-long celebration interspersed with the Ahuvati storytelling of what had been and was, and finishing with their Beloved sharing information of their future.

Lani's mind rolled around for a moment, but quickly settled on the day she found the inspiration for her honour story. She wanted the story to be unique and to be words that would touch her Beloved's heart. She remembered she talked to others to find out what they would talk about, but found no spark of an idea for her story.

She came to this private beach spot to review the year through her weaver's poems, to let her memories wash through her mind, to caress her stories and thoughts, rounding them to smooth ideas. She pondered the ideas to let her honour story take shape. At this inspiration spot, a wisp of an idea around her weaver's poems formed and took shape into the perfect story.

Lani leaned back into the warm sand, and the memories of that day so long ago came flooding back in detail…

2 | First Year Retrospective

Chapter Span: One Day | 0.12.30 |

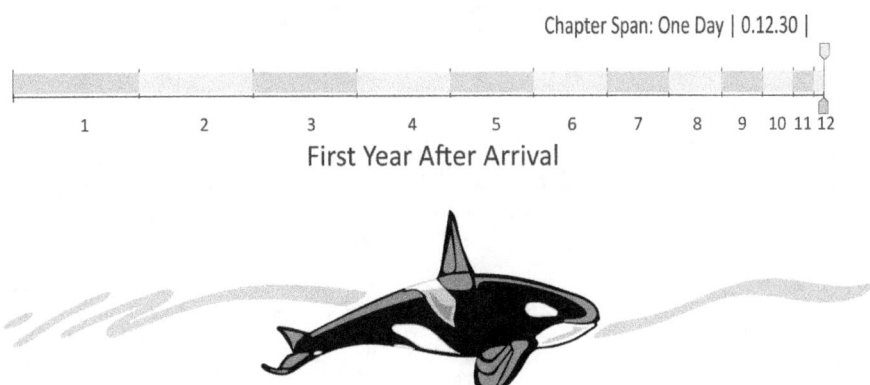

First Year After Arrival

Lani walked along her beach some distance from the entry to her gardens. She sought out her private spot, her inspiration point to pull together her honour story. The anniversary celebration started this evening and she still remained unsettled on a story. She thought a lot about what to say, but had yet to land on the right thing. She hoped by rumbling through her weaver's poems and letting the stories tumble around her mind like pebbles on the shore, one would emerge as the polished story she could share.

She sat down on the warm pink sand. After taking a moment to look out over the water and waves in the bay, she opened her collection of poems. Lani marked all the significant events or experiences she enjoyed by capturing her thoughts in the form of a poem. She needed to consider these special events. She sensed the inspiration for her honour story would come from these experiences, and she came to her favourite spot to commit the time to really contemplate the story behind some of the significant poems.

3 | Ocean's Celebration

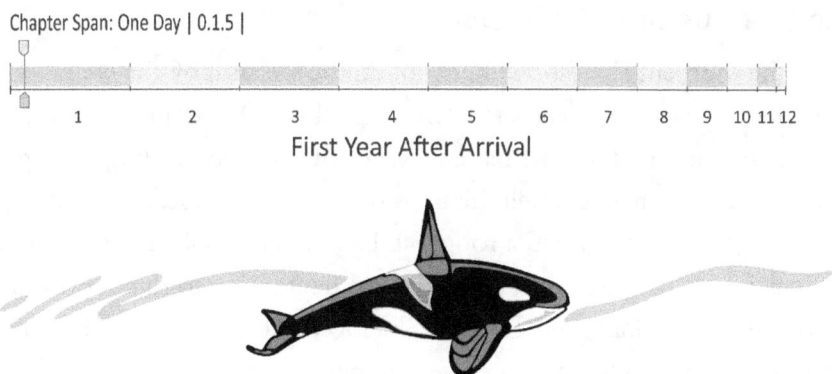

First Year After Arrival

Lani opened a tablet-like diary in which she recorded her thoughts, her weaver's poems. It structured her poems into a navigable timeline. She turned to an early poem she entitled "Ocean's Celebration," of the first time swimming in this ocean just days after arriving here.

The weaver's poem: Ocean's Celebration

I celebrate in the ocean,
I dance in joy.
I sing in delight.
I laugh in paradise.
Celebrate life.

Lani read the date and poem and smiled. In the long past she hadn't considered herself a writer or storyteller. In fact, she never kept a journal or diary, but in her first year here, she found herself writing reflective thoughts about various events. She wrote as she thought, conceptual snippets of ideas and feelings rather than structured sentences.

Lani wrote many of these mental reflections on remembrance stones and placed them throughout her gardens. As friends came to visit, they became known as weaver's poems.

The Story Behind the Poem

From the moment she dipped her foot in, the warmth of the water enveloped her in peace. She was totally enraptured with the depth and all-encompassing peace. It almost felt like waves of vibration rolling through her. She could taste and smell the harmony. It was intoxicatingly sweet, but more than sweet. It had a robust fullness in taste and smell. It was an internal wealth of bliss. She slipped in and floated out to the depths of the bay, gently rocking in the waves. She loved the sensation of floating. It reminded her of a life-changing event in her long past.

While lost in her attempt to put to words the sensation of this peace, she sensed another's presence. Quietly, gradually, she became aware of more than one. No, it was many. She knew "they" were a part of this peace. Almost timidly, they approached. They asked if they could visit with her. She lifted up her head, looked toward the beach to welcome her visitors only to find no one there. Yet still, they waited for an invitation. She focused on their presence to pinpoint where they were, and then she just knew. They weren't just a part of this peace – they were in the peace, in the water with her.

Lani felt struck with the difference of experience from her long past. In a far different world, in a far different ocean, she had been swimming in Hawaii and sensed something dark swimming beneath her. For a heart-seizing moment of sheer fear, she thought it was a shark. After all, a shark attacked just a week prior. She almost passed out from pure terror. She felt the blood drain from her face and could taste the rancid dread, a very different taste from the sweet peace of this new ocean. She recalled drumming up enough courage to look down into the water to face this dark shadow coming after her and to figure out what to do about it. Could she get to the shallow water? Barely able to breathe, she looked. Deep sigh. It turned out to be a sea turtle. Just a turtle.

Ah, that was long ago, in the time of long past. A year here, and the fear and rancid dread just seemed so foreign and not part of her world now. She no longer worried about life's sharks, or turtles for that matter. This place erased all emotional memory of the negative of her long past. Wiped away, never to be felt again.

Her first ocean experience here was definitely different. She felt immersed in peace and knew these visitors existed as a part of this peace. With a broadening smile, in anticipation of something wonderful, Lani looked into the blue and saw a pod of enormous orcas waiting for permission to advance.

She stretched out her arms and they joyfully approached like giggling children. Excitement emanated from the group. They spun and danced with each other as though Lani's laughter, like music, inspired a beautiful ballet. Slowly the matriarch came in front and bowed her head. The group quieted down. Lani reached out to touch the matriarch. Low murmurs rippled through the group. The younger ones barely contained their excitement. Lani smiled and welcomed them. And then it became obvious what caused their excitement. A new baby girl swam among them and they wanted Lani's blessing on their young one. Now part of her job, the ritual of naming and blessing animals went back to Adam. Lani called the wee one to her. Wee one! It was at least four times her height in length. Hesitantly, the baby approached. Lani spoke to her, welcomed her into her family. Lani placed her hand on the baby's head and offered a blessing. "May Yehovah smile on you and be gracious to you. May you have a happy life. May you take joy in flying through the waves, and dance with grace. May you bring happiness to your family." Then she named her Celebration. After all, the name is the nature. The group erupted in a cacophony of calls, announcing their baby girl's new name to other pods miles away.

Lani thought about her sweet Celebration. Since then, this pod visited just about every time Lani came to the water, and Celebration regularly came to her bedroom window for a morning greeting. She grew quite a bit over this past year and despite her maturity, she still lived up to her name.

She always whistled and called in delight upon seeing Lani, telling every whale of her joy at having Lani's attention.

Lani cherished the story of meeting and naming Celebration, but as a personal story she felt it lacked the meaning she wanted. This was not to be her honour story.

4 | Finally Home

Chapter Span: One Day | 0.1.4 |

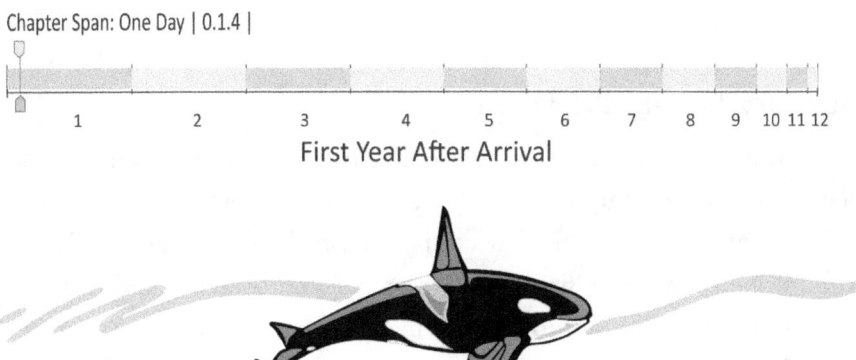

First Year After Arrival

Lani picked up her poems again and turned back a few to one entitled "Finally Home." She fingered the white stone around her neck with her new name Aha'La'anni, weaver of stories of what was, is and is yet to come, given to her exactly one year ago.

Time passed quickly and yet it filled with so many new and unusual experiences. Lani recalled her final years of the long past. She knew that one day she would leave her birth world to come here to her home, her inheritance. In the long past she spent most of her 55 years thinking about, longing for and waiting to move into her estate. Waiting for the time when she would be in the light and love of her Beloved.

The weaver's poem: Finally Home

Do not worry.
Trust me, my Beloved.
Consumed in my love
Over millennia,
I fashioned our paradise.
My gift to you, my heart.

Our eternal place
of peace and shelter,
of light and life.

The Story Behind the Poem

The arrival had been so exciting for everyone. They enjoyed a magnificent celebration feast lasting for several days. In the twinkling of an eye, millions arrived in the Majestic City courtyard, breaking through the door to eternity. She spent these first few days of her immortal life in the company of her mother, her grandmother and many of her ancestors. On arrival at the courtyard, she fell to her knees in awe of the glory around her. At the sound of her Beloved's voice, she wept at the enveloping love, so much more tangible than she'd ever experienced.

Despite being surrounded by more people than she could number, she found her saved loved ones and ancestors of the past. She found her mom already with her grandmother, a woman who had died when she was very young. She fell into their warm and welcoming arms, now exploding with an overwhelming joy of reunion. To think she would spend eternity with a long line of faithful women! With tears of joy, a paradox of peace and excitement, they headed to the feast together.

When the Haga'at feast finally broke up, everyone travelled in LAT buses (low altitude transport buses) to their inherited property. These vehicles operated without a driver, directed by thought programming. The bus Lani was on flew several hundred feet above the land, giving a good view across a distance, moving rapidly, yet silently.

Lani sat in the bus with a few dozen others headed for their properties on a beautiful coastal island. She met four of her bus companions on arrival and as neighbours, they would become close friends. As they approached the island, they dropped in altitude to just inches above the beach.

The island, a long strip of land varying from 2 to 10 miles wide, ran a couple of miles off the west mainland coast. The enormous properties spanned the entire width of the island.

As they travelled south along the beach, the group dwindled one by one. As they came to each estate, the group parted company with the owner, saying, "May the Light shine warm from within," as the person left to explore their new home. No good-byes existed here.

Lani's property stood as the last one at the south end of the island. Talking with her new neighbours and friends made the trip enjoyable, but she was now alone as her property was the southernmost lot.

As she approached the northern edge of her land, she heard some crashing through the undergrowth. Something was coming toward her at top speed. The bus slowed to a stop and Lani stood to get a better view.

Then Abbey, Lani's golden retriever from her life in the long past, from earth, burst through. She charged straight for Lani. She knocked her off her feet in her joy, crying, wagging furiously and licking Lani all over. Her reunion with Lani filled her heart with joy. And vice versa.

In the long past Lani owned several dogs over the years, but Abbey held a special place and truly owned Lani's heart. It took several minutes for Abbey's excitement and exuberance to pass and for her to comfortably settle beside Lani.

Together, Lani and Abbey continued on the bus along the beach of her property for at least 15 miles when the land came to a point and curved into a 4- or 5-mile-wide sheltered bay. At the far end of the bay the island ended in a spit of land lined with palm trees. Past this, a series of islands popped out of the ocean looking like huge stepping stones to the mainland.

About halfway down the bay, she could see an enormous mansion on the water that looked about 2000 feet long! It sprawled the length of six or seven football fields. Lani had never seen anything like this. It was more than she ever imagined.

Just before the mansion, two trees arched toward each other and joined into one trunk heading straight up, forming a stately entry with gardens beyond.

The bus rounded the point of land and turned north again to follow the shoreline around the bay. As the northern part of the bay opened up to her view, a marina came into sight. Passing the marina, Lani counted 10 Jet Ski-type watercraft, 18 speedboats and 30 sailboats of various sizes. It intrigued her to see no gasoline pumps or any other signs of fuel-like electricity to power batteries.

Further south, Lani looked out over the bay dotted with many small islands, shaped like tall pillars creating outstanding scenic views of land and sea. She could just get glimpses of the mainland because of the number of little islands in the northern part of the bay.

As they neared the two-tree entry, Lani saw an inlet of water and her enormous mansion beyond built on the water. A bridge spanned a river leading to a path heading southwest underneath the arch of the trees. She presumed this was the land path to her mansion.

Lani and Abbey left the transport and entered under the two-tree arch. Around the base of the two trees she saw masses of knee-high plants with deep blue-black, leathery leaves. A mist or cloud formed above each plant that radiated bright white light. Although not attached to the plants in any way, this mist seemed an integral part of the plant. Intrigued, Lani leaned over the plants and waved her hands through the mist, but the light or mist did not move or scatter.

Walking farther down the path, there were banks of bushes with three distinct bands of coloured leaves – dark blue at the base, medium blue in the middle and light blue at the top. The translucent long, thin leaves undulated in the breeze like waves.

Everywhere she looked she saw stunning, vibrant colour. Even the air was vibrant. No, not vibrant exactly, but Lani realized the garden exuded a whispering music. It sang to her! The garden literally hummed an invitation to her to wander through.

From these tri-blue bushes, the path rose up a hill covered in low green ground cover. These plants formed mounds of green ranging from dark olive to bright lime. In sections these plants sprouted tall stocks topped with a pom-pom of seeds. It looked like a miniature landscape, like looking out of an airplane at rolling hills and trees below. Lani slowly turned, gazing over the entire garden, and sensed something of great significance here.

She continued up the hill where the land levelled out. Plants with abundant velvety black leaves and a profusion of tiny white flowers throughout covered the flat land. As the leaves rustled in the breeze, the flowers seemed to twinkle. A well-formed, round mist-cloud of yellow light floated above the plants on the right, and on the left a smaller round mist of dim white light.

Lani made her way past the twinkling flowers. The path curled and twined among sea blue-green bushes. Drifts of flowers almost dripped off stretched branches. The flowers acted like weather vanes, moving to always face the breeze. Each flower displayed a unique mix of bright colours. Tall blue bunches of grass with each blade terminating in a wide flat section grew dispersed among the flowers. When the wind blew across, these flat ends rose up like kites in the breeze.

Winding around the path, the next section appeared quite different. Round plants covered in short hairs rolled about. The roots looked like fur in tones of brown, some with spots, some with stripes and some a solid shade. In a breeze, the plants moved like a herd across the African savannah. These plants didn't flower at all. Their beauty expressed in design, each plant having a unique pattern and colour. Young plants, miniatures of the mature ones, tumbled about, scattered among the larger ones.

At the end of this section rose a huge tree, absolutely glorious in appearance. Its branches stretched out back over the path Lani had come in on. Turning back to follow the branches, she could see they spanned back over the rolling herds of plants, and over the sea-blue plants with weather vane flowers and grass. Looking back over the plants and down the hill, Lani had never seen anything like this, and again sensed something more than just an ordinary garden.

Turning back to look at the big tree, its trunk formed from many strands of differing colours of light pink, yellow, olive and various shades of brown. These strands turned into the branches that formed the canopy sheltering the garden. To the left, Lani could see the shoreline followed the length of this garden, and she looked out over the inlet of the ocean and her mansion. She was getting closer.

South of the canopy tree, Lani noticed something that tweaked her curiosity. The land dipped into a huge section void of plants for several thousand feet east to west, and equally deep. Beyond grew an even larger forested area. She wondered about the reason for an entire section with no plants. She rounded the trunk of the canopy tree and looked out over the whole area of nothing except for several benches for groups of friends to sit.

As she considered the possibilities of why a vacant area existed in the middle of her garden, a movement above her head caught her eye. She looked up and gasped. The air filled with floating plants. They looked like jellyfish with their roots dangling in the air. They gently moved about in the breeze, gradually rising up in the warmth of the sun, then they exhaled and slowly dipped back down above her.

Large flat orange leaves shaped like a bowl and covered in silver hairs composed the body of the plants. Inside the bowl a translucent burnt orange balloon-like bulb swelled from the warmth of the sun. When full of air it would let out a sigh, releasing air full of fragrance. From the base of the bowl came red and purple fernlike roots waving in the air. The shades of orange and red dazzled like jewels against the backdrop of the sky and reminded her of a county fair ride of bejewelled carousel horses rising up and down.

Lani smiled to herself when she thought about what this Carousel Garden had become. She paused for a moment, then let the memories of her tour roll on.

Intrigued by the gardens, Lani wondered what other spectacular sights lay ahead and rather than turning to her mansion, she continued south through the Carousel Garden to a treed area. It appeared about 7,000 ft. wide and maybe 5,000 ft. long. Looking east, Lani could see this treed area continued all the way to the shoreline along the southern end of the island. She slowly turned her gaze from the east to south and then west. This forest filled the entire base of the island.

Lani studied the trees a bit closer. Really, it was one trunk in the middle with huge branches reaching out laterally in every direction. To support the weight of the branches, the tree dropped aerial prop branches to the ground that would sprout roots, much like the banyan trees of India. Initially she mistook these props as trunks, but no, one tree spanned the entire area. The lateral nature of the tree formed a dome over the entire end of the island. Amazing.

Turning west away from her mansion, the Carousel Garden ran parallel to the dome tree and eventually gave way to another river that flowed from the middle of the island to the west shore of the ocean. Lani crossed the bridge to walk among tall fountain-shaped purple and silver palms. Alongside the path she spotted several baskets of gathered silver fruit from the palms. She picked up a few. The fuzzy fruit felt delicate like a peach, and smelled a bit like a mix of pineapple and coconut.

She continued walking with Abbey, looking for a bench to sit and enjoy them. As she walked along the path past different plants, flowers and trees, the whispering music changed. Always harmonious, each plant hummed its own music. Lani soon discovered around her mansion a wide and exotic variety of gardens, some of just trees, some of grasses, some filled with her favourite colours, and some filled with a riot of colours.

As she followed the path, it rounded a bend and the main track headed north. The palms became a manicured jungle garden like a well-tended botanical garden, but far more exotic. She chose a smaller alternate path that headed back east toward her mansion. Many days lay ahead for her to explore the other paths.

The easterly path took Lani back to the river and another bridge. On the other side of the bridge the path opened up to a huge field of waving, dancing, humming grass. More than just grass bending with the breeze, it moved in a creative and ever-changing complex pattern of blues and greens. She heard it humming a familiar song, but the movement totally mesmerized her. Lani walked down a ways into the grass and reached out to let the tips of the grass brush across her palm as the grass progressed through its pattern of movement. Lani stepped back to the path to watch it more closely. She realized the patterns were actually letters and words. She started to read the message. "Praise God from whom all blessings flow, praise Him all creatures here below, praise Him above…" Thomas Ken, 1674. It was the doxology she sang as a child.

In the long past, her parents attended a beautiful old cottage-town church constructed of polished wood on the ceiling, walls, floor and seats. The service always closed with the doxology. Lani loved her time at the cottage, loved the beauty of the old church and the way the music echoed through it. The doxology became one of her favourite church songs because of her happy memories. Lani felt her heart swell to think of the care and attention to detail to have this song as part of her estate. Yehovah lovingly created a unique place intentionally made just for her.

And then from the side of the field Lani caught sight of movement. She spotted a real beauty galloping through the field straight toward her. In the long past, Lani considered Gypsy Vanner horses with their extraordinary manes, tails and socks the most glamorous of all animals. Oh, those Vanners looked like an old miner's donkey compared to this exquisite horse. This one moved with grace and elegance. Perfection, gracefully drifting like a pure white cloud blowing across the sky of blue grass. Not a blemish anywhere. She offered him one of the fuzzy silver pineapple-coconut fruits. She could feel his heavy breathing on her hand as he carefully took the fruit.

So many times in the long past when she dreamed of her future horse, she thought about what she would name him. She laughed at the memory of sitting in the bathroom and seeing him in the abstract design on the floor tiles. Back then, she thought often about the moment of meeting him for real. In fact, she thought about it every time she looked at the bathroom tiles.

Now here she stood with her horse. "What will I call you?" All the names she considered in the long past just didn't seem to fit. After a moment she thought, He seems to air dance, and then she had it! She said it out loud. "Ario." He quietly blew his approval through his nostrils, skipped in a circle, kicking up his heels. "Ario it is. My beautiful air dancer. May you always dance like clouds across the sky." He came up and rested his head on her shoulder. She thought, in the long past, Hebrew and Arabic tradition prescribed a name that reflected the nature, characteristics or spirit of the person. That was why people did not take someone's name in vain as they would be speaking in a derogatory manner of the person's nature.

Lani thought about her own name change. In the long past her parents named her Grace. One year ago, when she came to her inheritance land, her Beloved gave her a beautiful necklace with a large white translucent stone far more valuable than a diamond as a symbol of His eternal commitment. It was made of the most precious and rare gemstone in the universe taken from underneath the throne of the great I AM, known as thronestone.

Lani pulled off her necklace to look at it again. All the surfaces were smooth, yet etched deep inside appeared words that could be seen from viewing it at different angles. One, an etching of her new love name Aha'La'anni given to her by her Beloved and used only by Him. Her new name meant my weaver of stories of what was, is and is yet to come. But everyone called her by a shortened version Lani, meaning both creative and weaver. Some called her Lani the creative and others called her Lani the weaver. Here, last names no longer existed. When formally addressing someone, people used their new name followed by its meaning.

Turning the stone slightly, Lani read, "To my Beloved from your eternal love and desire," followed by her title of the order of Melchizedek meaning she was a ruler and priest. Finally, she saw a couple of beautifully crafted images. One image of a waterside tree with long branches and many trunks filled the length of the thronestone. She remembered her surprise when she realized what this image was. And the final image of the moed (the celestial markers of time and appointments) could be viewed from both the side and the ends. This provided a 3-D view overlaid with the moed of the current position of the celestial markers. This was a universal timepiece as well as having her name and identification.

She received it as an intimately meaningful gift given in tender love. Made of thronestone specifically for her before time and space. It also acted as her identification and her pass into the Majestic City. She always wore her thronestone because it symbolized so much that was precious to her. She put it back around her neck and thought about her charming Ario.

After Lani spent a few minutes loving on Ario, he stretched his nose out to Abbey and they shyly greeted each other. Lani watched the two of them make some play moves with each other, one in dog language and one in horse language. Eventually, Ario wandered off, and Lani and Abbey turned to follow an eastward path along the ridge and back toward her mansion.

As they made their way toward her mansion, five more golden retrievers and a black lab came bounding toward her – all the dogs she had ever owned. At their death her Beloved brought them all here to await her arrival. The massive greeting involved lots of dog crying, licking and wagging tails. All vied for her attention. They enjoyed a gregarious, joyous reunion. Lani felt happy and contented to her core.

This place expressed itself in such abundance and overflowed with peace and joy. Overwhelmed, she struggled to take it all in.

When the dogs settled down, they walked together skirting the dancing grass by weaving through the unusual Entry Garden. Lani could just make out her mansion. Curiosity propelled her to cut through the Carousel Garden directly toward her mansion. Her home. It seemed so perfect among the gardens, so – living.

She laughed out loud remembering the moment she realized this was no ordinary structure. It was actually alive. No wonder this took so long to "build." It needed to grow and mature into a mansion!

Beyond the scale of a mansion, it stood as a stunning edifice, unlike anything she had seen in all the years of her life on earth. In the long past construction materials came from clay heated in a kiln, and lumber from trees cut down and milled. But not here. This house exuded life. Two thousand years ago her Beloved took seeds and planted a special garden then gave the command, "L'hi'im benah bahyith," meaning to life, grow to a mansion. Over the next two millennia, a select group of plants and trees grew into the structure of her home. Regularly, He visited to tend the plants as they slowly grew into her mansion. It amazed her to think Yehovah prepared this mansion specifically for her even before her birth. Rather than simply commanding it into instant being, He lovingly committed time and attention to give her something He grew just for her. It was like a bonsai on a large scale. She loved this living house, and in return it loved her and responded to her presence.

It grew out of an inlet of ocean water. The mansion actually stood over the ocean. While on the shoreline, Lani looked at the entry steps hovering just above the water. The water sparkled bright and clear, and she saw brilliant coloured schools of fish swimming out and back under her house. The blue-grey plants and trees that grew into her mansion were sort of like mangroves of the long past growing directly out of the water. The schools of fish made their home among the roots of the trees.

It was most unusual growth. Rather than the trees growing in round trunks, these trees grew into flat walls, several covered in vegetation like a vertical garden.

Nearby, Lani spotted several transport vehicles. One looked very sporty and probably could really rip across the skies. Another looked something like a motorcycle. Yet another one was larger and looked as though it would serve the purpose of utility vehicle, although with nice lines. All the vehicles were blue with her name on them like the tradition of painting the name of a boat on the transom. Intrigued, she noted the motorcycle and the Ferrari-like sporty one had a steering wheel of sorts, but the utility vehicle did not. Learning to drive appeared an exciting endeavour.

Looking back at her new home, Lani walked across the steps with Abbey right beside her and entered her living mansion. The other dogs, distracted by something in the gardens, stayed outside. In the long past Abbey always stuck close to Lani, and it seemed that would be the case here too.

On entering the mansion she noticed a type of crystal formed the floor – a crystal so pure it looked invisible. It felt like walking on water like Peter. The many schools of fish gathered about her feet and followed her through the house. When she looked directly at them, they spun, pirouetted and showed off their best moves. The more she laughed, the better they performed. She reached down and placed her hand on the floor. They wagged their tailfins and swam off. And off Abbey went after the fish. The fish intrigued her and it turned out they loved chasing each other around the first-floor rooms of the mansion. In time they developed a game of hide and seek.

Light glowed throughout her mansion without light fixtures. The light outside invaded all space, as though air and light were the same thing. Sunlight lit the world during the day and created shadows, but this invasive air-light added to the sunlight and eliminated all shadow, all darkness. When the sun set, this light remained.

Water ran in every room. Abundant, flowing rivers of life streamed through her mansion. It flowed up through the trees to the top floors and flowed into each room, sometimes as a waterfall, sometimes trickling along a wall of mossy plants, and sometimes wending its way as a brook quietly running its course. Lani cupped her hands to take a taste of cool, sweet and clean water. These channel trees, by nature, channelled water to heights above the land.

All water originated and flowed from the Majestic City into mighty rivers and into the ocean. No salt or waste contaminated the water, even the ocean, but crystal clear, pure life-giving water irrigated the entire planet. It watered the land as a daily mist. And this same water channelled up to her top floor, flowing through every room of her mansion. Lani, a water lover from birth, enjoyed the look, sound and smell of water. She cherished the marvellous gift of a water feature in every room.

And the furniture was amazing. While chairs and such that Lani was used to filled her mansion, some seating formed out of branches and cushioned with large leaves. When she sat down, the leaves moved to hold her in the air, kind of like a hammock rather than sitting directly on the branches. It felt so weird at first, but she often chose leaf floating for its unbelievable comfort. When Lani moved, the leaves shifted to buoy and cushion her. The normal furniture was not so normal either. It could be shaped and molded for comfort with each person.

Lani thought about the times her many friends visited during the evening calm, and all the fun they enjoyed in and around this house. Many times she spoke her thankfulness out loud and the room responded with a blue-green light and the smell of fresh rain. Even after a year, it remained her favourite smell. It lingered so long, as though her living home delighted in her appreciation for hours. The power of words, her words, still astounded her.

Her home, her gardens, her property, this world of living water, living air filled with power. All fabulous, but this would not be her honour story.

5 | Melchizedek

Chapter Span: One Day | 0.1.4 |

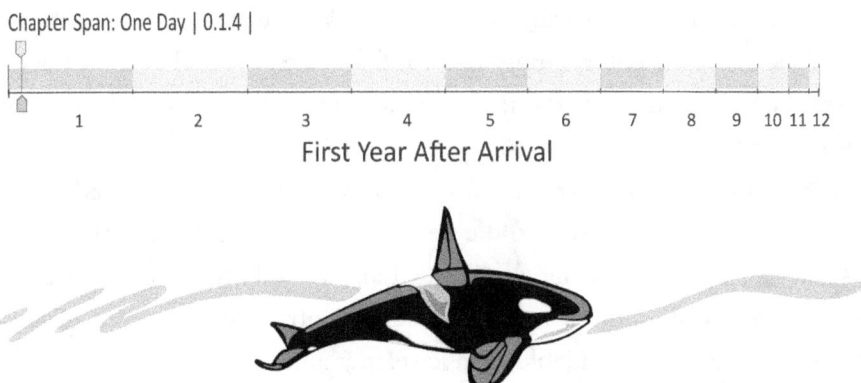

First Year After Arrival

Lani smiled in anticipation. She wrote the next poem in her diary when she first met her eh-bed. She settled in to read and recall the story behind it .

The weaver's poem: Ahuvati

Melchizedek,
I have become ruler and priest.

I am a safe harbour.
I am a chief.
I am a shelter.
I am a princess.

The Story Behind the Poem

As Lani explored her new mansion, she marvelled at the sheer size of it. What would she do with so much space?

She made her way through to the bay side. The first breathtaking room she explored spread open to the bay with no walls or obstruction other than an occasional tree trunk. A 30-ft. deep inlet of water invaded the room. Lani saw several sea turtles swimming in the inlet and sat on the edge, dangling her feet into the water for awhile to watch. Many of the turtles immediately surfaced to visit. Looking around, Lani thought it would be great for entertaining with food service bars and seating for well over a hundred. She smiled – this was the best room and would easily be her favourite.

Standing up, Lani became curious as to what the other bayside rooms were like and made her way to the next room to the north. It jutted out at a 45-degree angle to the main building. Lani walked out to the outermost point of the room. She spotted the unusual Entry Garden to the left and the bay to the right. Moldable lounge seating and comfortable hammocks along with a small dining table decorated this far smaller room. Trying out one of the hammocks, Lani reconsidered. No. This would be her favourite room.

Lani then headed south back through the inlet and turtle room to the next room on the other side, a rather large dining room with an unimpeded view of the bay. She smiled. "Rather large." This room easily stretched a few hundred feet long. *Funny*, she thought, *how quickly I became accustomed to the large scale of everything here.*

Continuing south, she entered a very intimate and casual dining room. While quite lovely, she passed directly through. Lani could see up ahead decking that stretched out into the bay and wanted to check it out.

She passed through a library and reading room and entered the living quarters. She headed directly toward the rooms at the far end on the bay side.

Stepping into the main bedroom suite she saw extravagance beyond anything she imagined. The bed was sink-into comfortable and positioned to watch the sunrise. The room opened to a deck out into the bay. A thatched roof covered the first half of the large deck and the far end remained uncovered and open to the sky. Luxuriant lounge chairs, hammocks, and an assortment of chairs that glided, rocked and swivelled covered the deck.

A set of stairs came off the side of the deck, extending down several feet to the water. Lani could go swimming every morning from her own bedroom and come back out up these stairs. Spectacular! She thought this might become her favourite room, and then laughed. All the rooms were perfect, beyond her greatest desires, and it would probably be hard to pick a favourite.

Inside her bedroom, a set of stairs led up to the second floor to an equally beautiful space totally open to the bay on three sides. There was a desk, shelves, closets, and comfortable chairs for reading and watching the bay. Another favourite place to spend time, she thought. Good thing she had all of eternity to enjoy her inheritance.

Every room included a viewing screen. She wondered what, if anything, was being broadcast or if it even worked that way here.

Another 20 bedroom suites filled the southern end of the mansion. Lani wandered through all of them, finding something special about each one .

While on the second floor, Lani wandered back north through several large, beautiful, but empty bayside rooms and wondered what these would be for. Entertaining, she supposed. She passed several sets of stairs and while she saw a third floor, Lani headed back downstairs. It was late afternoon and she wanted to find the kitchen to get something to drink and go settle in to explore the books in the library for a couple of hours. Then she wanted to watch the sun set and the changing colours of the sea and sky from her bedroom. She landed in another large room overlooking the dome tree and the Carousel Garden.

Lani briefly looked out to the ocean and thought. As she made friends and began visiting and working with others on projects, she found everyone had mansions with space for large gatherings. Evenings were often spent in commune with others, sometimes in small, intimate groups and sometimes in large parties. Everyone's mansion was unique and while she did enjoy spending time with others at their mansions and estates,

Lani loved her mansion and spent many, many hours in residence. And as it turned out, her estate would become a favourite spot for many, many others.

Standing there considering the size of her mansion, Lani heard a noise, a shuffling of sorts in the next room. Abbey returned from chasing the fish, so she knew there was someone or something else in her mansion. Since no fear existed here Lani wasn't concerned, just curious. She called out, but the only answer was more shuffling noises. Lani smiled. She sensed something quite shy behind all the shuffling, so decided to go to the other room and greet this visitor properly.

She entered the room to see a diminutive creature with head deeply bowed and eyes glancing up at her. This beautiful and delicate being gave the impression of a human butterfly. Big blue eyes and stiff blue-silver straight hair brushed up and back graced her elongated head. Delicate, butterfly-like wings, mostly purple and blue, slowly moved behind her. Bluish-purple skin covered her long, narrow human-like body. She walked on her toes as though her wings bore most of her weight. She carried herself with an air of sweetness and a desire to please. Her head bowed she quietly said, "I am your eh-bed, Aha'Kaiya," meaning I am your servant, my safe harbour.

Lani nodded to the creature, greeted her and asked, "What is your name?"

Shyly glancing up at Lani, the creature said, "Aha'Kaiya, I have no name. That is for you to give me. I am a mashqeh (cupbearer) and so just called mashqeh. Eh-bed were being prepared to be under the rule and reign of our masters, and so it would be appropriate for us to be named and blessed by our master."

Lani thought about what name would comfortably fit and please this delicate, cute creature. She seemed like a young, sweet girl, eager to please. She looked around the room. It was the kitchen and this creature was to be her cook. Honey was a fit, but not quite right. Nectar? That was it! "Okay, I name you Nectar, for you are sweet and you bring nourishment." Reaching out, Lani placed her hand on Nectar's head. "May you be an artisan with the seeds and fruit you prepare for me, my guests, the servants and pets. May you be honoured among your kind." At that, the wings started flapping in excitement like a puppy dog tail, flooding with red and orange colour. Lani smiled in delight at the sight of happiness displayed in flapping red-orange wings. Lani loved Nectar already and knew this would be a good relationship.

Since this was their first meeting, Nectar rather formally asked what Lani would like to eat that evening. Lani ate so well at the feast for the last several days that she wasn't very hungry. "Could I have something light? And please join me." Lani's exploration of her library and reading could wait. Nectar's head dropped in acknowledgment, but Lani could see a smile of pleasure, the flapping sped up and the wings shifted to yellow and orange. So adorable.

Nectar already knew what to prepare and it was ready to serve whenever Lani wanted. With a nod from Lani, Nectar led her to the small, informal dining room, presented the meal and waited for Lani to be seated before joining her.

They sat at a dining table for 12, and Lani positioned herself to look out over the bay, the Pillar Islands and out to the strait between island and mainland. She mentally sighed in contentment. She would dine in ocean breezes. They bowed together and Lani gave thanks for the bounty on the table, her gardens and mansion, and the gift of Nectar in her life.

Nectar served a selection of a few recipes for Lani to choose from. Each serving dish was beautiful in colour and presentation. The bowls looked like polished lapis lazuli, and the dishes in the dining set were in various shades of blue. Lani tried a sampling from each bowl. Each was exquisite in flavour and Lani complimented Nectar and asked, "What are these entrées made of?"

"Aha'Kaiya, this purple and orange one is a mix of two fruits from your garden, heated with the pollen from your carousel plants. This gold one is fruit from the bay out there," looking out at the ocean. "They grow underwater and when ripe, these fruits float up to the surface. This silver one is from the seeds from your silver palm trees. And this bread is made from the flour of nuts from the high hills."

Lani loved the bread. In the long past, she lived with gluten intolerance and avoided bread for many years. This tasted fantastic. Lani looked at Nectar and said, "You're a great cook and everything's delicious, Nectar." Then after a moment asked, "How old are you?" It was hard to tell looking at a creature that looked like a, butterfly and appeared to be like a young girl, yet seemed very competent in the kitchen.

"Aha'Kaiya, I was created a year ago specifically for you. Since my creation day, I have been taught about you and tutored in meal preparation for you."

"Do you have family? Brothers and sisters?"

"Aha'Kaiya, no. Eh-bed do not have family. Yehovah envisioned me while still unformed in the dirt of your estate. Yehovah formed me and commanded me to life. From my first breath my only desire is to serve and please you. My only thoughts focus on ensuring you and your guests are properly cared for and fed."

That gave Lani quite a bit to think about. She ruled over servants created specifically for her from the dirt of her inherited estate. And the single desire and delight of these beings was to serve her. This was another example of her Beloved's profound love for her and showed the value He had for her. It had not yet occurred to Lani that when Nectar said her single desire was to please Lani, it was at the exclusion of a desire for family and children.

In amazement Lani thought, *Her only desire is to please me, yet she just met me.* Lani asked, "Tell me, what do you know about me?"

"Aha'Kaiya, all mashqeh were told about our master's likes and preferences in food. And I knew you would have seven dogs here with you from your long past, and Abbey is your favourite. I know you were very creative and named a weaver of stories. I know your favourite colour is the cool blue of sky and the warm blue of the ocean, and yet you enjoy warm air and spicy hot food. I know your new friends are Honani, singer of songs, Kazhu, the reliable, Aymoon, the faithful, and Cheka, full of laughter that are and will be dear to you, but others will become your closest friends, and I have been informed of all of their food preferences."

Nectar bowed her head and said, "Aha'Kaiya, I met your dogs three days ago and can tell you are a good master. I know you have always been kind and thoughtful of those under your authority. I have eagerly awaited your arrival as I have loved you since my creation and I longed to fulfill my destiny as your eh-bed."

Lani thought about all Yehovah prepared just for her. The grass singing one of her favourite church songs, spectacular gardens, a mansion literally on the ocean with unbelievable rooms, good friends from the first moment here, the promise of close friends, sweet, loving servants, her mom was here and, of course, her dogs. It was all so perfect.

Lani always wondered if all those in heaven would know the time of arrival of the reclaimed, the redeemed, what were now called Ahuvati. With all the preparation necessary, she thought they must know when it was close at hand. Not the day and hour as that was known only by the Father. Lani asked, "When did you know the timing of my arrival?"

"Aha'Kaiya, we knew the preparations for your arrival were complete and a few days later we heard of the arrival of Ha'Ahuvati the moment you arrived. Excitement rippled through all the eh-bed. We knew we would meet you soon. We knew you would be at the Haga'at feast until today. Many of your servants worked on your estate for a long time now, tending animals and gardens. I was released to await you here at your mansion two days ago. I got busy gathering food and preparing for your arrival, and then I saw you coming along the beach. I watched you as you wandered through your gardens and my heart swelled with joy at finally being able to serve you. Thank you for my name and your blessing."

"You are welcome, Nectar," and they fell into a thoughtful silence .

So, many servants had been working here for a long time. Lani thought about that for a moment. Were they all like Nectar? She hadn't seen any in her wanderings, although the baskets of collected fruit evidenced the presence of labourers. After a few moments Lani asked, "How many other eh-bed work on the estate?"

"Aha'Kaiya, there are many, many servants. Over 300. I am the head of the mashqeh. You also have a head gardener, and a head herdsman who cares for your animals, a head of housekeeping, and one naqod servant who oversees all. Many eh-bed work under us."

"Where are they all? Are they here now?" Lani asked.

"Aha'Kaiya, yes, everyone lives here on your estate. Your head gardener, and the head one who tends your animals, and your head servant sit outside in your garden waiting to meet you. The others working under us will meet you tomorrow."

Lani smiled. "OK, I would like to meet them. Would you come with me, Nectar?" and Lani, Abbey and Nectar walked out the same door Lani entered. Across the steps over the water entry, Lani saw three creatures standing at the edge of the water, waiting to meet her. When they saw Lani coming, they knelt and bowed before her.

Looking at the three of them, a flash of familiarity triggered a vague memory from her long past. The memory passed as quickly as it arrived. She refocused on the creatures before her. The first one looked up from his bow with an impish grin. He had large eyes, pointed, long ears swept back, green hair that formed a mane around his neck and down his chest and around his hips. He had a strong set of wings, and a thick set of arms and hands, and lean, strong legs with a small wing off the back of each leg. His feet had toes like strong fingers and one like a thumb pointing back. Nectar said, "Aha'Kaiya, this is your gardener. He is a ganan. It is for you to provide a name."

Lani, smiling back at his impish grin, asked, "Tell me, what is your favourite part of the garden?"

"Aha'Qatsin, my chief, I love all of the garden, all of your estate, but I love flying to the tops of the trees to tend them and collect the harvest," the gardener said in a deep, resonant voice.

Lani was unsure about a name and took a deep breath. With her breath came inspiration. Her Beloved whispered in her mind. Lani said, "Okay, I will name you Gilad. It means happy or good gardener." Lani placed her hand on Gilad's head and based on the mental whisperings said, "May your gardens grow abundant with life and produce. May all who visit find the results of your labour beautiful and pleasing." Gilad was grinning from ear to ear.

Lani didn't know at the time the significance of blessing his labour as pleasing to all who visit. She would later realize how insightful and how meaningful to Lani's future that blessing would be. She thought a moment about how so many small seeds of something seemingly insignificant grew into something hugely significant and impactful. It occurred to her that maybe the concept of seed to fruition could be the foundation of her honour story. Tell about several seeds that burst forth into something big and meaningful, like the image of the dome tree on her thronestone, or the seeds of desire placed into the hearts of people at birth and left unfulfilled in life of the long past, or words of blessing and foresight spoken into a life. The idea intrigued Lani. She would tuck that as a possible approach to her story. For now, she continued to comb through for the gems that would be her honour story. Lani refocused on the story behind the Melchizedek poem.

"Aha'Qatsin, thank you for my name. I will do my utmost to fulfill it. I will ensure you enjoy my whistling, and you are pleased with the appearance of your gardens and they are a pleasure to your visitors. I am pleased to gather the produce for your table that brings life and energy to all." Lani smiled. She had not known that Gilad was a whistling worker, but her Beloved did. He now carried a perfect name.

Lani turned to the next being. He was short and stocky with short arms and big hands. His legs and feet were shaped like a cheetah. He kind of reminded Lani of a stocky troll or hobbit, but one who could run like the wind. He had a set of spiral horns like those of a ram, long white hair, bushy eyebrows, and a long Fu Manchu moustache flowing into a long, straight beard. He carried a flute-like instrument around his neck.

Abbey, quite enamoured with this being, circled, wildly wagged her tail and made play gestures. The creature lovingly petted Abbey, quietly spoke to her and gave a quick hand gesture. Abbey happily sat beside him, leaning in on his legs. Nectar said, "Aha'Kaiya, this boqer will be tending your animals. It is for you to provide a name."

He bowed deeply before Lani, saying, "Aha'Mo'ee, my shelter". Having seen how he handled Abbey, Lani suspected he was a being of few words. Looking at the pan-like instrument, Lani was curious. "Do you have a favourite tune you can play for me now?"

This creature straightened up and puffed out his chest with an air of being on an important mission. He brought the instrument to his mouth and played a very complex melodious tune. The birds, stunningly beautiful in Lani's garden, flew in close, some sitting on his shoulders, joined in the song. Nectar sang along and Gilad whistled. Even Abbey closed her eyes and wagged her tail in time with the music. When finished, the notes lingered in the garden for a time. After a few moments, the birds returned to their activities. Lani realized the boqer directed and led the animals in their care with their quiet presence, a melodious flute and a gentle hand.

"That was very beautiful," Lani said. "You've been given a great talent. I will name you Piper because you lead the animals in your charge through the music of your pipe." Lani reached out to touch his head and said, "May you be blessed with peace and harmony with the animals. May they mature to healthy adults and multiply under your care. May you be inspired with beautiful new tunes to bless our ears."

Piper considered his naming a solemn ceremony and held out his pipe in both hands in front, bowed deeply and said, "Aha'Mo'ee, thank you for my honourable name. I will bring honour to the Creator, you and your estate through my husbandry and shelter of your animals. They will be well fed, groomed, exercised and trained. I will ensure they are happy and love living under your rule."

Lani turned to the third being. She stood quite beautiful, with almost porcelain white, sparkling skin, a mane of long, white hair, small tubular, hippolike ears, and four large, deep brown eyes, two on the front and one on each side. She was quite slim. Even her hands and fingers were long and slim. Her feet had long toes each ending in discs that bore her weight. Nectar said, "Aha'Kaiya, this naqod is your head servant. It is for you to provide a name."

"I will call you Willow, for you are slender, lithe and graceful." Lani rested her hand on Willow's head and said, "May you bend to the needs of those under you with the flexibility of the willow. May you put deep roots in the wisdom of the living water. May you find joy in doing my bidding. May you grow in leadership and delight in the successes of those under you as they do your bidding."

Willow's eyes welled up as she looked intently at Lani.

Willow carried herself rather reserved, but Lani came to understand the depth to which Willow thought and felt. Deep roots, like her name. Lani found Willow to take direction well, think positive and act altruistically. Willow created a warm, nurturing environment around her, and as a result would build a close-knit team. All those working under her were extremely loyal. But at this first meeting, Willow remained quiet, soft spoken and rather formal.

In response to being named and blessed, Willow closed her eyes and slowly bowed, and said, "Aha'Sarah, my princess, I am very deeply honoured. I will work hard to please you. I am young to leadership and look to learn from you," and then seemed to recede into the background. Lani hoped this reservation and formality in Willow was due to unfamiliarity and would lessen in time.

Lani asked Gilad, Piper and Willow if they had eaten and invited them to join her and Nectar in a meal. They trooped to the small dining room to sit together for their first meal of many in each other's company.

Nectar turned out to be a great chef. She was the best chef around, but then everyone thought their mashqeh was the best. Each eh-bed was created specifically for their master, so it made sense that their masters viewed the results of their work as the best.

Lani enjoyed everything Nectar prepared and Nectar seemed to always know the right thing that would satisfy. And no matter whether it was just Lani, Nectar, Gilad, Piper and Willow eating together, or a spontaneous big party gathering, or a small group of Lani's friends or just the servants alone, Nectar always prepared the appropriate dishes to please and had just the right amount of everything. Lani quickly came to love and treasure Nectar and enjoyed her presence in her home.

Lani thought, back then, she had no idea how important these four would become in her future.

With Gilad, Piper and Willow joining them, Nectar brought out more prepared food and they gave thanks for the food and each other. Lani asked Piper if she could be introduced to all of her animals the next day. She knew Piper would have groomed them to a shine for her arrival and she wanted to acknowledge his preparations. She suspected they were waiting for her to give them a name and bless each one.

She then asked Gilad for a tour of the estate as she would like to know the plants, and their produce and nature. She knew Gilad immaculately prepared the gardens, like the animals, for her first viewing and he would want to impress her.

Lastly Lani turned to Willow. "Have you spent much time with the servants with whom you will be working?"

"Aha'Sarah, yes. Prior to your arrival, all head servants worked with the servants under them to prepare for your arrival."

Lani said, "I would like to spend some time with you to go through the list of servants and what work each is good at performing. Then I would like to meet each one and give them their name and blessing. We should discuss what work needs to be done right away. Let me know when you are ready with this information and we can discuss plans."

"Aha'Sarah, as you wish. I am prepared with the information you require and await your instructions." Some might have considered this an aloof or haughty attitude, but Lani knew in her heart that Willow was a creature ready to grow into a leadership role with her mentoring.

It would be a busy few days getting caught up on her obligations as the master of the estate. After dining she bypassed the library and wandered upstairs. On the north side of her mansion, she walked up another flight of stairs where she discovered the governance room. She carried the title Melchizedek, a ruler and priest. This would be the room from which she would fulfill her role as ruler and provide leadership in the running of her property. There was an elevated seat made of seastone, a water blue-green colour.

This room afforded beautiful views in all directions and she enjoyed the time she spent here. To the side of the room sat an imposing desk and some cabinets and cupboards made of the same seastone. One or two mornings a week, she met with her head servants here, discussed the happenings of her estate, gave directions and shared her plans in the management of her property.

As time passed, when Lani saw the second full moon appear in the sky, she marked it as time to thank her servants, acknowledge their accomplishments and provide direction for their growth. Yehovah gave wonderful servants and they deserved to receive good leadership. Over the last year Lani saw her own development into a graceful, supportive authority.

Yes, the first time she met her servants and stepped into her role as ruler and priest was another fond memory, but this would not be her honour story either.

6 | Six Days of Creation

Chapter Span: Two Days | 0.1.4 to 0.1.5 |

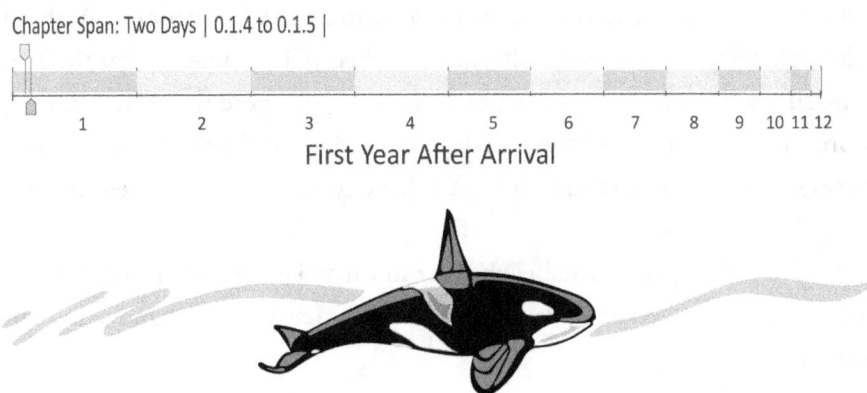

First Year After Arrival

Lani spent many hours with her friend Kazhu, the reliable. His first visit and the revelation that her garden had an eternal remembrance of what drew her to her Beloved in the long past inspired the next poem in her collection.

The weaver's poem: Creation

By Word, light.
By Word, life.
The cosmos.

In six days,
By divine purpose, Man.
His intended.

The Story Behind the Poem

Lani thought about her first visitor with a warm heart.

Shortly after she started to look around the governance room in her mansion, her neighbour Kazhu came by for a visit. She heard a commotion coming from the garden below. He had come through the Entry Garden from the beach and was making quite a bit of noise. In response, Lani hurried downstairs and out the front door to run right into him. Without acknowledging her or their collision, he asked if Lani knew what the Entry Garden really was. Lani said no, but had a feeling there was something more to it than just a garden. Kazhu grabbed her by the hand and ran through the garden to the beach. "We have to start from the beginning," he said.

When they got to the beach, Kazhu turned around to look at the entry arch. He asked again if she could see it. Lani laughed and said, "No, but please tell me."

"Okay, it is a representation of creation. You have the creation story as your entry! See this arch formed of two trees merging together at the top? It is symbolic of time and space coming together. At the base are plants with deep blue-black leaves and a light mist above. That is day one. The creation and separation of light from dark. Everyone enters your place at day one, the first day of the cosmos.

"Next we see the tri-blue waving plants. The dark blue base represents the waters below, the medium blue the air, and the light blue the waters of the heavens, all moving like waves. This shows the creation and separation of the waters into sea, air and firmament of day two.

"The hill of green mounds with tall seed stalks is day three and symbolic of the creation of the rolling land, the plants and trees."

Looking up the hill, Kazhu continued. "The velvety black-leafed plant with twinkling flowers represents day four, the creation of the stars, and the yellow mist and white mist represent the sun and moon. When a breeze blows across, you can see the stars twinkling.

"The blue plants with the colourful dripping flowers always moving in the direction of the wind is day five, symbolic of the creation of the fish of the sea. The grass with blades that fly like kites represents the creation of the birds of the air.

"The plants that don't flower, don't have roots and aren't anchored to the ground represent the creation of animals. Look at the unique patterns and markings and how they move like herds of animals. That is a part of day six.

"The spectacular tree at the far end symbolizes mankind. Humans come in all colours and form branches of relations. We were given authority and dominion over the animals and plants, so this tree with strands of different colours forms a canopy over the herds of animal-plants, the fish-flowers, and over the bird-grass." Kazhu finally looked at Lani, positively glowing with his excitement.

Lani stared. When viewed from the beach, when you looked through the window of time-space, you really did see the story of creation: day one, light and dark; day two, separation of water from the air; day three, the land and vegetation; day four, the sun, moon and stars; day five, the fish and birds; day six, the animals and man. Kazhu was absolutely right. This was spectacular!

Lani hugged and thanked him for sharing this with her. They stood quietly looking, quite amazed. After a few moments, Lani asked Kaz if he had an Entry Garden with meaning. He laughed. "Yes, that is what made me look for something meaningful in your garden. Mine's symbolic of the big events in the life of Peter, the disciple. That's a deeply meaningful story for me."

Kaz went quiet, lost in thought. After looking over her Creation Garden again, Lani invited him to come inside and stay for awhile, confident Nectar could prepare something for them.

Lani made a mental note to tell Gilad to take special care of her Creation Garden. It should always be a showpiece. The story of creation was an important part of her long past. As soon as she realized the meaning of this garden, she knew her Entry Garden told the story of her entry into relationship with her Beloved. It ushered her into her inheritance both figuratively in her past and now physically to her estate.

When Kaz and Lani got to her mansion, Nectar led them to the room jutting out on the north side overlooking both the Creation Garden to the west and the ocean bay to the east. She already prepared drinks and seasoned seeds for the two of them to enjoy. They lounged in the hammock seating, looking out to the bay.

Lani asked, "How did you know the garden represents the six days of creation?"

Often Kaz was spontaneous, but when he took time before speaking, it meant he would say something worth the wait. When in this mood, he provoked a line of thought that would lead to something profound. Kaz's brain was just wired a little differently and he would see connections many others would miss.

After a pause, he said, "History merely repeats itself. It has all been done before. Nothing under the sun is truly new. Sometimes people say, 'Here is something new!' But actually it is old. Nothing is ever truly new." Then he paused, again looking at Lani.

Lani recognized it as words from Ecclesiastes. "Okay," Lani said, "so you expect to find nothing new here? Have you seen a Creation Garden before?"

After another pause, Kazhu said, "We all saw the original ark of the covenant, its lid, the mercy seat, in Yehovah's temple when we walked through the Majestic City on the first day. It is a symbol of Yeshua representing the promise through Him that people would be granted mercy. Under Yehovah's direction, Moses made a replica for the Hebrews as a foreshadow or promise of Yeshua. Even though Yehovah-Yeshua has now fulfilled the promise of mercy, the ark remains in Yehovah's temple as a remembrance of the provision of mercy. When I saw that, it got me thinking. I figured there would be lots of original symbols here that we saw replicated on earth in the long past. When I realized the meaning of my garden, I knew there would be many memorials here of the important events of history.

"When I came to visit you, I too felt there was something more to this garden. I walked through a couple of times, then stood on the beach, looking through the arch. I thought there was a pattern. Each plant grouping had to represent something. Then it came to me. As soon as I realized what it was, I came running in to see if you already knew. And here I am."

Lani thought this over for a few minutes, then wondered since both she and Kaz had a meaningful Entry Garden, did everyone? Then she wondered if all the mansions were like hers. "What is your house like? Does it grow out of the water too?" Lani asked.

Kazhu laughed. "No. You love being on the water, so you have a floating mansion. I love being near the water and I enjoy the smell of water, but like to be a bit above it all. My house is really a treemansion. It is more than I ever dreamed of. I look forward to hosting wonderful parties, sort of gatherings in the air."

At that he burst out laughing. "Get it?" he sputtered out. Before Lani could answer he said, "Gatherings in the air! It is another symbol of remembrance. We were just gathered in the air, and I will have remembrance parties where we will again gather in the air! Thank you, Lani, for helping me realize my gatherings will have great meaning."

Lani looked at Kaz quite fondly, then moved to sit right beside him. She rested her head on his shoulder. When they met a few days ago, Lani knew they would be great friends throughout eternity. They sat quiet for awhile, staring out over the ocean in a companionable silence.

Then Lani said, "I can hardly believe we're here. In the long past I knew this would come, but on a given day couldn't imagine that would be the day. And yet the day did come and we came home. This really feels like home and all the things that I longed for have been satisfied. I know I was made for life here. And I know this is more real than the long past. The long past seems so superficial now. But still, I just can hardly get my head wrapped around the fact that all the pain, grief, loss, angst, loneliness, emptiness, self-doubt, disease, fear, darkness and evil are gone."

Kaz reached for her hand and said, "My sweet Lani. We – you – will never be alone again. We are now Ahuvati, His Beloved, His eternal mate. We are no longer human, but transformed. The first stage of the transformation occurred in the long past when we chose Yeshua. Once we chose Him, we became a new creature. When we were removed from the long past, the transformation to incorruptible and immortal completed, we no longer live as human. We are Ahuvati.

"Our Beloved gave each of us a place in this paradise made specifically for us, and brought us here. It's bursting with life and filled to overflowing with food, living water, clean air, everlasting youth and health. We will be in eternal peace and sensory richness beyond imagination.

"Lani, we now live in incorruptible abundance. There is so much richness here, even the economy is one of overabundance. I am humbled by His care and deep love that prompted the formation of a perfect paradise. There's no comparison to the pain of the long past, and this grandeur and greatness of our home. All the misery of the long past was so worth it."

Kaz turned out to be one of her really good friends. Often they rode their horses together in the mornings, enjoying each other's company, sharing events of the day and more importantly, their thoughts.

When Kaz left, Lani went to her bedroom and sank deeply in her bed, looking out over the ocean, and fell asleep in minutes. The next morning she got up early to greet the day at the end of the deck off her bedroom. She'd never felt so uninhibited in the long past, and was inspired to write her thoughts and feelings of this new world down. It was the first weaver's poem she wrote, and started her writing about the many significant things that had happened over the first year.

The weaver's poem: Morning, A New Day in Paradise

Evening is almost over.
The air becomes thick with silence
As the living water rises to water the land.
Looking east, standing on the edge of a new day,
Then the first brush of the colour palette on the horizon, giving announcement.
I stand in hope, quiet excitement, anticipation of what this new day

promises.
Finally, the first ray of light bursts forth – a new day in paradise.
Light and life lighting across the expanse of the sky,
Diamonds dancing across the sea,
Uncontained excitement swells my heart beyond capacity.
With all my being I raise my voice to thank you, my Beloved.
I stand before you on the cusp of my destiny, my night long past.
Filled to overflowing, I sing my heart's thoughts to you.
Stars, angels, creatures, the sea and sand
All join to sing their tribute,
Praise echoes across eternity.
I dance under the sky painted in Yehovah's love.
May this offering fill your heart.

The air filled with the scent of rain and earth. Lani didn't know it at the time, but the air about her filled with different scents depending on what she was thinking. In the long past people said "you are what you eat." Here you were what you thought. When expressing love, joy, peace, patience, kindness, goodness, faithfulness, gentleness and self-control, the scent of fruit, particularly coconut, emanated from her like a subtle perfume. When thinking and doing creative things, the scent of the ocean encompassed her. But on mornings like this, when immersed in praise, the scent of rain and earth surrounded her.

Her morning dance, with the scent of rain wafting from her, became her way to greet the day and thank her Beloved for another day in paradise.

Such sweet and tender memories. Lani shifted position in the sand and turned to look east out toward the mainland where the sun rose every morning. The third moon started to rise for the third day. All three full moons in the sky for the third day signalled the start of the Haga'at feast that evening. Yehovah placed the three full moons as a moed – a reminder. She intentionally came here to prepare her honour story. The story of the Creation Garden and her dancing on the deck were great events and full of meaning, but really did not rise to the level of an honour story to share with all Ahuvati. This would not be her honour story.

Bonus Content

You can read how the story of creation turned Lani to Yehovah at www.serenitymclean.com/bonus-content/ Use the password soulsailing.

7 | Treasure Hidden in Plain Sight

Chapter Span: One Day | 0.1.5 |

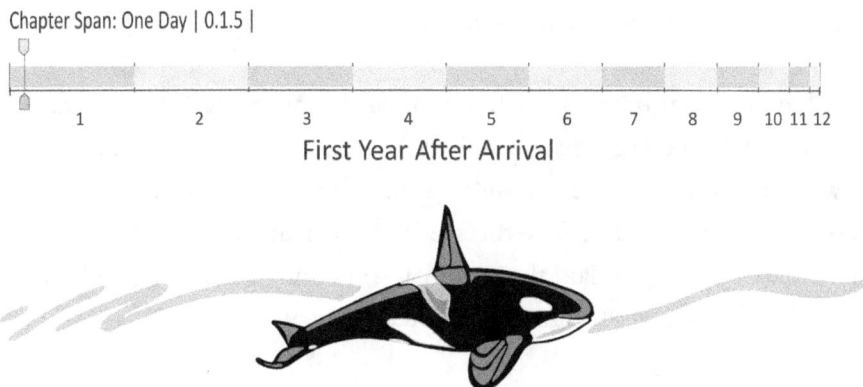

1   2   3   4   5   6   7   8   9   10 11 12

First Year After Arrival

Lani thought about the day that followed her first deck dance. She toured her property, met and named all her animals and servants. In taking an in-depth tour the scope and grandeur became apparent. The many unusual property features left her feeling Yehovah created this land for a significant, meaningful purpose she just didn't understand. Lani turned to the poem about her property features she wrote in her eighth month.

The weaver's poem: Mayan, the Oasis

Dome Tree, a place of private meditation,
Meaningful moments marked with remembrance stones.

Carousel Garden, contemplation of inspiration and creativity,
Deep and enduring stories of love on display.

Paradise, of synthesis, accord, beauty, creation, and pleasure.
Blue Rock, immersive experience.
Coconut Stroll, meandering relaxation.
Water skimming, riding with the giants of the deep.
Bucking Horse Chute, bound together in adrenaline.

Sunrise, creative expression of praise.
BlueWater, at one with living water.
Savannah flying, sweeping view of Yehovah's gift.
Blue Cliff, intense focus, intimate thought.

Lani thought back to her first tour of her property. Oh, was she in for a surprise when she discovered what her place would become. On first view of her property, she marvelled at her inheritance yet remained blind to the property's destiny. Like the seeds that germinate into big things, this first view of her estate laid the seeds of something grand. A good memory lay in the story of her tour as a seed of destiny.

The Story Behind the Poem

Lani awoke to the day she would meet the animals, the gardens and the servants in her care. She decided to take the same approach as Yehovah-Word, and follow the pattern of creation. She learned of her land and gardens first, then the animals, then her servants, and finally laid out the direction and plans for the operation of her estate.

As soon as the mist rose from the land, Lani called Ario and met Gilad. Knowing the size of her estate, Lani decided to travel by horse. It became her first morning horseback ride of many. Piper had Ario tacked up and ready for her. Gilad, of course, flew alongside. They started from the beach and travelled through the Creation Garden. Lani asked what Gilad knew of this garden.

Gilad replied, "Aha'Qatsin, I know the names and nature of the plants in all of your estate. I know the care each requires. I know when each will come into fruit and when is best to harvest the fruit and seeds. Of this garden, it is your Entry Garden and therefore is important. The plants of this garden only grow here on your estate. I do not harvest from this garden."

Lani asked if Gilad knew of the story told in the plants. Gilad looked at the garden and thought for a long moment. "Aha'Qatsin, no, I didn't know there was a story told by plants. The possibility never occurred. Can you tell me the story?"

Lani walked him along the path, telling how each plant represented the days of creation. After her explanation, Lani explained the importance and sentimentality of the garden to her. Just like the story of creation acted as the entry to the heart of her estate, in the long past Yehovah used the story of creation as an entry to her heart and to bring her back to Him.

Gilad looked over the entire garden and said, "Aha'Qatsin, I'm amazed to see the creation story here in my care. I'm committed to keeping this garden beautiful in remembrance of the creation of the Melchizedek, and in honour of your redemption."

They travelled between the Creation Garden and the singing grass toward the southwest river. Gilad happily shared information about the plants and the care he was providing. They crossed the river and headed to the west coast of her property. The silver palms ended at a beautiful sandy beach. The quiet bay looked south out over the ocean as far as the eye could see. Gilad mentioned turtles often frequented this bay. Because of the orientation of the land, and the gentle drop-off of the ocean floor of the bay, a gentle surf rolled in.

They continued northward, climbing steadily upward through what could only be described as a tropical botanical garden. A collection of quite unusual and remarkable plants filled the large, very well-tended garden crisscrossed with many paths.

The land opened up on the west side to another larger bay with steps down to the beach. Unlike the last bay, a large surf steadily roared. Ahead the land opened to grassy, level land for at least a mile, maybe farther. In the distance, Lani saw a distinctly blue-coloured ridge rising up with low rolling mountains on top of it. The ridge or escarpment looked about 500 ft. high with equally high hills piled on top.

Beside the escarpment, Lani saw a grove of channel trees channelling water to their dark blue crowns resulting in water raining out of the leaves. This gave new meaning to rainforest. Under beautiful, sunny skies, this forest provided a sunshower.

Looking right, Lani spotted the river that branched into two rivers near the singing grass. She thought about Nectar's words the previous evening about her favourite colour being blue. It was true. And here on her estate, so many shades of blue. The escarpment, the water, the silver-blue palms, the singing grass. And yet a feast of other colours for the eyes. Lani quickly grew to adore her property. They headed north toward the ridge, gradually tacking east toward the river flowing from the escarpment.

When they neared the river, she saw it widened into a bit of a small lake at the base of the escarpment. At the north end of the river the water thundered over the ridge in a waterfall. The west half of the falls dropped straight down unimpeded and looked like a bridal veil. The east end of the falls dropped in stages over outcrops of the ridge. She stared at these spectacular falls rivalling anything on earth. And they belonged to her! In the long past, she grew up on a property in the country with a river running through. She often visited a small waterfall and pool on the neighbour's property in the summer, but that paled in comparison to these 500-ft. falls over a blue rock ridge. She hardly comprehended the breadth of love that would create this and give it all to her.

She asked if they could readily get to the top of the ridge. Gilad nodded and smiled. "Aha'Qatsin, yes. Underneath the falls."

Lani laughed. "Under the falls? Really?"

"Aha'Qatsin, yes. There's a cave and a ride up to the top." And off they went. Sure enough, at the side of the falls they found the opening. She forgot about the light that leaves no shadow and expected it to be dark and dank, but once inside she could easily see. The cave continued deeper into the ridge, ending in a set of glowing circles on the ground. She also saw a tunnel to the right continuing behind the falls to the other side of the river. The tunnel opened in several places to view the falls from behind.

Gilad led Lani and Ario to stand on one of the circles which lifted them up to the land above the ridge and once there, the view left her speechless. Then she thought she shouldn't be stunned. Everything here was spectacular.

At the top a deep, clear lake fed into the waterfall. Although a lot of water flowed over the edge, the depth of the water kept the lake mirror flat, reflecting sky and land. The lake disappeared into the distance, weaving its way around several mountains.

Turning back to look over the ridge, Lani had a great view of her lower property. Looking west over the flat grassy land, it looked like the African savannah with many animals grazing. A number of cumulus clouds formed over the savannah in what used to be called a cloud street in the long past. A cloud street always indicated strong thermals birds and gliders used to ride the air.

Turning to look south, she followed the waterfall and river down to the familiar gardens. Even from this vantage point, the dome tree spread huge, covering the entire southern part of the island. The spit of land at the south end curled toward the mainland and terminated in several small islands filling the distance between the spit and the mainland. These islands popped out of the water like tall pillars dotting the bay to the east.

Lani turned back north, and as Ario walked along the shoreline, she asked about what appeared to be coconut trees. In the long past, she knew coconut trees didn't grow at higher elevations and to see them atop the ridge surprised her. But then again, nothing here should surprise her. Gilad said they were indeed coconut trees and they grew all the way to the top of the mountains alongside pineapples and other fruit and nut trees. All produced a bountiful crop.

Rounding the mountain, Lani could see two rivers feeding into the north end of the lake. Gilad said they both came from the same source, but wended their way around different mountains. He described the one on the east as quiet and slow flowing and the one on the west as fast flowing through rough rapids. It reminded her of Jacob and Esau – twins of opposite nature.

Also at the north end of the lake she found another marina filled with speedboats and Jet Skis. They followed the western river around to another lake that was the source of the two rivers. They returned following the east river back to the main lake.

They took a staircase back down to the lower land, walking through a large bowl-shaped area at the base of the ridge with the ridge of the escarpment forming tall walls on three sides. The land naturally stepped down to a flat area. In walking through the bowl, listening to Ario's foot-falls and talking to Gilad, Lani realized she owned a natural amphitheatre.

Walking up and out of the amphitheatre, Lani could see the marina at the north end of the bay. Gilad led them south through an area of tall plants with giant 20-ft. leaves and beautiful flowers. This brought them back to the singing grass and the Creation Garden.

Throughout the tour, Gilad pointed out many trails for Lani to ride, all the different plants, and talked about the edible fruits and seeds he and his servants gathered for Lani, the servants and animals to eat. He educated her on the seasons of growth and fruiting for each plant. It was a lot to take in. She developed a real appreciation for all the knowledge and skill Gilad had in keeping all this property growing and producing. Lani could tell the estate was quite productive from the baskets upon baskets of food she had seen collected throughout the property.

Upon return to the Creation Garden, Lani thanked Gilad for the tour of her property and the information he shared. She praised him for the beautiful condition of the estate. Gilad left her, grinning ear to ear and happy his efforts pleased her.

Lani then rode out to the savannah to spend time with Piper. He organized his team to bring the animals to the savannah grasslands be-fore Lani to name. It took awhile, but she met and named a wide variety of birds and mammals. First came the birds including paradise-worthy parrots, herons, several types of toucans, owls, eagles and kites, sparrows, swans, ducks and geese, and a large number of songbirds, all in colours unimagined in birds. In flight, it looked as if the air absorbed the colour from the feathers, leaving a lingering trail of colour behind them, kind of like condensation trails behind the jets that flew high across the sky in the long past. To see a flock in flight was a spectacular sight.

Next came a vast collection of mammals including familiar ones from the long past like lions, giraffes, kangaroos, jaguars, squirrels, sheep, zebras, pandas, otters, and several completely unique to this world.

Ario joined a herd of horses as they arrived. The sight thrilled Lani. "Horsie" was the first word she said as a toddler and loved them ever since. While a few of the horses were much like Ario in elegance, the majority of the herd was quite large and stocky, rather like Shire horses. All with spectacular conformation, beautifully long, arched necks, powerful sloping shoulders, equally sloping hindquarters, well-sprung ribs, long, wavy manes and tails, strong and compact bodies, and strong legs with feathering. While the structure appeared compact, overall these were large horses, at least 18 to 19 hands high. One of the large drafts, a black beauty, caught Lani's eye. He had an aristocratic carriage, amazing presence and spacious, powerful gaits. He approached Lani for his name and won her over with soft, low horse talk in her ear. She decided to name him Bentley because of his beautiful carriage. He was an absolute gentle giant.

Lani always loved the appearance and nature of the Clydesdales and Belgian draft horses of the long past, and fell in love instantly with her herd. She generally took her morning rides with either Ario or Bentley along trails, both on the beach and up in the hills above the escarpment. Very often she would meet up with Kaz and they rode the trails on both of their estates.

The last and largest animals to arrive for their names, Ta'onka, looked much like elephants, but were significantly larger. The females came in shades of blue and the males in shades of purple. The largest and oldest female approached Lani first, her skin a stunning, saturated blue. Reminded of the colour of sapphire, Lani decided to name her for her beautiful colour. Sapphire came right up to Lani and wrapped her trunk around Lani's shoulders as Lani rubbed her chin. Sapphire's breathing tickled Lani's neck, making her laugh. Once satisfied with her chin rub, Sapphire lifted her foot, inviting Lani onto her back. Lani stepped up and Sapphire used her trunk to help Lani up atop her neck. As soon as she was seated, Sapphire trotted proudly around the herd. Clearly Sapphire loved having Lani on her back.

Lani saw the young Ta'onka running together, moving quickly, then abruptly changing direction as a group, and after a few moments making another abrupt turn. Lani could tell they were having fun playing some kind of game and thought about long past videos of animals playing. She had seen bears sledding down a snow-covered mountain and a crow using a jar lid to slide repeatedly down a roof.

Lani guided Sapphire to get in the game and as they approached the youngsters, Lani spotted a ball they were all chasing. As a team, Sapphire and Lani gained control of the ball, but quick-manoeuvering youngsters soon regained control, and Sapphire and Lani wandered along the beach, with Sapphire trumpeting her pleasure the entire time.

Piper had all well trained, well groomed and beautiful for their presentation to Lani. When she finally met and named all the creatures, she complimented Piper on his fine work. They were all in great shape, well fed, well mannered and very happy. Thousands of animals and all gentle and sweet to each other. The promise of the lion lying in peace with the lamb was true here.

Finally, Lani met with Willow in her governance room. She wanted to meet all the servants, find out about each of them, what work they were doing and what they loved to do. Although Lani didn't realize at first, this would take quite awhile as there were well over 300 servants working on her property. She never managed this many people before and felt the responsibility. It would be important to develop Willow into a strong leader.

After meeting and naming everyone, Lani asked about what Willow spent her time on, what consumed her time and attention. Willow started, "Aha'Sarah, most of my time is determining what work needs to be done each day and dispatching servants to complete the work."

Lani thought for a moment and said, "So really, focused on the co-ordination. What do you see coming up that could change the daily routine or require reallocation of resources?"

"Aha'Sarah, I haven't thought about what's coming up." Bowing her head, Willow quietly said, "I have much to learn about leadership and management."

"Oh, Willow. My dear, sweet Willow. Yes, you do have much to learn. So do I. So we will learn together, okay?"

"Aha'Sarah, yes, okay." Looking Lani in the eye, she finished. "Thank you."

"Okay, let's start with this. Is everyone busy? And is there any additional or different work coming up because of the harvest, or the care of the land and animals?"

"Aha'Sarah, everyone works for a few hours a day. Sometimes there is nothing to do, but we all would be happy to fully work in your service. For what is coming up, there is always a steady amount of harvest work and maintenance to be done, but that doesn't keep us busy."

"And what else does everyone do with their time?"

"Aha'Sarah, many just spend time where they work. The ones tending animals just spend their time with the animals, and the ones who are gardeners spend time wandering around the gardens." Lani wondered why she would have so many servants when there was nothing for them to do many days. There must be something coming up that would require so many.

"Ok, let's talk about you. What do you like to do?"

"Aha'Sarah, if you are asking what do I desire in my heart, well, I love to help others grow and develop. I would like to make a difference in each life, every day, if I could." Willow had spoken from her heart, quite excited and enthusiastic, then realized who she was speaking to and bowed her head again and said, "Maybe that is too grand and too much for me."

"Willow, I believe you can be all that. Before we talk about my plans and how you and I are going to make your dreams come true, I am curious about something. Can you tell me about the marinas, the boats and how they are powered? Who uses them?" Lani was wondering if she could figure out the need for so many servants by sorting out why there were so many boats.

"Aha'Sarah, the marina on the upper lake has 15 personal craft that I am told are meant for one or two Ahuvati to ride around the lake. No one has ridden any of the boats. Everything is waiting for you. All the craft just run. I am not sure what you mean by how they are powered."

"So there are 15 Jet Skis just for me? Huh! Do you have to put fuel in the Jet Skis to make them run? Or charge a battery?"

"Aha'Sarah, I do not know what a battery is. There is nothing you need to put in the Jet Skis to make them run. Like everything here, they just run."

Lani thought about that for a moment, then concluded there must be something in place to transmit or absorb power through the air. She remembered reading about the concept of wireless electricity and concluded it must be something like that. Power comes from the air, from the light. Talk about green!

"Aha'Sarah, the marina in the ocean bay has Jet Skis too, another ten. There are also boats that hold several Ahuvati, up to ten at a time. There are 18 of those. And there are sailboats, different-sized sailboats, and there are 30 of those. No one has used any of those boats either. They are for you."

What would she do with all those boats? She would have to have friends over for a sailing party. She smiled at the thought.

After a moment, Willow continued. "Aha'Sarah, there are other things too. There are these triangular wing-things at the upper lake marina and boards to put on your feet. I was told you go in the water and the Jet Ski pulls you across the water on these boards." With her head down and smiling, she said, "I would really like to see that, if you wouldn't mind."

Laughing, Lani said, "Yes, you are welcome to watch us ski. Some people are quite good at it. The wing-things, well, they might be gliders Ahuvati use to glide in the sky. Is there anything else? Other equipment here that you don't know what it is for?"

"Aha'Sarah, yes. There are these circles of rubbery material filled with air and boats made of the same rubbery material. These are kept at the source lake up above. And there is something similar at the two marinas, but not circles or boats. These other ones are flat squares and rectangles. And then there are these really long boards with a fin at one end."

"So that sounds like inner tubes and rubber rafts for floating on the water, and inflatable beds for floating, and maybe some for towing behind a boat. The boards sound like surfboards. They're used to go out into the ocean waves and stand on the board, letting the momentum of the wave bring you back to shore. It's called surfing."

It amused Lani to watch Willow take in this information about how people play in the water. Finally Lani asked, "Is there a map of the entire property with names of the lakes, rivers and such?"

"Aha'Sarah, no, there is no map and nothing has been named. It is for you to name."

"Alright. First, can you draw me a map for tomorrow and I will put names to places? Next, put together a list of all that needs to be done every day to maintain the property. Talk to Piper, Gilad, and Nectar to get a list of tasks they see in the near future that is different from the day-to-day work, and how much help these tasks will require. Then you and I will put together a plan for everyone so they know what they will be doing ahead of time, and you will not need to be figuring it out every day. Do you think you can have all that information for tomorrow?"

"Aha'Sarah, yes. That'll be no problem."

The next day, Willow gave Lani a map and she named the features of her property and included the map in her diary.

Lani's Property

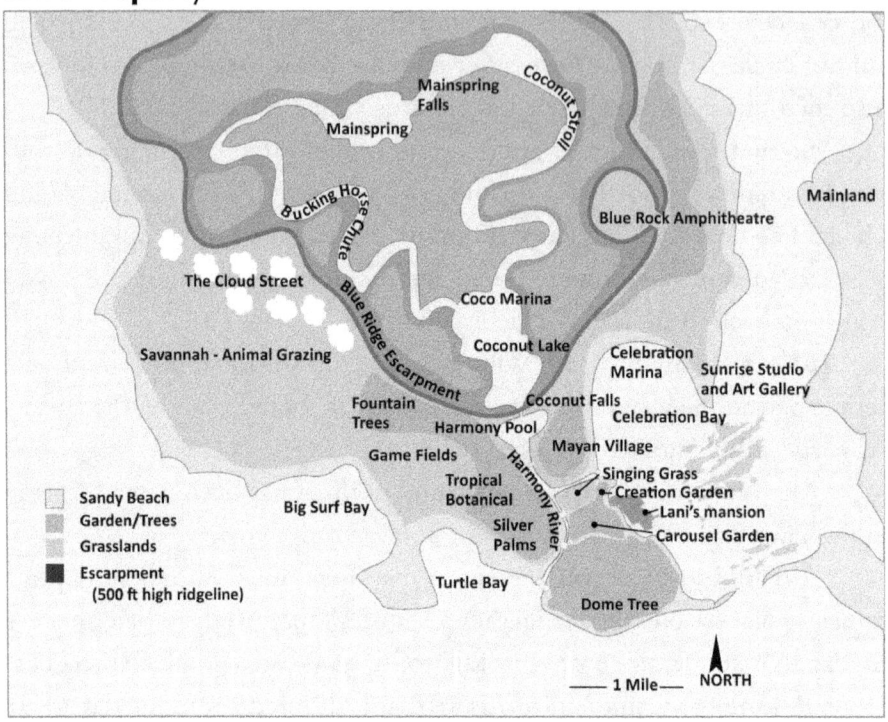

Lani thought about her property and all occurrences here this first year. Her tour was just the seed. In a few short months, she discovered the purpose for her property and pursued that purpose. Lani used the work of property development to help Willow grow into a fine leader. Willow quickly became indispensable and they established a deep and trusting relationship.

The story of finding the purpose of her property carried great meaning for her. The purpose and development of her property became a project that truly started her toward her mission. The story of the seed, the germination and the big thing at the end could be a good honour story, but she wondered if she should focus her story on her mission, or one of the projects, or the whole thing from seed to implementation. She decided to consider all the poems and stories and decide later what she would use as her honour story.

A fun morning lay ahead.

8 | Corruption of the Intended

Chapter Span: One Day | 0.1.6 |

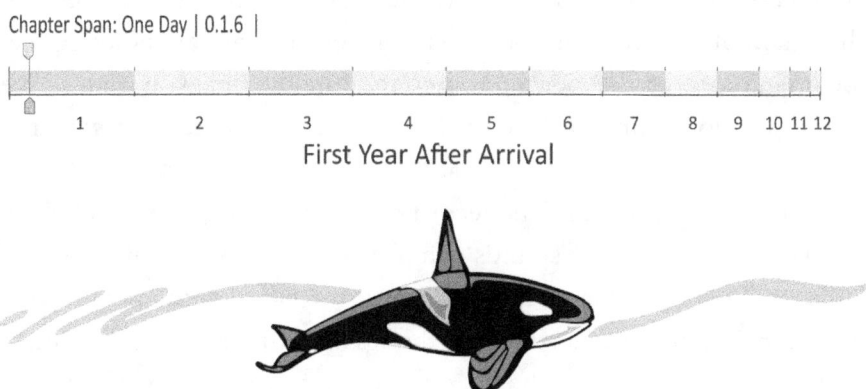

First Year After Arrival

A morning spent with Aymoon, one of her first friends, inspired one of Lani's early poems. In the long past, Aymoon studied the Hebrew language and the exhaustive library here excited him. This day, he invited her to visit the library with him.

Unlike any library she knew in the long past this was more like a multiplex cinema filled with volumes upon volumes of history. While she really enjoyed the visit, Aymoon shared information afterward Lani found particularly interesting and really quite illuminating, and the inspiration for her weaver poem.

The weaver's poem: Corruption of the Intended

In jealousy,
purity corrupted,
beauty twisted to vile,
love poisoned by lechery,
light fouled by evil.

The intended were lost and ignorant.

The Story Behind the Poem

When they arrived at the library in the Majestic City, Aymoon introduced Lani to how it worked. "All of this is the history of everything, everywhere, and of all time right up to today. The recordings are holographic. You go into one of the viewing rooms, indicate the time you want to see, and the location from which you wish to watch, and it feels like you are really there.

"It's pretty intriguing. The recording of time is like a thick rope composed of strands, and the strands composed of threads. My life is a thread in the story of time. Put a bunch of threads together, say all people of earth, and that becomes a strand of the story. Put together all the various strands of the story across the universe, and you have the rope of time.

"Yehovah is everywhere, existing throughout time all at once, and takes it all in. In fact, He is outside time and space, like it is a ball in His hands." Smiling, Aymoon continued. "We are definitely not nearly as sophisticated and capable as the all-knowing and ever-present Yehovah-El Shaddai, God Almighty, and can only watch a thread of the story at a time."

Aymoon took her into one of the viewing rooms and asked what she would like to watch and from where. Lani thought for a moment and asked to see the creation of the cosmos from the vantage point of the moon.

Aymoon input her request and the two of them settled in to watch. Suddenly, they sat in the vastness of nothing. There was no moon. There was nothing. Lani felt the emptiness of the abyss. But even in this recording, she also sensed the immense presence of Yehovah.

Yehovah-Word, in whom existed light and life, expressing the desire of Yehovah-El Shaddai roared, "Hawyaw or!" or "Be light!" Hawyaw! This is the very part of God's name. "I AM" or "Be" is His name. Yehovah-Word commanded His name (I AM/be), then His nature (light), and the light formed

In amazement, Lani said, "Yehovah-Word used His name to bring His nature into existence!" The power within His name formed the cosmos. It would be like Lani shouting her name and suddenly one of her characteristics bursting into a physical, tangible thing.

Even though they watched a recording, the words "Be light" vibrated through her chest. It echoed through the vast nothingness that would become the cosmos. And in the very moment of the command, "Be light!", light separated from darkness and came into being, shining on the void, formless earth.

Lani found it interesting that in the original language used by Yehovah it wasn't "Let there be light," as her Bible stated. When Lani read that, she wondered who formed the light. "Let there be light" seemed as though Yehovah-Word, the great I AM, made a request of another entity to create the light.

No, it was not a request, "Let there be." It was very clearly a command, "Be." It was a command to the nothingness to form light, and the light formed. At His command, His nature spread throughout the cosmos!

Lani recalled her favourite part of this story thread.

It was the fourth day. Yehovah-Word commanded, based on the design of El Shaddai (God Almighty), "Hawyaw maw-or rawkeeah shawmahyim" (Be lights in the expanse of the heaven), and countless billions of suns formed in the vast expanse and instantly began to shine their light.

Lani paused and thought about subsequent visits to the library. She fast-forwarded the recording to watch the stars march along on their prescribed pathways. Because these recordings contained the threads of the story from all conceivable locations in the cosmos, creation could be viewed from anywhere in the expanse. At first, she watched from earth or near earth. She could see the story of redemption clearly written in the marching lights as moed or markers of Yehovah's appointments with humans, set in place even before humans were created. Before Adam was formed, Yehovah put the lights on their paths in a perfectly timed symphony with each other to tell a story and act as a calendar of appointments perfectly in sync with Yehovah's plan and mankind's history. Oh, if she'd only known and understood the majesty, power, and love for mankind to put this complexity together. Such a rich knowledge came from these recordings. She learned something new every time she watched.

Later she watched a different thread of this recording, one from the vantage point of her new home. What she saw amazed her. There were moed or markers in the sky here to mark the appointments on Yehovah's calendar. If Lani wanted to watch the six days of creation, she had to slow down the recording to catch all the detail because creation really was just six days that had passed from here. Watching creation from the vantage point of her new home caused everything on earth to pass very quickly.

In the long past, a lifetime seemed so long, but when Lani watched the recording from this home's vantage point, a human lifetime seemed so fleeting. It flashed in a bare wisp of a vapour. Here with eternity stretched before her in paradise, time didn't matter.

Lani thought about the nature and importance of hours and minutes here. It really didn't drive or dictate life, unlike her life in the long past. Other than the feasts and the signs or moed in the stars, and the evening calm, people just didn't bother to track time down to the minute. No watches, no clocks. Everyone just knew what time it was. Deadlines were not discussed – everything completed when intended.

According to the moed, today was the third day of three moons, tomorrow, the first Haga'at feast. When Yehovah created the moed for the earth, He also ensured appropriately timed signs in the skies here. In fact, Yehovah placed moed to be seen and understood throughout the cosmos. Here, the moed indicated the festivities would begin at the start of the day, the evening calm.

Lani returned to her memories of the story behind the "Corruption of the Intended" poem.

On their way back home from the library, Aymoon and Lani stopped by a group of fruit trees to enjoy a snack. "Lani, I thought about what you said when watching the recording. You said Yehovah used His name to spread His nature of light throughout the cosmos when He commanded, 'Be light.' It made me think, when Yehovah introduced Himself to Moses,

He said His name was 'Hawyaw asher hawyaw' and literally means "Be that be," or "I am that I am." Then He declared to Moses that His name, I AM, would be His memorial for all generations."

Lani thought about this for a moment and said, "What a memorial! We all live in His creation. We look at it every day. His creative work each of the six days came from a command starting with His name, 'Be.' By His name He created the universe and all that is in it. Every generation of creatures exists in the cosmos, living within and surrounded by the memorial of His name. His name is indeed a memorial. That's amazing, Aymoon." After a moment, she asked, "Have you spent a lot of time at the library?"

"Actually, yes. I've been intrigued with all the different living things existing here, like us, the cherubim and seraphim, all the eh-bed like the mashqeh our cooks, the ganan our gardeners, the boqer our herdsmen, and naqod our head servants, and then all the animals. I wanted to understand how they all came to be, the meaning of their names, the nature and the purpose of each. I discovered some unexpected things I would like to share with others. I'm still thinking about how."

"Like what?"

"Well, we are really no longer human. We were spiritually changed into a new creature, then physically transformed, putting on incorruptibility and immortality. We are now Ahuvati. First, Yehovah placed a piece of Himself in each of us, making us Man-Yehovah and called it new creature. Then we were given new bodies and changed fundamentally and permanently when we put on immortality and incorruptibility. We took our place as kings and priests, and as the one and only mate of Yeshua, His Beloved. That's why Yeshua calls us Aha'Ahuvati, meaning *my* Beloved, but other beings call us Ha'Ahuvati, meaning *the* Beloved, and why we refer to ourselves simply as Ahuvati or Beloved."

Aymoon continued. "The concept that the name reflects the nature also extends to titles. In the long past where I lived, a title was a category or classification like Ato or Weyzero, your Mr. or Mrs. It reflected little intimate, personal characteristics, but here all our titles hold deep and personal meaning, as much as your name is personal.

"So, we have the title Ha'Ahuvati. When someone uses that title for you, Lani, they honour you as the Beloved of Yeshua, and so acknowledge you are prized. It affirms the dear price paid for you to be here. And it implies, as Yehovah's mate, we are of His kind.

"Then when someone calls you Melchizedek, they honour your character and acknowledge your authority as ruler and priest.

"I don't know if you noticed, but the only ones that use your name 'Lani' are other Ahuvati. Yehovah has a special name for you, given to you on your thronestone and only He uses that name. And all other beings like the angels and servants have too much respect for Ahuvati to be so familiar as to use our name. They will always use a title of respect for who you are."

Lani thought about that for a moment and said, "That explains why my servants all have a title for me, but there are many different titles. Like Nectar calls me Aha'Kaiya, her safe harbour."

"Yes, what's interesting is Nectar is of the mashqeh. The word mashqeh means cupbearer, butler or cook, and so they have been created to prepare and provide nourishment. The origin of the root word means a well-watered region or a fat pasture. Mashqeh means abundant provision and is a perfect name for them. The mashqeh are a beautifully delicate race built like a butterfly, or rather, Yehovah placed butterflies on the earth as a shadow of the delicate servants that awaited us here. Because they're so delicate, they prize an unbuffeted, safe life above all. A safe harbour. It's critical to their existence. Their title Aha'Kaiya for us reflects a deep honour and trust in us. They feel safe with us and this title reflects respect deep to their core."

Evidently Aymoon spent quite a bit of time in research. Wanting to learn more, Lani prompted him, "My gardener always says, 'My Qatsin.'"

Aymoon smiled. "The ganan always use the title Qatsin, meaning chief. The really interesting thing about the ganan is that they inspired the Bene Ha'Elohim, the fallen angels, to generate the mythical Hermes or Mercury. In the long past Hermes was said to be the god of finance, particularly the grain trade, one of eloquence and communication, but a trickster. Now think about the ganan's long ears swept back and pointed, the strong set of wings, and legs with a small wing off the back of each leg. You can see the similarities in their physical construction to Hermes."

She recalled her flash of memory when she first met Gilad and her other head servants. He reminded her of the logo for an express parcel delivery company.

Aymoon continued. "Isaiah tells us that Lucifer wanted a throne above the stars of Yehovah and to be like the Most High. So he desired to be worshiped as Yehovah was and is, by the same multitudes of creatures. To be just like Yehovah, Lucifer desired to accomplish three things – be worshiped, to be a creator of living beings equivalent to those Yehovah created, and have all of Yehovah's creation worship him."

Lani recalled in the long past she heard some discussion about the fallen angels actually experimenting with DNA to the point that replication on earth was no longer after its kind. And that's why Yehovah brought the flood. That's what was meant in the Bible by the fallen angels taking wives of the daughters of man and their progeny became the heroes of mythology. Yehovah stepped in to preserve a pure genetic line of both animals and humans on the ark to ensure a pure human line to redeem mankind through Yeshua.

Just before all the redeemed arrived here, scientists performed a lot of genetic experiments, pushing past the species boundaries, mixing human genes with everything imaginable as well as mixing animal genes with plant genes. This was done in total defiance of the command, "Each after its own kind" for plant, animal and mankind. Yeshua promised, "When the Son of Man returns, it will be like it was in Noah's day." So genetic tampering prior to Noah, and at the end, mankind, both a violation of this same command.

"Lucifer, intent on replicating the diversity of creatures worshiping Yehovah in heaven, led the fallen angels to abandon their first estate, and mess with human genetics. The resultant bizarre creatures called the Nephilim or giants became 'heroes' of old renown. Between the Nephilim, the genetic tampering of human and animals, and the stories told by the fallen angels, Lucifer brought about the ancient pagan religion we now call mythology. It satisfied some of his desire to be a creator and to be worshiped.

"In trying to replicate Yehovah's gardeners, Lucifer twisted the beauty and purpose of the ganan and authored the mythological lies we knew as Hermes or Mercury. Instead of the happy-hearted flying gardeners tending Yehovah's land, and growing crops of provision, Lucifer twisted the character of the ganan to one of an erratic, volatile creature of provision that was a trickster, a thief who guided souls to Lucifer's underworld. With all his genetic tampering, Lucifer couldn't quite replicate the wings attached to the legs, so in storytelling and imagery Lucifer added wings to the shoes and helmet.

"So when the ganan give us the title Aha'Qatsin, it means my chief or my ruler. This emphasizes their reverence to Yehovah, and their happy obedience to the Ahuvati, who have been designated their rulers by Yehovah. They want no part of being aligned to a pagan religion where they became the object of worship."

"Wow!" Lani exclaimed. "I had no idea. Lucifer corrupted everything he touched and really tried to corrupt all of mankind. The ganan are such happy, honest, straightforward beings, it is sad to think that ancient man worshiped a wicked, twisted distortion of the ganan as a god."

Aymoon replied, "Yes, Lucifer tried to replicate a bunch of Yehovah's heavenly beings on earth to equal God in creative ability and build realms of beings to serve and honour him. This is the reason for the mythical creatures and the reason for the flood."

After sitting quietly for a moment, they got up to head home. Lani asked, "Tell me about the boqer, the ones attending the animals. Piper has quite a way with all the animals in his care."

"Ah, that's another interesting story," said Aymoon. "Think about the mythical Leshy, a mischievous male woodland spirit protector of the animals who has a special bond with the wolf. Or even better, think about Pan, or the satyrs, or Faun, the forest god. They were half-human with the hindquarters, legs and horns of a goat. Pan was the god of shepherds, flocks, hunting and rustic music, always carrying a reed flute with him, which he played to provoke uncontrollable lust. He presented as a highly sexualized god inspiring rape and sex for the sake of lust, and was against monogamy. He was lecherous and of questionable parentage. The caves and grottoes used by shepherds for shelter became Pan's temple.

"Lucifer took the tender heart and gentleness of the boqer, and twisted them into a horrible creature to bring people to worship him. Instead of caring for the animals, Pan encouraged people to be consumed by lust and rape. Do you know of the origin of the scapegoat?" asked Aymoon.

Lani replied, "Yes, as part of the Days of Atonement ceremony, the high priest would sacrifice a bull for his own sins and one goat as an offering to Yehovah. The high priest would then confess all the sins of the nation of Israel and place them figuratively on the head of a second goat. The second goat, the scapegoat, was then released into the wilderness to carry their sins away, never to be seen again."

"Right," said Aymoon. "Lucifer chose the goat as the lower half of Pan because the scapegoat was a foreshadowing of Yeshua's removing our sins to be remembered no more. Using the scapegoat as the base of Pan is pure blasphemy. Lucifer chose the hindquarters, and specifically the genitals of the scapegoat animal, the very animal used to symbolically carry sin away, and debased it into a repulsive, depraved creature seducing humans into worshiping him, and worshiping and engaging in sin.

"And Lucifer distorted the sweet, melodic music of the boqer that calms and pacifies the animals in their care, and created a legend of wild and erotic music, bringing birds and squirrels near and lulling them into a stupor, and causing trees to dance and humans to fall into erotic sexual relations. What an abhorrent perversion of Yehovah's herdsman, their music, and their nature to love and care for animals.

"The boqer always honour their rulers with the title Aha'Mo'ee, meaning my shelter. They are a tender race whose sole purpose is to provide shelter and protection for the creatures in their care. This is so important to them that, to the core, they value the shelter and protection we provide for them. It was a deep insult to both Yehovah and the boqer for Lucifer to use the earthly shepherd's shelter of caves and grottoes as Pan's temple."

Lani had her hand on her chest in response to her dismay. "How arrogant! What a prideful and twisted affront!"

After a long pause she said, "I almost hesitate to ask, but I assume there is a story behind the naqod and their use of Aha'Sarah."

Smiling, Aymoon said, "Of course! This is another story of a twisting of Yehovah's divine creation. Maybe the worst one. Pan was an offence against Yehovah's promise to remove our sin and His defeat of death, but this was a direct offence against our Beloved's very nature.

"Think about elves," Aymoon continued. "They were considered pagan gods, unbelievably beautiful, with magical powers. They were associated with sexual threats, seducing people, and were said to be dangerous and harmful. The origin of the word elf meant white swan, suggestive of the white feathers, the grace and beauty of the swan. Obviously the white skin and hair, the beauty and grace of the elves, was stolen from the tall, slim naqod. The naqod have beautiful porcelain-white skin and long, pure white hair and move with the grace of a swan.

"Many pagan worshipers felt elves were divinities of light. In building the legend of the elf, Lucifer tried to steal from the very nature and character of Yehovah. Yehovah is the one who is the true Light, who gives light to everyone. Yehovah, not Lucifer, and certainly not elves. In the long past, there were even some that believed there were elves of heaven and elves of the underworld.

"The naqod were created to be the head of the other eh-bed servants and in that place of leadership, it is essential to them to acknowledge our position as their rulers and priests. So they honour us with the title my prince or princess. They are being very clear they are not following the fallen angels and taking honour for themselves, but rather giving respect to our position and place."

"Oh, they are noble and righteous beings," Lani said. After a moment of thought, she asked, "What is the difference between sons of Yehovah-God and sons of man?"

Aymoon replied, "All the boqer, ganan, mashqeh, and the naqod are all created by Yehovah like the angels were created. Yehovah formed them from the dust of the land and commanded them to life, and because He directly formed, created, and ordered life into them, they are called sons of Yehovah-God. Adam too was formed of the earth. The difference between Adam and the angels is that Yehovah bent down and breathed His breath directly into his nostrils. So Adam, along with the heavenly creatures formed of dust, are considered sons of Yehovah-God.

"With the exception of Adam, all mankind comes from either Adam's side or a union or mating of a male and female, so all humans but Adam are considered sons of man."

Aymoon continued. "What is interesting is that all the sons of Yehovah-God, those He formed and created from the dust, are called holy or qadosh, which means set apart for a special purpose. And so were we who accepted the gift of redemption. We were also considered holy or set apart. Those that were set apart infuriated Lucifer. His heart filled with anger and jealousy against all set apart beings. He set out to destroy all mankind, to prevent us from being set apart. And he used a double whammy by first twisting the beauty and purity of the heavenly creatures into something vile, and second enticing humans into worshiping the vile in place of Yehovah."

Lani remembered thinking, *This was powerful information.* At the time, she felt sure Yehovah had a reason for Aymoon to learn about the past and pressed it on his heart to share it with others. It would be several months before she understood the purpose.

Lani came to a deeper understanding of Yehovah's plan and Lucifer's twisted, evil intentions. This information laid the foundation for her relationships with her servants and all of this played into fulfilling the purpose of her property. But it didn't resonate as her honour story.

9 | I AM

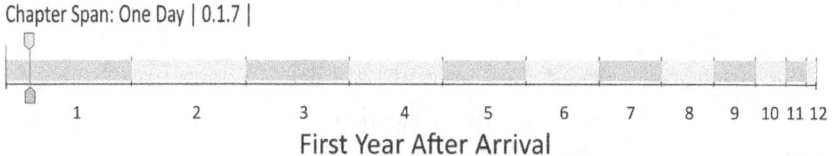

First Year After Arrival

The Weaver's poem: Who is I AM?

Yehovah.
YHVH.
LORD.
I AM that I AM.

Yehovah-Father,
Yehovah-Son,
Yehovah-Spirit.

Yehovah-El Shaddai, the almighty,
Yehovah-Elohim, the God,
Yehovah-Adonai, the master.

Yehovah-Word
Yehovah-Life, Light,
Yehovah-Yeshua.

Yehovah-Air and Yehovah-Breath,

Yehovah-Inspiration,
Yehovah-Education.

I AM that I AM, my Beloved.

The onshore breeze kicked up and Lani drew a deep breath. Refocus. Everyone would head into the Majestic City later today. This evening would be the first anniversary of their arrival here. Every year at this time, on the third day of the third moon, everyone joined in the Feast of the Haga'at, which means arrival or touch. Then every 50 years they enjoyed a weeklong festival celebration, the Jubilee Haga'at.

In just hours, she and her friends would head to the Majestic City for her first Haga'at, her first anniversary since arriving. She needed to have her story chosen by then. She thought if she reviewed weaver's poems and the stories behind them, she could easily pick out one to share. It turned out a longer process, kind of like rolling pebbles around in your hands, exploring the size and shape of each pebble looking for the right one. Lani rolled around the stories in her head, explored the impact and meaning, searching for the right one. And that took longer than she expected.

She momentarily felt the pressure of picking her story. Her friends would be gathering in a few hours. They wanted to arrive in the Majestic City long before the evening calm. She felt the excitement about the feast build, but took in a deep breath to settle herself.

There was time enough. She wanted to spend time fondling these memories, turning them over in her mind. She wanted to give appropriate honour and appreciation at the feast, she wanted to pick through the memories for something meaningful and yet different and unique to her.

The first year held many stories to pick through.

She thought how things differed here from the long past. Even the days were marked differently. First, no darkness existed here. No darkness, no fear, no bump in the night! She never worried about being alone, being hurt, the whales from the deep would not swallow her like Jonah, the lions would not try to eat her like David, she would never die. Oh, so different, and now no stress, worry, care or burden.

Second, in the long past, a full day started at midnight. A day started with morning and ended with evening. The approaching end of a day was marked by dusk then darkness, and the day ended in the middle of the night at midnight. But here, as established in the beginning, the evening and the morning made up a full day. Here, the complete day started with the evening. Sunset marked the start of a new day.

Third, the sun rose after the evening and lit the daytime. In addition to the sunlight, everything was bathed in "the Light." Light emanating from the Majestic City, from the throne. From the glory of Yehovah. Yehovah-Lamb. This Light was continual and everywhere. It eliminated all darkness, all shadow. It was the light of the evening after the sun sets.

Because there was no darkness, the word evening meant a time of calm, not a time of darkness. During the evening the Light filled space with warm, apricot-coloured light. It deluged everything in tender, almost passionate warmth. The air filled with the smell of sweet fruit. The Spirit and the Light brought Ahuvati together to share a meal and spend time reconnecting and exchanging thoughts, events of the day and stories. It was a time of community, sharing and reflection, and a time of relaxation. Some days she spent this time communing with the creatures, servants and life around her. Like today down at the beach. What a great start to the daytime!

As the evening started to wane, a mist would rise to water the land, trees and plants. This mist rolled in along with the sunrise, and the warm light of the evening shifted to a bright sunshine yellow. Then as the sun climbed higher in the sky, the light shifted to clean green light over the land. The evening passed with the mist dissipating and the light finally shifting to a vibrant, bright white light. The air tasted of strength and fed power, energizing Ahuvati for the work of the day. The Light carried such life and flooded everything with deep saturated colour.

The Light was life. Over the course of a day, it brought love and benevolence in the evening, then energized for the day's activities. Now it all seemed normal, but Lani remembered when she first encountered the air-light, the Ruach-Light that brings life to all it touches.

The Story Behind the Poem

Her first breath in was astonishing. She drew in a deep breath. Like a newborn baby, every breath was a breath of life. With every breath, she sensed the presence of Yehovah-Word and Yehovah-Spirit. The air was a part of the Light, the Light was the life, and here the two together had scent, colour and life. Every breath became a part of you, bringing love, tenderness, life and strength right inside you. It was food for the soul, so much more than air and light as she knew in the long past, when they were two separate things with no colour that expressed mood, and certainly not a living entity.

Astounded by the air-light, Lani set about to study more about the names and natures of the Light and the Breath to gain a deeper understanding of God. Aymoon discovered so much about names, titles and history with his research, Lani excitedly dug in to a little research of her own and returned to the library the following day. She learned of the many sides or aspects of Yehovah.

Living as physical beings in the long past limited people's understanding of or view into the spirit world. To help humans understand the different aspects of Yehovah, He provided His name along with different titles to help our physically limited minds understand. The big takeaway from her study was:

Yehovah is the name of the God, the One who was, is and will be. It is used by people who are in a relationship with God (not His enemies); by people with whom He shares His heart. This is His name spoken in love and respect. It also suggests His unerring morality. Everywhere in Lani's Bible where it said LORD (a title), the original Hebrew text stated His name, YHVH pronounced Yehovah.

Elohim, a title, emphasizes Yehovah's might, creative power, justice and rulership, sovereignty, and is used when talking about the mighty works done on behalf of Israel. It presents Yehovah as the transcendent being and Creator of the universe. Usually the heathen used this title of God as a general title of power. The description of creation used this title, as God had not yet shared His name with His people – they were not yet created until day six. The Ahuvati or heavenly beings rarely used this title.

El Shaddai, a title meaning the almighty. Yehovah was known by Abraham, Isaac and Jacob as El Shaddai rather than by his name Yehovah. Here, when Ahuvati wanted to reference Yehovah in His might and power, they said Yehovah-El Shaddai.

Adonai, the master, owner, sovereign ruler, exalted position for Yehovah, focuses on Yehovah's position of master, authority and all-provider. While this affirms Yehovah's position of elevated authority and creator, it includes Yehovah's revelation and interaction with His creation. Here, when Ahuvati want to express Yehovah's authority while in relationship, they say Yehovah-Adonai.

The Word. In the book of John, it is clear that in the beginning was the Word. The Word was with Yehovah and the Word was Yehovah. All things were made by the Word and in the Word was light and life. When the Word in human form was asked who He was, Yeshua replied, "I am the voice…" I AM – He is Yehovah, the voice – the Word. Lani cane to think of the aspect of Yehovah that is the voice, the aspect that brings things into existence, as Yehovah-Word.

Yeshua. This is the human form of Yehovah. He was predicted as and was called Immanuel or God with us. Joseph named him Yeshua, a version of Yehoshua, which means Yehovah is salvation. Yeshua is the Yehovah-Word who took on the form of man (Yehovah-Man) to redeem man from the death penalty of sin. Yeshua became the human kinsman redeemer, in that He made His believers His bride, His eternal mate.

The Father. Isaiah declared, "Surely you are still our Father! Even if Abraham and Jacob would disown us, LORD, you would still be our Father. You are our Redeemer from ages past." So Yehovah has a side Yehovah-Father. This is the mind, the designer, the caring, yet disciplining parent-like aspect. Isaiah 63:16.

The Spirit of Yehovah was named Ruach, pronounced Roo-ahk. It means wind, spirit of inspiration, teacher of knowledge, teacher of what will be. If you looked at creation, Yehovah-Father developed a creation plan, Yehovah-Word spoke creation into existence, and Yehovah-Spirit moved on the face of the water.

Man made in the image of God has a mind, a body and a spirit. Three parts that make the whole of a person. It is similar with God. Three parts that make the whole of God but unlike man, the three parts can operate separately. Yehovah is a complex, difficult-to-understand being.

The Father is like the mind of God. This was reinforced when Yeshua said, "No one knows the day or hour when these things will happen, not even the angels in heaven or the Son himself. Only the Father knows." Matthew 24:36.

The Son, the Word, the light, the life, that became flesh, the body. In the beginning Yehovah-Word was with Yehovah-Father, and Yehovah-Word was God. All things came into existence through the commands of the Yehovah-Word and in the Yehovah-Word are life and light, and truth.

The Spirit, the wind, the teacher that moves through creation. In the beginning of the cosmos, the Spirit moved on the surface of the waters. Lani learned of the presence and scent of the Ruach. Sometimes she smelled something like pine, and other times a delicate flower scent and yet other times something like fresh cut grass.

Lani saw how these were different components of God. Yehovah, I AM that I AM, is the name of the Lord God. El Shaddai is a far less intimate title referencing His might and power. The Word is the part of Yehovah that brought all into existence. The Word was and is light and life. The Word took on human form and died to redeem His intended from our sins. Here, this light and life are tangible. Ruach is the Spirit, the teacher, the wind. Here, the spirit is in the wind, the air, bringing with it knowledge and inspiration.

In speech and thought, Lani followed the practice of using His name Yehovah followed by the aspect she was referring to. The first word was the primary being Yehovah, and the second word described the aspect (Primary being-Aspect). For example, when speaking of the mighty and powerful aspect, she said, "Yehovah-El Shaddai." When she wanted to acknowledge His authority while in relationship as her master, she said, Yehovah-Adonai. When speaking of the Word, the Son, "Yehovah-Word," "Yehovah-Yeshua" or "Yehovah-Man." One God, different aspects.

The air-light is the Yehovah-Light (the way, truth, life), and Yehovah-Spirit (the wind, teacher, inspiration, breath). Different aspects of the same Yehovah. The Word and Spirit make up the air-light that filled her new world. It is the spirit of inspiration. Just breathing it in would bring ideas. It is alive (the Life) and shares its moods of courage, energy, and wisdom. Sometimes it would bring and share knowledge of what will be. It was the source of quick knowing. It is how Ahuvati knew other Ahuvati even though they never met. It is one way Ahuvati gain wisdom and insight.

Interesting, but still not her honour story.

10 | First Friends

Chapter Span: One Day | 0.1.1 |

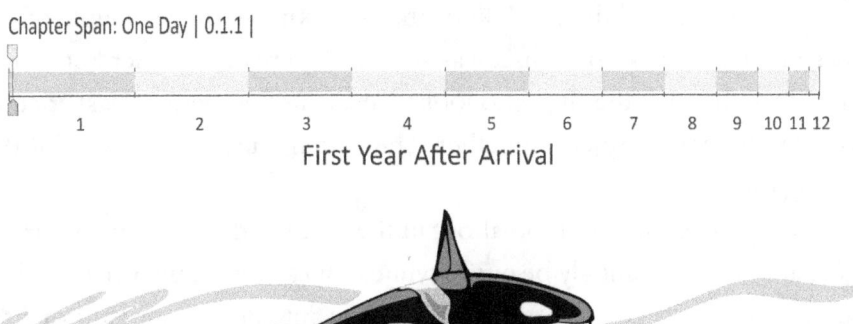

First Year After Arrival

Lani navigated back to the poem about their arrival. The first feast she celebrated here occurred on this first day. Unlike the long past where you introduced yourself to others, here Yehovah-Spirit, the Ruach, provided a quick knowledge about the person you were meeting.

Lani let out a quiet sigh, remembering when she met her first friends here. The arrival day.

The weaver's poem: Arrival Friends

Aymoon, from Africa: Faithful.
Cheka, a Samaritan: Joy.
Kazhu, from Asia: Reliable.
Honani, a Polynesian: Song.
Lani: Weaver, Creative.

The Story Behind the Poem

All the Ahuvati had just arrived from earth and gathered in the courtyard.

As they moved to the Majestic City to celebrate the first Feast of the Haga'at, several in her immediate vicinity turned in unison to look at each other.

She experienced the quick knowing she'd known only a couple of times in the long past, but oh, it was so much deeper and richer knowing here. Since that day, the five who looked at each other became fast friends, working on several projects together. They often joined each other for the evening calm.

Everyone excitedly stood about in the courtyard. They'd finally arrived, and wore stunningly beautiful white stones around their necks with their new names. They all breathed the exotic, intoxicating air-light of life. They looked at each other, then at their stones, then back at each other. In that brief moment they knew each other by their new names. Aymoon, a beautifully handsome Ahuvati with a wonderfully rich African accent. They all knew his nature as one of faithfulness throughout his long past. His name matched him perfectly, an honour to his character and longstanding commitment to Yehovah. He smiled, opened his arms to the rest of them and in joy, they embraced each other in such rich love, joy and trust.

After a long moment, they all turned to the fine-featured Cheka, a Samaritan. Although physically small her presence boldly revealed itself in joy personified. She gurgled with happiness and laughter, and wore a contagious smile. Her name fit her perfectly. They all broke out in joyful laughter, the purest joy Lani ever experienced.

They all turned to Kazhu, probably the best-looking Asian man Lani ever met. They knew him as the rock, a steady, reliable fellow. Since that day, Lani spent many, many hours with Kaz talking through her projects. He provided uncountable steady insights and reliable foresight and advice. She so enjoyed her time with him.

The fourth member of her little group was Honani. Nan had deep brown eyes, high cheekbones, blue-black hair and a beautiful Polynesian complexion. Lani came to know Nan as a warm, sweet, graceful woman, but when she spoke for the first time, they heard the most rich, melodious sound. Nan's voice made everything she said sound like a song.

Finally, they all turned to Lani. She remembered thinking they were all so perfectly gorgeous, profoundly and indescribably beautiful. And so young. Looking around, everyone seemed about 30 years old. In the long past she lived for 55 years, and now she shined with the gift of eternal youth. She then realized everyone exuded beauty and perfection from inside.

Lani always struggled with accepting herself and her looks. The long past world had been so judgmental and she always felt she just didn't measure up. But not so here. No one judged her by her appearance.

And then the revelation washed over her like a tidal wave. She equaled everyone else in beauty. With all her characteristics perfected she exuded a beauty, shining out from within her. She too was 30 years old again, and would be for all eternity. Putting on immortality ensured she would never age. And she was astoundingly beautiful, shaming the most gorgeous person of Hollywood or magazines.

She smiled at everyone as they came to know the meaning of her name. She spent time thinking about what the future would look like, and since arriving here, she still thought about it. She loved her new name. She felt it reflected her inner life. Her earthly name was the name of her physical being and her carnal mind. It turned out that the physical being and the carnal mind was not who anyone really was. She was Aha'La'anni, the weaver of images and stories of what was, is and is yet to come, known as Lani, the weaver or the creative.

They held each other with their eyes, knowing more and more about each other without sharing words. They all knew an eternal friendship started at that moment, never to be broken. Never to have anything that would bring tension between them. They would love each other and be loved by each other forever.

Overwhelmed by the depth of promised friendship, they turned to follow the crowds to the Majestic City, knowing they would always have each other. At that moment, she first realized this knowing they all just experienced was the Ruach.

Lani thought for a moment about this unbelievably exciting, life-changing moment. Certainly one worthy of mention as an honour story. But everyone would have the same story. Lani really wanted to live up to her name as a creative weaver of stories. She decided to keep this in mind, but to keep looking for the right one. So far, she leaned toward the seed, germination and development of her estate tied to her mission. But many additional stories contributed to this one. She need to continue reviewing her poems and stories to pull together the right honour story.

11 | The Promise

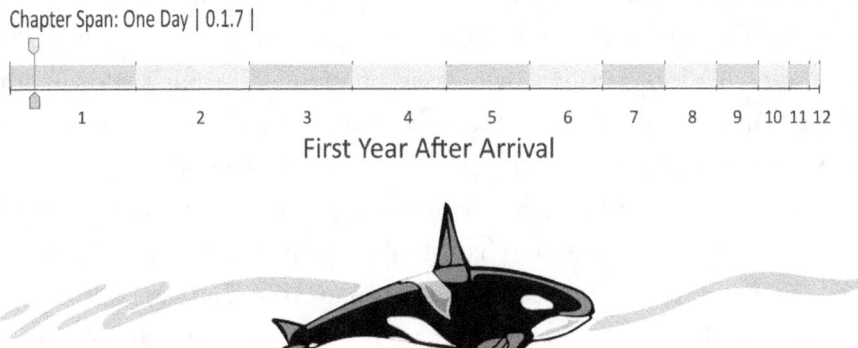

Chapter Span: One Day | 0.1.7 |

1   2   3   4   5   6   7   8   9   10 11 12

First Year After Arrival

The weaver's poem: Cosmic Romance

The desire from before time,
A bride, a mate of His own kind.

The betrothed.
A choice to be made,
A covenant to seal the deal,
The price to be paid.
Love gifts.
Prepare paradise.
Snatch away.

Consummate.
A wife, a mate of His own kind.

Lani wrote this poem in her sixth month here, but a moment of contemplation early in her time here actually inspired it.

The Story Behind the Poem

Lani took the seventh day to contemplate all that had happened over the first week. She wandered down the beach south of her mansion. She came across a quiet little alcove protected behind by a ring of palm trees. It looked straight out into the bay, but when sitting there, it would be difficult to see her from up or down the beach. A vague recollection of a beachside location of her long past briefly crossed her mind. She didn't know it at the time, but this would become a favourite spot for her. It would be her place in nature where she would go to think, to find inspiration.

She settled in and became lost in her memories when Abbey nudged her arm, bringing her attention back to the beach. She was looking for some attention. Lani wrapped her arm around Abbey, inviting her to sit with her awhile. Stroking her golden fur, it amused her to think of the long past when she worried about the fate of her beloved companions. She often worried about leaving them behind. Had she only known, she could have saved herself much worry. She always felt Yehovah created her youngest dog specifically for her. Abbey turned out to be such a sweet, loving girl, smart and funny. She and Abbey truly loved each other very much. Abbey slept with her, wrapping her front legs around her. She was so bonded with Lani and it ached to think of leaving her behind.

In the long past Abbey always came to the door to see her off in the morning. And every morning Lani placed her right hand on Abbey's head and spoke a blessing over her and all in the household. And Abbey looked out the window every evening, waiting for Lani to return.

Years prior, Lani's mom saw a satanic being in their home and together they prayed in the Name of Yeshua that the house would have Yehovah's protection. Since then, Abbey often turned to look up and down in the corners of rooms or edges of the property, staring at unseen things. Both Lani and her mom believed, like Balaam's donkey, this wee dog saw the angels dispatched to protect the house and all those in it. Sometimes Abbey tracked the angels' rapid movements. Never, not once, had Abbey been fearful of what she saw. Lani often wondered if Abbey would sense a change in the angels when the time to leave neared.

Yehovah was truly good and knew the desires of Lani's heart. Since their arrival Abbey became a part of just about everything Lani did. Everyone who met Lani came to know Abbey. The two were rarely separate. If Abbey wasn't with Lani, she could usually be found in one of three places – swimming in the ocean with Celebration, running the fields with the lions Jareo and Jalao, or just hanging out with Piper. Abbey led an eternally happy life.

Stroking Abbey brought to mind the concept of a constant companion. Living in a marriage with Yeshua was not at all what Lani expected.

In the long past, it seemed a really weird concept to share your husband with thousands of other people, both men and women. She was always glad she was not a man having to deal with what she thought would be emasculating to think of being a bride and wife for all eternity. And besides that, the promise that He went to prepare a place for us so that we would never be separated equally puzzled her. How could He be present with all of us all the time? Would it be like a bunch of five-year-olds playing soccer, just everyone moving as a big blob, doing everything together with Yeshua surrounded by thousands upon thousands of others? That didn't seem right, but she just couldn't imagine how that would all work.

Life in the long past only allowed for naïve, narrow thinking. Back then, her limited thinking and understanding of what this new and eternal life would be like left her confused.

Lani remembered hearing the traditional Jewish wedding foreshadowed her future role of Yeshua's bride. In a traditional Jewish wedding, the groom's father chose a bride and the son approved of the choice. They gave covenant in writing to the bride as a promise that marriage would be fulfilled. If the bride accepted the proposal, the groom and bride broke bread and ate and drank from the same cup to seal the deal. The groom then paid a price to show the depth of his love for her, gave the bride some love gifts, and then made a speech or proclamation that he was leaving to prepare a place for his bride at his father's house, but would come for her soon. The groom's father also gave the bride some gifts, like an inheritance. This sealed the betrothal, known as the kiddushin (which meant sanctified and set apart for a sacred purpose, to be the wife of a particular man). At this point the woman was legally the wife of the man. The only way out is death or divorce.

The groom and father returned to the father's house where the father oversaw the groom's preparations, and when the father was satisfied, he gave permission for the son to go and collect his bride. Therefore, no one knew the day nor the hour, except the father.

When given permission, the groom came as a thief in the night to snatch his bride away. The groomsmen ran ahead and blew the shofar to announce his coming. The bride and groom returned to the father's house to consummate their marriage, known as the nisuin (meaning elevation), and then they celebrated. The celebration was followed by the marriage supper with the wedding guests.

And all that helped her understand the stages and the concepts, but she lacked understanding of what consummation really meant in this situation.

Yehovah-Adonai is the mind, the designer, the power and the authority. Yehovah-Spirit is the breath and teacher. She could sort of see how the mind and spirit could be everywhere at once for the multitude of people, but she really didn't get the groom thing. She understood that the Yehovah-Word became flesh, became a man. But this just seemed to make consummation more confusing. How can one man possibly be married to all of the saved people? How would each person get His time and attention to maintain an intimate relationship? And how does that intimacy take place? But now that she was here, it all made perfect sense.

First, Yehovah-Father (Adonai, the mind and designer), Yehovah-Son (the Word, Light, life, truth and physical flesh), and the Yehovah-Spirit are aspects of one being named Yehovah. Second, humans were made in His image each with a mind, a physical body and a spirit, yet we functioned as a single person in the long past. And while Yehovah packed His power and eternal and continual presence in all time and all space into a mere human vessel, Yeshua the man was still mentally and spiritually God. As a man, He was Yehovah-Man.

Third, like a body of water is an aggregate of water droplets, Ahuvati are an aggregate of spirits and minds. In the long past the joining of bodies consummated a marriage. Here, joining the minds and spirits consummated the marriage of Ahuvati to Yeshua. Yeshua entered into and become one in mind and spirit with each Ahuvati for all eternity.

Ha'Ahuvati, the Beloved, the multitude of transformed people, express various characters, skills and functions. If any one were missing, the group would not be whole. Everyone's a necessary component of the whole. And while a physical group of bodies would be doing one thing and another group doing something else, it was like a hand and foot, each with a different purpose and objective, but still part of the spiritual and mental whole.

In the long past, a couple fell in love when a man entered and filled the heart of a woman, and once married they would consummate by his entering her body. They would renew their connection through physical intimacy.

Here, this relationship started with Yeshua entering the hearts of the people, and on consummation He entered the minds of His Beloved. Now, consummation was a meeting inside the mind of each Ahuvati. Sometimes, they shared a leisurely experience of sharing thoughts of love and acknowledgement. Other times, they wildly chased thoughts, bounded through green meadows of possibility and leapt to mountaintops of impossibility. And yet other times explored the nuances of notions.

Lani took the morning mist as an opportunity to mentally share or exchange her intimate thoughts and feelings in both the mental and spiritual level with her Beloved.

She thought of it this way. In the long past, the shadow of a person was not the real thing, but an outline. A shadow didn't have life, personality or dimension, but was a hint of the shape only. The life and detail were missing. So too the physical intimacy of the long past was just a shadow of the spiritual and mental intimacy she had now. The physical was a mere hint, an outline of the real intimacy.

From before time and space, Yehovah was a nonphysical entity. He created the physical cosmos and physical beings within the cosmos for a future purpose in the nonphysical realms. The richness of life here was in the spiritual and mental realms, and the mingling of mind and spirit in consummation was not limited by a short, physical joining.

Lani thought of the physical consummation of the long past like bouncing two balls off each other. It offered a brief connection, but they were still two separate balls. Here, the spiritual-mental consummation was like mixing water and grape juice concentrate. Once mixed, they could never be separated again.

Adam walked with Yehovah and talked with Him face to face, in the physical. Ahuvati finally returned to interfacing with Yehovah, but now the interaction was instant in each one's mind. Although all Ahuvati are mentally and spiritually joined to Yehovah-Son, it is an entering by Yehovah into the individual minds of Ahuvati. Ahuvati haven't entered the mind of Yehovah and are not all knowing as Yehovah is. No Ahuvati could take in the rope of all information from all time and space, just a thread.

Because Lani joined to the mind and spirit of Yehovah, she was constantly connected both mentally and spiritually, yet she retained her free will to focus or tune into what she wanted. Like Adam chose to physically walk and talk with Yehovah, Lani could choose to do the same, but really the intimate relationship was built on spiritual and mental togetherness. And unlike the limitations of physical togetherness, both spiritual and mental togetherness is instant, constant and on demand. Lani thought it was quite different to have someone else inside your mind. In the long past, this was the one place you were always alone, sometimes desperately alone. It was totally extraordinary to have an independent, all-powerful mind sharing the same mental space, to have another's thoughts occurring in your own personal and private mind.

Lani still lived as an individual, and was free to come up with her thoughts and take on things, but moment by moment she could tune into her Beloved. And her Beloved could reach out and talk to her, share His thoughts and feelings. This was not mind control. It was a two-way relationship, just like in the physical where each partner lived as their own person, but continually loved deeply with their heart and sought out time to talk and share. Both Yehovah and Ahuvati were separate entities, loved each other deeply with their hearts, and predominantly shared and talked mind to mind and communed spirit to spirit.

Lani had a rich mental relationship with Yehovah. It was very cool to share her mental space, but a common experience for all the Ahuvati.

Right. This was not an honour story. Lani moved onto the next poem.

12 | Concert Canyon

Chapter Span: Two Days | 0.1.8 to 0.1.9 |

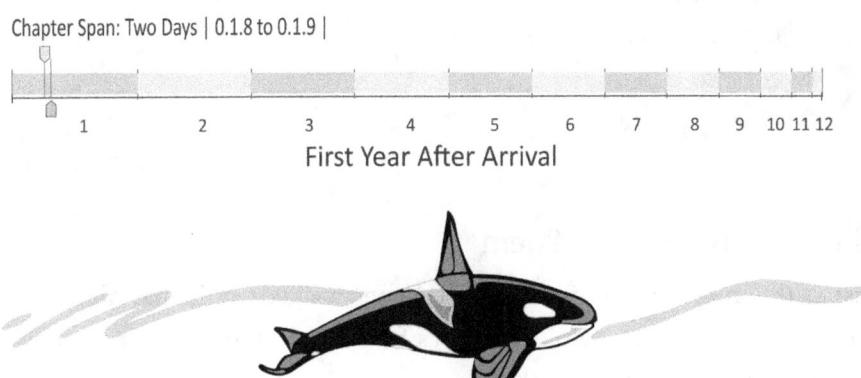

First Year After Arrival

Lani took a deep breath and closed her eyes. Life in the long past was spent predominantly alone because life was based on the physical being and physical presence. Absence of physical presence meant absence. But even when Lani was with people, she felt different and alone, sometimes even lonely.

Mankind was created for the ultimate purpose of mental and spiritual joining with Yehovah. Adam and Eve lost their intimate relationship with the introduction of sin. Mortals had physical joining as a placeholder, but it could never satisfy the deep, longing desire for fulfillment of what we were created for – spiritual and mental joining.

Here, Lani was never alone. Every breath brought light and life into her being. Her mind and spirit permanently mingled with Yehovah. The relationship never experienced a low nor did she struggle to stay in relationship. And Ahuvati always played a part in her days.

Following this train of thought, Lani flipped through her poems to find some based on her time with her friends and settled on one titled "Joy."

The weaver's poem: Joy

I celebrate with music,
wings to the mind,
flight to the imagination,
swept into dance.
It is gaiety to life.

The Story Behind the Poem

Just as the mist burned off, Lani and Abbey walked up the bay along the beach. She saw Cheka, two of Cheka's friends and four dogs up ahead, looking at something in the sky.

Lani looked up and saw shimmering, prismatic flashes high in the air. When she joined the group, Cheka introduced Lani to her two companions. "Lani, this is –" Before Cheka could finish, Lani was smiling and gave them the standard greeting. "Elia, the one who rises, and Hanna, the graceful. I welcome your eternal friendship."

Laughing at herself, Cheka said, "I just can't get used to the fact that introductions are unnecessary here." Hanna hugged Cheka and said to Lani, "We were watching the eder flying up from the south. Elia and I live across the bay on the mainland. We spotted these distant flashes of colour and decided to come out to the island to watch. As they got closer, we realized they were giant birds. Thousands have flown by already in flocks."

"Here comes the next flock," said Elia. It looked like there were eight or ten in this group. They flew nearly silent. You wouldn't know of their presence unless you noticed the flash of colour across the land and looked up. As they neared, the eders let out a call that sounded like laughter, then turned and banked, changing their course to head toward the group standing on the beach. Still quite high in the air, it took several circles to lose altitude. A kaleidoscope of colours coloured the land and ocean. They were coming in for a landing!

Lani watched as they circled. They were each at least 25 ft. long with a wingspan of about 80 ft. Their heads looked like a jackal with tall, thin ears. A beautiful ruff of feathers ringed their necks. They had a stocky body with rather thick legs ending in huge webbed feet. The wings were see-through and iridescent. Sunlight shining through them resulted in a myriad of multicoloured lights flashing in bursts of colour across the land and water.

They came in over the ocean on their final circle above. Nine birds, each with 80-ft. wingspans coming straight in toward them made for a spectacular sight. Their webbed feet spread to look like 10-ft. paddles. They glided slowly and quietly in, landing gracefully on the water, slowing to a stop at the edge of the beach. A perfect landing. They tucked in their monstrous wings and waddled on shore, bowing before the group.

Two moved in front of Lani. She walked up to the closer and smaller of the two and petted her head. The head alone was 2-ft. across. The creature let out a light breath and closed her eyes. Lani scratched around her ruff and she let out a long sigh from the depth of her lungs, triggering the laughter sound they heard earlier. The larger eder pressed in close for some of Lani's attention. As Lani petted the larger one, Abbey approached the smaller one and they nuzzled each other.

In their presence Lani knew they were here for a purpose. She thought for a moment, then when she realized why they were here she gasped and turned to her friends. They just received the same revelation and looked equally surprised.

Elia said, "These are our eder! For – " and he paused, almost too surprised to say out loud what he realized.

Hanna had three in front of her and smiling said, "Oh aye, they're our trusty steeds and we're the jockeys." One rested its head on the ground and Hanna climbed on board.

Lani turned back to the two in front of her. Both were smiling. She wondered if they had names and then knew, like her servants, it was for her to name them. She put her hand on the head of the larger male one and said, "I will call you Boz, for you are swift and sure. May you be happy living under my leadership and take pleasure in my riding."

Lani turned to the smaller female one and said, "I will name you Makani, lover of wind. May your days be filled with joy in flying." Lani paused, then added, "May you be steady and sure in the air." Then she realized why she had been given two. For a moment, she was unsure, but felt a warm confidence as reassurance.

In the long past Abbey loved swimming in their pool. When she became tired, she would start crying and running around Lani, "asking" for her to get out the inflatable beds. Abbey loved floating and napping so much that Lani labelled one of the floats "Cleopatra's barge, Queen of the Nile." Abbey became surprisingly good at balancing, even in waves.

Lani had no idea that was preparation for Abbey to fly on the back of a giant bird. Now she knew why she felt an urge to add the blessing of "steady and sure in the air."

Lani turned to pick up Abbey and help her get aboard, but Abbey and Makani worked it out between them. Makani lowered her one wing, allowing Abbey to gently use it as a step up. Abbey circled on Makani's back to face ahead and lie down. Makani untucked a couple of "fingers" from the base of her wings and wrapped them around Abbey. Lani cupped Abbey under the chin and asked if she was okay. Abbey gave her a big lick on the face and a happy tail wag.

It was her turn to get on board. Lani looked over at Hanna to see how she was positioned. Hanna looked like a racing jockey aboard a thoroughbred, with the biggest grin imaginable.

Lani didn't wish to be left out of this fun. As she approached Boz, he lowered his wing for her to use as a step up. She got on his back and slid right into place. Her legs almost locked into position at the base of his wings. Boz's fingers untucked and wrapped around her hips, allowing her to sit up or lie along his back. She fit quite comfortably and felt secure. Two very large tufts of feathers came out of the back of his ruff for Lani to hold onto.

Lani looked over at her friends. All people and dogs were on board and ready to go. Lani leaned forward and said, "Okay Boz, lead us out on a gentle flight over the island." With that, Boz stood up on his legs and stretched out his wings, giving them a test flap. Lani felt the lift of about 20 ft. up just from this one light wingbeat. Boz squatted down, jumped straight up about 30 ft. and gave a light pump down with his wings, and they were off. In a few powerful thrusts, they rose to hundreds of feet in the air.

Lani looked over at Makani to be sure Abbey was still doing okay. Abbey sported a huge goldie grin and a wagging tail. *For a dog, it must be like driving in the car with an open window.*

Lani found this view of her property interesting. She noticed the escarpment ran the entire length of the island. She saw Kaz's treemansion built off the edge of the escarpment high at the top of the tree canopy. He would have a spectacular view of the strait between the island and the mainland, and probably saw quite a distance across the mainland. Now she understood what he meant by gatherings in the air.

Gliding provided a surprisingly quiet flight, but even when Boz pumped his wings, she still heard her friends' chatter. They circled the island in a matter of five minutes. Lani discovered that Boz responded to just the slightest tension on the ruff feathers, providing him guidance on which direction she wanted to go. Hanna and Elia came near to talk about their destination. Cheka suggested they ask the eder to take them somewhere not yet visited by Ahuvati. They all agreed and gave verbal instructions to their eder. In turn, the eder called to each in a series of laughing calls and then headed directly east across the coast, deep into the heart of the mainland.

The coastlands gave way to foothills and eventually high mountains. The eder knew passages along fertile valleys through the mountains. Lani spotted many mansions scattered through the foothills and valleys.

They came to a line of very high mountains. Boz glided down to circle along a huge waterfall that must have been a couple of thousand feet high. They flew up along the river toward the falls then banked away, flying through the mist and spray.

Past the huge waterfall the mountains gave way to foothills. While the valleys filled with abundant vegetation, the hills lay bare. Lani saw the structure of the foothills in layers of transparent gemstone. It looked like a rainbow of colour, starting with purple at the base, progressing through blue, green, yellow, orange and ending with red peaks. The beauty of the light shining through the stone totally fascinated her.

After the gemstone foothills the land levelled out and they could see for hundreds of miles. In the distance there looked to be a scar on the land. It seemed that was the destination. As they approached, Lani saw a circular canyon. The eder slowed as they neared the edge. They glided in, slowing their speed by tilting their wings slightly up. When just feet from the ground, they tucked them in and landed gently on their feet.

Boz released his hold on Lani and leaned forward for her to dismount. They all gathered at the edge of the canyon and looked down on an amphitheatre carved out of the rock with a platform at the north end. They headed for a nearby set of stairs. Once inside, Hanna headed straight for the platform. Everyone else sat down, awaiting her performance.

Hanna looked around thoughtfully, then said, "My heart's in the Highlands a-chasing the deer – A-chasing the wild deer, and following the roe; My heart's in the Highlands wherever I go (Robert Burns, 1789)." The words echoed around the amphitheatre. Hanna cocked her head and thought for a moment, then turned her head to the left. She sang out a note while turning her head all the way to the right. It not only echoed, but seemed to repeat in a harmonic resonance, amplifying the sound. Hanna tried it again, this time singing a sliding scale. The resonance frequencies seemed to be aligned to the Ahuvati voice with all sound being amplified.

It didn't seem extraordinarily loud sitting in the amphitheatre, but the sound magnified as it escaped and carried across the flat lands above. Shortly, they saw several new eders flying overhead, bringing more Ahuvati.

One of the new arrivals was Honani, Lani's friend. Nan headed straight for the stage to join Hanna. She listened to the results of the sounds Hanna made, then sang O Holy Night. The harmonics of the canyon made for an absolutely beautiful sound, probably the best performance of that song Lani ever heard. Shortly after Nan began singing, Hanna began to dance, closing her eyes and expressing the music in movement.

After trying out the Christmas carol, Nan paused for a moment, then sang a new song she wrote about their arrival here. It moved from hauntingly beautiful to joyous, in complex patterns and strains of notes. As she finished the second verse, a man Nan seemed to know joined her on the platform.

He sang along with her, providing a deep bass harmony, equally complex. The experience went beyond sound. The music moved like waves washing through Lani's brain. She almost sensed the wave of delight moving from her ears through to the front of her head. Lani loved music in the long past, but that now seemed like garbage compared to the depth and rich sound of music here.

The duo sang quite a number of songs, the last ones brought everyone to their feet and dancing broke out throughout the now large audience. Lani met Lisha, sweet, honest truth, and Elkanah, Yehovah has purchased, when dancing. She discovered they lived as messianic Jews from Europe of the long past, and taught her some good Jewish dance steps. Laughter and joy rolled throughout the audience.

When the impromptu concert ended, Hanna invited everyone nearby, people and dogs, back to her place for the evening calm. Chattering together, the group climbed the steps to the mesa to locate their eders among the huge collection of eders. It looked as though everyone chose to ride their eders here instead of vehicles. With everyone leaving at once, it could have been a challenge locating Boz and Makani, but Lani told Abbey to lead the way.

Without a misstep, Abbey went directly to their group of eders. After ensuring she was safely aboard, Lani mounted Boz for the return flight. Hanna took the lead, getting them back to the coast before the sky shifted to the colour of the calm. Upon setting down at her friend's property, Hanna's eh-bed approached with food prepared for all the eders and dogs. All the animals had tucked into their food before anyone moved off the beach.

Curious, Lani paid attention to the Entry Garden. She loved that entry gardens all had a story to tell. Kazhu was so good at this and nailed the story every time. Lani found it easier just to get Kaz to visit the garden and tell her the story than to try to figure it out herself, but he wasn't there.

At the entry Lani saw three trees. One big old gnarled tree in the middle of the path. Two smaller trees on either side, each with equal ground between them. The big tree in the middle extended its branches the full length of the garden with abundant branches and leaves. The one tree on the left extended almost the full length of the garden, the branches fully leafed. But near the end of the garden, the branches sharply veered left away from the big tree branches.

The right tree also had branches that extended the full length of the garden, but had a big bare section in the middle where the branches didn't have any leaves and fell low to the ground. Further along the branches, the leaves started again and the branches rose back up to their proper height.

At the start of the garden, the big old tree intertwined its branches with the other trees, creating a beautiful canopy. On the left, the intertwining connections continued almost to the end, but stopped when the branches of the left tree twisted away, stretching out of reach of the middle tree.

On the right, these connecting, intertwining branches stopped abruptly before the bare branches. They connected and intertwined again further along the garden. Once the intertwining with the middle tree resumed, the branches of the tree to the right began to leaf again and the intertwining connections with the big tree raised the branches of the right tree up to normal height.

Underneath the trees the undergrowth started at the trunks with abundant plant life. The groundcover continued under the left tree until its branches diverged, then the undergrowth petered away to nothing. Under the right tree, just after the intertwining connections stopped, the undergrowth erupted with abundant flowers of all imaginable colours. This quickly gave way to bare ground underneath the bare, drooping branches. Once the intertwining started again, the undergrowth became rich and abundant again.

Lani looked at it for a long while, knowing the trees represented people, but she couldn't quite figure out the story. She would have to get Kaz to figure it out.

Hanna watched Lani study the garden and caught up to her to ask what she thought of the trees. Lani laughed. "Well, I know it is a story about three people. The big one and the one on the left seem to be connected until near the end where it leaves the relationship. The one on the right seems to leave the relationship, but then comes back. The big tree picks it up off the ground and gives it life again. It seems familiar, but I'm just not quite identifying the story."

Hanna laughed and said, "You done a braw good job. I didna have a clue. I have a pure brilliant friend Kazhu, who came to spy my garden and figured it out."

"Kaz!" Lani exclaimed. "He figured out my garden too. He must be on a mission."

Laughing, Hanna answered, dropping her heavy Scottish accent. "Aye. He discovered this garden tells the story of grace. It symbolizes the story of the prodigal son. The tree in the middle represents the father. He gave his wealth equally to his two sons, one on the left and one on the right. The branches tell of their relationship with the father. You're right about the meaning of the intertwining branches. The plants underneath tell of the wealth and abundance. At first all is equal, but you can see the son on the right left his father and the connections stop. There was a wild abundance of flowers in a riot of colour that shows he spent his wealth in wild, riotous living, then quickly lost it all, fading to empty, bare land. This illustrates when the son dropped in stature and lived below his heritage, and the tree branches dropped low to the bare earth. When he reconnected with his father, his father elevated him and shared his abundance with his son.

"When the tree on the right reconnected with the father, the tree on the left deserted the relationship in anger and in absence of relationship felt the absence of wealth and abundance. The father, eager for relationship, reached out to both trees and offered his abundance to both regardless of the past. I love this story because of the grace provided to me in my life of the long past." With that, Hanna left Lani to walk the garden path by herself to contemplate the meaning.

Lani watched Hanna, the graceful, walk on and wondered about a garden of grace for the graceful one. She sensed a deeper meaning there. Turning back to the Entry Garden, Lani noticed how the branches intertwined. They were so interwoven that nothing short of cutting down the trees would separate them. When she got to the end, Lani paid particular attention to the left tree. The old tree was reaching out with its branches to connect, but the tree on the left had branches deflected as far away from the old tree as possible.

In the long past, once connected and in relationship with Yehovah, you really had to be deliberate to turn away. But anyone who returned was welcomed back with abundance. Looking at the branches above, Lani pondered her fully intertwined and abundant life.

Abbey finished eating and caught up with Lani. She petted Abbey's head and Abbey leaned in heavily against her leg. Lani bent down to hug and kiss her, and together they headed into Hanna's mansion.

A story of gifts and the joy in life here. A good story. Actually this story laid seeds for both Hanna and Nan, but this would not be her honour story.

13 | Memorials

Chapter Span: Two Days | 0.1.9 to 0.1.10 |

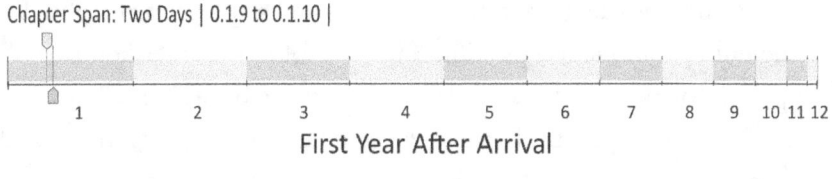

First Year After Arrival

Lani sat back for a moment to look out over the ocean. She remembered being intrigued by what she saw while travelling to the impromptu concert in the canyon. She moved to the next poem inspired by when the hills of gemstone sparked a grand idea.

The weaver's poem: Remembrances

Memorials
Formed of the land,
The Light, the heart, from a wound in the side.
Echoes of Adam,
Echoes from the cross.

The Story Behind the Poem

Since the flight to Harmony Canyon, Lani thought about the foothills of beautiful gemstone. Something intrigued her and the next morning she felt prompted to visit the Ahuvati living there. She considered flying in her sporty vehicle, but then called the eders Boz and Makani to fly her and Abbey to the gemstone hills. She thought the open air flight would be better to view the landscape.

In the early morning light, the hills provided a spectacular sight. The air of the entire valley shimmered in rainbow colours. Lani asked Boz to fly up and down the range of hills to soak in the beauty. In what Lani considered the most beautiful valley, she spotted several Ahuvati out and about, and asked Boz to land nearby.

The Ahuvati spotted them and drew close to greet her. The first one gave the standard greeting. "Lani, the creative, I welcome your eternal friendship."

"Adi'el, the jewel, I too welcome your eternal friendship," Lani replied. She then turned to the other two and said, "Asher, the happy and blessed, and Keshet, the rainbow, I welcome your eternal friendship as well." Looking down at Abbey, Lani said, "We flew over to go to the concert at Harmony Canyon yesterday and I felt an urge to come to meet you and learn about these gorgeous hills you live among."

"We've been looking forward to visitors and you and Abbey are the first," said Adi'el.

"We know there is a grand purpose in us living here and have been talking about what that might be. All of us feel the purpose will be revealed through our friendship with other Ahuvati, so we are pretty excited to have you as our first visitor," said Keshet.

Asher stepped forward and invited her and Abbey on a tour of the nearby gemstone hill. They just finished scoping out a trail and were keen to take their first visitors on a tour. With Abbey running out front, the group made their way to the base of the hill. They asked where Lani lived and wanted to know about her life on the water.

As they approached the purple base of the hill, the brilliance of colour astounded Lani. The colour layers were not distinct, but rather the stone gradually progressed through all the colours. This meant that every stone pulled from the hill was unique in colour.

114

As the trail turned up through the purple base, Lani bent over to pick up a stray violet-coloured stone and held it up to the light. It captured light, then sparkled and twinkled, and shot out bright light of vivid violet with ebbing and flowing violet sparkles dancing in the beam of light.

Lani decided to hold onto the small violet stone and followed her new friends up the trail. They stopped for a rest about halfway up in the yellow section. Lani now carried a collection of stones and pulled them out to look at them.

Adi'el said, "Hold two of them up to the light and see what happens."

Lani looked over her assortment of colours ranging from violet to yellowy-green. She picked out a cobalt blue one, leaned down to pick up a pure sunshine yellow one from the ground and held them together in the sunlight. A beautiful pure emerald green light burst out with sparkles of both cobalt and yellow in the light. It looked absolutely spectacular.

She tried a different pair. The violet and the yellow, wondering if it would be a dull grey, but no, shafts of orange and blue with twinkles of yellow and violet. The light and colour didn't act the way she expected, as it had in the long past. No, it behaved sometimes additive and sometimes split into colours a quarter way around the colour wheel. Quite bizarre, but totally spectacular. She had never seen light behave this way. She became quietly thoughtful for quite awhile and then felt the hatching of an idea. Another seed.

"Do you think it'd be possible to carve this stone?" Lani asked.

Asher grinned. "I hadn't thought about carving it. I just collected a few stones that I thought were beautiful and took them home as decoration."

Keshet laughed. "They call me rainbow, but Asher's home looks like a rainbow with all the stones he's collected."

Asher said, "We could take a few pieces back with us, if you would like to try."

"Yes, I would like that if you don't mind helping," said Lani. They decided to go to the top and collect on the way back down.

At the top, Lani picked up a red stone and held it to the light with a yellow and blue stone. Out of the stone burst a brilliant white light with bits of dazzling white sparkles. She looked over the area carefully for a stone of a colour that moved her. She moved from the crimson toward the cerise and selected an area between the two. They worked a bit to pry loose a stone about double the size of her hand. It was as spectacular as Lani expected.

On the way down Lani selected several different coloured pieces, her friends happily helping to pry loose just the right ones. When they got to the bottom of the trail, Adi'el invited everyone to her place for some food and drink. As they were lounging, Asher asked, "What do you hope to carve from these?"

"I had done a couple of sculptures in the long past out of clay and soapstone, but I am quite inspired by the effect of light through the stone and how it blends in colour. And the way light is amplified and sparkles. I'd like to do a series of sculptures, each telling an old story or parable," Lani said, confident it was possible. "I'll take these pieces home and experiment, then come up with a plan. Once I figure out how this will work and get my designs put together, I'd like to come back to collect what I will need, if that is okay with you."

Immediately, in unison they agreed. Keshet and Asher packed up the pieces of stone they collected in some palm leaves and strung them together into a pack they could load onto Boz's back for the flight home. Meanwhile, Adi'el gave Lani and Abbey a tour of her garden. Lani, out of curiosity, asked if there was a story in Adi'el's entrance garden. Adi'el wasn't sure, but she felt it was the most intriguing part of her estate.

Lani wanted to approach the garden from the outside in, as the story would be told that way.

At the entry stood a large tree, rather grand in stature with brownish-green leaves, and beautiful red and gold flowers on the top branches. Beyond this tree stood three smaller trees. Two of the smaller trees were the same species as the large tree, but without its crown of flowers on top.

Unlike the large tree these two were twisted and gnarled grotesquely. The third tree, different from the others with rich emerald-green leaves, stood quite upright and straight. Lani knew trees represented people and said, "This story is about four people, one in authority over the other three. Of the three smaller trees, two people were of a twisted and cruel nature, and the third person honest and true." Lani looked further into the garden for more of the story.

Next, there were three identical trees to the one small, straight tree at the beginning, but these three were most unusual trees. The branches of all three were limited to the top and north side of the tree only. Adi'el stepped beside Lani and said, "In the morning all the branches wave in the breezes. Then shortly after sunrise this first one draws its branches and leaves tightly together and the base loses its stiffness and the whole tree leans down toward the north. In doing so, even the topmost branches pull down into a tight bunch with the other branches. It stays like that for half an hour, then the base stiffens and the branches open to their normal shape. At midday, this next one does the same, and near the end of the day this last one bends down, bunches up, and then relaxes half an hour later. Look! There, see? The third one is starting."

Sure enough, just as Adi'el said, the base bent over, the branches bunched together, and the top branches bent to join the tightly gathered side branches. Lani watched as the tree assumed its new shape. She thought it looked like it was kneeling in prayer. Wait! She had it. "These three represent someone praying three times a day!"

"You're right!" Adi'el exclaimed. "That's exactly what it is."

Lani looked ahead to see an area enclosed by raised land except for an entry which was blocked by a large round stone. Inside the enclosure was a large pure white tree intermingling its branches with a small tree of the same type as the small straight tree at the beginning of the garden and the three praying trees. Lani contemplated this for a few minutes and concluded it represented the same person throughout. The white tree was unlike anything she had seen. As a tree she knew it represented a person, but pure white suggested not a normal person. "This white tree represents purity and light. Oh, it represents Yehovah in close relationship with a person," said Lani. Adi'el became excited to hear what her garden symbolized.

Just then, Keshet and Asher joined them and Adi'el said, "Lani wanted to see this Entry Garden of mine that we have all wondered about." Pointing back to the start of the garden, Adi'el said, "Look at those four trees. They represent four people. The big one is in authority over the other three. These two twisted ones are wicked, evil people, and this different one that is straight is the honest and true person."

Moving Keshet and Asher along the path, Adi'el continued. "These three identical ones represent someone praying three times a day, and Lani thinks because it is the same kind of tree as the honest person at the beginning, it represents that same person praying."

"Now here, this white tree with its branches intertwined with the straight tree represents Yehovah in relationship with the straight tree that prays. And the two are standing together."

They all gathered to look in the enclosure. Around the two trees were rolling ball plants like what were in Lani's garden that represented animals, except these seemed to have spines sticking out. Adi'el said, "What is interesting about these rolling prickly plants is that they never get near the two trees in the middle. But look over here at this next enclosure. This one does not have the white tree, Yehovah, nor the straight, honest person. Instead it has the two twisted, gnarled trees with a bunch of smaller baby trees. But in this enclosure, the rolling plants have severely damaged these trees. In fact, they no longer grow. The living water does not flow through its trunk and branches."

Lani looked the whole garden over, and ran through from the start. One person in authority with a crown – a king! This was a story with a king in authority over three others, two of whom were evil and one godly who clearly prayed three times a day. This godly one ended up in an enclosure with dangerous animals, yet stood with Yehovah and was preserved. Later the evil ones were in the enclosure and were destroyed by the animals.

Lani smiled. "I know what it represents! This is the first time I have figured it out on my own! Normally I have to ask my friend Kazhu to figure it out, but I got this one on my own!"

Laughing, Asher said, "Don't keep us in suspense! Come on, spill."

"Okay, it's the story of Daniel, one of three working for the king. He was honest and prayed three times a day facing Jerusalem. The other two were evil and sought to get rid of Daniel. When they threw him into the den of lions, Yehovah stood with him and kept him safe. No lion even touched him. But when the evil men and their families were thrown in, the lions destroyed them."

"Oh Lani, thank you," said Adi'el. "You've shared an awesome gift with me. I loved this story as a child. It meant so much to me as there was a time in my childhood that was dominated by a very bad man. I trusted Yehovah stood with me as He stood with Daniel, and that He would protect me like He protected Daniel. And He did. This story became a precious part of my childhood. I cannot thank you enough for letting me know that my Beloved gave this to me. I loved Him for so long, and He protected and cared for me." Adi'el hugged Lani, and without another word stepped away from the group to be alone with her Beloved.

They all quietly left her to her private moment with Yehovah, her guardian of her long past.

Lani mounted Boz and positioned the load of stones on his back. She looked over at Abbey and Makani and they seemed ready to go. She asked Boz if this would be too much weight. Boz lifted his head and answered with a loud, laughing cry and a light flap of his wings, and they were off.

The next day, Lani took the stone bundle to the Carousel Garden and unwrapped each stone. She held up combinations of stones and made note of the colour of light that came out of the combinations.

She then went down to the beach. In the long past she did some of her best creative thinking on or near the water, so she stepped into the water to float on the waves and think. Within minutes, she knew she had a visitor. Celebration. Lani rolled over to look down into the water and saw Celebration waiting for an invitation. Laughing, Lani called Celebration to her. She grew so quickly. She could see a difference in just a week.

Lani rubbed her nose and Celebration moved close alongside drifting and occasionally blowing water out and breathing in through her blowhole. While Celebration enjoyed a good rubbing, in her youth and exuberance she preferred racing and dancing through the water. After a few minutes, Celebration nosed Lani onto her back and dashed across the bay, giving Lani the ride of her life. Lani loved the water, loved speed and loved animals. It just couldn't get any better than this. After a few runs across the bay, Lani slid off and faced Celebration. She held Celebration's two fins and they danced together for a couple of minutes.

Lani thought about this past year with Celebration. Over time their dance became longer, more creative and complex. They loved rehearsing together, often during Lani's early morning swim. Many mornings Celebration waited in the water at the base of the open wall from Lani's bedroom.

Lani patted Celebration, thanked her for the fun and sent her on her way. With a deep smile in her heart, Lani rolled onto her back again to think about her stones and the sculptures she would like to create. The gentle waves rocked her as she drifted across the bay.

She closed her eyes and thought about Adi'el's garden and her reaction to learning its meaning. Such a tender, loving Ahuvati. Their Beloved truly loved each of them very deeply and clearly loved them long before they were even born. All of this could not have been prepared in just her lifetime, but had to have been planned and started long, long ago. That love was heartwrenchingly pure and boundless. Hard to even put into words what it was like to live with a Beloved that desired her, planned for her long before time began. He paid a very dear price to have her as His mate. Amazing. Almost overwhelming.

She thanked Him for His love and told Him how much she loved Him – for all of eternity. After mentally talking with her Beloved, her mind wandered back to the long past. She contemplated why she failed to understand the depth and breadth of His love and desire for her backthen. The Bible told stories to show mankind, but she just didn't get the depth of that love.

Like the story of the shepherd with a hundred sheep and one little lamb who wandered away and got lost. The shepherd left the 99 sheep in safety to find the one lost sheep. With an increasing ache in his heart, he searched and called well into the night. Finally, he heard a faint, pitiful bleating and found his precious little lamb in a deep pit. He climbed down into the pit to rescue the wee one, rested it on his shoulders and climbed back out, laughing and rejoicing that he had found his Beloved sheep. Such love. So tender and caring. So joyful when reunited.

There were several old stories that illustrated His love for His Beloved. Hmm. An idea began to take shape in her heart and mind. The stories of Yehovah, the Light of the world, and His love. Light and love. Made from the stones that light bursts through.

That's it! She would create sculptures of the old stories of love that represented Yehovah, the Light of the world, using light and gemstones. Brilliant! *Thank you, my Love,* she thought, thanking her Beloved for a great idea.

Back in her study, Lani researched the multiple stories to determine which ones she wanted to carve and settled on what she would call the love series. She started with the good shepherd, laughing and rejoicing after he rescued his beloved sheep from the pit. She'd position the finished piece so light would burst forth from the heart of the shepherd.

She would do one of the father embracing his wayward son who returned home desolate and destitute. The father would be positioned as the source of light shining through to the son who collapsed on his knees, embracing his father.

And one of the good Samaritan who stopped to bind the wounds, clothe, and house the man who had been robbed and left for dead. The light would be from within the Samaritan, shining through and out to the man on the road.

Another one would be of the woman at the well being offered a river of living water and desiring it because of the love and care of Yeshua. The light could be bursting forth from Yeshua and His river of living water.

Lani produced a few sketches with ideas of colours. She decided she wanted these to be large life-sized sculptures.

The next day she set out for the valley to collect the stone required for the first sculpture. On arrival, she learned from her friends that they had more visitors who wanted to bring home stone to use as decoration like Asher had done. This small group had been busy helping Ahuvati collect the stone.

All three friends wanted to walk the trail with Lani to help collect the various stones for the first sculpture, the good shepherd.

With the demand for stone, Adi'el, Keshet, and Asher made some discoveries about the stone and brought in some improvements to help make the job of collecting easier. First, Adi'el discovered fresh-cut stone started quite soft and hardened with exposure to the air. Keshet discovered the hardening process significantly slowed down if they used palm leaves to wrap the stone. And Asher found he really enjoyed helping Ahuvati select pieces, loved the feel of the stone, and turned the removal of just the right piece into an art in itself, choosing the right colours and stones for his visitors.

They travelled up the trail in Asher's utility vehicle to carry his stone-cutting tools and bring the selected stones down the hill. Lani shared her plans and design with Asher. Her idea was to create her art more like the way stained glass was assembled than a typical sculpture carved down from a large stone, like the statue of David or those of Easter Island. Her plans involved cutting pieces of stone to layer on other stone, building up the shape.

Unsure of how much she needed of each colour to create the good shepherd, Asher studied her plan, did some quick calculations for the amount of stone needed, and suggested she pick out the colours she want-ed and they would collect only the pieces she wanted to start with today.

He would take his time to cut the best pieces for Lani's sculpture over the next days and bring them to her.

Lani was stunned at his kindness and helpfulness. Asher, as usual, laughed and said, "Oh, it's a great satisfaction to me to work with the stone and deep joy to spend the time laughing and talking with my All while I work. Don't get me wrong, I enjoy your company too," and he hugged Lani. "I don't have any artistic talent, but I feel I am a part of creating great artwork. Please don't think I feel it a burden. It's a joy to me. I would like to be the first to see your sculpture when it is finished, if that'd be okay with you," Asher asked.

"Of course! You will have been a big part of the completed work. It is only right that you get to see it first. In fact, you're welcome to come by and see it as it develops, if you would like. And I'd love to show you around my place," said Lani.

She continued. "The good shepherd called together his friends and neighbours to celebrate with him when he found his sweet lost sheep. I think you and I should call together our friends and neighbours to celebrate the completion of the good shepherd sculpture. I want you to be a part of the unveiling party."

They looked at Lani's plans again and discussed what stone she would like to take back with her. Lani shared that she wanted light to shine from the heart of the shepherd, but hadn't quite worked out how to make it work.

Asher went quiet and thought for a moment. "I think I know how. It wouldn't take a big source of light because this stone amplifies the light and it would still burst out like you want."

Lani thought about it briefly and said, "Yes, you are right. So now I just need to find a long-lasting source of light that I can put inside."

"A couple of days ago, I was visiting a friend a few valleys south of here. I was telling her about what I was up to and about the beautifully coloured stone in the hills about our valley. She took me to a stone she had picked up from her hills. She displayed it in her garden in a place that received maybe an hour of direct sunlight a day, yet it emitted light for the entire day. It's like it has a solar panel in it. I think this would work for your sculptures," said Asher.

"Oh Asher, that sounds perfect. Would you mind going with me to check it out? I'd love your company," said Lani

After identifying the colours of stone for her sculpture and collecting some initial pieces, they went back to Asher's mansion to pack up the stone in palm leaves to keep the stone soft. Then they were off to visit his friend with the light-emitting stone.

They both flew in Lani's utility vehicle over several valleys to land in a large valley with a huge lake in the centre. On the far side of the lake a large flock of flamingos waded along the shoreline. The valley had a peaceful, pastoral look about it.

As they dismounted, a beautiful Ahuvati of Middle Eastern heritage approached and greeted Asher with a warm hug. Turning to Lani she said, "I welcome your eternal friendship, Lani, the creative."

"And I welcome your eternal friendship, Liora, light for me," replied Lani. "This is an absolutely beautiful valley. Do the flamingos live here or are they just visiting?"

"It's lovely, isn't it? I really enjoy living here. The evenings are spectacular. The orange light of the evening calm bathes the entire valley in warmth. I'll never tire of it. And yes, those flamingos spend quite a bit of time here, although often in the early evening they fly to the lake in the next valley. I look forward to seeing the mass of pink birds against the orange sky every evening."

Turning back to Liora, Lani asked, "Asher mentioned your valley has stones that collect and emit light?"

Before Liora could answer, Asher added, "Lani is carving a life-sized sculpture of the good shepherd out of the coloured stone of my valley. She would like to build her sculpture around a source of light to really enhance the light burst that shines through the stone. And I thought of the stone you showed me in your garden."

124

Excited, Liora answered, "Yes, yes! I think that is a great idea. Come on, let's try putting some of the coloured stone in front and see how it looks." Off Liora ran to her garden with Asher and Lani trailing behind. Lani pulled out a few small stones she had with her and selected a red one and a blue one, and held them in front of the lightstone of Liora's garden. Just as Asher thought, light burst through, amplified by the coloured stones. It was beautiful and just what Lani wanted for her artwork.

"Would you mind if I collected a few stones? I have several sculptures I want to do," she asked.

"No, please come anytime and take what you like," replied Liora. "I've found a place in the hills just loaded with these stones. In fact, I went searching for this place because I saw it glowing in the evening. This stone is throughout the hills here, but there is one area I find interesting. Let me take you to some beautiful pieces." And off they went into the hills.

Liora directed them to the base of a hill with an area that had many stones just lying below a large exposed seam of stone in the side of the hill. As they climbed, something in that scene caught Lani's eye and she paused a moment before looking over the stones. She bent to look over some of them, but something still tickled her mind and while Liora and Asher discussed different stones, Lani stepped back to really study the area. She wanted to figure out what it was about this scene that was poking at her mind. She sat down some distance away to take in the whole area. After a couple of minutes, Asher and Liora noticed Lani and came to sit with her. Asher, worried that something concerned Lani, asked, "What is it, my dear?"

"That seam of lightstone across the side of the hill. I think there is something maybe significant or meaningful about it," Lani replied. "When we rounded the corner, I first thought it looked like a slash in the side of the hill. It makes me think of a wound. In the side. With light pouring out."

After a long pause, Lani gasped. "We need to take stone only from the wound, not from the ground."

"What is it, Lani?" asked Liora

"Oh, my heart. Thank you so much, Asher and Liora, for bringing me here. This is truly the right source of light for my sculptures. I can hardly believe how authentic, how significant, how perfectly symbolic a lightstone from this wound on the side would be," said Lani.

Asher started laughing. "Lani, you are not making sense. Tell us what you see."

"Oh Asher, I am sorry. I am just so rocked by this. Okay, sit down. Let me explain."

Asher and Liora settled in, expecting an interesting story and Lani, the weaver of stories, would not disappoint.

"Yehovah formed Adam from the dust of the ground and leaned in close to breathe life into his nostrils. Adam lived in the garden, with beautiful trees, loaded with exceptionally pure gold, onyx, rivers, and plentiful with animals each with their mate. Except Adam. Adam who had no mate, made in the image of Yehovah, who had no mate either.

"On day three of creation, Yehovah commanded the plants and trees to mate with their own kind and reproduce after their own kind. And He said it was good. On day five, He created the birds and sea animals and commanded they mate with their own kind and reproduce after their own kind. And He said it was good. On day six Yehovah created the land animals, and again commanded they mate with their own kind and reproduce after their own kind. And He said it was good. Yehovah declared it was good and proper for all to mate with their own kind and reproduce after their own kind. We now know that DNA is the genetic marker that identifies one of its own kind.

"Yehovah knew Adam longed for a mate of his own, but had no one of his own kind to be his mate. Yehovah determined to take this opportunity in birthing a mate for Adam to foreshadow what He would do approximately 4000 years later to birth His own mate. He put Adam into a deep sleep symbolic of when He would give Himself to death on a hill not far from where Adam lay. Yehovah opened up Adam's side, reached in and pulled out a rib, a piece of Adam by which He would form Eve, leaving Adam with a scar on his side. That piece of Adam was the very core of the formation of Eve, made of Adam's DNA.

"Eve, of Adam.

"The scar on Adam's side showed Eve came from Adam, was of Adam's kind and therefore qualified to be his mate.

"About four thousand years later, Yehovah took the form of man, often called the second and final Adam. As Adam birthed a mate of His own kind from His side, this second Adam would birth His mate of His own kind and from his side. Look to Yeshua crucified on the cross. He declared, "It is finished," and released His spirit from His beaten and bruised body. He died. Much like Adam in a deep sleep.

"Next, like the wound Yehovah created in the side of Adam to create Eve, a soldier then pierced Yeshua's side with a spear, creating a deep wound, and blood and water poured out, evidence of his death.

"The blood from His side was His new covenant carrying His DNA by which He would birth a new creature that would become His mate of His own kind. Remember, the life of all flesh is the blood. When He declared, 'I AM the light of the world, the light of life,' He knew His life and light would be poured out and it would become the new creature in us, the light of life, given to those who accepted Him as saviour. When we accepted Him, He placed in us a piece of Himself, His light and life, so we could be the light on the hill. His light shining through us.

"Look at the side of this hill. You see a deep wound by which pieces of light pour out. It represents our redeemer and His pierced side, through which He created a mate of His own kind.

"It's fitting the stones I use, the light within the sculpture, come from a wound in the side, just as the Light within us came from His side. My sculptures will represent His love and light. The light will have come from a wound as His Light in us came from a wound."

"Oh, Lani. You are utterly correct. He intended the light within your sculptures to come from this wound in the side of the hill. What a deep symbolic representation of His love," said Liora.

Asher chimed in. "I like that these stones will absorb His light of the day, reflect it, and emit it just like His light in us. Yes Lani, this was meant to be. Let's get you the perfect stones from the wound."

With that, they went to work to collect four stones for her good shepherd, the father and the prodigal son, the good Samaritan and the woman at the well. When they cut out four perfect stones, Asher and Liora moved to leave, but Lani hesitated.

Asher, always full of joy, laughed and asked, "Lani, there is something on your mind? What are you thinking?"

Lani replied, "I really think I need a fifth stone. I can't say what the fifth sculpture will be, but I know there will be another one. I really feel I need a large stone for the fifth artwork. Can we cut a piece deep from the wound?"

"Gladly, Lani. I know this is important and you are being directed to gather the right stones that will achieve His end," said Asher. Asher and Lani set to work to dig a stunningly beautiful piece deep from the wound in the hill while Liora went to get a transport to help carry the stones down the hill.

The piece was quite large, about half her height, and Lani wasn't sure how she was going to manage getting it in place at home. Asher noticed the concern on her face and said, "Lani, ask your servants to help move it into position for you. And I am always glad to help you. Just let me know what you need and when you need it, and I will be there."

Lani hugged him. Quickly, she counted him a good friend and a happy fellow to share in the successful execution of her idea.

When she got home, loaded with her lightstones and some of the coloured stones for the good shepherd, Gilad and Piper and several of her servants stood waiting on the beach for her. They knew she was coming and needed their help. They unloaded all the stones and carefully carried them to the Carousel Garden where Lani would create her sculptures.

This story caused Lani to pause. It was a personal story and had deep meaning and symbolism, which appealed to her. It had the makings of an honour story.

Or maybe she could use this as part of her honour story. Yes, this felt like a good direction to take her thinking. Rather than tell just one story, she could weave together aspects of several stories into one. She thought she might be onto something.

14 | The Cherished

Chapter Span: Thirty Two Days | 0.1.12 to 0.2.14 |

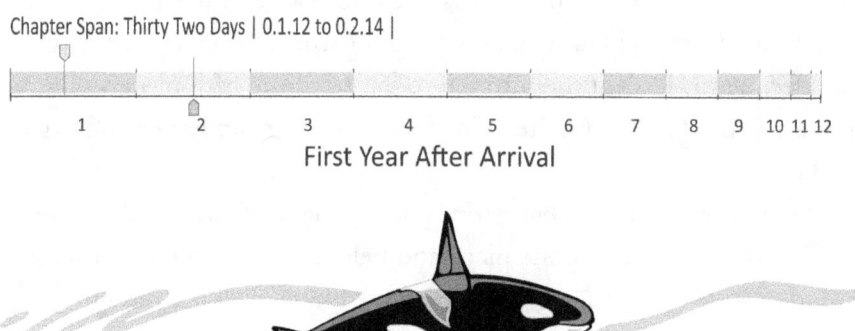

Chapter Span: Thirty Two Days | 0.1.12 to 0.2.14 |

| 1 | 2 | 3 | 4 | 5 | 6 | 7 | 8 | 9 | 10 11 12 |

First Year After Arrival

Lani turned ahead in her poems to the first one about her sculptures. She considered weaving a story of the gathering of stone and the resulting sculpture.

The weaver's poem: The Cherished

> *A shepherd's love, tender, seeking and finding, rejoicing.*
> *A breath of life to one near dead.*
> *In return, innocent love for its All in All.*

> *Lost and fallen,*
> *Alone,*
> *Battered and bruised,*
> *Encroaching predators,*

> *Found and rescued from the pit.*
> *Cherished, rejoicing,*
> *Embraced and kissed,*
> *Together again.*

The Story Behind the Poem

It was her twelfth day here. She placed the lightstones in the Carousel Garden where they could be seen as she came out of the Creation Garden and into the Carousel Garden. She wanted them to be in a place where she could frequently look at them to figure out what the fifth piece would be. All the coloured gemstones remained wrapped in palm leaves and organized nearby.

Lani looked over the lightstones for the light of the good shepherd. She picked up each lightstone piece and held it in the sunlight, turning it around to watch how the light was emitted. She had all her designs with her and was deciding which stone would be the light for which design.

Lani looked over her designs and realized all the sculptures were a snapshot of a critical, memorial moment of contact between two beings. She would be careful to use the light as the heart, the source of love, as well as a focus of the brightest beams to bring attention to that point of contact.

The good shepherd design showed the happy shepherd holding the found lamb high in the air in front of him, kissing the lamb's forehead. The lightstone would be the heart of the shepherd with the brightest beams shining through the tender kiss, the expression of his love for his lamb.

The next design was of the good Samaritan, kneeling on the ground with the beaten, near unconscious man pulled into his lap, one arm supporting the man and one hand smoothing olive oil over his head wound. The light would be the heart of the Samaritan shining through his arm and hand to the beaten man's head. The tender touch of love for the damaged and dying.

The third design was of the good father embracing his destitute son. The father's face expressed pure delight and love. He bent over to kiss his son's head. His son, collapsed on his knees before his father, bowed his head in humility. The lightstone would be the heart of the father with the brightest beams shining downward through the tender kiss, his expression of love and joy for having his son back.

The fourth one was of Yeshua offering living water to the woman at the well. Yeshua was casually sitting on the edge of the well. The woman knelt in front with her water vase in her lap. Yeshua had His outstretched hand resting on her head, and living water flooding from His hand over her head and pouring onto her heart. This would be the most challenging of the four. Lani wanted the lightstone as the heart of Yeshua shining brightly through His hand, and she wanted all the water to have lightstone within it, shining out from the water. Yeshua was giving a piece of Himself and placing it within the woman. The living water was the essence, a part of Yeshua, and needed to have its own light. Lani also wanted a small lightstone in the heart of the woman – with the woman accepting the offer for His living water, His eternal life, so a piece of Yeshua's light would need to be in her as well.

In turning over the lightstones, Lani noted the light shone brightest through flat-angled cuts, so for the good shepherd she would need a stone that had a cut to shine the light upward to his head and the lamb he kissed. She found the perfect piece and set it aside.

Lani next picked up the largest of the four lightstones. If she cut off the long piece, she could use it in pieces to be the light of the living water, and the end bit would be ideal for the light within the woman. The main part of the stone was larger than the good shepherd stone and would be a perfect symbol of the heart of Yeshua. Lani set about cutting this stone into the needed pieces.

Finally, the last two stones would be the heart of the father and the heart of the Samaritan, both shining downward. She looked the stones over and decided which would go inside the father and which inside the Samaritan.

Lani sat back, looked around the Carousel Garden and decided to place these sculptures along the edge of the dome tree and the Carousel Garden, in progression from her mansion west. She picked up the lightstones to be used in the woman at the well sculpture and placed them about 1,000 ft. west from her mansion. It would be the fourth one in the lineup. She placed the good shepherd's heart nearest her mansion, the heart of the good Samaritan second and next to the shepherd, and the heart of the father in the third position. Lani stood toward the middle of the garden to slowly turn and look at the stones in their location to confirm she had it right. After a few turns Lani determined all was where it should be.

She rested her hand on the large lightstone in the middle and wondered what this was intended to be. She still wasn't sure and wondered if she wouldn't know until all four sculptures were complete.

Lani turned her attention to the wrapped coloured stone. They were predominantly shades of reds, oranges with some yellow, a few blue, green and purple ones. Lani held up a red and a yellow stone to the sunlight and a brilliant orange light burst out with sparkles of both red and yellow. So she could use orange stone, or layer red on yellow stone and get orange with sparkles of the original two colours. She tried purple and orange and was surprised to see red light burst out. She wanted the sculpture to be mainly composed of reds followed by orange shades with white highlights.

She thought about the good shepherd and decided to use the pure colour on the areas of the sculpture that were less important, like everything from the hips down. But she would gradually introduce the combination colour in layers starting around the hips so that all the light coming out from the chest, head, and hands would sparkle in two colours. For the sheep, she would do the same, having the two-colour sparkle light predominantly on its head where the shepherd was kissing and the chest where the shepherd was holding it up.

Lani set to work on the shepherd's sandals and feet, carving them of solid stone. She found the stone quite easy to carve, almost like clay. The feet came along quickly and she moved to start on the lower part of his robe. Since she wanted to make this of bigger blocks of stone, she would need long pieces of various colours to form the folds and bends of the cloth. The pieces she brought with her would not get her too far.

Just then she heard a commotion coming from the beach. As she stood up to take a look, Asher came jogging up through the Creation Garden, smiling broadly as usual. He warmly hugged Lani in greeting and said he had brought with him all the stone she would need for the good shepherd. Lani moved toward the beach, but Asher held her back and said it was being taken care of by their servants.

He looked down at the sculpted feet and bent down to take a closer look. "Oh Lani, this is beautiful. You captured so much detail. Look, even smudges of dirt! It is perfect. I can't wait to see the finished piece. Was it hard to carve to this level of detail?"

Lani answered, "No, it was surprisingly soft. I think the palm leaves somehow soften the stone, making it pliable. I wonder how long it will take to harden though, as I don't want to build on top of the feet, put too much weight on them too soon."

"Then I think you should give me a tour of your gardens while we wait for the eh-bed to bring all the stone up, and give the stone some time to harden," Asher said grinning.

They walked down to the beach to start from the beginning of the Creation Garden. They wandered around the Carousel Garden, Lani explaining which sculpture she planned to put where. They headed under the dome tree and Asher shook one of the aerial prop branches reaching to the ground, and down fell several fruits loaded with juice. They seemed pure liquid because when they hit the ground, they splattered shades of colour.

Gilad, her gardener, saw what had happened and hurried over, bowing before Lani to apologize for not having picked the fruit sooner. Lani smiled and rested her hand on his shoulder. "Oh Gilad, if you had, we would not have discovered the land under the dome tree could be decorated like a floor of beautiful tile. I love the look of this. Please just harvest what we need for food, and let the rest fall and decorate the whole area under this tree. It will be a beautiful and natural piece of artwork you will have your hand in designing."

Gilad looked a little puzzled, so Lani explained. "By determining what fruit to pick and what to leave, you will be determining the colours of the dome tree floor. You and the tree will be equal artists."

Asher reached out to rest his hand on Gilad's other shoulder and said, "Gilad, I look forward to seeing the results of your work every time I visit. Under the leadership of an artist," nodding toward Lani, "I am confident you will create a beautiful space for Lani and her visitors. May you be favoured with wisdom in deciding what fruit to leave for the floor."

Gilad bowed, having the honour of a second Ha'Ahuvati speak a blessing over him. "Thank you, Aha'Qatsin. You have indeed honoured me. I am deeply thankful." With that, Gilad stepped away and flew off, whistling a happy tune.

"Asher, you made his day. That was very generous of you to acknowledge him and bless him with wisdom. Thank you," Lani said.

Asher replied, "My dear, words are such small, inexpensive things that have the power to move mountains. They are but a breath, yet they have big impact and can change minds, hearts and actions. A thoughtful, well-timed word can make someone's day. A blessing can change the outcome of a life. My blessing for Gilad was but a breath, inspired by the Ruach, but has the immediate impact of joy and honour. It will surely have the long-term benefit of Gilad striving to be a wise gardener. You empowered him to be creative, and he will require wisdom to fulfill your request. In a moment of his day, he has been given the responsibility to make creative judgments by you, and blessed with the wisdom to do so by me. Between us, we have changed the direction and impact of his life. With just words."

After hesitating, Asher continued. "But most importantly, I believe there is something quite important, quite significant, about this dome tree."

Lani could still hear Gilad's whistling. Everyone heard a happy heart. She would try to be sensitive to noticing the moment and giving the gift of timely words. "Thank you, Asher. Your well-spoken words made an impact on me as well. I would like to do as you, and look for those well-timed moments in which I can impact and honour others."

Asher said, "You are kindhearted, even tenderhearted." Resting his hand on Lani's head he spoke a blessing over her. "Lani, may you be a wise leader. May you be sensitive to the Ruach and provide blessings that move others into their intended future. May your words carry life and light. May they have positive impact and swell hearts with joy. May many find peace and shelter in you and your estate."

Lani stood there in awe of him, speechless. No, this was not a moment to be speechless, but one that required a response. It required her words.

"Asher, you – are –" Lani paused to gather her thoughts and focus on what should be said. "You are good through and through." Lani placed her hand on Asher's shoulder, and waited for the Ruach to give her the right words. "Thank you for this blessing and your wisdom in knowing what to say in your blessing to me."

She wanted her blessing to be meaningful and on target for Asher's future. She tuned to Ruach's voice. After a moment, she started her blessing, hesitantly at first. "Asher, may you be a prince among the Ahuvati. May Yehovah reveal deep and secret things to you, endow you with the wisdom, skill, ability and knowledge to carry out every assignment."

Asher knew there was more and encouraged Lani by looking directly into her eyes, giving her a slight nod. She began to feel an inner assurance to step out further and speak to Asher's future. "May you increase in stature, walking in the paths of great leadership. May the Ahuvati find favour under your leadership and may the blessings you speak bear fruit in those under you."

Asher held her close and whispered a broken thanks, a sign her blessing had moved him deeply. They held each other a little longer, then Asher pulled back and said, "You delivered that right from the heart of Yehovah. You fill my heart and give me much to talk over with our Beloved. You spoke some great things into my life and I am deeply honoured to receive such a noble and monumental direction through you, Lani. I love you much, my friend." He bent to give her a warm kiss on her cheek.

She took Asher's hand. "Let me show you the rest of my place. You live in the mountains and you should see my mansion on the water." She showed him the rest of her gardens, then they went into her mansion to be greeted by Nectar, who directed the two of them to the small dining room overlooking the ocean. They lounged and talked right through the evening calm to the next morning, nibbling on an assortment of sweet fruits and spicy seeds.

Lani thought about Asher. In the past year, he became a regular and very welcome visitor, and had indeed risen to great leadership positions. He was honoured among the Ahuvati and well loved. Lani counted herself among the many that flourished under his leadership and came to love Asher deeply.

Lani paused her stroll among her memories to consider if the story of finding and gathering stones and creating the first sculpture would be her honour story.

The good shepherd took a few weeks to complete. She spent her time totally absorbed in her work, talking through her decisions on colours and shape with her Beloved. She found the process very demanding, requiring her full concentration, but she cherished the intimate time.

As a result of this deep mental intimacy, the good shepherd turned out to be an expressive, emotionally stirring piece of artwork. It powerfully exhibited both the shepherd's exuberant joy, and his quiet, tender love for his helpless and lost lamb he had found. Even now when she looked at her sculptures, Lani knew they showed a mastery far beyond her ability. Yehovah truly worked through her.

Yes, this could be the story, but only in part. She possessed a bigger story. Lani sat back to recall when she completed the sculpture.

The combination of the coloured stone and the lightstone achieved the effect Lani hoped for. It looked like a stained glass sculpture, something that couldn't be accomplished with glass or stone from the long past. With the lightstone in place, light emitted from the coloured stone, resulting in brilliant beams of coloured light and sparkles like coloured fireflies flashing bursts of colour.

There was never a sculpture done like this in all of time and it was a breathtakingly beautiful piece of art. She felt deeply humbled that Yehovah chose her to forge new ground and invent a new art form, and to create something that carried such impact.

As Lani promised, Asher was the first to see the finished piece. Reds and oranges dominated, and with the lightstone it had a beautiful, warm glow. When approaching from the beach, the warm glow expressed the tender and deep love before the detail could be seen. The warmth enhanced the message of the compassion of the shepherd.

Asher studied the good shepherd in silence for quite awhile, then said, "Lani, this is quite remarkable. You captured the deep feeling of the shepherd. It moves me deeply to look at it and see my All's heart for us. This is so beautiful and so meaningful. I think this is meant to be seen by everyone. You mentioned having a party with friends to celebrate, like the shepherd who called together his friends to celebrate finding his little lost lamb. Is it okay if I bring my friends? I would really love Keshet, Adi'el and Liora to see it."

"Definitely! Let's plan for two evenings from now," said Lani and they were off making plans.

Lani's regular visitors, her friends, stopped in their tracks when they saw the good shepherd for the first time. With the sculpture being life sized, visitors felt like they stood in the presence of the good shepherd. She discovered her visitors purposefully spent several minutes with the sculpture before seeking her out.

Every time Lani saw this happen, she gave a silent thanks to her Beloved for His direction and help in the design, and in guiding her hand in sculpting, and her mind in making colour and layering decisions.

When Lani thought over events since arriving here, the sculptures played a significant part. A turning point. A critical event that would put her on the intended path for her life. The collection of stone and sculpture would be a good story only because of the outcome. The purpose and value of her property became exposed through the work and unveiling of the sculptures. The unveiling should be an important part of her story.

A couple of evenings after Lani completed the good shepherd, a group of invited friends came to spend the evening together. Kazhu came with many Ahuvati he met in his quest to visit Entry Gardens and document their meaning. Lani's mom and grandmom from her long past came. Cheka came with many in her family. Honani came with some of her musical friends. Aymoon came with his library gang. Asher, Keshet, Adi'el and several from the valleys came. Elia, Hanna, and many from the mainland. Lisha, Elkanah and many formerly Jewish Ahuvati. There were probably close to 50 gathered in her garden.

All were quite taken with the good shepherd. They asked Lani to tell them about it. Lani thought for a moment. Although she understood they asked for her story of how she found the stone and carved it, and how she got the idea for it, instead she felt inspired to tell a story of the characters of the sculpture.

"This sculpture captures a moment in time for this shepherd and his sheep. A moment he would never forget. A moment of pure joy and pure selfless love. Let me tell you how he came to be so happy and kissing his lamb in love.

"A long time ago he lived as a poor young man. A lonely man looking to improve his situation. He sold the few things he owned including the coat off his back and bought five little lambs of fine wool.

"The only protection these little animals had against predators was to flock together. It was such a little group of very young animals, so this young shepherd became everything to these little lambs. They stayed close, following him to the fields every day. They came to know his voice and skipped to him when he called.

"All sheep need interaction and touch normally provided by the ewes, but these lambs only had the shepherd. Every night he cuddled his innocent and vulnerable little wards like they were his children. He loved each one dearly and cared for all their needs.

"Over time, the lambs grew up, giving birth to new babies. His little flock grew to a hundred sheep and lambs. One warm spring morning a ewe struggled to birth her first lamb. The good shepherd became worried and stepped in to help her. He reached into that exhausted young mother and helped pull out the wee little lamb. The mother ewe had struggled so hard to birth her lamb that she let out a long moan and never took another breath. She'd not survived the ordeal. The young shepherd grieved over the loss of her.

"The little lamb came out tiny and lifeless. The good shepherd picked up its little body by the hind legs and gave it a spank to dislodge any fluid in its airway, but it remained still. So he cleaned off the little lamb's nose and breathed a steady breath into its nostrils and it kicked. Another breath and the lamb answered with a little bleat. His breath revived this little one. Soon it was standing on its feet and looking for food.

"He milked another ewe and held this newborn lamb in his arms to feed it. The good shepherd dearly loved this wee lamb. It was just so tiny, so fragile, so dependent on him for life. This wee life he shared his breath with completely commanded his heart. It followed him everywhere. They would walk side by side as it built up its strength and when tired, he would scoop it up into his arms, hold it close to his chest and stroke its head until it fell to sleep. This wee lamb ate from his plate and drank from his cup. He'd not loved anything so much as this little lamb.

"After a few weeks his lamb gained strength and played with the other lambs, climbing and chasing each other. Despite the fun it enjoyed with the other lambs during the day, it still spent the nights curled up in the good shepherd's arms, sleeping, soothed by the sound of the shepherd's heart-beat.

"Knowing it had the care and protection of the good shepherd, this young lamb became curious and as with all young, explored farther afield. But every evening it sought him out to curl up with to sleep. And truth be told, he looked forward to the evenings when he could stroke the soft baby wool and feel the life in his hands.

"One day as he settled in for the evening, his wee lamb did not show. He called among the flock, but it did not come skipping up. He walked among the flock calling again, but his little one just wasn't there.

"Fear seized his heart. His little lamb was not there. Not with him. Lost in the fields somewhere. Out with the predators. He could not let himself think how bad this could be. He could not face finding the half-eaten remains of his beloved little lamb.

"He hurried out the gate of the shelter, leaving his flock of 99 in the safety of their shelter to find his precious little one. The one he saved. The one that shared his breath. The one that had his heart.

"He headed in the darkness to find his lost little one. He called and called, but no answer. He was brokenhearted. He could hardly see clearly past the welling tears in his eyes. How could he live with himself if he lost his precious, sweet little lamb?

"He kept on through the fields, calling. It had been hours and it was late into the night. He really should've gone back to his flock, but just couldn't give up on his beloved, sweet, helpless lamb. He called again, and this time thought he heard something. His heart skipped. He called again, and listened intently.

"Yes!" He heard it again. A faint little bleating. He ran toward the muted call, tripping over a stone and cutting his knee open. He didn't notice his injuries. He pressed on toward that little muffled voice calling for his help.

"He came to a steep ravine with wolves crouching in the darkness, and saw his beloved little lamb, dirty, scared, perhaps badly hurt at the bottom. Without a thought of the danger or risk to himself, he scraped and crawled down to his sweet lamb. He carefully picked it up and held it to his chest, inspecting its limbs. The little lamb bleated, licked his face and dropped its head to his chest to rest in the safety of his arms.

"The good shepherd was ecstatic. He found his loved one and held it tightly in his arms. He carefully pulled himself and his little lamb out of the pit. The wolves dared not approach the shepherd and faded into the darkness to find a meal elsewhere. He held the wee one close to himself, stroking its head as he had done when it was a newborn.

"He was absolutely delighted. His heart sang. The way back to the shelter seemed to pass without awareness. His joy overflowed, he couldn't contain himself. It finally spilled out and he shouted out in jubilance, waking the little lamb sleeping in his arms. It bleated in protest.

"The good shepherd laughed at the innocence of his sweet lamb, so unaware of the danger it was in. He wrapped his hands around the lamb's chest, holding it up in front of him, face to face, with its legs dangling. They looked at each other, his little lamb wagged its tail and licked his face. Laughing, he kissed the forehead of his dear lamb.

"And so you see before you that moment of love and joy between the good shepherd and his beloved lamb captured in this sculpture. I call this sculpture The Cherished."

Lani focused inward to tell this story, but now that she had finished, she glanced at her audience. Everyone stood quiet, deeply moved by the story and the sculpture. The reflection of Yeshua's love had just been laid out before them.

Asher stepped forward and said, "Lani, you captured the heart of our good shepherd in your story and in this sculpture. I think I speak for everyone here when I say I'm beyond words. You moved me emotionally to my core. I'm broken by the love of my All and you expressed the depth of His love for each of us. You definitely enjoy a gift of expression through story and art. Thank you for sharing with us."

At that everyone clapped and cheered for their Beloved. Lani bowed in appreciation for their response, then Kaz and Cheka pulled into a group.

Visitors wandered about her property, deciding where they wanted to spend the evening. Several congregated under the dome tree, on the ever-increasingly fruit-decorated land. Some preferred lounging inside, in the room with the inlet of water. Nectar prepared plenty of food and drink.

Moved by the sculpture, many spent time looking at it, repeating their favourite part of the story and sharing their feelings with their friends.

Their interest and emotional response inspired Lani to move ahead with her remaining sculptures.

Ahuvati mixed and mingled, enjoying the opportunity to meet new Ahuvati and establish new friendships. Many asked about the large lightstone standing unadorned. Lani explained it had a purpose. There was a sculpture she would be creating that would use it to light up the artwork. She just didn't know what that sculpture would be yet.

When the party broke up with the morning mist, everyone asked to come back and visit again. Many remarked on her Creation Garden, on the dome tree and Carousel Garden. But all commented on The Cherished, and how they enjoyed their restful and peaceful time under the dome tree. They loved the artful designs of colour on the ground underneath the tree. They felt they had spent the evening immersed in art and in the warm arms of their Beloved.

The crowd began to make their way back home with the morning mist. Asher, the last to leave, held Lani close and thanked her for a wonderfully restful evening. Lani said, "Asher, much of how this turned out is because of you. You provided all the stone, cutting it all from your hills, and delivered it here. You showed me the lightstone and helped cut that as well. Thank you so much, I really appreciate all your help. In fact, I really feel you are a part of the success." Asher looked ready to deny that he had any part, but Lani continued. "No Asher, we talked about what colours I wanted, but you chose all the stone for me, and it turned out the perfect colour."

"Thank you, Lani. You're very generous in including me in your innovation and your creation. But the success of the evening goes beyond the artwork and includes the tale you wove around the sculpture. You brought to life the story of the good shepherd. You showed us his love, his heart, his passion for his little lost lamb. I will never look at this sculpture again without feeling his passion and commitment, his tender love. Thank you, Lani, for that gift."

Lani's eyes now welled up. Asher pulled her into a warm embrace.

When he sensed she was able to talk again, he smiled at her and asked, "So when are you going to get started on the next one?"

Wiping away tears, she replied, "Right away, I think. I am going to work on the good Samaritan next. Could I come by and select stone later today?"

"My dear, today would be fine," and with a kiss on the cheek, he left.

So that was the story of the collection of stone and the good shepherd sculpture unveiling. Lani thought for a moment, and decided if this was to be her story, it was bigger than the one sculpture.

15 | Desperately Needed Hero

Chapter Span: Forty Two Days | 0.2.14 to 0.3.26 |

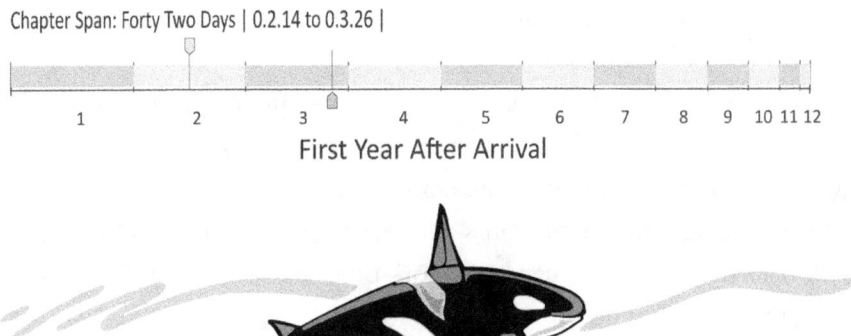

First Year After Arrival

The weaver's poem: Desperately Needed Hero

Eagerness and excitement dashed.
Evil brought innocence to the edge of death.
Left for dead by the religious, the pious.
But One still cares.
Love overcame.
Reclaimed from the filth,
Healed and housed.

The Story Behind the Poem

The morning after the unveiling of The Cherished, after the mist had burned off, Lani started for Asher's valley. And he was waiting for her when she arrived. Together they headed up the trail to the coloured stones. Lani decided to carve the good Samaritan primarily out of shades of purple. For the critical areas like the chest and head covering, she would use a combination of red and blue to get a purple beam of light, but sparkles of blue and red. She also wanted highlights of white and that would require more red and blue as well as yellow. The man on the road would be stripped down to just a loincloth. She'd need red for the injuries, and greenish yellow for the oil.

It would require quite a bit more stone as this sculpture was of two people. It would probably take quite a bit longer to complete as well. But it would be time spent in intimate conversation with her Beloved, sharing and exchanging intimate thoughts and feelings on a mental and spiritual level. And Lani would be happy to work on sculptures for eternity just to spend time in communion with her Beloved.

"I can have all the stone to you in a few days. I will send the initial load later today, if that's okay," said Asher.

"That'll be great, thanks Asher. And thank your servants for me," replied Lani.

"I will. Lani, do you have some time today? I'd like to talk over some things on my heart."

"Sure."

"Do you mind if we go back to your place?"

"The dome tree?"

Laughing, Asher said, "Yes, the dome tree. I love what Gilad is doing with the floor!"

Leaving instructions with his servants, and passing along Lani's gratitude, they left for Lani's dome tree. Nectar greeted them with refreshments already set up for them under the tree.

They talked for awhile about the gathering the previous evening, discussing the various conversations each had and the many new Ahuvati each had met.

"Lani," Asher started. "Everyone really enjoyed themselves, really connected."

"Yes, I enjoyed the evening too," Lani replied.

"I feel something more happened, something of significance. Everyone really connected in an evening of harmony enjoying an immediate closeness and warm fellowship. We all attuned to each other. More intimate than usual. Did you notice?" asked Asher.

"I did, but I thought I had imagined it because it meant so much to me," said Lani.

"No, you didn't imagine it. You are creating something special here. For awhile, I pulled away from everyone and sat and watched. I looked at all the Ahuvati and I looked at your sculpture and thought 'The LORD is my shepherd; I have all that I need. He lets me rest in green meadows; He leads me beside peaceful streams. He renews my strength' (Psalm 23:1–3).

"I think everyone felt this dome tree you have by the ocean, with the coloured floor, brings refreshment like a green meadow beside a peaceful stream. The evening of harmony and unity and everyone left refreshed. Everyone spent time under the tree.

"I think Yehovah has plans for your place and the sculptures you are working on play an integral part of something significant."

Lani replied, "I don't know what that could be. I don't even know what the final sculpture will be yet."

"Yehovah will reveal His thoughts at the right time, Lani. But in the meantime, I'd like to ask a favour of you."

"Anything, Asher. I count you a good friend. I would be happy to help you in any way I can," Lani replied.

"Would you mind if I came here regularly? I want to spend some time in this space of harmony and peace and seek my All's guidance on some thoughts I have around the direction I should take." Asher paused, thinking of how to frame his words. "Lani, your blessing over me spoke of leadership among the Ahuvati, and that is the second prompting I had to move in this direction. I want to spend time away from the distractions of my estate to really commune with my All. You spoke of Yehovah revealing deep and secret things, granting me wisdom. Lani, I am asking if I could use your gardens, the dome tree, as a retreat. A place of quietness, of harmony, of art, of Light and Love where I can really spend time seeking His will and His direction. I have several seeds of thoughts, but need to really talk it all over with the master. I really feel tuned to the harmony, shelter and sanctuary of this place. For me and for everyone here last evening, it is a harbour or haven to really connect.

"I am not expressing myself well, but for me, I find this a place of retreat particularly rich in peace, a shelter from distraction wherein I can really focus on seeking His will. I know you will be busy with your sculpting work, and I won't disturb or distract. I look to be alone with my All. It would be a great favour to me."

Lani pulled Asher into a warm hug, and while holding him said, "First, you are my dear friend and on that alone, I am happy to put my estate at your disposal." Pulling back to look Asher in the eyes, Lani said, "But secondly, Asher, I believe great things fill your future. Important work to be done for Yehovah. I know leadership can be demanding. Now I realize Yehovah gave me a place that will be your Mount Sinai, your place of intimate revelation. You and Yehovah honour me to be a part of your work in this small way. Of course you are welcome to anything I have, Asher. I will ensure you will not be disturbed. And feel free to come and go as you please."

"You are precious, my dear. I see great things ahead for you. Just keep working on the things He put before you, and He will direct your path. Thank you for your gracious acceptance of my request."

Hearing noises from the beach, they both looked down the path to see a large load of stone had arrived and both Lani's and Asher's servants began to haul it up.

Lani said to them, "Thank you all for your help with my project. I appreciate your work in cutting and delivering stone. Please leave it at the edge of the Carousel Garden under the dome tree. I see Nectar put out some refreshments for you all. Please stay and relax for awhile."

They thanked her for her kindness. As the group enjoyed the refreshments, they gathered around The Cherished. They talked among each other in low tones, quite taken with the sculpture, many reaching out to touch the heart of the shepherd and the little lamb.

When Asher's servants turned to leave, they stopped in front of Lani, bowing before her. She smiled gently at them and asked what they wanted. They looked at each other, and Asher's head boqer said, "Aha'Mo'ee, I, we," indicating those with him, "would like to say that we never dreamt the stone of our hills could be turned into a likeness of Yeshua. You captured His heart, His love, His light. We've never seen artwork like this before and feel deeply moved by this and honoured to be a part of gathering the stones to pay homage to the One who is Love and Light. We would like to ask if we would be allowed to see your next sculpture when it is finished?"

Lani and Asher exchanged a glance. She saw this as confirmation Yehovah was indeed doing something special with this place. "Of course, you are all welcome whenever you would like to come and visit. I have four more sculptures to do, so you will all have to visit at least four more times. I know Nectar will be ready for every visit. And again, thank you all so much for your help in gathering and bringing the stone. You are all very generous."

"We will bring the remaining stone tomorrow, if that is okay. Oh, and thank Nectar for us. The tea, sandwiches and cookies were great," said the boqer.

Lani nodded, and with that they all bowed again and headed down the beach, chattering among themselves.

Asher looked at Lani and said, "This is a beautiful place Lani. Thank you for sharing generously with everyone. You are a good, kindhearted love." Asher took in a deep breath and held it momentarily as though he wanted to take in as much of this place as he could, and said he would head back with his eh-bed, but would be back the next day to spend some time with their Beloved, and with a kiss he disappeared down the hill.

A few hours remained before the evening calm and Lani picked through the stones to select the ones for carving the next morning. That evening she ate an early supper, took a couple of hours to work on her poems on her deck, watched the sun set, then headed to bed early.

The next morning after the mist burned off and she finished deck dancing, she started the next sculpture, the good Samaritan. She settled to work where she wanted this sculpture to be when it was finished. It would not be possible to move a completed sculpture, so she created it on its final resting spot.

She decided to sculpt the good Samaritan and the injured man as two separate pieces and started with the good Samaritan. He would be kneeling on the ground with the injured man pulled into his lap. Her work deeply absorbed her attention when Asher arrived.

He quietly made his way up the hill and entered the Carousel Garden before Lani noticed him. She got up and dusted herself off to greet him.

"Good morning, my dear Lani. I see you are busy at work. The colours of the robe look quite beautiful, but I thought we collected purple for the Samaritan's garments."

"Good morning, Asher. I changed my mind a bit with the colours. I'm carving the robe in purple and blue, with red and gold on the hem. A second equally beautiful robe in the same colours will lie beside him on the ground, ready to put on the injured man. I started to work on the Samaritan first.

"Please Asher, make yourself at home. Gilad set up a hammock and variety of chairs for you. Please feel free to move them to where you would like. I see you brought some reading material and note tablet with you. If it won't disturb you, I'll ask Gilad to bring you a table as well. A private and quiet bedroom awaits you inside to store your things, if you wish. Also, Nectar will ensure you have food and refreshments, but won't disturb you."

"Oh, a room would be great, Lani. Thank you." Looking over at the chairs, Asher added, "This will be perfect. Again, thank you for giving me this retreat." Nodding toward the stones scattered about he said, "I will leave you to your work, and may your hands and heart be guided in achieving His purpose." And with that Asher moved to organize his new space. He chose to position the furniture to look out over the ocean, and still see the good shepherd.

Lani left to ask Gilad to provide a table for Asher, and returned to her work. She glanced at Asher and saw he settled in comfortably, so turned her attention back to the good Samaritan.

She worked several hours quite absorbed and in deep conversation with her Beloved over every stone choice, and every cut and carve. She heard Nectar nearby with refreshments and took a break to sit back and examine her progress.

Nectar headed over to Asher to drop off some refreshments for him as well. Lani glanced at Asher and noticed a slight glow about his face. All Ahuvati shone with the righteousness, from inside, from the Light placed within. But the Light from Asher's face looked brighter, stronger somehow. As Nectar approached, she did so bowing deeply. She quietly set down the refreshments and backed away, still bowing.

Returning to her work, several hours passed before Lani took a break. She got up to stretch and gather more stone. She glanced at Asher standing with his hands on his hips, looking out over the ocean. She noticed a distinct aura about his head, a depth of Light expressed in a ring about his head.

Lani spotted Gilad moving about the palm trees beyond the dome tree, whistling one of his happy tunes. In the distance, she could just make out the melodic harmony of Piper's pipes accompanying him. The birds added to the chorus as gentle background. She noted the easy way they all joined the spontaneous concert with no rehearsal, yet in perfect harmony with each other, creating a peaceful environment.

Yehovah gave her a sanctuary of rest and peace.

As Lani finished her work for the day and headed into her mansion, Asher bowed in deep conversation. Lani quietly whispered to her Beloved that He would grant Asher wisdom and understanding as He revealed His plans and assignments to him.

After her evening meal, she looked out to check on Asher and he was gone. He silently slipped away to his home. Lani hoped he found the peace and stillness he desired to seek Yehovah's direction.

The next morning, after the mist lifted and she deck danced her praises, Lani got another early start to her work. This became her practice when working on the good shepherd and continued for all her sculpture work.

Shortly after starting, Asher came quietly, gathered some materials he left in the private room set aside for him, then headed to his space under the dome tree, stopping briefly to greet her. Lani noted he seemed very distracted. Clearly his thoughts centred on his conversations with Yehovah and what He revealed to him. They held hands for a moment, and Lani said, "May you find the peace and quiet you need to talk through your assignments, and may Yehovah give you the strength and courage to fulfill your mission."

Asher looked deeply into Lani's eyes, then simply nodded his agreement and headed to stand for a long time under the dome tree, looking over the ocean, deep in thought.

Lani bent to her work and after a few minutes could hear the faint strains of Asher singing an old African American spiritual, "There Is a Balm in Gilead," a song he sang in his long past.

Each day went like the first with Lani absorbed in her carving and Asher in deep communion with his Beloved, and as each day passed the glow about Asher increased to a very obvious radiance. He sought deep communion and the increased intimacy shone from his face. After the third day, Asher stayed over the evening calm, and Lani arranged additional supplies to accommodate a prolonged stay without disturbing him.

The good Samaritan developed quite nicely. She followed the same approach with this carving as the good shepherd, using pure coloured stone for the lower parts of the robes, and layered stones for the critical focal areas to get the multicoloured sparkles. She completed as much as she could on the good Samaritan and started the injured man in his arms. The carving progressed more quickly this time because of her experience with the first sculpture. She expected to finish the two people in another week, but she wasn't sure how to create the liquidity of the olive oil, the wine and the blood. This would be an important technique for carving the living water of the woman at the well.

The liquidity took a bit longer than expected to complete, resulting in 40 days for the entire sculpture. Out of it she figured a way to create the look of liquid. For the olive oil she started with a thin layer of white made of red, yellow and blue. On top of the white, she carved a thin layer of varying thickness of yellow-green stone. It really looked wet and runny and the result pleased her. She thanked her Beloved for the idea.

By mid-morning Lani packed away the leftover stone. Asher spent the entire 40 days in meditation and communion, staying through many evenings. She noticed he had not yet appeared when she heard him coming up the path.

As he made his way toward her, Lani asked, "Good morning, Asher, how are you today?" His face shone with a bright radiance. Lani came to realize, in spending such concentrated, intimate time with their Beloved, the Holy One's splendour settled on Asher's face, shining like the sunrise, with rays of light flashing as he moved.

Smiling, Asher replied, "I am very well today, thank you, Lani." He gave her a very warm hug and kiss on her forehead. "I want to thank you again for the space of quiet retreat." Lani saw Yehovah on his face, felt the splendour of Yehovah about him and the heart of Yehovah-El Shaddai. She felt a paradox of Yehovah's might and power combined with His heart of love resting on Asher. Standing near him, Lani felt enfolded in love and courage.

"Asher, you know you have Yehovah-Adonai's splendour shining from your face. His presence is thick about you. You seem settled," said Lani.

"Come sit with me for awhile," Asher said and took Lani to his space under the dome tree. They sat down, looking back at the two completed sculptures in the Carousel Garden.

"I see you finished the good Samaritan. It looks exquisite and equal to The Cherished, Lani. It really struck me, the meaning of colours of this one. The rich purples and blues carry the subtle message of king and priest. I don't know if you thought about this when you selected the colours, but the Jewish priests of the long past wore robes of pure blue with a hem of red, blue and purple pomegranates and gold bells, and the kings wore purple robes. The colours of your good Samaritan and his second robe are those of both king and priest. This subtly shows the underlying story of Yeshua, the Melchizedek king and priest, picking mankind out of the mud and dirt, nearly dead, cleaning him up, anointing him, and clothing him in robes of kings and priests as he is king and priest. With your colours you added a richness to the sculpture. It is the underlying story of us, Lani. It is really beautiful."

Asher continued. "I watched with interest every day to see this underlying story unfold. It really spoke to me. You have no idea what it meant to me to watch this particular sculpture develop. As I came to see the underlying story of man's redemption to kingship and priesthood, Yehovah revealed to me His plans for me. My time here has been most precious to me. I cannot put into words what these 40 days have meant to me." Laughing out of pure peace, joy and delight, Asher said, "Because of my time here in communion, Beloved Adonai set me firmly on my path!"

Lani said, "You know it is probably not coincidence that Moses dwelled on Mount Sinai with Yehovah for 40 days and returned with the splendour of Yehovah on his face, and the directions for His people."

Looking down, Asher said, "Yes, I realized that on my way home last night. I thought about my experience here and about its completeness. His purpose for this communion time had been fulfilled. And I thought about this radiance and then it hit me. It is just like Moses. I too have a great commission from my Beloved Adonai that will define my eternal destiny. It will direct my words and path just as the instructions Moses was given were to direct his path and the path of Israel.

"Yehovah revealed much to me and gave me a commission to share what I have learned and assume a leadership role among Ahuvati. I am deeply humbled and spent many days resisting as we discussed if there was a better choice than me.

"I've not shared my past with you or anyone here. I wasn't from your time in the long past. I lived hundreds of years before you. I was born in what you knew as Nigeria in 1626, the oldest son of a powerful chief. Slavers kidnapped and sold me to a slave ship when I was 14 years old.

"I sobbed at being ripped from my family, my father, my brothers, my mother, my home. On the ship's crossing many around me died from the appalling conditions. They provided little food and what was given was mouldy and rotten. Men bigger than me generally took all the scraps and left little for the women and us younger ones. Many nights I silently sobbed alone with a broken heart. I slept little for fear of being raped. I just wished I would be granted a reprieve from this horror through death. I was a frightened, lonely little boy.

"The slave traders sold me to a plantation owner in Georgia. I learned quickly to keep my angry and vengeful thoughts and feelings to myself. I lived as a very unhappy young man in a state of contained rage.

"I heard several stories of this God that loved me. I was conflicted. Although I was angry, I was starving for love. Reluctantly intrigued, I saw this as the only sign of love in my world.

"I finally committed to Yehovah when I heard the story of Joseph's brothers selling him into slavery, and how Yehovah preserved him and elevated him to power, second only to the Pharaoh. I couldn't read and didn't understand all the aspects of the story. I lived for the day of my freedom like Joseph when I too would be a ruler of many. I paid attention to all the stories of the Bible to learn all I could about this promised freedom and authority.

"On that first day I accepted Yehovah, He gave me eternal freedom. I was a new creature, I just didn't understand what that meant. And though I never knew freedom or leadership on earth, I continued in trust that Yehovah would work it out for me.

"Eventually, I had a wife and young family. All were taken from me with the yellow fever. I died shortly after their deaths from injuries as a result of a vicious and undeserved beating. In all, I lived a very pathetic, short life.

"To be named Asher, 'one of happiness and blessing,' is a treasure beyond measure. It means more to me than anyone can imagine. For all of eternity, I am happiness. I will not just feel happy. No, I am happy. My character, my essence is happiness. And I am named 'one of blessing.' I cannot imagine a better name.

"I wasn't an educated man. I lived the lowest of earthly lives. I do not bring much to Yehovah but my heart. My commitment. Thankfully, that's all He asked for. I'm so humbled by His love, His righteous holiness. Outside of what He gave me, I remain nothing before Him. Anything I offer now to Him, He gave me for His purpose.

"You remember your blessing over me to 'increase in stature and walk the paths of great leadership'? That was all I wanted in the long past. But I am now so humbled." Laughing, he said, "Like Moses, I feel there should be someone better equipped to lead. In fact, I have less going for me than Moses. At least he received the best education possible. My All reminded me of His promise that everyone who lost their home and family will receive a hundred times in return, and that the least will be greatest. I stand in faith and trust.

"Lani, in return for a short, unhappy life in the long past, He gave me an eternal one. And like Joseph, He elevates me to high leadership. I am so broken and humbled before Him."

After gathering himself, Asher said, "Lani, I have another favour to ask of you. As Jacob and Moses did when they had a powerful meeting with Yehovah, I would like to build a simple altar of remembrance as a testimony of Yehovah's presence in my past and more importantly, His restitution, faithfulness and strength in this life. He wove it all together into a great destiny and I want to mark this place with stones of remembrance. And I would like to ask if it is okay to come back regularly to renew and refresh here at this place of intimacy under your dome tree."

"Oh Asher, I put my estate at your disposal the last time you made your request. I see on your face Yehovah met with you in a very intimate and meaningful way. I would love to see an altar of remembrance. I think that is a fantastic idea. You demonstrate leadership in honouring Yeshua in such a visible way." And laughing, Lani continued, "And you're always welcome to visit your Mount Sinai, your remembrance altar anytime. You never need ask permission." Smiling, she said, "There will always be a room at the inn for you."

Asher laughed and thanked her and said, "You know there will be another gathering here this evening. Word got out that you completed the second sculpture and Ahuvati want to come for another evening of harmony and connectedness. I would expect a far larger group, Lani. I heard about the last gathering from many, many who were not there."

Lani smiled as she saw all the preparation work going on in the kitchen, and told Asher based on the kitchen activity she expected lots of Ahuvati. She said she planned to spend some time down either in her inspiration beach alcove or in the ocean seeking inspiration for her story about the sculpture. Asher smiled in understanding and left for his estate to gather 40 stones to mark the place where he received his commission.

Just as the sky started to fade to the warm tones of the evening calm, Asher completed his altar and Ahuvati started to arrive. Over the next hour numbers swelled to over 500. Asher was right. So many more attended this evening than last time.

With the gathering well under way, they asked Lani to repeat the story of The Cherished. And when she finished, there was not a dry eye in the crowd. She then moved in front of the good Samaritan and started.

"You see here a Samaritan, considered a half-breed, heathen dog with a near-dead injured Jewish man in his arms.

"How did it happen that these adversaries came to be here? An old rivalry between Judah and Israel brought Jews and Samaritans to be contemptuous of each other. Jews considered Samaritans as inferior and of little value. A Jew would accept no hospitality from a Samaritan. To eat his bread as a guest was as polluting as to eat swine's flesh.

"The Samaritan left his home, his family, and friends in the north to head south to Jerusalem, passing through Bethel more than a week before. He carried on business with several merchants in Jerusalem and Jericho that brought him south several times a year. He never enjoyed these trips. He missed his family, but he could deal with that. His bigger reluctance centred around this ancient conflict. The businessmen despised him, yet were glad to purchase his goods.

"And then he feared the dangers of the trip. Ever since Herod the Great dismissed thousands of men from building the temple, many resorted to highway robbery. On his last trip descending from Jerusalem to Jericho, he heard a band of men rushing out from the rocks toward him, but he ran for his life and escaped their evil intent. He escaped the fate of many travellers on the 'way of blood.'

"Having completed his business in Jerusalem, he summoned the courage to walk this dangerous highway to Jericho. He would have liked the protection of an escort, but he did not have the money to do so. He brought back with him just enough to clothe his growing family for the coming winter and regularly set aside for his son's betrothal. And as a Samaritan he was not permitted to walk with groups of Jews also making this journey. Yes, the Jews would exchange money for goods with him, but would never walk with him because of the contamination of association.

"This young injured Jewish man," pointing to the injured man in her sculpture, "was heading to Jericho to become betrothed to his childhood love. His wealthy father passed away the previous month, leaving him the oldest male to negotiate his betrothal on his own. Excitedly he looked forward to seeing his beautiful girl again, to gain her official consent, to sign the marriage contract with her father and give her gifts of silver, gold and expensive garments. All was packed onto his donkey and he left home with a light heart.

"He chose the short route as he eagerly wanted to get to Jericho. Indeed, it was the 'way of blood,' but he couldn't believe anything bad could happen on such a joyful day. Lost in dreamy thoughts of his beloved, his heart ached in his excitement. He wasn't paying any attention to his journey when more than a dozen evil, violent men encircled him.

"The men were excited. Here was a young man alone with a donkey and a big, carefully packed bundle. Easy pickings.

"Seeing the burden on his donkey, they tightened their circle around the young man as he backed into his donkey to keep distance between them and him. He pleaded for his life. The lead gangster hit him in the mouth, popping out teeth and screamed at him to shut up. Another ripped his packages from the donkey, his gold and silver spilling all over the road. The thieves fell on the ground, fighting each other for the precious cargo.

"Seeing an opportunity, the young man grabbed his donkey's lead and took off running, trying to make good an escape while the thieves distractedly fought among themselves. Several noticed him hurrying down the road and rallied the gang. They would punish him for trying to get away.

"The head thief pulled the lead from the young man's hands, growling at him. Someone hit him on the head from behind with a stone and his knees buckled under him. The thieves converged on him, kicking and punching. The violent explosion of anger and rage was only satisfied when these evil men thought him dead. They took his gifts, his donkey, they removed his rings and even stripped him of his fine garments he wore for the betrothal ceremony. The only thing they left was a cloth about his loins.

"The bandits left him bleeding into the earth, delighted in the money they would get from their booty.

"They left the young man with a broken arm, broken ribs, several broken bones in his hands, internal bleeding, a large wound on his head, the blood flowing freely down his face, and from his broken nose and mouth. He could hardly breathe through the blood. He tried pushing himself up, but his chest screamed in protest, his head reeled and he lost consciousness.

"He came to briefly to see a Jewish rabbi coming toward him. He raised his hand and pleaded for his help. But this rabbi crossed to the other side of the road and looked straight ahead, not even acknowledging this injured man's presence. He would not sully himself with this stranger. He would probably die anyway. To justify his position, he thought, *If he were a good man like me, YHVH would have protected him. No forces of evil would touch him if he were as good a Jew as me. He probably deserved what he got. I should not interfere with the justice of YHVH.*

"The young man let out a gurgling moan and passed out again.

"Along came a temple assistant. He approached the young man and noted his laboured breathing and all the blood and thought, *I am too busy today to stop and help. He shouldn't have been travelling so early in the day when the evil ones are roaring, looking to see whom they may devour.* And he too went on without helping.

"Then along came this finely dressed Samaritan man. He too was hurrying to Jericho, hoping to complete his business quickly and be on his way home. When the Samaritan crested the hill and saw the young man naked and lying in his own blood, his heart went out to him.

"He stopped and got off his donkey and grabbed his travel bag. He called to this injured man and heard a moan. At least he still lived. He set his bag down beside the young man and knelt down at his head. Carefully he turned him over and cleaned the blood off his face. He was about the same age as his oldest boy. His heart ached to think of the potential of this young man, and all that evil nearly snatched from him.

"The young man began coughing out the blood still gathering in his mouth. The good Samaritan pulled the young man onto his lap to elevate his head to help his breathing. He reached into his bag, pulled out some oil for his wounds and wine to help revive him enough to transport him to an inn.

"Look at the good Samaritan's robe. It is of the colours of priest and king, and the second robe he will give to the young Jew was of the same priest and king colours. Yehovah-Yeshua was and is our priest and king, yet He was despised as much as the Samaritans. Mankind rejected Him. And still He pulled us out of the dirt and filth. Like the good Samaritan, He too gave us oil and blood for our healing and redemption. He protected us and brought us to safety. He gave us the honour of ruling with Him as priest and king.

"The moment you see here is a moment of deep compassion. The good Samaritan, abhorred by the Jewish people, knelt in the filth and dirt to rescue the damaged, nearly dead Jewish man who would despise him on an ordinary day. In love and with care, the good Samaritan pulled the man onto his lap to help him stay alive. Here you see him gently cleaning and caring for his wounds.

"He would put this young man on his donkey and bring him to the nearest inn. He would give all he had to ensure the innkeeper would look after this injured man. His family could do without to save this life. He did not see an enemy. He did not see filth and death. He looked past all that and saw a young man in need. He saw the similarities with his own boy and knew someone loved this man. I call this The Desperately Needed Hero."

When Lani finished her story, the crowd erupted in joy and cheering. All were applauding, not for Lani, but Yehovah-Adonai, their Beloved, for His love and care for people while they were nearly dead, wallowing in vile and filthy sin.

Several Ahuvati wanted to talk to Lani and she spent quite awhile talking about how the sculptures were made, the coloured ground underneath the dome tree, what the other sculptures would be, and when she thought they would be finished.

When she finally had a break, she became aware of Ahuvati who brought their instruments and played beautiful music for the party. She looked around for Asher and spotted him resting at the far end of the Carousel Garden where he was enjoying the music. She went and sat beside him.

"Lani, this is another wonderful evening of joy and harmony. It is good for Ahuvati to spend time together like this. You delivered a good story for your sculpture. I like that you concluded with the symbolism that links to Yehovah. Your Sculpture Garden is really taking shape. And more than Ahuvati love to visit, to ponder what they see in the sculptures and meditate on Yehovah. I have watched our servants intentionally coming by to look and think about their Creator. It all points to Yehovah. This is a good thing, Lani.

"Look, see over there? Those folks have been dancing since the music started. I have been watching them and thought about what Yehovah said.

"Praise the LORD!
Sing to the LORD a new song.
Sing His praises in the assembly of the faithful.
O Israel, rejoice in your Maker.
O people of Jerusalem, exult in your king.
Praise His name with dancing,
Accompanied by tambourine and harp.
For the LORD delights in His people;
He crowns the humble with victory.
Let the faithful rejoice that He honours them.
Let them sing for joy as they lie on their beds.
(Psalm 149:1–5)

"I see music, dancing, rejoicing, singing and joy to the delight of Yehovah. And look under the dome tree. Many wandered about over there. Some go with a purpose to spend some quiet time with their Beloved and others go to check out the fruit-decorated ground and the structure of this unbelievably huge tree. They wander about for a few minutes, but soon they bow in conversation with their Beloved.

"The next chapter in the Bible starts,
Praise the LORD!
Praise God in His sanctuary;
Praise him in His mighty heaven!
Praise him for His mighty works;
Praise His unequaled greatness!"
(Psalm 150:1–2)

"They spend time under the dome tree, thanking and praising their

Beloved as we are told to do. Here, we are all drawn to give praise and thanks, and He is crowning us with missions of victory. "This is a special evening and a special place."

Lani remained quiet for a long while, watching the Ahuvati and thinking about what Asher said about this place of harmony and connectedness. The seed of an idea just cracked open, ready to germinate. Lani needed to mull things over until she felt settled and aligned with the direction and intent of her Beloved. But for this evening she wanted to mingle with this happy, warm group.

"You are right, Asher," Lani said. "Everyone is having a – " she paused, unsure of the word she wanted to use. She thought to say anointed, but that meant applying oil to consecrate for holy office. She still felt prompted to use that word, but was this really a place where the Yehovah-Spirit, the oil in our lamps, consecrated Ahuvati for holy office? Was there a choosing or assigning happening here? Asher hinted at this with his comment about being crowned with missions of victory.

She looked more closely at different Ahuvati and saw cheer, contentedness, delight, joy, jubilance, peace, rest and happiness. She witnessed life. But she wondered if an unseen event occurred underneath this life. Was there something happening within, leading to this expression without?

Lani looked Asher in the eye and said, "I will finish that sentence later. I felt to use a particular word. Also I'm experiencing the germination of a great idea, but I need to check a few things to ensure I say and do the right thing. I want to talk to my visitors to find out what is happening on the inside. I wonder if something unseen happens here."

Asher smiled one of his relaxed, understanding smiles. "Yehovah be with you, Lani. I will talk to you later," and with that he left her to her investigation.

Lani saw Aymoon and Cheka at the refreshment table and went to talk to them. They both had a very warm greeting for her and thanked her for the wonderful evening. Aymoon said, "I really enjoy coming here, Lani. These evenings refresh and renew me. And I love getting to know all these new friends."

Since the arrival of the Ahuvati, Cheka and Aymoon became good friends. While they didn't know each other in the long past, they lived on earth at the same time and shared acquaintances and friends among the apostles and several of those ministering with them who taught in Samaria and Africa.

Cheka, full of laughter, joined in. "I do too. You know what I really notice? My abundant joy overflows here. Paradoxically, everyone seems really grounded and yet in a flight of jubilance. I hadn't thought about it, but for me, I feel the meaning of the sculptures." Laughing, she continued, "As you know I was a Samaritan, so I feel a personal attachment to the story. I'm reminded of all that Yehovah has done to redeem us, to show His love for us, and His eternal commitment to us. This place brings all of Him to the forefront of my thinking and moves me deeply. It pulls both toward quiet meditation, some alone time with my Beloved, and at the same time moves me to connect to and celebrate with the other Ahuvati."

Aymoon said, "I too feel the pull to quiet time with my Beloved and connected harmony with Ahuvati. This place points us and leads us to intimacy with our Beloved, both as an individual and as a corporate group. I am not saying this place is 'magical,' but Yehovah led you to create a place that in every way moves us, draws us into closer relationship with our Beloved. It is the drawing near to Yehovah that is so special.

"Lani, remember when we went to the library together? And I discovered some things I wanted to share with others, but the path just was not clear for me? Well, I spent some time seeking the will of our Beloved here both this evening and the last one with the unveiling of the good shepherd. He gave me the start of an idea and as I spend more time here, surrounded by evidence of His eternal partnership with me, the idea is clarifying. It is a stretch for me, but I am ready to put plans in place to implement.

"You know what I would really like?" asked Aymoon. Lani shook her head, and he continued. "I'd love to come back here another day and meet with other Ahuvati who want to talk about and share the projects Yehovah put on their hearts. I think now is the time to share, as I believe there will be synergies with each other's plans and projects."

Cheka said, "Oh yes, Aymoon, I'd really like to do that! Lani, would that be okay? Could we come back to share our plans?"

Lani replied, reaching for Cheka's hand, "Of course you can. I appreciate both of you sharing what you are thinking and feeling. My friend Asher and I talked about these evenings as well. I see such harmony and joy, but wanted to get to the root of it."

Aymoon answered, "Lani, I think the jubilance you see and the harmony all are feeling results from each of us discovering our purpose, our direction through our increased intimacy with our Beloved. With all of us gaining insight into the path we should walk, and the courage and strength to do so, we are all living in elation. Because this is the place we moved into deeper intimacy and commitment, we express exuberant joy and feel connected and in harmony."

Cheka said, "Okay, so let's decide when we will come back, and then we can talk to people here this evening to see who is interested. How about tomorrow after the morning mist? Is that too soon, Aymoon?"

"No, I think it is time to connect with each other about our missions. Tomorrow is good for me. Lani, is this too soon for you?" Aymoon said.

Laughing, Lani said, "I have the rest of today and the evening tomorrow to prepare. Tomorrow is great! I look forward to these discussions too as I feel I have an idea about to germinate."

"Okay, we have a mission to talk to everyone tonight. If I don't see you before, I will be here after the next morning mist." And off Cheka went to talk to as many people as she could.

Lani thought for a moment. She identified a few select people she'd like to have come and share their project or mission. And off she went looking for Kaz, Nan, Hanna, Elia and particularly Asher. She really felt it was important for him to join this group.

She spotted Honani first talking to a few friends Lani had not met. As she approached, Lani overhead their conversation. One of Nan's friends said, "All evening I wondered what those stones were under the dome tree." The other one answered, "I wondered about it too. I think they are a marker of some kind."

As Lani joined the group, she said, "Yaara, sweet as honeysuckle, and Bayla, the beautiful, I welcome your eternal friendship. I couldn't help overhearing your conversation. You're right. Asher created the stone pile as an altar of remembrance. He spent some time here seeking the will of the master and preparing himself for His commission, and wanted to mark the place with 40 stones for the 40 days he spent in close communion with our Beloved."

Nan asked, "Asher? Isn't he the Ahuvati who lives in the hills of the stone that you created these sculptures from?"

"Yes, he is the one. He's been an essential part of the creation of the sculptures. We discussed the colours I wanted and he selected and collected the stone for me, and he suggested using the lightstone."

Noticing Yaara and Bayla looking at the coloured ground underneath the dome tree, Lani asked, "Have you enjoyed the evening?"

Bayla was the first to answer. "I have been thinking about this evening. I missed the first sculpture evening, but this evening touched me. I enjoyed the nearness I felt with everyone, like an intimate connection to everyone here. And while I enjoy the deep and joyful relationship with others, I spent some time wandering under the dome tree by myself and felt a warmth, a feeling of being cherished, a closeness to Yehovah. Yes, I really enjoyed my evening."

Nan added, "Yehovah decided to bring us to this place to remind us of His commitment to us. We see it in the love and passion of the good shepherd, the care and love of the good Samaritan, the serene beauty of this place under the dome tree, and the life and harmony with others in what I understand you call the Carousel Garden. Two different spaces, yet both leading us to connection. Lani, I enjoyed both evenings and look forward to the unveiling of your remaining sculptures. It gets better and better."

Lani said, "Thank you for sharing your thoughts and feelings. A few of us plan to gather back here after the mist rising tomorrow. We want to share with each other what our Beloved put on our hearts as a mission, project or commission. Everyone is welcome. I wonder if that interests any of you?"

"Oh Lani, what a great idea! I'm in," said Yaara. "I too felt the presence of Yehovah here and although my direction remains unclear, I want to hear what everyone else will be doing as inspiration, if that's okay."

Lani answered, "There are no rules and no reason for you not to be a part of the meeting. Please feel welcome."

Nan said, "I too would love to participate. For me, I experienced several affirmations, one this evening, that confirm for me my next steps, and would appreciate the opportunity to share it with friends. Count me in."

Bayla chimed in. "Count me in too! I feel the same as Nan and Yaara. I have some clarity on some work our Beloved has in mind for me, but need to connect with others to accomplish His mission. This would be a great place and great Ahuvati to share with."

"Ok, enjoy the rest of your evening and I will see all three of you next day," Lani said as she noticed Kaz with Hanna and Elia near the good Samaritan.

Kaz spotted Lani making her way toward them and waved at her to join them. "Lani, this is great! I love the depth of meaning the story brings to the sculpture. I like that the good Samaritan-Yehovah wore the colours of priest and king, and offered the same prestige to the bloody, filthy man regardless of who he was. That speaks to me. I told Hanna and Elia something of my life in the long past.

"I now carry the name Kazhu, the reliable, but I wouldn't describe my life in the long past as steady and stable. I felt like the disciple Peter before Pentecost. Always keen and eager, but always failing Yehovah. I grew up as an orphan in China living in a Christian mission in the late 1650s. Although fervent in my belief, I found myself to be short on faith. I jumped into anything Yehovah put in front of me, but quickly lost my faith and sank into the rough waves of circumstance. That is why I like to be near the water, yet live above it. It reminds me I will never sink below those waves again.

"And in the long past, like Peter, I denied my Beloved three times when confronted by the army staging a revolt where I lived. I feared for my life, but afterward my denial saddened me. In my own strength I failed to live up to what the missionaries taught was a good Christian.

"I struggled my whole life, never attaining Peter's status as a pillar of the church. When I see this man in the filth unable to help himself, and on the edge of death, I see myself. And despite all my failings Yehovah, with no requirements from me other than belief in Him, saved me and made me a king and priest in His Kingdom. Yes, Lani, I'm deeply moved by the meaning of this sculpture. It is a powerful reminder of what He has done for me."

Laughing, Lani said, "Kaz, I cannot picture you as anything less than keen and enthusiastic. You hardly stopped to say hello when you figured out the creation meaning of my Entry Garden. Surely Yehovah enjoys that enthusiastic nature He gave you as much as we do. I see you following in the footsteps of Peter. And like Peter, not ending at a failing, but fulfilling your destiny as a pillar. Steady and reliable."

Looking at all three Lani said, "Several of us plan to gather here after tomorrow's mist to share what Yehovah put on each of our hearts. We are all finding out what He would have us do, our mission or project, and we think there may be synergies. It should be interesting to hear what He has in mind for everyone, and how we can support each other. I would like to invite the three of you to join us."

Kaz, Elia and Hanna answered at the same time, confirming their interest and with his usual enthusiasm, Kaz asked if he could invite some of his friends. Lani could just imagine how many some would become for this exuberant Ahuvati. Laughing, she said, "Yes Kaz, you can invite whoever you wish. It is open to everyone who wants to come. And thanks to all of you for coming. I look forward to hearing about the great things ahead for each of you."

The evening continued with many conversations and invitations to gather again in a bit more than a day. Lani finally caught up to Asher to invite him. He began laughing. "You are about the fifteenth person to ask me. And I told each I would be happy to participate in this gathering. I think this is a fantastic idea."

Lani answered, "Well, it was Aymoon's idea, not mine. But I do think it is from Yehovah and now is the perfect time. I'm glad you're coming, Asher. I look forward to hearing all the great things others will work on, including you.

"I think I'm ready to finish my sentence. You know how you remarked on the dancing, how people are moved to spend time with our Beloved under the dome tree, and how you feel this is a special place?" Asher nodded and Lani continued. "And I said, 'Everyone is having – ' and didn't finish? What I almost said was anointed, but that suggests the dedication to a divine purpose. I talked to several people and yes, this is an anointed time. Many came to understand what Yehovah would give them as a mission, a purpose."

Asher answered, "I came to seek the will of my Beloved and found an intimate place where I shared and exchanged deeply intimate thoughts and feelings with Him. The environment, saturated in things that point to Yehovah, focused me on Him to the exclusion of all else. He and I had the quiet and privacy to really talk through what He would have me do now and into the future. For me, it was an anointed time, and He did commission me."

The gathering, the lightstone, the sculptures, the stories, they were all part of a bigger story – seeds of an idea would burst forth with life at the gathering. It felt the bigger story would be perfect for her honour story.

16 | The First Gathering

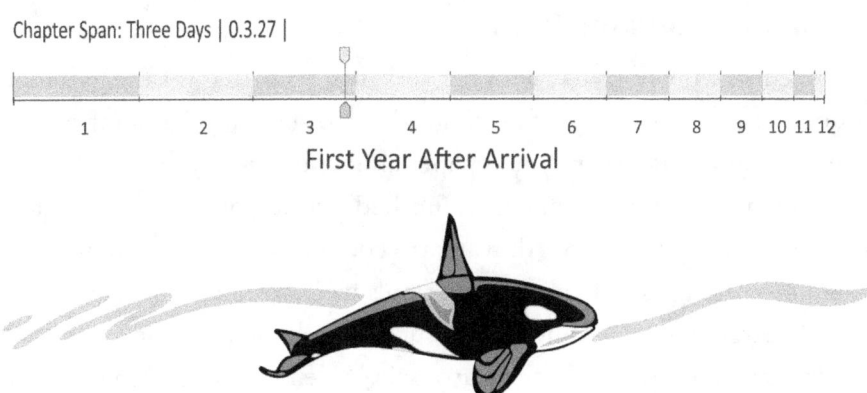

First Year After Arrival

Lani turned to her poem of the first gathering, a significant day in her first year. She intended to review all the poems and stories that would help her decide on the breadth and scope of her honour story. Although she felt the passing of time sitting there reviewing her history, an idea began to formulate.

This poem and story became a turning point for her. The gathering. This might develop into the heart of her story.

The weaver's poem: Desires of My Heart

Seeds of desire planted in the young heart.
Life crushes,
Dreams unfulfilled.

Creatures transformed,
A new name that speaks to the nature,
A new mission that fulfills desire and dream.

Praise Him,
Thank Him,

My faithful Beloved, my All in All.

The Story Behind the Poem

Lani spent the previous day with her servants, preparing for the gathering, setting out a large number of seating, tables to serve food and refreshments, and a few tables with notepaper and writing tools.

The next morning as the mist finished burning off, the light shifted from yellow to green when Ahuvati arrived. Lani was not sure how many would be coming, but if these first arrivals were any indication, she expected a large number. Ahuvati came up through the Creation Garden in a steady flow and gathered in the Carousel Garden with refreshments set out by Nectar and her team.

Once the light shifted to white, and Ahuvati no longer arrived, Lani scouted out Asher as she wanted to spend the day at his side. Many Ahuvati gathered, more than for the sculpture unveiling. Lani smiled. Word spread.

Ahuvati assembled into roughly a circle. Lani stepped forward and encouraged everyone to find a comfortable seat. When everyone settled, Lani said, "I thank you all for coming. I would like to acknowledge Aymoon for the idea of this gathering." Ahuvati broke out in cheering, with those near Aymoon thanking him directly. In response to this recognition, he shouted out, "Not my will, but thine, oh Yehovah!" And that brought an even louder cheer from the crowd.

They could only be described as happy, comfortably relaxed, and enthusiastic to take time to share with each other. An excitement simmered alongside anticipation. Lani also felt this would be a meaningful gathering.

Lani continued. "I'd like to open with acknowledgement of the reason we're gathered here – to share our mission or project and to support each other. Some of you may not know your project yet. We still support you. Where is my friend Honani? Please Nan, would mind singing us a song?"

As Nan made her way to the centre of the group, she asked Lani, "Is there anything in particular you have in mind?"

"No, your choice," replied Lani.

Someone from the back shouted, "Nan, how about that Psalm I heard you singing with Shelomah?"

"Okay. Shel, are you here? Yes, there you are. Please come join me."

As Shelomah joined Nan and conferred for a moment, Lani realized this was the man that sang so beautifully with Nan at the Harmony Canyon. Their voices matched beautifully.

Praise the LORD!
I will thank the LORD with all my heart
As I meet with His godly people.
How amazing are the deeds of the LORD!
All who delight in Him should ponder them.
Everything He does reveals His glory and majesty.
His righteousness never fails.
He causes us to remember His wonderful works.
How gracious and merciful is our LORD!
He gives food to those who fear Him;
He always remembers His covenant.
He has shown His great power to His people
By giving them the lands of other nations.
All He does is just and good,
And all His commandments are trustworthy.
They are forever true,
To be obeyed faithfully and with integrity.
He has paid a full ransom for His people.
He has guaranteed His covenant with them forever.
What a holy, awe-inspiring name He has!
Fear of the LORD is the foundation of true wisdom.
All who obey His commandments will grow in wisdom.
Praise Him forever!

(Psalm 111)

Everyone joined in clapping and dancing. They really had fun together. When finished, Nan said she wrote a participative song based on the sculpture unveiling the other evening. She taught the crowd the participant part. "Shelomah and I will sing a part, then when I point to you, everyone answers with 'My faithful Beloved, my All in All.'"

The crowd rehearsed it a couple of times and were ready to go.

Give thanks to our Shepherd, for He is good.
He gave us breath, He gave us life,
My faithful Beloved, my All in All.

We slept in His arms, drank from His cup.
He entered the pit to ransom us,
My faithful Beloved, my All in All.

And gave us a seat by His side.
Give thanks to our Redeemer, for He is good,
My faithful Beloved, my All in All.

He lifted us out of the filth and sin,
His blood-wine our redemption,
My faithful Beloved, my All in All.

His radiant light our timeless life,
In robes of priests and kings,
My faithful Beloved, my All in All.

Give thanks to my All, for He is good.
Our communion for Your pleasure
My faithful Beloved, my All in All.

Our utterance be Your delight,
May our unity and harmony edify,
May Your desire be our mission,

My faithful Beloved, my All in All.

A hush fell over the group as they considered the words and testimony of the sculptures to the heart of Yehovah. Everyone sat in contemplative silence while each considered the great Yehovah who loved before time.

After a long pause Lani got back up and said, "Nan, that was beautiful, thank you. You gave us a perfect start to our gathering. I know we all seek what we can do to glorify our Beloved All in All. As His prized mate we still enjoy our free will and fervently seek His commission. Some of us know their commission, for others it remains hazy, and still others still seek His wisdom and direction. Is there anyone who would like to share their experience and direction first?"

Liora stepped to the centre of the gathering. Lani remembered her fondly for her kindness in helping her collect the lightstones. Lani introduced her friend. "May we all welcome eternal friendship with Liora, which means light for me." Many offered their encouragement for Liora as she prepared to speak.

"I don't have much of a story or testimony from the long past like many of you. Although born in Solomon's day to Israeli parents of the tribe of Judah, my parents didn't worship Yehovah, but chose the ways of the Ammonites and worshiped Molech. It was a vile god fashioned of brass, hollow inside, bull headed with outstretched arms, ready to receive a sacrifice. The sacrificers first kissed the brass, then kindled and stoked a fire in the hollow belly. Once the arms reached a red hot temperature, they laid their child in the arms as a sacrifice. Drums and cymbals erupted loudly to drown out the screams of the child. Yehovah called it passing their seed through fire to the god of Molech by burning their children alive. The saying 'fire in the belly,' originated from this practice.

"I was one of these children. I never saw my first birthday. My parents cut my life off as an offering to Lucifer. Yehovah, in His great lovingkindness and grace, took my spirit quickly from my defiled body. I had no say in becoming a sacrifice and my spirit groaned under that burden — destruction of my life as a sacrifice directly to Lucifer. My precious life graciously given by Yehovah. It was an evil, detestable practice that Yehovah specifically told the Israelites not to do. And yet, Solomon himself built an abomination in honour of Molech. Child sacrifice came straight from the heart of Lucifer, intended to break the heart of Yehovah.

"At my death my spirit was taken to paradise where I waited for my redeemer. Yeshua came and gathered us up from paradise and took our spirits to heaven with Him. Yehovah-Father held me to Himself, comforted me and whispered sweet promises. Here we awaited the day we would be given our new bodies. As you can see, my new and eternal body shows no scars from the vile start I had in life

"So unlike many of you, I didn't live a life in service or obedience. I come to this day with no skill or experience to offer. I have no developed talent. And yet Yehovah-Father whispered some powerful promises of my future, and I am standing in faith that He will provide me with all I need to fulfill my destiny.

"I was the seed that was passed through the fire, a mocking of Abraham and Isaac and the foreshadowed sacrifice of Yeshua. It was not for humans to try to sacrifice their children to blot out their sin. Yet Yehovah does not see the mockery in me because Yeshua bore the debt of that sin on the cross.

"So that's my history. Like many murdered babies through human history, murdered by our own parents, forced into death against the intention of Yehovah as a sacrifice to Lucifer. We were an affront to Yehovah and His redemption plan because our sacrifice was a mockery of Yehovah's sacrifice of Himself for our redemption from sin, and it was a forced human sacrifice.

"Even though I was used as a mockery of Yeshua, Yehovah loved me and promised I would be used in a mighty way to remind everyone of His grace and love. How out of His deep love and desire, Yehovah-Yeshua gave His own life to remove even the stain of sin and change us into new eternal creatures. A reminder that nothing any human could do would remove sin and make us righteous. He promised to use me to bless the nations, like He blessed the nations through the descendants of Isaac.

"I feel a lot like Isaac, but not for the reasons you might expect. Like Isaac, I have no great achievements, yet am obedient and trusting. And like Isaac, although neither he nor I offer a great gift or talent other than tenacity, both of us now sit in His Kingdom.

"I know of His plans to use me as a blessing to others, yet I don't know how. But I trust Yehovah will reveal it to me at the right time. I love my Beloved so much for rescuing me despite being an abomination, and preserving me for eternal purposes. In abundant joy I will stay in obedience to His will."

When Liora finished her story, Asher sang, with many joining in who knew the hymn:

All hail the power of Jesus' name!
Let angels prostrate fall;
Bring forth the royal diadem,
And crown him Lord of all.

Ye chosen seed of Israel's race,
Ye ransomed from the Fall,
Hail him who saves you by his grace,
And crown him Lord of all.

Let every kindred, every tribe
On this terrestrial ball,
To him all majesty ascribe,
And crown him Lord of all.

Crown him, ye martyrs of your God,
Who from his altar call;
Extol the Stem of Jesse's Rod,
And crown him Lord of all.

O that with yonder sacred throng
We at his feet may fall!
We'll join the everlasting song,
And crown him Lord of all.
(Edward Perronet, 1780)

Liora sat down beside Asher and he lovingly hugged her as they finished singing.

Lani decided to leave the flow of this gathering to people's inspiration. She quietly waited for the next person to speak. Several Ahuvati stepped up with their story in the long past and shared what they knew about their commission. Lani enjoyed hearing all the great things assigned.

After a long pause a familiar figure quietly headed to the centre to speak. Lani could hardly believe it. Here was someone from her long past. She hurried to the centre to meet him and introduce him. She wore the biggest grin on her face as he approached. He looked at her and although he did not know her from the long past, he realized she knew him. He sheepishly smiled back at her and they embraced each other. Lani's eyes welled up to think he would be here at the gathering. She was excited to finally meet him face to face.

Choking back emotion, Lani said to the gathering, "I lived in the last days of the long past and was caught up alive to be with Yehovah for eternity without facing death. These were dark days and few people spoke the truth from the Bible, but this man did. And he spoke it to the world every week. I called him my Hawaiian pastor and he gave a prophesy update every week, watched by thousands of people. He never knew me. I attended his online church, just like thousands around the world."

Lani greeted him with his new name. "Remi'el, Yehovah's mercy and compassion, I welcome your eternal friendship." As she stepped away the crowd parted, and Yehovah-Yeshua walked directly to Remi'el and held him close. Remi'el grinned like a little boy.

Yehovah-Yeshua said, "This is my Beloved Arab pastor in whom I am well pleased. He stood up and spoke truth in the last days. He ministered through faith and trust in me, to people around the world, many he never knew. He led his sheep in my mercy in the face of persecution with a heart of compassion for the lost of the world. This is a man of my mercy and my compassion. My 'Jesus disciple.'" (Remi'el changed his name in the long past from what his parents named him to JD to honour his master.)

"Remi'el, I entrusted you to shepherd a small congregation. You proved faithful and I entrusted you with a global congregation. Well done! I now release to you far more responsibilities in my Kingdom.

"Remi'el, I chose you for a great purpose before you were born. I put you in the womb of the Arab people, I brought you to a land of freedom, I blessed you with a ministry. I gave you healthy, smart children in the face of the impossible. I gave you a congregation and a mission. You showed yourself a faithful steward with all I gave you, a good and honest shepherd to the people I entrusted to your care. All of this was for my purpose, and you grew and developed in faith, trust and obedience. You are rare in my Kingdom – an Arab pastor with a love for the work of leading my people in the ways of righteousness and a love for the Jewish people. You aligned your heart with mine. I now appoint you as a prince, a ruler and priest over nations around Israel for my millennium reign. I will assign Ahuvati to rule and minister under you, but for now, prepare."

Remi'el, humbled by our Beloved's words said, "Excuse me a moment here," and he bowed his head as he worked to gain control over his emotions. "Wow. I love you so much that it humbles me to hear how you see my life in the long past. I know you look at the heart, not the works. But I struggled so with the flesh, my passionate anger would often get the better of me and I found myself shouting about the evil injustices becoming ever increasingly worse, and apologized time and time again. I had all the human failings and could never measure up." Becoming emotional again, Remi'el continued. "I would not be here if it were not for your grace and mercy. All good that I did or any degree of goodness of person I was, it was because of you. Eternity doesn't contain enough time to thank you, my Yehovah-Lamb. I dreamt of the time when you would say, 'Well done, good and faithful servant,' and now I'm broken by those words." With that, Remi'el bowed before our Beloved and master.

Yehovah-Yeshua reached down and blessed Remi'el, then said, "Stand beside me, my Beloved, my partner and mate for eternity. My heart."

Turning to everyone in the crowd, Yehovah-Yeshua said, "You are all so dear to me. Regardless of when and where you lived, you all chose me. I put my heart out there and asked for your hand in marriage and your heart. And you are the ones that chose me. I love you as no other and will love you forever. I am pleased to join you in your gathering." And with that He moved through the crowd, gently resting His hands on Ahuvati's heads and shoulders as He passed, looking for a comfortable spot among His Beloved.

Lani sat back and thought for a moment. In the long past, she thought everyone would clamour to be in the physical presence of Yeshua, like people pressing in on him during His three-year ministry. But the long past was a physically dominant world. There was little understanding of the spiritual, and each person lived an independent mental life. It was so different in a world where the physical life was not where the marriage connection occurred. All the Ahuvati lived in a conjugal mental and spiritual relationship with Yeshua. It felt so fulfilling that to enjoy the physical presence of Yeshua was good, but not a necessary part of the wedded relationship.

In the long past people lived with their mate. They spent plenty of time together. While people needed to spend time with friends, it was not the same as a mate. Lani thought because she spent time with Yeshua in the mental and spiritual, His physical presence was like the visit of a good friend. She valued the spiritual and mental time far more than a mere physical visit. Mental and spiritual relationship was far more intimate, immediate and satisfying.

That's not to say everyone didn't enjoy Yeshua's physical visit to their gathering. He used this time to publicly tie everyone's new name, their experience and growth in the spiritual to their millennial commission.

Lani recalled the part of the story when she started to realize her purpose.

All she knew at the start of the day was that she was chosen to create the sculptures as a tribute and witness to the love of Yehovah for His intended, and the grace and mercy He extended to make it possible to transform from betrothed to mate. But she knew there was something more, something significant that would be her commission.

While others shared their background, their name and what they knew of their commission, Lani saw how the past prepared them for their future. But it was more than that. No one learned all they could have in the long past. Many lives were cut off early. Many lived in circumstances that prevented them from achieving their dreams – *their* dreams.

I get it! she thought. Yes, Yehovah placed those dreams and desires in the hearts of each human, but those dreams and desires could not be fulfilled in an imperfect world. Those dreams gave each person the impetus to grow and develop in preparation for their future when they would be living in a perfect world.

A few people learned deep spiritual lessons while living in that imperfect world and became skillful in faith, trust and pressing into the heart and mind of Yehovah. Most people struggled and made mediocre gains.

She thought about Asher and the difficult life he led as a slave. How the slavers ripped him from his family to live out his life in very difficult circumstances. But through those circumstances, despite those circumstances, he met Yehovah. The story of Joseph, who also was sold into slavery and taken to an unknown land as a lad, inspired him. This sparked a desire within him to rise to leadership. But like King David, Asher needed a time of growth and development. And like David, it was not easy. But also like David Asher was prepared to take on great leadership in Yeshua's Kingdom. Not everyone could have taken those hard lessons and developed into this generous, quiet, and steady man already an expert at learning and trusting. Life hardened, tempered and prepared him for great leadership.

Listening to the various histories, names and commissions, her mind wandered to thinking about the dome tree and its beautifully coloured floor, the Carousel Garden, the sculptures and the Creation Garden.

She thought about Asher's blessing on her. He spoke into her life a variety of things: wise leadership, the ability to speak success into a future path, that her words would bring light and life, that she would have a positive impact on others, and that many would find peace and shelter in her and in her home.

Providing peace and shelter stuck in her mind. Lani mulled this over and over when she realized the significance.

She took her thronestone from her neck, her identification. Turning it she could see her name. She turned the stone past the words "To my Beloved from your love and desire," and "Melchizedek", past the moed, and there it was. The image of a waterside tree with branches providing shelter to many.

This was the third touch on her life that told her like a large waterside tree, she would provide comfort, rest and shelter to many. The first was a prophesy spoken over her in the long past. The second was here on her identification. It was so important, it was included on her thronestone. She would be identified by others because of the peace and shelter she would provide. And the third time was Asher's blessing over her.

A large tree by the waterside.

Lani looked out to the dome tree. And then she knew. She finally knew what the prophesy, her identification and the blessing meant. A paradox of emotion swept over her. She felt both excited and settled.

It all came together in her mind. The dome tree under which Asher found a place of contemplation, quiet time with the presence of Yehovah. She looked at the stones of remembrance Asher placed there.

This gathering. Ahuvati wanted to be here. The peace and harmony everyone enjoyed gathered together here. Hesitatingly, the purpose clarified. Yehovah wanted to use this place as an oasis, a retreat for Ahuvati.

She rapidly turned to look at Yeshua. He casually looked back, smiling gently. Knowingly. All her external awareness dropped to nonexistence. A moment when time stood still while she took it all in.

Yeshua, breaking the moment, said, "Lani, please share with us what's on your heart." He attended her thoughts and knew it was time to birth the idea, time for the seeds to burst forth with life.

Lani slowly stood up, still dazed. She started. "Like I mentioned earlier, I lived in the last days before we were brought here. I grew up in a Christian home, but challenges led to the family fracturing. Hypocrisy in the home and church left a bitter taste for all the human failings in the church. And when I was old enough to make my own decisions, I quit attending church. And for awhile, I quit on Yehovah too.

"But He pulled me back to Him through a Christian scientist who spoke about creation. Yehovah used my interest in space and time to draw me back to Himself. I am so moved when I think Yehovah knew long before I lived to give me an Entry Garden that tells the story of creation as a marker or reminder of what brought us together. The entry to our relationship. I know all of you also have Entry Gardens that illustrate the story of His entrance into your hearts. Asher, you have the story of Joseph. Adi'el, the story of Daniel. Kaz, you have the story of Peter. Hanna, the story of grace to a prodigal son. Nature greets us singing the story of how Yehovah brought us into relationship. It is just so amazing to think this was planned for before time and prepared before I existed."

Turning to speak directly to Yeshua, Lani said, "I love you so much." Her eyes welled up as she paused to let the emotional wave pass.

Yeshua gently said, "I know, my sweet love, my La'anni." He nodded encouragement to continue her story.

Taking in a deep breath, she continued. "Yehovah provided a comfortable life, allowing some challenges to draw me in closer. In my stubbornness and perhaps stupidity, I took a long time to learn His lessons.

"Like all of you, I bring little to the table. Spiritually, I was immature in faith, trust and obedience. I struggled with knowing Yehovah loved me. My father didn't love me and I survived two failed marriages, so I felt unlovable. I mostly retreated and quietly held onto my belief. I determined to be glad just to make it here.

"When growing up, the church left me terrified I would be left behind. If my mom, a godly woman, was late getting home, I became fearful I didn't make the cut and faced the horrors of the antichrist alone.

"Many years later, I came into assurance listening to Remi'el on the Internet every week." Turning to Remi'el, Lani said, "I can't thank you enough for making your messages available around the world. I counted you my minister and you never knew me, but faithfully and diligently followed the direction of Yehovah.

"Not being married, I needed to work. For a period of time, I lost my job and couldn't find work. That drove me to my knees. I learned Yehovah is my provider, not me. Afterward, a minister spoke prophesy over me that I would be like a tree by the water, providing shelter and peace to many.

"I had a heart for teaching and supporting others in their development, and sought out opportunities to be that tree, but none of my jobs ever satisfied my desire or fulfilled that prophesy.

"My thronestone has an image of that tree of shelter. A second confirmation that my destiny still includes providing shelter and peace. And my friend Asher spoke a blessing over me that, among other things, many would find peace and shelter in me and in my home. A third confirmation.

"So sitting here listening to everyone share their story and commission, I realized here is this huge dome tree under which Ahuvati spend quiet, focused time in the presence of Yehovah. The stones of remembrance mark the place and time for one person. The sculptures are a witness. They exemplify love and commitment of our Beloved, drawing us into communion. I now realize Yehovah planted eternal desires in us at conception, which life in the long past could not fulfill. I see my path to fulfilling that planted desire.

"My immediate commission is to open and develop this property as a retreat for Ahuvati to withdraw from their business, have a time of quiet with Yehovah, create an environment where they can gather to speak of the great things He has done and is doing in their lives, and gather together in deep harmony to recharge and celebrate, a place of fun, a place of rejuvenation."

Laughing in delight, Lani concluded saying, "I have to laugh. Master, I love your sense of humour. From a distaste for church life in the long past, you now ask me to run your eternal tabernacle."

The crowd broke out cheering and laughing with Lani. Yeshua came to Lani and held her close to His heart. Bending down to speak into her ear, He said, "I so love you, and really love to hear you laugh. I gave you the heart and property to create an oasis for my Beloved to refresh and rejuvenate mentally and spiritually. Lean in and lean on me, and I will guide and inspire you. This will not be tainted by human failure."

Looking and speaking to the crowd, Yeshua said, "I am well pleased with my sweet Aha'La'anni. This is but a stepping stone on her path of eternity. Aha'La'anni, I have great plans for you, my Love. You are my weaver of stories and images of what was, is and is yet to be. I will inspire you in your stories to bring light and life. My stories, through you, will spark ideas and energize. I will instill the ways of wise leadership in you and give you the faith, boldness and insight to speak words of counsel, visionary words that speak to the heart and destiny for my Ahuvati. You will forever be a tree of shelter for many.

"Before time I set aside this place for a purpose. A sanctified place of gathering together and a place of individual retreat to spend intimate time with me. An oasis, a mayan for my people. I will inspire many pieces of art as remembrances of my love, faithfulness, grace and mercy. I will inspire many remembrance stones as a sign, a memorial forever of the great things I do with my eternal Beloved. I will inspire many stories that will speak to my unchanging nature and embolden my Beloved to move into their destiny. Many will come to listen to the inspired stories, or look on the inspired art and marker stones, and will celebrate my abundant love and provision.

"Like the good shepherd, I will lead my Beloved here to still waters and times of refreshing both with me and with each other.

"May you find shelter to seek my direction, my strength and courage, and my boldness to step out into the unknown. May you be invigorated by gathering together to testify of the great things I am doing through you. May you be revitalized in contemplating the art and stones as witnesses to my unchanging character and my great accomplishments. May you find friendship, share joy and laughter, have fun together here. May this mayan be a place of shelter, peace, refreshing, harmony, camaraderie, entertainment and celebration."

Lani sat back and thought about all her Beloved said. He gave her things to do, made promises of things He would do through her, and finally the results He would bring about as a result of the things she would create and convey.

He created her property as an oasis, a spring, a mayan, for His mate to draw near to Him and to each other. He would provide fresh words, the bread of life and living water. And finally, He would commission His people.

Her mission – to create a mayan, a retreat of peace, shelter, refreshment, harmony, fun and celebration. A place to display His abundant love, faithfulness, grace, mercy and provision. A place that declared and attested to what He has done and will do. A place filled with emblems of Yehovah, a collection of reminders to His greatness.

He promised He would fill her with stories of His unchanging nature that inspire, bring light and life. He would enable her with wise leadership through which she would speak words of counsel and speak to inspired vision.

And through the environment and her words, He would use this place to bring Ahuvati together in joy, and strengthen, energize and embolden them to move into their destiny.

The next day Lani saw Asher at the beach with a huge blue stone and more lightstone. He came up to ask her to show him how to carve the stone without explaining what he wanted to do. Lani showed him the basics and loaned him her tools. Asher thanked her and returned to the beach.

Later that afternoon, Lani saw him coming up through the Creation Garden with a piece of lightstone and a piece of purple stone. He said, "Lani, let me show you what I have been up to," and continued toward his remembrance stones. He rearranged the stones to make room for this lightstone in the centre, and carefully put it in place with the purple stone on top. Lani read the writing Asher carved on it:

"You met me when I was lost.
Through a difficult life, you molded me.
Offering nothing more than my heart,
You elevated me to your helpmate.
Here, you asked and I committed .
My mission.

Forever."

Asher

It shone like a beacon of royal light. Beautiful words from Asher's heart to mark the remembrance stones, reminding both Asher and Yehovah what occurred at this place.

"I like it, Asher. It looks great and very honouring to Yehovah," said Lani.

"Thanks. I have something down at the beach for you. May I show you?"

Lani nodded and off they headed for the beach through the Creation Garden. A number of Asher's servants milled about on the beach, staring just off to the right of the entry. Lani became curious, but Asher only smiled in answer.

When she got to the beach, the servants moved aside and Lani saw what he had been up to down here. He brought a huge boulder of blue stone and carved out the word Mayan in huge letters, and filled the carved-out letter spaces with lightstone. Mayan – the perfect name for her oasis.

Yehovah-Yeshua graced it with a name and Asher put the sign out like a billboard.

Underneath, Asher quoted the Bible. "There is nothing better for people in this world than to eat, drink and enjoy life. That way they will experience some happiness along with all the hard work God gives them under the sun (Ecclesiastes 8:15)."

Lani started to laugh, then held her hands to her face and just stared with her mouth open, stunned. "Oh Asher, it's beautiful. I hadn't thought about naming this place and even when Yehovah-Yeshua called it Mayan, I still thought nothing of it. This is perfect. It's a perfect word of description and a perfect name." Turning to him, she was deeply moved. "Thank you so very much. Every time I'm on the beach, I'll remember the gathering when Yehovah-Yeshua gave me my commission, and I will think of you."

Asher gave her a hug and said, "I feel the same way about the remembrance stones. You gave me a mayan – an oasis to intimately talk over what Yehovah would have me do, and a spring of refreshment. I will always think of Yehovah and you when I look on those stones. Thank you for giving me an intimate place of meeting."

Lani determined in that moment to complete the remaining sculptures as the first step in developing the Mayan. She would continue with gatherings and take this time to really think through what the Mayan could and should be.

She wanted to include this intimate experience as part of her honour story. It was a good story, but she wanted her honour story to be worthy of her name, weaver of stories. As a weaver, she wanted her story to be unique, creative and reflective of her style. The stones and sculptures, her purpose and mission, sort of felt like the basis of a perfect story, but she needed to explore her poems and stories some more to really round out her honour story.

You can read the story of the prophesy of the water tree at www.serenitymclean.com/bonus-content/. Use the password soulsailing

17 | The Mayan

Chapter Span: Two Hundred and Seventy Days | 0.4.1 to 0.12.30 |

First Year After Arrival

Lani heard the sounds of her estate's daily activities. In the distance she heard sounds of people in unity, kinship, in true affection for each other. The Mayan had become a place that brought people together, developed togetherness and built close relationship.

It occurred to her maybe she should include something in her honour story about the expansion of the Mayan, the addition of amenities and the significant impact on the people involved. Seven or eight months passed since she considered her estate as a mayan – a spring of refreshing and renewal. And just about every month, she added a new way to build togetherness. Lani turned to her poem about the impact the development of the Mayan had on her companions and sat up to read.

The weaver's poem: The Mayan, the Year of Impact

Kaz, reliable, discovers authentic steadiness and strength,
Cheka, full of laughter, on her journey of touching all with joy.
Adi'el, Yehovah's jewel, on her journey of touching all with spatial jewels.
Nan, singer of songs, leads into His presence.

Shelomah, man of peace, leads into peace beyond understanding.
Elia, one who rises, steps into role of leadership.
Aymoon, faithful, steps into role of knowledge bearer.
Asher, happy, accepts the mantle of Yehovah's prince.
Remi'el, Yehovah's mercy and compassion, accepts the mantle of
Yehovah's prince-shepherd.
Aha'La'anni, weaver of stories –
I am a weaver of people.

The Story Behind the Poems

The day after the first gathering, Lani grabbed her digital notebook and went to the beach early in the morning. She itched to get some thinking time in on what she would do to turn her property into a place where people would come to be refreshed, to learn, to rejoice, to eat and have fun.

She found her favourite inspiration alcove in the sand and settled in. She loved this spot because of the privacy and the familiarity to a significant place in her past. Here she could work undisturbed. She thought about Yeshua's words and decided to focus on three things.

First, create a place of quiet meditation and communion where people could spend time alone. Second, create a place of gathering together and harmony where people could sing, dance and learn together. And third, create a place of joy, laughter, and fun where people could engage in activities that satisfied creative desires and the desire for fun together.

She was well on her way with the first, a place of quiet. The dome tree had become a place of communion, a place where Ahuvati came to spend quiet time undisturbed. Asher built the first altar of remembrance and Lani suspected many would follow. Thinking about how Asher stayed overnight to really immerse in his quiet time, she could build some small huts near the beach on the bay side as a quiet and private place for those seeking time alone.

Second, she also had a start on creating a place of gathering and harmony. The Carousel Garden with the sculptures, the unveilings, and the first gathering had become a place where people and eh-bed gathered in harmony and celebration. Lani thought for a moment and it occurred to her the natural amphitheatre would be perfect for teaching, concerts and shows, and for larger gatherings.

And third, to create a place of joy, laughter and fun, she could leverage the natural features of her property. She could set it up for people to take a lazy float down the east river, or go white water rafting on the west river. She had enough boats to organize Jet Skiing, sailing and wakeboarding. Then there were the two bays on the west coast that would allow for surfing for beginners and experts. She finally understood the reason for all the boats and equipment.

Maybe she should have some activities that were not water based. Art, for example. Maybe she could build a studio for people who wanted to learn and create in an inspiring environment. She could have someone design a really interesting open concept building for artists to work in. It could be along the shoreline at the north end of Celebration Bay. It could be a unique design like the opera house in Sydney of the long past, or even better like Fallingwater in Pennsylvani, only built for artists to work. And then she could have an art gallery for visitors where the artists could display and give away their work.

Maybe some land sports like rock climbing. Yes, the ridge face would be perfect for climbers, and then she could take that flat area along the shore of Big Surf Bay and turn it into sports fields. People could use it for whatever spontaneous game they wanted.

To do this resort thing, she should make sure she built enough facilities for visitors to stay over if they wanted.

Okay, maybe I should stop thinking up new ideas. Implementing all these developments would take quite awhile. She could aim for releasing one new thing a month, but she would really need a lot of help from Willow.

She would be busy for the next couple of months finishing her sculptures. So she could wait until she completed them before starting with her

Mayan project. She really wanted to get it going, though. She thought for a moment, then wondered if she started with releasing some of the less complicated features first. Willow could probably handle it with just a bit of help from her.

She decided to start with the natural amphitheatre. It required no work to prepare it for use. Naturally tiered seating existed for a few thousand. She would need to do a bit of planning to organize and schedule events, and to organize food and refreshments for people attending them.

Sitting with Willow after the morning mist, Lani laid out some of her thoughts around the purpose of the property and what help Willow thought she could provide.

"Willow," Lani started, "did you notice the big sign Asher put down on the beach at the start of the Creation Garden?"

"Aha'Sarah, yes. You named your property Mayan. I know the word means oasis, but what does it mean for your estate?"

"Yeshua gave me this property to provide an oasis, a place of refreshing for Ha'Ahuvati. Think of it like the way a spring of water refreshes those who drink.

"I want this place to be a retreat for those who want to be alone with Yehovah. Everything will be provided ☐ meals, refreshments, privacy and a beachfront place to stay overnight. I also want to use the property's natural features to provide a place where Ha'Ahuvati can come to have fun and recreation with others. And it will also be a place of gathering, learning and sharing. It is this third aspect I want to start with.

"Here, look on the map. See this area here?" She pointed to the natural amphitheatre. "I am going to call it Blue Rock Amphitheatre. This evening I invited Honani, Shelomah and Hanna to talk with them about setting up a series of concerts. I also invited Aymoon, Remi'el and Asher to talk to them about using this space to offer teaching. Would you be interested in helping with this? I'm still busy with the sculptures."

"Aha'Sarah, yes I would!" Willow said, beaming ear to ear. "What do I need to do? I am not sure what needs to be done and what you would like me to do."

"Awesome! Thanks Willow, you'll be a great help. Some of the things will require that we identify the servants who will be involved and get them some training. And for Blue Rock, we'll need to organize events and dates with the help of those coming tonight, then plan food and refreshments, and servants to prepare and serve.

"Today, could you think about which servants would like to be involved in food preparation and serving? Also identify at least a hundred that can help with construction work, and another 60 to 80 who really like being in and around the water. We can talk tomorrow morning about who would like to do what.

"This evening, I would like you to join us for dinner. I won't talk about Blue Rock until after, so you can enjoy your meal. Then we can take everyone to Blue Rock and sit around talking about ideas and dates. You will want to take notes of what is decided and any event needing support.

"You will need to follow up with each person to ensure we provide everything they need. I would like you to be the main person they go to if they have questions or need anything. You and I can meet several times a week so I can help you with what needs to be done. Would you be okay with that?"

"Aha'Sarah, yes. Thank you for giving me so much responsibility. I know this is Yehovah's desire and I will not let Him or you down." Willow looked down, then directly at Lani with a smile full of eagerness and excitement. "Aha'Sarah, I am really excited. I never dreamed I would be helping with such an important project. Thank you so much. I can't believe it. It is going to be wonderful to have so many Ha'Ahuvati here. It will be like the unveiling of your sculptures and the gathering. And good food. I will make sure we have good food for everyone."

Laughing, Lani said, "I am glad you're excited. It is going to be a lot of work at first to get things organized and I will need to lean on you to make it happen."

Reaching out, Lani rested her hand on Willow's head and said, "Willow, may you find wisdom and confidence in Yehovah. May He give you good judgment in organizing the servants, that you give each one opportunities to bring joy and happiness. May you be astute in anticipating needs and insightful in resolving problems. And may you find this work fulfills your desire to grow and develop those you manage."

"Aha'Sarah, thank you. I will never forget this day. I will talk to the servants to find out who would like to help with construction and who would be happy working around the water." Bowing, she stepped away. Lani noted a lightness in her gait and smiled to herself.

That evening, Asher arrived first. Lani heard him talking with Gilad in the garden and came out to greet him. They sat for awhile in the Carousel Garden talking about the progress of the prodigal sculpture.

The sun had just set when Nan and Shelomah arrived and joined Lani and Asher. They talked about the gathering when Hanna, Aymoon and Remi'el came up through the Creation Garden.

Lani invited them into her mansion. Nectar was ready to serve dinner in the ocean-facing dining room. Happiness pervaded their meal. They chatted about the fish under the floor following them, and the ocean view.

Lani introduced Willow to everyone and they all welcomed her warmly to their mealtime. When everyone finished dining, Lani shared with them her idea for her Mayan and wanted to show them something. There was much laughter and chatter as they piled into the utility LAT.

When they arrived at Blue Rock, Shelomah led the way to the front and began singing. His voice vibrated deep and rich, the walls of the ridge encompassing the sound and naturally amplifying it throughout the amphitheatre. Intrigued, Nan joined him at the front to sing a catchy tune about the beauty of this, their new home world. Hanna joined them on stage, gracefully dancing like the birds of spring, incorporating expressive hand and body gestures.

When Nan and Shelomah finished their song, everyone stood, clapped and cheered except Willow. She stood as though in shock. She had never seen dancing like Hanna had done, and never heard Nan and

Shelomah sing before. Her face showed her amazement and she became overcome with emotion. Lani immediately went to her side and wrapped her arm around her. She was such a sweet, tender soul. It occurred to Lani that the Ahuvati would do many things that eh-bed would find stunning, amazing and unexpected.

Speaking to her friends, Lani started. "Okay, so now you have seen the Blue Rock Amphitheatre and heard the way sound carries. I would like to open it up as a venue for theatre, concerts, gatherings and learning. What do you think? Is this something you would like to do? Could you make use of this space? Or do you know of anyone who would be interested?"

Willow quickly gathered herself and sat down to take notes. Remi'el with an impish grin immediately responded, knowing Lani had subscribed to his YouTube channel. "I miss doing my weekly message and prophesy update."

Lani laughed at first, then said, "We could broadcast, if we wanted to. That is a great idea, Remi'el."

"I was just kidding, but now that I think about it, it would be a good idea to set this space up for showing visual material. I could get the guys that helped me in the long past to get it set up."

Lani thought, Yay! Remi'el is in.

Asher replied, "Regardless of when we get set up to put on a visual show, I think it is a great idea to run events from here. With people already attracted to spending time under the dome tree, and coming to the sculpture unveilings, this is a natural place to hold concerts, and I could use this space to teach and prepare my team for what is ahead."

Aymoon was next. "As you know, Lani, I have been doing quite a bit of research and have a number of things on my heart to share with Ahuvati. This would be a great venue for me. Thank you for thinking of me. I think everyone will want to use Blue Rock and it will fill up fast."

Shelomah then said, "The sound's remarkable here. I wrote a number of songs and thought about giving some concerts. This would suit me perfectly. I'm in."

Nan followed. "I agree, the sound is spectacular. I would love to have a series of participative concerts where the audience joins in and Hanna leads in dancing." Looking at Hanna, Nan said, "I hope you are okay with me volunteering you." Hanna nodded, totally on board. Nan continued. "I think this would be an instant hit. Everyone is going to want to come. Just look at the response to the invitation to the sculpture unveilings and the first gathering. Everyone really enjoys being here and spending time together. This is a great idea, Lani. When were you thinking of having the first event?"

"Well, how soon would any of you be ready?" Lani replied.

Shelomah and Nan answered in unison, "Now!"

Asher, always the voice of reason said, "How about the fourteenth? That would give Lani time to prepare, and give the rest of us time to get the word out."

Remi'el said, "Two weeks? That works for me. Who gets the first event? Lani, do you have any preference?"

Lani thought for a moment, then said, "No. Actually I wasn't expecting everyone would be ready so quickly. What do you think about Willow putting together a calendar and you can pick dates that work for you? And it can be morning, afternoon, all day or evening. Whatever works. I will make sure to stock up on food and refreshments. So we're a go?"

With everyone's agreement, Lani thanked them for their support. She let them know this was just the first thing of many she would offer.

Together, they headed back to Lani's mansion, using the time to further their plans. They sat around the inlet room into the wee hours of the evening, discussing what each could do with Blue Rock.

Asher was the last to leave. Lani was glad to have some time with him as she wanted to share all her plans with him and get his thoughts. They discussed building a village of small houses for Ahuvati to stay in if they were going to be here for more than the day.

Lani mentioned she thought Kaz would be able to help get that work done, but she would like someone to design the buildings as she wanted a relaxed feel and a unique design. Asher suggested his neighbour Adi'el. She produced some really inspired designs for her property and would probably welcome the challenge. Lani remembered Adi'el because of her Daniel garden, the first one she figured out on her own. Maybe Adi could design an art studio and gallery as well.

They chatted awhile longer, then hugged each other and Asher left for home.

The following evening Lani invited Adi'el, Kaz and Cheka over for dinner. She explained about Blue Rock and what she planned. She asked Kaz if he would be willing to lead and take care of the construction work she needed done. Kaz immediately agreed. He was looking for something to do since checking out Entry Gardens no longer kept him busy. They talked about the village of small houses she wanted built, and the Sunrise Studio and Art Gallery.

Kaz asked if she already organized a crew to do the work, and Lani mentioned about a hundred of her servants were excited to help, but suspected they had little experience. Kaz assured her he would arrange for skilled people to help as well. Through his Entry Garden investigation, he met lots of Ahuvati and knew many skilled in building construction.

She then asked if Adi'el would be able to help with designs for several buildings. Adi'el said she really didn't have a background in architectural design, but she did love looking at magazines and always sketched out her ideas. And she had been studying engineering and design at the library. She said she would be honoured to help and they made plans to meet with Kaz in a couple of days to review her sketches.

Lani then turned to Cheka and mentioned she heard she was a phenomenal chef, both in the long past and now, and wondered if she would create some recipes unique to the Mayan experience and teach them to Nectar and her team. "Of course," Cheka said. She asked if Lani would mind if she spent a bit of time in the morning with Lani's ganan Gilad to find out about the produce on Lani's property. Cheka discovered everyone had unique fruits and seeds on their property and she would be sure to incorporate those into her Mayan recipes.

They travelled out to the bay and walked north along the Celebration Bay shoreline to look at where Lani wanted the houses, and then continued all the way to the point where she wanted the art gallery and studio. Adi'el loved both locations, and asked what kind of mood or feeling Lani desired or particular look she wanted. Lani said the village should be casual and tied to the beach, and she wanted something memorable and artistic for the studio and gallery. And it should look like the village and the studio/gallery belonged together on the same property.

As they prepared to leave, Lani said she couldn't thank them enough for their help, and they hushed her up, saying she offered an exciting project and they were pleased to be a part of it.

Willow did a great job organizing and preparing for the first events at Blue Rock Amphitheatre. When Lani looked at the schedule, Blue Rock was already booked almost half the time. She asked Willow to follow up with both Gilad and Nectar to ensure they were ready to provide food and refreshments.

Aymoon booked Blue Rock one morning a week to launch his study group. He planned on bringing visual materials from the library and worked with Remi'el to get the amphitheatre ready to show their materials. Several of Remi'el's friends, interested in the art that could be produced from the technology used in the library, helped Remi'el and Aymoon equip Blue Rock to display enhanced holographic visuals throughout the entire theatre.

That was the explanation given to Lani as to what they were doing. In time, Lani discovered the explanation didn't do justice to the reality of what they achieved. Not only could enhanced visuals be displayed, the guys recreated the totally immersive library experience at Blue Rock. And they set it up to broadcast live and record events for the Mayan video library. And they did one more thing for Lani. She could tune in to watch or simply listen to the live events, and could replay any event from the screens in all the rooms of her mansion.

Remi'el continued his study of the Bible twice a week. In the long past he focused on the prophesy of the bride. Now he focused on the prophesy of the millennium. The big difference from what he did in the long past would be that he created an immersive experience for his millennium teachings. And he showed things from different points of view, really enhancing the depth of the study.

Shelomah and Nan would perform an evening concert, with new and familiar songs celebrating the story of redemption. They worked with one of Remi'el's friends to produce artistic supportive visuals for the concert. This was planned for six evenings over the first two weeks. In addition to the joint concert, both Nan and Shelomah scheduled several evenings to give their own concerts afterward.

Shelomah booked additional time for choir practice and choir concerts. And Nan booked time once a week for a sing-along where people could come and request their favourite songs.

Asher booked Blue Rock twice a week for a learning study on leadership and once a week to meet with the people he was gathering to form his team of leaders for his millennium work.

In just a couple of days since asking for help from her friends, Adi returned with ideas for the village, studio and gallery. She came with a few very different ideas for the studio and gallery, but Lani instantly fell in love with one. It had the linear structure of Fallingwater by Frank Lloyd Wright, similar to the linear nature of the dome tree and her mansion. It would be anchored to the land and three floors high. She designed the first floor with a rather open concept of no walls, a river starting with channel trees at one end would run through the middle of the first floor to the ocean and a very wide walkway on either side of the river. The first floor would be about a 1,000 ft. wide and 2,500 ft. long. Trees, contained gardens and sitting areas decorated the sides and back of the main floor.

The second and third floors would be lined with a series of sliding glass doors. These floors would be the length of the first floor, plus extend out over the water, ending in a semicircle of glass walls. The second floor would extend out about 500 ft. and the third floor would extend about half that distance with the remaining floor space as an outdoor deck. There would be a set of stairs leading to a roof deck. Lani expected the view would be great from both the second and third floors, and spectacular from the roof deck. She thought the second floor could be the studio and the third floor the gallery. The decks would be a nice feature for gallery shows. Adi planned to use lightstone and coloured stone to light the gallery and studio like a jewel on the water.

Having chosen the linear style for the Sunrise Studio and Art Gallery, Lani then looked over the proposed designs for the village. Adi gave her three options, but Lani loved the first one she saw. It was a combination of land-based and water-based huts. Each hut would be like a linear-styled cottage with lots of windows and flat roof. Adi'el had designed the village around a central building that would be used for dining.

The design included 50 huts built out on the water. A couple of long docks would be built like roads, so people could walk out to steps up to the back of the hut. The front of the hut had a walkout upper deck with steps down to a relaxation room and private dock at water level. Lani profusely thanked Adi for her designs, and gave Kaz the approval to go ahead with both the village and the art gallery

A few days after Kaz took on the building projects, Lani heard the unmistakable sounds of construction. She took a break from her work on the prodigal sculpture to zip down to see how things were going. Kaz organized a huge crew of experienced builders teaching an even larger crew of eh-bed the skills of construction. Posts were going in for the two docks of the village and the foundation for Sunrise was started. Talking with Kaz Lani learned the village could be finished and ready for use in a couple of months because of new construction technology some of his engineering friends developed. Confidently he promised Sunrise, leveraging the same technology, would be open in four months. Lani would follow the progress of both with great interest.

A week prior to opening Blue Rock, Lani discussed with Willow the plans to provide food and refreshment, and how it would be delivered. Having confirmed Gilad was ready with produce, she asked if Nectar was ready with recipes and the ability to prepare the required volume of food every day. Willow walked Lani through the kitchen, showing her the preparations in progress and what she had set up outside Blue Rock to feed the visitors. Lani was impressed and comfortable they were ready to open Blue Rock in one week.

Lani thought of one last thing. There would need to be signage throughout the estate indicating what was open, what would be opening soon and when.

Looking ahead three weeks, Lani wanted to open inner tubing down Coconut Stroll. She talked to Willow about getting ready for opening this part of the resort. It would require training eh-bed to drive the Jet Skis as Lani wanted to have the visitors towed on the inner tubes up the river to the Mainspring Falls and let them float the river down to Coconut Lake. She wanted refreshments at Mainspring Falls, halfway down Coconut Stroll and at Coconut Marina.

A couple of Remi'el's friends, Annikki, full of grace, and Eden, delight, who helped set up Blue Rock, came from Hawaii and were experienced in all things water. They offered to help with the training required around using Jet Skis, boating, and surfing. With their help Coconut Stroll was well on its way to opening in a few weeks.

The two weeks passed quickly and Remi'el's study group opened Blue Rock without a hitch. In the long past about 20,000 followed him online, and word got out that he would be leading a study a couple of times a week. Hundreds showed up including Asher and his leadership team on the first day of his study, and if it went the same way as the sculpture, there would be thousands soon.

Asher started his study on leadership the next day and Aymoon his in-depth study on names and natures a couple of days later. Asher also regularly met with his growing leadership team. And lastly, the joint concert by Nan and Shelomah ran three evenings with huge attendance.

After the first week, several approached Lani about arranging to use Blue Rock for several popular musical groups from the long past that wanted to put on a few concerts. MercyMe, NeedToBreathe and Casting Crowns, to name a few, booked several time slots. The schedule quickly filled up and it surprised Lani who came to the Mayan to contribute to the oasis. With the broadcast station set up, all of these events would be seen across planet heaven. It grew so quickly to a scope and scale Lani could not have imagined. Amazing to think she was a part of something so important, so global.

Signs announcing the upcoming opening of Coconut Stroll had been posted and seen by all the Blue Rock visitors for a couple of weeks. Asher and his leadership group took the first float down. It took several hours to have a leisurely tow to Mainspring Falls and float back down to Coconut Marina. They spent the day floating down and getting another tow to float down again, then led a study in the evening.

Two weeks made a big difference in the construction projects. The docks were done, posts for all the water huts were in, along with five completed huts. The dining hall was also completed. The first floor of Sunrise was also well on its way. Kaz was a fabulous construction manager and organized his experienced people to lead each building's construction. Lani hadn't thought about it earlier, but Kaz also organized the preparation and delivery of all construction materials, and all logistics.

Looking around she found him looking after a delivery of materials. She waited for him to finish, then went to speak with him. "Kaz, I can't believe how much has been done. Everything looks great. I just wanted to thank you for taking care of everything, the construction, the materials, the workers. You are fantastic!"

Kaz started to blush, "Yes, it is coming along nicely. Adi'el was here earlier today and very happy with how we are building to her design. The guys are doing a great job leading and teaching the eh-bed, and the eh-bed have been fantastic to work with. They learn so quickly, yet are careful and accurate in their work."

Lani could see he enjoyed this work. She looked over the progress in the village. Then prompted to speak into Kaz's life, she turned back to him. "Kaz, you're amazing. May you be known for your ability to get things done. You are a leader of people, a developer of eh-bed. You develop strong friendships that enable you to deliver. You are reliable, strong, steady and true. May you be a leader in management and organization."

It was the first time Lani had seen Kaz speechless. He sat down and looked out to the ocean for a long time, then said, "Lani, you know of my past. No one described me as steady and solid. I caved in many circumstances. This is the first I have thought about how things are going here.

"You knocked me off my feet. I realize who I am now. Lani –" He paused, and took in a shaky breath, clearly moved. "You have no idea what leading this work has done for me. I left that old me behind. This work seems so easy, but it is not about the work. I have become the person Yehovah always intended me to be. You gave me the opportunity for me to see this. You – this work put me on the road to my destiny. And I almost didn't notice. You showed me what a change has happened in me."

Turning to look Lani directly in the eyes, "I'll never be able to thank you for what you've given me. I appreciate your words more than you will ever know. Thank you, sweet Lani."

And he got up to walk the beach alone with his Beloved. He changed and had just realized it. Lani smiled watching Kaz stroll onto one of the docks. He would spend some time thanking Yehovah.

Elia attended Remi'el's studies and caught up with Lani one day. He asked if she had plans for the sailboats. Lani shared her timeline with him, showing him the lead time she thought the eh-bed would need to learn to pilot the boats. In the long past Elia instructed sailing and water skiing with his country club gang, and volunteered to teach the eh-bed both sailing and power boating. With Elia's help she could offer water skiing, wakeboarding and maybe even surfing (what Willow called water skimming) by the start of the sixth month and sailing by the ninth.

Elia asked Aymoon for help in finding nautical charts and after the fourth day was out on the water. In a few days Elia invited Lani for a late afternoon sail. After asking her if she had any experience in sailing, Elia decided to take them out on one of the smaller sleek vessels. A steady breeze blew once they were south of the island. They put the sloop through her paces, Elia giving the wheel to Lani for most of the trip. Lani always loved flying across the water. They raced at top speed, cleaving a path through the waves, leaving the land far behind them.

Lani made a mental note to spend more time with Elia to really learn how to sail. She loved being out on the blue water in the warm sunshine, whipping across the whitecaps. As they sailed back into Celebration Bay, she navigated around the Pillar Islands with Elia's help. She turned the wheel back to him once they were in the bay. She sat back and looked over the growing village and the construction on Sunrise.

They completed the framing for the second and third floors and started installing the floors. Already, she loved the lines. The village and Sunrise looked great together from this vantage point.

Lani thanked Elia for all the help he gave to the success of the Mayan. Elia told her he always loved blue water sailing in the long past. It was his place of retreat. He then made some poor decisions and had left it behind, but was very glad to be back on the water.

Lani thought about the sad life story where the only happiness was found on the water. Blue water sailing. That's what she would call it! Blue-Water Sailing! In remembrance of its restorative nature.

Over the next few weeks, Lani watched Elia teach the eh-bed to pilot the powerboats for skiing and wakeboarding. Many Ahuvati volunteered to ski behind as the eh-bed learned. With the increased traffic coming to Blue Rock and Coconut Stroll, and those working on the construction projects, there was no shortage of volunteers. Lani took pleasure in watching people enjoy themselves together. She knew the land fulfilled its intention. A wave of thankfulness washed over her. She loved this place and what it was becoming.

208

At the beginning of the sixth month, Lani officially opened the water skiing feature. With all the "volunteering" going on, it really opened prior.

She stopped in to see how Nectar was doing. With the increase in visitors to Blue Rock, Coconut Stroll and water skiing, Lani wanted to be sure Nectar was okay. She didn't want this delicate creature stressed.

On entering the kitchen, Lani saw Nectar had things well in hand. Nectar immediately came over to talk with Lani. "Aha'Kaiya, can I do anything for you?"

"No, nothing Nectar. I came to see how you are doing. Are you able to keep up with all the extra preparation and cooking?"

"Aha'Kaiya, thank you for asking. Willow made some great suggestions. I organized my team into groups, each focused on either prepping, cooking or delivery. I just provide oversight and I also personally take care of your meals."

"Good plan. Is there anything not working well or anything you think might become a problem?"

"Aha'Kaiya, I'm a little concerned that as we get busier, I may not have enough room in here to prepare all the food."

"Yes, it's already pretty busy in here. You know of the construction on the bay? One of the things built is a large kitchen and dining hall. Would you like to see it?"

"Aha'Kaiya, yes, I would!"

And they headed to the dining room in the middle of the village. Kaz and his crews had completed about half of the village. Lani went straight to the dining hall and led Nectar to the kitchen area. Based on Cheka's input, Adi designed it for streamlined organization with a large pantry to receive and store food, many prep tables with shelves above filled with a wide variety of serving dishes, multiple stoves and two huge staging areas, one opened to the dining area and one on an outside wall for sending food out to various locations throughout the estate. This would become the main kitchen for all the food prep associated with Mayan visitors.

Nectar's wings filled with orange and red as soon as she saw it, which pleased Lani. It always warmed her heart to see Nectar happy.

Nectar asked when her team could move to this new kitchen and Lani let her know that she was welcome to use it whenever she was ready, but should work out the timing with Willow to ensure co-ordination of the delivery of produce.

Nectar returned to the mansion and Lani continued to take a look at the progress of Sunrise. Two months remained before the completion date Kaz promised. As she passed Celebration Marina, she noted many of the power boats were out on the bay.

Elia had come back from the docks as Lani passed. Clearly in his element, Elia chatted about the success of offering skiing. He said all was going great, the eh-bed learned quickly and ensured all the visitors enjoyed themselves. Many Ahuvati learned how to ski and wakeboard, now they had their young, strong bodies. It was fun to watch.

After a couple of moments, Lani asked if Elia knew of someone who knew about white water rafting as she wanted to open Bucking Horse Chute. It would require an expert to train the eh-bed to act as guides for the rafts. Elia smiled.

He pointed to one of the wakeboarders out on the bay. Lani turned to watch. This person was really good. Elia said, "There's your gal. In the long past she kayaked all the wild water. Her name is Eliana, my Lord responded. She'd be great."

"Ok, thanks Elia. Could you let her know I would be interested in talking with her?"

"Sure thing. Hey, want to go sailing again later this afternoon?"

"Absolutely! Thanks, Elia." She continued to the point and Sunrise, and turned back to wave at him.

Sunrise looked close to finished. Lani thought maybe another four weeks and it would be done. The guys were working on finishing the walls and ceilings. Kaz and Adi'el organized the delivery of the lightstones and coloured stone for lighting the building. Several worked on cutting the stone to size.

Lani walked through the first floor. It looked like an atrium with beautiful spaces for people to meet and gather. She took one of the sets of stairs up to the second floor. It too was gorgeous. Daylight streamed in through the windows. Cupboards and racks of shelves filled the storage rooms at the back. Lots of space to bring in supplies and places for people to store their work.

Next to the storage, electronic equipment for digital work, both video and audio filled several studio rooms. Annikki and Eden equipped one room as a broadcast station for Blue Rock. Next she saw a couple of rooms equipped for classes and a couple of tables for framing work. And at the front many individual stations for sculpture work and painting. The front half of the floor, the part that hung out over the ocean, was all windows and sliding glass doors, offering a spectacular view of the channel between the island and the mainland. This would be an amazing space for artists to work.

She then headed up to the third floor. It too was a spectacular space. Lots of standalone wall space for displaying finished work, including digital work, stood around the floor. The length of the third floor split between an enclosed part and an open deck out over the water. This too gave a breathtaking view of the channel.

Heading up another flight of stairs to the roof deck, she looked back over her property and could slightly see into the Blue Rock Amphitheatre. Looking southwest, she could see the marina and the village with the ocean huts on the water. Looking straight west, she had an excellent view of Co-conut Falls. Adi'el and Kaz had done a fantastic job with this building.

As she looked out over the water, Adi'el came out on the third floor deck, spotted her and headed up to the roof deck. Lani called her over and said, "Adi, this is stunning. I love how it is all coming together. Did you know the view would be so spectacular up here?"

Adi replied, "I'm glad you picked this design. It was my favourite because of the views. I really love it up here. My favourite is the view of Coconut Falls."

Lani said, "Sunrise is so much more than I thought it could be. I always loved the linear look of Frank Lloyd Wright and this is even more spectacular than I had imagined. I cannot thank you enough. You were the perfect choice to design this building."

"Oh Lani, thank you for trusting me. In my long past, I was a nobody. For much of my life, no one loved me. No one cared whether I lived or died. I dreamt of what life could be, but never lived to be anything more than a nobody.

"Yehovah gave me the name of jewel to remind me I'm precious and important. And you gave me the opportunity to express my creative ideas and see them come to life. You gave me the chance to contribute to something important, something that will be significant in many lives. While I know Asher suggested me as your designer, I know Yehovah is behind all of this. But Lani, you, you trusted me and you gave me the opening to be more than a jewel, but a creator of jewels. Thank you so much. You impacted me very deeply. I'm unable to tell you adequately what you have done for me."

Lani reached out and rested her arm on Adi's shoulder, and in the silence of each of their thoughts they watched the sunlight dance over the bay.

Later in the afternoon, Lani returned to the marina and she and Elia took out another sailboat. This boat was a bit larger, a cutter trimmed as a sloop. Elia navigated through the Pillar Islands and this time headed north up the channel. Elia turned the wheel over to Lani to tack her way up the channel and he acted as crew.

When they turned to head back south, Elia took over to steer the boat as they coasted back down the channel, leaving Lani to relax. She thought about what a difference Elia made to the Mayan and to her life. It then occurred to her. She found experts, and simply turned over the work and the decisions to these people, and they had done extraordinary things.

Lani said, "You know, this is not really my resort. You, Kaz, Adi'el, Cheka, Aymoon, Asher, Nan, Shelomah, and Hanna have all taken on the responsibility of building a part of it. Whatever success is totally due to you guys, not me. I had some ideas, but you all took on a piece and made it happen. I really think of you all as part owners."

Elia broke into an easy laugh. "This has been the greatest thing for me, Lani. I made some stupid mistakes in the long past and lived in deep regret. This place and this work has been a balm. You trusted me with so much responsibility and I discovered who I was always meant to be. I know this was by Yehovah's design, but I cannot thank you enough for letting me contribute, letting me grow, letting me become who I was designed to be. Lani, you have affected me more than any person in my life. I love to take you sailing because clearly you love being on the water, and it is a way I can give back to you."

Lani just looked at Elia with her heart aching for the pain of his past. He was such a good-looking man, loaded with talent and knowledge. Life had been a challenge for so many of them, but they hung on. They persisted. "Thank you, Elia. I think you're great. You're fantastic in managing others, and a great teacher. You are so level and calm. A great quality in a sailing instructor," she said grinning.

And then following a mental prompting, Lani said, "Elia, may you rise to heights of joy and happiness spilling over to all around you. May you steer a clear course to your place of leadership. May you find yourself and help lead others to their destiny."

Elia's emotion welled in his eyes. "Lani, I have no words to tell you what that means to me. Thank you so very much." He looked off to the distance and became quiet in his thoughts.

This conversation made Lani think she should give a celebration dinner for the "owners," all those who led the development of her estate. Maybe every month to recognize everyone's contribution. She decided to schedule these for the first of every month as they released another feature.

Elia and Lani became good friends, and at least once a week they sailed together. Elia always knew what the best sail would be. Sometimes they flew over the water, racing the wind, and other times they would quietly sail, watching the sunset, listening to the steady lap of water against the hull. And every type of sailing in-between. Elia taught Lani to become a competent skipper. While she occasionally sailed without him, she enjoyed the time they spent together on the water.

As they drifted along the coastline, they watched the sun quietly set and with the evening, the luminescence of the ocean sparkled blue across the bay. Elia easily piloted the boat back into the slip leaving a wake of swirling blue luminescent ocean creatures marking their path. Lani watched the pattern dissipate slowly and thought, All aspect pleaseth.

When they returned to the marina, Lani spoke with Eliana. She was glad to take on the preparation and training required for white water rafting. And on schedule Bucking Horse Chute would open the start of the seventh month.

As Lani left the marina, she ran into Cheka. She was just leaving the village dining hall and heading to Blue Rock, but stopped to talk with Lani. "Hey Lani, this new kitchen in the village dining hall is fabulous. The food flows through as easy as the breeze."

"Oh, I am glad things are going so well. Thank you, Cheka, for all the training you provided and the wonderful recipes you created. All the guests commented on the great food being served. The Mayan signature dishes, your creations are quite beautiful in presentation and over-the-top delicious. I love all you put together for the Mayan. And all the recipes reflecting the land perfectly. Again, thank you so much, Cheka."

Smiling, Cheka replied, "You're very welcome, but I should thank you. I never received an education and always wanted to study, learn and ultimately teach. I never had any opportunity to do so in my long past. You opened the door to a great, exciting path. I studied the various foods available here, and I loved researching the fruits and nuts unique to your land. I did a few experiments inspired by what you are doing with your property. And I adore working with the mashqeh. Nectar is great, by the way.

"Because of the opportunity you gave me here, I see my destiny lies clear in front of me. I now know my purpose and I am fulfilling a lifelong desire. This allowed me to see a beautiful, shining future of combining my kitchen skills with newfound teaching skills to contribute to the lives of others. I now make a difference. Oh, Lani," Cheka grabbed Lani's hands. "This has been the best thing that ever happened in my life. Thank you so much for trusting me. You let me see my happy future. I'm so happy, I'm going to burst. Thank you, thank you, thank you. You are so precious."

Cheka kissed her cheek, then said, "Gotta go. The concert will be starting shortly and I promised Nan I would be there. See you!" and off she went.

This day gave Lani a lot to think about. Kaz, Adi'el, Elia, and now Cheka had all commented on how their help with the development of the Mayan impacted their lives. Everything happened as was intended. Lani turned and followed Cheka to the concert.

In the Carousel Garden the next morning, as Lani brushed down Bentley after her ride, Remi'el came up through the Creation Garden and stopped to talk with her. This morning he would lead a study, but had a few minutes to chat.

"Lani, I don't know if you've had a chance to join our study. I know you used to watch every week in the long past. Back then, the next thing we awaited was the reclamation of the believers, the betrothed. I spoke about it every week, in addition to studying the Bible verse by verse. Well, we still progress through the Bible at one study. For the other study, we focus on the upcoming millennium of peace. We supplement our study with materials from the library. Aymoon helps with some of the research. He is brilliant at digging into the vast materials there.

"All that to say thank you, Lani. In the long past I loved my role as a shepherd. I delighted in the study, following current events and bringing them together to show how the Bible was coming alive before our very eyes. You have given me a place to meet the people I was shepherding face to face. I loved my online church and I am now favoured with their physical presence. We are together at last.

215

"I have new meadows to take my sheep into. I can't wait to share the new revelations and understanding. We are all on such a new path compared to the long past, and I get to be one of the few called to lead in these new meadows. Lani, this is my calling, my mission. To share Yehovah's compassion and mercy to the people of the millennium, to my Arab people who survived. Yehovah called me His shepherd. I love your story of the good shepherd and the sculpture. I come this way every time to look on it. It reminds me of the high calling of a shepherd.

"Thank you so much for this place and for opening Blue Rock to me. The Mayan is the perfect setting for study into the depths of Yehovah and His plans and purpose.

"I don't have a lot of time now, but wanted you to know what coming here means to me and what a great opportunity this place allows me to pursue. Thank you, Lani." And with that he was off. He turned back to say, "I would love to have you join us!"

Lani returned to brushing Bentley when Aymoon's loud call broke the quiet. "Lani!" She glanced in his direction just in time for his welcoming hug. "I have to tell you how much I enjoy my study group here. In the long past, I studied Isaiah in great detail before I had access to writings by the other prophets and the apostles. I and my little group of young men who worked for me, well, we dug deep into the layers of meaning and learning to be gleaned from those few writings. Here, there's endless study material. And the whole holographic, immersive, captivating experience the library materials bring to Blue Rock makes the study come to life before our eyes.

"Just wanted you to know what a great opportunity it is to study and share what I learned with people here at Blue Rock. I now live my dream on a grand scale. More grand than I ever dared dream. All because of you and your willing development of this place. This place is fantastic. You, Lani, are fantastic. Thank you. This means more to me than anything before. All I hoped, all I ever desired, is now real for me."

As Aymoon turned to leave, he said, "You are a precious weaver of many things. Love you, Lani."

A few hours later Shelomah came along. He was heading to Blue Rock to lead a choir practice. In getting ready for their first concert in a couple of days, they practised regularly.

"Lani, I hoped to see you today. I would like to personally invite you to our concert. We call it the Mayan Peace concert and we're pretty excited. We shot enhanced holographic video of experiences all over your estate of Coconut Stroll, the waterfalls, the dome tree and all the piles of remembrance stones, a quiet walk through the botanical gardens, a sunrise from one of the village huts, and a sunset from one of the sailboats. All kinds of scenes. It will be a Mayan immersive musical event. I really want you to come to our first concert."

"Oh Shelomah, what a cool idea. I'll be there for sure. Thank you for the invite."

Shelomah reached for Lani's hands and held them in his. "I need to tell you what this place means to me. In the long past I lived a life of torment as a public spectacle. I ached inside and yearned for privacy and peace. I sang only to quiet my tormentors. Lani, you can never know what a medicine to my wounded soul and a lift to my courage my singing has become here, and you provided a place to put on a spectacle, but not *be* a spectacle. I no longer yearn for peace, I am peace. I live in peace, I overflow in peace, and now I can share peace. I am becoming the person I was meant to be. A leader in front of people, with no fear or humiliation, but actually happy in my role.

"Oh Lani, my life in the long past was so far removed from peace. Putting on that first concert with Nan, and taking the lead to create the music and the visuals for the Mayan Peace concert showed me my purpose. You gave me the opportunity to use my courage to express my delight and share what total immersion in peace is like for me. You gave me the place where I can immerse others in my peace and tranquility. My life is on a new path, a very happy path for me, all because of the opportunity you gave me. Thank you. I really want you at the concert because that is the best way I can express my thanks."

Lani felt near tears, but was no longer surprised to hear what this place meant to her friends, what an impact it had. Shelomah kissed both of her hands and was on his way to Blue Rock. Lani returned to her work only to see Nan coming up out of the Creation Garden.

This was the day of thanks and Lani knew looking at Nan that she came with the same idea as all the others. "Lani, I am heading to Blue Rock to help Shelomah put the final touches on his concert. Has he invited you yet?"

"Yes, he came by here a few moments ago."

"Oh good. I saw the visuals a couple of days ago. Lani, it is stunning. He worked with some very creative folks and they recorded some impressive footage. It's really an inventive use of the enhanced holographic technology and quite sensational. All of it was shot here on your estate. And then he wrote absolutely fantastic music. The two together are breathtaking. He talks of nothing but how you gave him the opportunity to discover his path of leadership. I just wanted to be sure you see the results.

"And what is happening here impacts a great number of people, Lani. The people in his choir all have a story to tell of how coming here, putting on the concert and working with Shelomah made a difference in each of their lives. For that matter, all of this made a big difference for me too.

"In my long past I did some pretty horrible things in the name of a pagan religion. When I discovered Yehovah, the God of love, I went to the beach every morning and sang my thanks to Him. I had a ghastly voice. People ran away, suffering from the dreadful noise. But I didn't care. I was just so thankful. When given my new body, Yehovah gave me what I longed for, this beautiful voice. You gave me opportunity after opportunity to use my gift. And because of you, I now step into my leadership. I write songs, design concerts and lead an ever-growing group in a sing-along.

"Because of this place and the people you bring together, I found what I am meant to do, my role in leadership. This has been a place of life, harmony, connection, joy and laughter. It has been so refreshing for me. I have grown so much in working with everyone. I just want to say I am very grateful for you promoting me, for meeting so many wonderful people and forming such deep relationships. Oh Lani, I found my life here. Mayan is a spring of refreshing and while I will soon be doing things in the Majestic City, I will always come back to spend time renewing and refreshing. This is such a special place and you are such a special person, the perfect person to run the Mayan. Thank you so much. You will never know how deeply you and this place affected me.

"I really need to get going. Thank you for being my friend from the first moment we arrived and making such a difference in my life. Love you!"

The concert was all it was touted to be, and more. Shelomah introduced the evening by dedicating it to Lani, explaining what a blessing the opportunities she offered had been.

Then all went quiet for a long moment, the visuals started and Shelomah began singing, followed by a low, slow introduction of the choir. The music seemed a part of the visuals. Both picked up on the pulse, the heartbeat, the life of the Mayan. The concert mesmerized and deeply engaged. Lani felt the land and sea. The nature of her land enveloped her into its existence, its movement, its reflection of Yehovah. The experience mentally and emotionally engrossed her. She lost awareness of herself and others, and was swept away into the life on her estate and the encompassing, deep peace that invades all who visit.

Lani laughed when she saw a clip of her morning deck dance to Yehovah. She loved that Shelomah felt free to share all of the Mayan. And she smiled inside, acknowledging how remarkable it was that she didn't feel embarrassed, but pleased to see that clip.

Shelomah set a new bar for concerts. When the concert finished, the audience went wild with their appreciation. Shelomah looked surprised and perhaps a bit overwhelmed. He had a hit on his hands and this concert would be in demand for many months.

The next night, Lani attended a packed-out concert put on by Need-ToBreathe at Blue Rock. They played all their popular songs from the long past, many of Lani's favourites, as well as several new songs. Not only was this live and the sound was great when you were right there with the band, but the sound in Blue Rock was spectacular. The concert was phenomenal, maybe because Bear's voice was in great form. Lani would contact Annikki afterward to ensure she had a copy of the broadcast to play for her morning deck dance.

A few days later, she stopped by the marina looking for Elia one early afternoon. It was warm, sunny and a good breeze. Perfect for sailing. Elia spotted her coming and came to meet her. "Sailing?" he asked with a smile. She answered with a wide grin and together they headed for a sleek, fast sloop with great upwind performance.

She was a little puzzled. Elia seemed contented, yet rather reserved this afternoon and didn't have much to say, yet his eyes were filled with happiness. She thought he was acting intentionally mysterious. *He must be up to something.*

It was a great breeze and they were rapidly leaving Celebration Bay behind as Elia headed around the base of the island and out west into the ocean.

It was an absolutely perfect day with a perfectly steady wind. He steered to sail close hauled and they raced the wind. Lani, utterly joyous, watched the sun dance across the water. He looked at her, and with a wink set the boat on autopilot, took her by the hand and headed for the bow. Standing together, he commanded, "Music on," and the sound system he rigged up turned on. He looked up to the sky, raised his arms to the air and began to sing "Multiplied," a song he heard NeedToBreathe sing at their concert at Blue Rock. Elia had a strong, beautiful, raspy voice, a quality of voice Lani always loved.

It was one of Lani's favourite songs and she joined in after Elia had finished the first chorus. The rocking of the boat and the waves off the bow splashed in time with the beat. A pod of dolphins joined in the celebration, leaping the bow wave in rhythm. A legion of angels arrived to sing background. The sound truly multiplied across the skies.

It was a spectacular, spontaneous, joyous tribute to Yehovah with wind, water, animals, Lani and angels all joining with Elia in expressing his happiness, love and devotion. The unmistakable scent of rain and earth surrounded them. Lani looked at Elia and thought, *He's living up to his name as one who rises.*

And there, speeding across the middle of the ocean, Yehovah-Adonai settled His loving presence on the group. Unaware of how much time passed, she stood on the bow of the speeding boat, singing with angels, water, wind and dolphins. When Elia finished singing, the blazing fire of the glory of Yehovah surrounded him.

She now understood his mysteriousness. What a gift! She felt so deeply honoured that he wanted her to share in his intimate tribute. She loved him deeply. He became one of her best and dearest friends. She felt she could share anything with him and clearly he felt the same way.

On the way back, he explained the lyrics really moved him deeply and seemed to have been written for him and for this moment in time. When he heard this song at the concert, he closed his eyes and his mind went straight to sailing. He heard the waves and felt the rhythm of the boat, and just knew it would make for an unforgettable experience to play the music and sing, standing facing the vastness of sea and sky, and he had to take Lani out to be a part of the experience.

The experience emotionally and mentally stretched her, inspiring her to write one her favourite weaver's poems.

The weaver's poem: Soul Sailing – Standing in Infinity

Leaving land behind, a freedom from anchors,
Sharp wind straining the sails, a path to unrestraint.
Rocking in the cadence, the joy of the ocean,
Sea spray mingled with sunshine on face, pure elation.
Enter into the vastness of sea, sky and air,
Endless blue, endless joy, endless Yehovah.
Cast away in time and space, vanished

In the breath of His nearness, awareness of His strength, His power.
Facing Yehovah in the enormity of His realms, without dimension,
I am small in the immensity, His unbounded presence.
I surrender my praise, my heart, my desires,
Magnified to fill the cosmos with the music and incense of offering,
I stand in infinity.

Without discussing, they both committed to time to continue their musical sails. They called it soul sailing. They discovered they enjoyed very similar tastes in music and Lani came to treasure this time together. She felt utter joy standing in the wind and waves, on the expanse of the ocean, facing a big sky and singing out her thoughts and feelings. It was particularly special to share the journey with a trusted friend. Elia renamed his favourite sloop Surrendered and set it aside for their soul sailing. They sailed in many of her boats, but Lani knew when they went out in Surrendered, they would be soul sailing. Together they spent many afternoons lost in music, surrounded by nature and angels.

On the first evening of the seventh month, Lani brought together all those involved in the unveilings, the gathering, and the Mayan development to a dinner in her large dining room in her mansion. Kaz, her nearest neighbour, lent his servants for the day to prepare for this meal, giving all of Lani's servants a day off, and they spent it having fun together.

Before dinner, she thanked each and every one individually and they all rose to toast themselves. Lani made it very clear the success was down to the leaders of the different areas and all those who worked under them.

After the meal Lani invited the leaders Asher, Remi'el, Aymoon, Nan, Shelomah, Hanna, Cheka, Kaz, Adi'el, Elia and Eliana to the inlet living room looking out over the luminescent ocean. These people made the Mayan wildly popular and put it solidly on the path to what it was intended to be.

As they all settled in, Lani asked if they would be interested in acting as the board for the operation of the Mayan. She wanted this group of people to continue to make decisions about each of their areas. It would be a loss to have anyone take their hand off the tiller of leadership. Everyone happily agreed as they all felt an attachment. This place had been special to each of them, in unique ways. It made a difference in each of their lives and met a need.

Kaz discovered he was reliable and responsible. Cheka stepped into teaching. Remi'el received a new teaching direction and his following increased for this shepherd of people. Elia became comfortable with his leadership role. Aymoon shared what had been put on his heart to share, to teach. Shelomah, the man of peace, stepped into his role of public concerts and leadership in developing singing talent. Nan, too developed into a public talent, but took on the leadership of creating a place and space of worship through song. Adi'el realized her dream of architectural designer. And Asher confirmed his role of leadership and built his team.

Yes, all had grown through this place. These were indeed good leaders for the Mayan.

It was a comfortable evening, everyone enjoying each other's company. They agreed to meet like this once a month. As time passed, the time spent over the leadership meals divided between discussing Mayan business, sharing their growth in leadership and what was upcoming on their roads of growth and development. Generally, the conversation circled back to how the Mayan could support each of them in their projects. Often they discovered how they could help each other achieve their dreams and as a result, they formed a tight-knit group.

Lani spent the next month bringing in supplies and tools for the opening of Sunrise. Even before it was officially open, several artists worked in the studio. The Mayan refreshed and inspired many. They initially came to spend time under the instruction given at Blue Rock, attended several concerts, drifted down Coconut Stroll, spent time under the dome tree, and simply slipped into expressing their hearts and minds through art.

Lani smiled to herself. This was the second feature that was in use before it opened. She counted this as confirmation she was on the right track.

Shelomah's Mayan Peace concert acted like advertising. Many, many people wanted to spend time here to be a part of the refreshing and renewing experience. So many good relationships formed, and people stepped into their roles of leadership. Yehovah used the Mayan as a launching point for many of His projects, and used events and activities to knit together the teams needed to accomplish His purpose.

As Sunrise prepared for opening, Eliana worked with servants who would guide the white water rafting down Bucking Horse Chute. Lani visited a couple of times and found everyone laughing and having fun together. Lani joined the first group they took down Bucking Horse Chute and found it thrilling. The run mixed class one to class five rapids, making for an exciting ride. Stretches of calm meandering to enjoy the scenery and chat with fellow riders separated the wild white rapids. A couple of class five rapids had huge, intimidating standing waves with the water shooting between narrow cliffs, one followed by a couple of large drops and a class four rapids. It was challenging, exciting and just plain fun.

During one of the calm stretches, they stopped with the other rafts for a catered meal including some warm dishes. The guides shared a deep camaraderie and they created a companionable environment for the riders. Everyone enjoyed each other's company.

A second raft going down ahead of Lani impressed her with the tricks these river guides performed □ a pirouette, a nose dunk and lots of surfing. The whole experience was a total adrenaline rush. Lani could see Bucking Horse Chute becoming quite popular. She thanked the servants that acted as guides, those involved in catering, and those supporting the guest experience. They created a culture of companionship and fellowship. This became a team-building experience for many groups embarking on projects together.

A month later and right on schedule, Sunrise Studio and Art Gallery opened on the first day of the eighth month. She issued an open invitation to come to the opening of Sunrise followed by a Planet Heaven concert by Shelomah and Nan. The artists who used the studio gladly put their work on display for the grand opening.

Shelomah and Nan organized a stunning display to go along with their concert centred on beauty and creation. They worked with Remi'el's friends and had an enhanced holographic display of scenic views from across the planet Heaven. The projection put the audience right into the setting. Lani felt like she no longer sat in Blue Rock, but flew through a rainbow, glided through the changing colours of sunrise over a canyon, felt the light breezes washing over a meadow of flowers, dove to the depths of the ocean with Celebration's pod of whales, rode a surfboard through the tunnel of a wave, and so much more. The audience raved about it so much afterward that Nan and Shelomah decided to put the concert on quite a few more times.

After the concert they served refreshments on the upper decks of the gallery. It was evening, and the tinted lightstones lit up the windows of the second and third floors, making the building shine like a jewel floating over the bay. Many people commented on how dazzling it looked, often asking about the designer.

With the village complete, a large number of visitors stayed over for several days. A couple borrowed surfboards to try out the waves on the west coast. The surf on Big Surf Bay was moderately big with waves ranging up to 15 ft. high.

That evening Jarmo, lifted up by God, and Lisi, promise of God, after spending their afternoon surfing on Big Surf Bay, had quite a story to tell Lani. Lisi said they rode two or three waves in, paddled back out, and had just caught the next wave when she saw a huge whale appear beside her and it rode the wave in with her. She waved to Jarmo to show him the whale and he pointed to another one beside him.

As they neared the shore, both whales powered straight up and back into the calm waters behind the wave. Both Jarmo and Lisi immediately paddled back out to see if this was an unusual thing or just normal behaviour. Sure enough, on the next big wave three or four whales surfed in, then popped up out of the back of the wave at the last second and breached into the trough. It was a spectacular sight from shore, seeing the immense bodies gliding through the midst of the waves. But even more so from the ocean side, from beyond the churn of the surf, seeing these enormous bodies rise up out of the back of the wave and appear completely out of water as they broke away from the shore.

Lani knew instantly this was Celebration's pod and made a point to check it out the next big surf day. News of this spread quickly and not only surfing became popular, but watching the whales surf became a big attraction. Without any effort or really thought, whale watching became another feature.

Elia trained several servants to pilot the sailboats and at the first of the ninth month, BlueWater Sailing opened. Quite a few visitors wanted to watch the surfing whales from the ocean. On high surf days, at least one sailboat could be seen drifting past Big Surf Bay with visitors hoping to catch a view of the dramatic full-body breaching.

The sailboats were in steady use from the moment BlueWater opened. Asher took a larger boat and skipper out for several days as an opportunity to build his team. They made the trip around the island, each day enjoying a leisurely evening together, studying and planning in the morning and learning sailing in the afternoon. Since then, many groups followed Asher's example using the time alone with their team to develop, learn, laugh, dine and draw close together. Even with all the demand for the boats, Elia always kept Surrendered available for him and Lani, and they both found a settledness, a strength and renewal on the waves.

With the steady stream of visitors, Lani found a large number spending quiet time under the dome tree every day. Like Asher, they came to seek out and discuss the will of Yehovah. And all left stones of remembrance to mark it as a significant event. It became a trend to create remembrance seats as markers, encouraging others to linger.

Blue Rock was now almost fully booked every day by musicians, leaders, teachers and video artisans. Sunrise provided a space for artists to bring honour to their Beloved with creative and stunningly beautiful works of art. Teams preparing for the millennia took the Coconut Stroll to discuss and lay out their plans and then developed team connection by taking a run down Bucking Horse Chute. With all her friends' help, her estate developed into the spring of renewal it was intended to be from before time began.

Two artists, Gilam, joy of a country, and Evron, bearing fruit, borrowed one of the Jet Skis on Coconut Lake. Gilam rigged up one of the hang gliders with pontoons. Evron towed Gilam to launch the glider, rising to a few thousand feet. He glided west past the escarpment and out over the savannah into the afternoon thermals. Both Gilam and Evron, gliders from the long past, spotted the cloud street over the savannah and plotted a way of getting a glider out into the thermals.

Savannah Flying opened at the start of the tenth month under the direction of both Evron and Gilam and quickly became another success. The view from 2,500 ft. above the hills of the escarpment allowed the gliders to enjoy a perspective of animals grazing across the grasslands running along the west coast. In the thermals the gliders spent a couple of hours in the air before landing in the ocean.

Shortly after Savannah Flying opened, Matea, God's present, brought with her some ropes and equipment and asked Lani if she could try climbing the rock face of the escarpment. She already scouted out several climbs that would offer various levels of face climbing experience. Lani's response was, "Of course!"

Matea, fantastic at climbing, used finger holds, edges, toe hooks and smears to make her way up the face of the escarpment. Within days, she formed a group of climbers and news rippled out that another activity would be opening. It took a couple of weeks to scout out the routes and another couple to ready the equipment for use by guests. Blue Cliff Rock Climbing opened the start of the twelfth month.

Lani should have expected to meet well-known biblical personalities visiting the Mayan, but it surprised her the first time a famous person showed up. Probably the most ironic was when Jonah boarded a sailboat to watch the whales in the surf.

Methuselah visited often to spend time under the dome tree and attend both Asher's and Remi'el's studies. It still made Lani laugh to recall when Methuselah tried out waterskiing. Obviously he'd never seen or known anything like it, but he was a young man again and discovered a love of water sports. He quickly became quite good, and loved to delight the many visitors that would gather at the shore to watch the oldest man of the long past perform tricks on skis.

David frequently visited both Blue Rock for concerts and the Sunrise for art shows. Adam became a regular visitor to Sunrise studios. He worked on a digital visual project with Eden, coincidentally about the Garden of Eden and heaven. Philip the apostle became a competent rock climber, and Boaz loved Jet Skiing.

Perhaps the one that touched Lani the most was Ruth. In her long past Lani's mom's middle name was Ruth, meaning friend and companion. That was indeed what the original Ruth was and in the long past Lani's mom had become her Ruth, living together to the last day. Lani always felt quite tender about her mom, and took great pleasure in seeing her mom now best friends with the biblical Ruth. Lani spotted them here together quite often.

Most of these biblical people came to spend time under the dome tree, leaving markers of their experience with Yehovah. At first being around them felt like being near celebrities, leaving Lani tongue-tied. But that quickly passed. These famous personalities wanted the same as everyone else – to be one with everyone. All were redeemed. All were Ahuvati, each with their special role and project, yet equal to each other.

As remarkable as it was to have famous bands playing at Blue Rock, and famous Bible people as regular visitors, the significant part of the Mayan development was really the story of growth and development of Ahuvati, not the property, or the celebrities. Really, the land was just a means for so many Ahuvati to rise to their potential. This was indeed a fantastic story. A story of many. Lani loved the emotion, and meaning, and impact of this story. This was her destiny. To be a tree of shelter and refreshing for others. Without straining or stress, Lani realized she began to fulfill that prophesy of long ago. She actually impacted the path and destiny of others. Not just a weaver of stories, but a weaver of Ahuvati too.

Oh, now a decision. Should her honour story be the story of impact on so many lives through the development of the Mayan? Should her story be one of a weaver of Ahuvati? Or should her story be the story of the love series sculptures, the love of their Beloved?

She really thought the love sculptures was the answer, but the story of changed lives would be very powerful. Maybe she should finish the poems and backstory of the sculptures. Oh, but there was also the Love Project assignment.

This required more consideration.

**Bonus
Content**

Do you have a preference as to which story should be her honour story? Share your thoughts here: www.serenitymclean.com/bonus-content/. Also, access a bonus chapter entitled "The Stone Turtle". The password is soulsailing
Check out the lyrics of "Multiplied" at
www.azlyrics.com/lyrics/needtobreathe/multiplied.html, Rivers in the Wasteland (2014). Bear and Bo Rinehart

18 | The Love Project

Chapter Span: One Day | 0.6.4 |

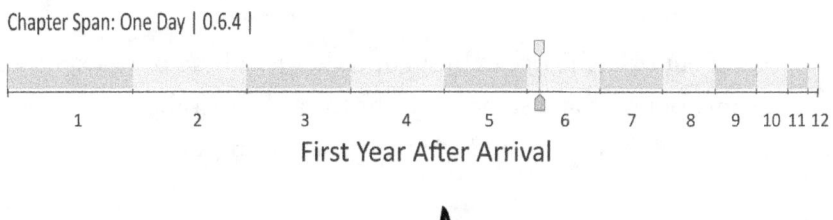

First Year After Arrival

Many people told Lani the weaver's poem on the Love Project was their favourite poem. It was inspired by one of her favourite stories. Before moving ahead to the poems of the remaining sculptures including the unveiling of the fifth sculpture, she would take some time to read this poem and consider the story behind it.

The weaver's poem: The Secret Plan Finished

The history and future of love

With the Holy One on His throne,
Transported to before time,
The story of longing, love and desire.

A secret plan,
The unfolding process of gaining a mate,
All evil turned for a good purpose.

It is finished.

A choice made,

A commitment,
The final Adam's rib implanted,
A mate of His own kind.

Looking out over the ocean brought to her mind the time a spectacular sight came out of the distance straight toward her. Yehovah travelling
through space and time aboard His living transportation.

The Story Behind the Poem

Lani took a long walk along the western shoreline early one morning when
in the distance she saw fire and lightning in the sky in the far distance. As
she watched she could see this phenomenon approached at supersonic
speed. Within seconds she distinguished a whirling wind of fire and bright-
ness with lightning flashing out from the fire like solar flares. Creatures
with six wings flew about the top of the whirlwind cloud. They used two
wings for flying and the remaining to cover their faces and feet. In their
hands they carried fire and coals.

The loud rumbling sounded like multitudes of voices as it neared.
The shining, rich amber fire coming from the centre of the whirlwind
cloud transfixed her. From within the fire appeared four living creatures in
the shape of a human, each with four faces, one face in front like a human,
one on the right like a lion, one on the left like an ox and like an eagle at
the back. The creatures each outstretched two of their wings and inter-
locked with the other creature's wings. Their other wings wrapped around
their hips. She had difficulty in determining whether the creatures had
two or four wings wrapped around their bodies. Under their outstretched
wings rested human arms and hands. Their legs were straight like a human,
but their feet looked like a bronze calf's hoof. It looked like coals of fire
burned within them with static electricity flashing between them.

Beside each creature was an enormous rumbling wheel. It was made
of gemstone unlike anything she had seen before. It was as though it had
the appearance of liquid, sparkling, sunlit sea and covered in eyes. These

wheels seemed to be a living part of the creatures. Inside each wheel was another wheel turning crosswise to the main wheel. With this wheel arrangement, the creatures could move in any direction without turning. They moved at the speed of light and at the will of Yehovah.

Above, the four creatures carried a crystal, glittering surface on which sat a throne made of blue lapis lazuli. It stunned Lani to see the throne room on the move powered by the four living creatures.

Yehovah sat on the throne. He appeared like gleaming amber, flickering like a fire. His bottom half looked like a brilliant flame burning white, all shining in splendour. Around Him a glowing rainbow halo. As the creatures flew, their wings sounded like waves crashing on the shore.

The wheels touched down on the beach in front of her. When the four-faced creatures stood still, they lowered their wings and she heard the praises from the creatures flying above emanating from behind their wings covering their faces. The living beings constantly praised and honoured the One on the throne. She realized this was much like the scene described by Ezekiel.

Yehovah lifted her onto the crystal platform and rested His hand on her shoulder. "Let me show you the history of my heart." The air felt thick and heavy with His holiness and presence. She knelt before the throne in the glow of Yehovah's splendour as the thunderous wings took flight. In a breath they travelled in both space and time.

He took Lani to watch the implementation of His plan right from the beginning. Before time and space Yehovah's desired an eternal helpmate to rule and reign with Him. One who could think creatively. One who would share His mind and desires. One who would have the option to choose or reject Him and out of their free will choose Him. One who equalled Him in perfection and righteousness. One with whom He could share a deep and passionate love, forever. One of His own kind. And yet there existed none of his own kind. He was alone. Alone and longing for a partner – a mate.

The challenge in gaining a mate was threefold.

First, He wanted to be chosen. He did not want His mate to love Him because He created it to love Him. Everyone wants their mate to choose them above all others.

Second, granting choice to a being introduced corruptibility. Granting choice meant choosing between righteousness or sin, between Yehovah or not Yehovah, between life and death. The corruption of sin and death stood as far from holy and righteous as east is from west. His mate need-ed to equal Him in holiness and righteousness in spirit, body and mind. In granting choice, those who didn't choose Him rejected righteousness, perfection and life and therefore became corrupted. Even before deciding between Yehovah and not Yehovah, the possibility of choosing something other than Yehovah meant that being could become corrupted. Unaccept-able in a mate.

Third, and perhaps the most challenging, His mate needed to carry his DNA, made in His image and bearing His essence. His mate, as is true for all mates, would have to be of His kind. After all, He declared it was good for all to have a mate of their own kind.

To achieve His goals would require an incubator and a plan.

Viewing Yehovah before time and space existed, Lani saw His glow-ing desire driven by deep longing. He created the incubator of time and space and within He created the cosmos. Lani watched these recordings so many times, but now she watched from Yehovah's perspective. From before time and space. She felt the heat of His desire as He created the environment that would bring about His mate, His love, His passion, His desire.

Then contained within His cosmos incubator, Yehovah first created everlasting spirits, creatures who were incorruptible. This meant they could neither choose nor reject Him. Without the choice to turn from Yehovah, they were incorruptible. He appointed them to serve Him forever. These creatures failed to fulfill even His first criterion. They could not satisfy Ye-hovah's need to be chosen. So these creatures, the cherubim and seraphim, could not and would not be His mate.

Next Yehovah created the angels, eternal spirits able to take physical form. To these He granted the ability to choose. With choice came the capability of corruption. Through rejection came unrighteousness and unholiness. They could never equal Him in perfection and righteousness because of choice. The fallen angels demonstrated this corruptibility. Even those who chose Him still retained choice. They could still reject and thus were still corruptible. As soon as the door opened to choice, the perfection of incorruptibility Yehovah required in a mate no longer existed.

These creatures could never be His mate, but they served two purposes. Those who chose Him became His top servants. The creatures who rejected Him faced eternal death for that choice, as God could not in His perfection exist throughout eternity with imperfection. But from the beginning, the corrupted beings played a part in His plan to bring about a helpmate that would choose Him and be equal to Him in perfection and righteousness. It just couldn't be these creatures.

Kneeling in front of Yehovah, Lani felt His desire and longing increase. Yet within the incubator she saw no sign of a being who qualified as His mate. In the long past she knew the desire to be wanted and loved by someone who chose her, and she knew the loneliness of not being chosen. As she knelt watching, the depth of Yehovah's desire to be chosen, His need to have a helpmate choose Him, overpowered her. Only Yehovah could accomplish such a thing and it would require something surprising.

Yehovah let Lani watch the angels and His other creatures as they observed His plan come to fruition. They all watched closely to see this mate who had free will, who would choose Him and be equal to Him in incorruptibility, perfection and righteousness. Before His audience of countless creatures, Yehovah created a frail creature made in His image, with a physical, potentially mortal body, and granted the option of choosing or rejecting Him.

Man.

The angels and other living creatures looked on in awe of this physical being that housed an eternal spirit. The animals were physical beings, but didn't have an eternal spirit. This man stood unique. One of a kind. A physical being made in the image of a spiritual being. And not just any spiritual being. Made in the image of Yehovah!

They had never seen anything like this and knew Yehovah created man for a higher purpose, to be His helpmate for eternity. What remained unclear to the angels and creatures watching was how this frail, potentially mortal creature, who had the option of choice and was corruptible, would make the choice of righteousness and somehow become incorruptible. Further, how would this creature carry the essence of Yehovah? How could this being carry the DNA of the Creator of all? How could it be of Yehovah's kind?

Of course, the creation of man, Yehovah's intended mate, generated intense jealousy in the angel Lucifer. Lucifer desired to hold the elevated position of Yehovah's helpmate. But that could never be. From the beginning the plan dictated the angel's purpose in servitude. Lucifer boiled in envy and covetousness. In pride and jealousy, he determined to position himself above Yehovah. He and his underlings set out to accomplish four things.

First, turn man from looking to Yehovah and cause these frail creatures to worship anything but Him. Anything would do – rock carvings, wood totems, abhorrent chimera creatures like men with jackal heads, half-man half-goat things. But as mankind tired of paganism, then cause them to chase after money, or best of all, restructure their belief of meaning of life in the cosmos and negate Yehovah. Bring them to choose an abhorrent philosophy or agnostic belief system. Simply, they set out to separate mankind from Yehovah. The pain of this man creature rejecting Yehovah would be deliciously delightful.

Second, prevent Yehovah from getting a mate, break His heart and leave Him alone and lonely. They intended to make Him pay for not choosing them.

Third, build their own creatures to worship Lucifer. He then would claim himself above Yehovah.

And fourth, perhaps the most vile part of this plan, corrupt and destroy Yehovah's precious man. That should be easy. Make the pure creation, man, genetically impure. The most repugnant thing they could do, they would. They would contaminate human DNA with their own. They would mate with Yehovah's precious man, His intended mate. Even if Yehovah had a way to meet the requirement of man carrying His essence and being of His kind, they would get in there first and contaminate him. Yehovah would not place His essence in a contaminated being. This would be a slap across Yehovah's face as man would be contaminated with the genetics of the ones not chosen.

Ininitally in a rage whipped up by Lucifer's jealousy, a third of the angels, exercising their choice, followed their leader and chose to leave the leadership and protection of Yehovah, turned from righteousness and followed Lucifer. If they could not have the position of helpmate, they intended to do all they could to ensure man would never have this desired position either. In their corruption, raging anger and hatred filled their hearts and minds. Lani watched their fury. Like a pair of wild, insane, rabid cats wheeling and reeling, all the fallen ones turned on each other screaming, ripping and clawing in a frenzied storm of violence. When Lucifer shared this plan with his underlings, they danced and reeled in delight. This would be their profane justice.

Yehovah's heart ached at the loss and betrayal. But it was all in the plan. He knew of this rejection and fall from before time.

Turning her attention back to Yehovah and man, she knew He planned to create a lowly creature with free will, and in its frailty, allow for sin and mortality to corrupt all of mankind and all things under the leadership of mankind. This corruption meant mankind and all those under him would have to suffer death along with the corrupted angels.

At the moment mankind became obedient to Lucifer, the serpent, and bit into the fruit of knowledge of good and evil, the deed of ownership of the earth slipped from man and into the hands of Lucifer. Now under Lucifer's ownership and rule, all of mankind, all life, the entire earth, fell under the curse of sin. The destructive nature of sin would be horrible for life on earth if Yehovah, in His mercy, did not cut short the physical life. No, it would not be good to let man living in sin to live indefinitely, so Yehovah removed man from the Garden of Eden and denied access to the tree of life. And with access to the tree of life removed, so came death to all living things on earth.

Lani heard the continual groaning of the entire creation under the burden of both sin and death. As the sin and death piled up, the agonizing sound stretched across the universe. To think Yehovah listened to this torment, anguish and misery from the time of Adam's fall through the decades, centuries, and millennia to the time of Yeshua's return to earth and subsequent peace. Lani looked at Yehovah. *How could He bear it?* She realized His desire and longing far outweighed His aching heart for the agony of His creation. He knew how this would end and knew it was worth the agony.

Lani turned back to look at man. She watched as Lucifer tempted man into sin. She saw Yehovah's precious creature, made in His image, fall into corruption. The beauty of man became black in sin and the stink of death hung on Adam and Eve. They became vile creatures about as attractive as a rotting carcass. Not only would man face a physical death, but in their corruption they would face an eternal spiritual death.

It all seemed lost.

Lucifer and the fallen howled and shrieked in delight at defeating Yehovah's plan so easily. They saw this as ensuring Yehovah would have no mate. If not them, then no one!

But this was all part of Yehovah's plan. This was known before time.

Again, Lani turned back to look at Yehovah. He said to Lucifer, while in the Garden of Eden in the form of a serpent, "Because you have done this, you serpent are cursed more than all animals, domestic and wild. You will crawl on your belly, grovelling in the dust as long as you live. And I will cause hostility between you and the woman, and between your offspring and her offspring. He will strike your head, and you will strike his heel

(Genesis 3:14–15)."

What a statement of His plan, right there in the garden. There would be hostility between mankind serving Lucifer (Lucifer's offspring) and an offspring man, born of a woman alone (not of a woman and man). Woman's offspring, this promised man, would strike Lucifer's head and destroy him. Lucifer got it. This promised seed of the woman, a future man, would destroy Lucifer, but the cost would be this man's death. Lucifer initially screamed in rage at Yehovah commanding his destruction, then paused. He grinned a heinous grin dripping in evil, gathered the fallen and slinked away.

The air hung thick with Yehovah's pain and loss. He saw His intended in their detestable state and knew He had to remove them from their garden paradise and from the tree of life. And yet Yehovah expressed His intimate love for each human and gave His full attention to each one as they lived their lives. His heart swelled with pleasure as He became madly in love with mankind. Each person who chose Yehovah brought joy to His heart and a celebration among the throne creatures. Lani knew with each choice the promise of His fulfilled desire grew.

But Lucifer determined to thwart Yehovah's plan at every opportunity. And yet Yehovah steadfastly turned every destructive effort to good.

The evil thought that quieted Lucifer's scream soon played out. If Yehovah expected a seed from the line of Eve to crush him, he set out to destroy that genetic line before this redeemer man could appear. He first attempted his destruction of the line by tempting Cain to let jealousy take root in his heart over Yehovah's acceptance of Abel's offering and the rejection of his own. His jealousy boiled over causing Cain to kill Abel, eliminating the genetic line of Abel.

But this murderous termination of the line failed to stop Yehovah's plan.

Yehovah gave Adam and Eve another son Seth, who would become the genetic line through which the redeemer would come.

With Seth's line destined to strike his head and destroy him, he next attempted to corrupt all human DNA. Then no children would be genetically pure and after their own kind, as was commanded by Yehovah. There could be no redeemer out of something not quite human. So the fallen angels tried to corrupt the genetic purity of mankind by mating with human women.

Yehovah let out a deep sigh. He grieved in His heart. But that did not stop His plan.

He looked over all life and found Noah and his family to be godly and genetically pure. He brought the remaining pure in the animal kingdom to the ark, and saved them from the flood.

The waters He commanded to keep their place at the time of creation He now commanded to erupt from the earth and fall from their place in the sky. Yehovah cleansed the earth of this evil impurity, flushing away the evil, abhorrent corruption of His creation's DNA with the fallen angel DNA, like flushing a toilet.

The fallen ones could not have seen that coming and hissed in frustration. Yet they determined to break Yehovah's heart for eternity. If destined to destruction, they would ensure Yehovah was destined to face eternity alone.

So the human genetic corruption didn't work, but the fallen ones could corrupt man's heart and turn mankind to worship them or anything else instead of Yehovah. That would surely grieve Yehovah to the point of abandoning mankind. They inspired Nimrod to introduce a false religion. But Abraham obeyed Yehovah. He did not go the way of the false religion, and Yehovah blessed him richly and rewarded him with countless descendants.

When Yehovah promised Isaac that through his descendants all nations would be blessed, Lucifer determined to end that genetic line of blessing. This blessing sounded like it could be the genetic line from which the redeemer would come and destroy him. So when Isaac blessed Jacob instead of Esau, proclaiming that he would be the master of his brothers, the fallen ones conspired to make Esau attempt to murder the favoured and blessed Jacob. Another fail.

They inspired the Egyptian pharaoh to forget about how Joseph saved them from famine. Ingratitude and hatred arose in his heart, whipped up by Lucifer, and he enslaved the Hebrews. Pharaoh ordered the slaughter of all young boys in an attempt to kill the man that would bring the Hebrews out of slavery. In reality, this was the work of the fallen ones. They wanted to cut off the Hebrew line. There would be no rescue of the Hebrews out of slavery if Pharaoh slaughtered all the boys. There would be no redeemer of mankind if Pharaoh wiped out this line.

Yehovah preserved His man Moses, and the Hebrews were delivered to the promised land.

In Esther's time, they inspired Haman to attempt the slaughter of all Hebrews. Again, another fail.

And then the most stunning thing happened. Yehovah himself, through His spirit, impregnated a woman. This child would be the off-spring of woman as promised. The child would become the man, born of a woman, but not of a man. The seed of the woman. Yehovah-Man. The second Adam and promised redeemer who would destroy Lucifer.

There were signs in the sky indicating the promised redeemer arrived. Lucifer, realizing this was the seed of the woman promised in the garden that would crush his head, inspired yet another slaughter of male children, this time by Herod, to prevent the survival of the reported king.

But Yeshua (Yehovah-Man) was not found. He was not slaughtered. He lived.

Okay, if not death of the redeemer, then corruption. What does the Creator desire? Yehovah intended to use this Yehovah-Man to destroy Lucifer and redeem His precious man. Lucifer determined that would not happen.

Lucifer attempted to corrupt Yeshua by tempting Him in His hunger to change rocks into bread. Where Israel failed in the wilderness, Yeshua did not. Yeshua made it clear that Yehovah would supply Him in His need, not Lucifer.

Knowing this redeemer would face death, Lucifer tried to entice Yeshua to jump, claiming Yehovah would protect Him from harm. If he could bring about this redeemer's death prematurely, he might not face his own death. But Yeshua denied Lucifer, instructing him it was a sin to test Yehovah. And He would not sin.

In his third and final attempt, Lucifer offered Yeshua the world without having to die for it. Just bow before Lucifer and worship him. There was just so much wrong with this one. First, Yeshua was Yehovah in a physical body. Yehovah would never bow before Lucifer and would certainly not worship him. And Lani understood Yeshua wouldn't violate the promise made in the garden – the destruction of Lucifer and the fallen ones, and the death of the man who would cause his destruction ("He will crush your head and you will strike his heel.") Yeshua declined to bow and Lucifer failed again. He raged.

In cruel spite, Lucifer tempted the Jewish religious rulers to harden their hearts against their redeemer, this Yehovah-Man. Lucifer, delighted with his treacherous idea, determined to cause Yehovah's chosen people to kill the one born of a woman, not from the seed of man, but the seed of Yehovah.

Lucifer smiled. All things were finally going his way. The Romans beat Yeshua to a pulp and sentenced him to die. Lucifer cried in delight. He and his horde danced in triumph around Yeshua as He dragged the cross to Golgotha.

Looking back at Yehovah, Lani saw deep and emotional grief, but He remained resolute to see His plan to completion. The angels stood stunned. How could Yehovah allow Yehovah-Man to be treated so?

While Yeshua climbed Golgotha, Yehovah commanded the angels to gather all laws, religion, rituals, all principalities and powers, and all sin and disease of the past, present and future. At the moment Yeshua willingly lay on the cross, the angels laid this loathsome, perverted, stinking, wicked mess on Him. In the briefest of seconds, the nail plunged through Yeshua's wrist and with that first strike, all evil was pinned to the cross with

Him.

In His perfection, Yehovah-Man would not be required to die as He was not corrupted. Yet here He was on the cusp of death, nailed to the cross, joined to a foul, repulsive load of evil from all time. Before time began this was the plan. Before the cosmos, He chose to become man, and to bear all of mankind's corruption into death.

Hanging on the cross, a deep darkness fell across the land. Angels turned away and wept. They couldn't bear to look at Yehovah-Man suffering under the burden of all sin, nailed to a cross. Even the wood of the cross and the metal of the nail cried out to Yehovah of the violence they were made to be a part of.

At the appointed time Yeshua claimed, "It is finished!" and gave up His life.

Because He was Yehovah-Man, man born of Yehovah's seed, because He lived a righteous and perfect life as a human, He had no debt to pay. He was not required to face death and the grave because He was not corrupted. He had to give himself to death as death had no hold on Him. He chose to take all evil and all our corruption on our behalf, and die bearing all our corruption.

Hanging on the cross, under a blackened sky, Yehovah-Man died in degradation.

The heavens erupted. The angels keened and lamented. They were inconsolable. Lucifer screamed in delight. Thinking he had defeated Yehovah once and for all, he roared and danced in a vile ecstasy of triumph. All those saints of the past, now his. All those waiting in paradise, his! He positioned himself in front of Yehovah, bringing his fallen ones with him and sneered, "It is finished," then howled to the cosmos, "And I am greater!" The fallen ones repeated, "It is finished and Lucifer is greater!" bowing before Lucifer.

Decisively, Lucifer and the fallen ones felt satisfied. Their howling finally ceased. Indeed they were appointed to destruction, but they saw to the death of Yehovah-Man and prevented Yehovah from having a mate.

They counted it a win.

Lani looked at Yehovah and He met her gaze. He then looked into the temple. The curtain in the temple preventing entrance to the holy of holies ripped in half from top to bottom. She then looked intently at the cemetery. Lucifer, the fallen ones, or even the angels failed to notice the opened tombs and the many godly men and women who rose from the dead and walked about the city. They missed the torn veil. They didn't notice man could now go directly to the holy of holies. They didn't realize the first evidence of the defeat of death walked about Jerusalem.

Although Lani knew how things turned out, she was caught up in the emotion. After a moment of watching the grief of the angels and the delight of the fallen ones, she turned to Yehovah. He smiled! Well pleased! He hushed His angels, telling them to watch.

Yehovah-Man went to Hades to declare His victory over Lucifer and the fallen ones. He informed them of their destiny in hell. Well, they expected that news. From the garden they knew when Lucifer bit at the heel of the promised seed of woman, they would be destroyed. They indeed faced their destruction as promised, but as they intended, Lucifer accomplished more than a bite at Yehovah-Man's heel. Yehovah-Man was dead. And that was worth celebrating. Lucifer stopped Yehovah from having a mate. And by His people's own hand. How perfect!

Lucifer's celebration slowly quieted. He saw Yehovah's smile. He caught on there was something more here than he thought. Looking to the temple, mankind now approached the holy of holies? How could that be? Saints erupting out of their graves? Saints he thought belonged to him?

The fallen ones watched in stunned silence. While He carried all the sin of the world to the grave, the power of the purity and righteousness of His shed blood flushed the vile load of sin from Him. It washed even the stain of sin from Him. Yehovah-Man stood in Hades now pure white in holiness and righteousness. And in His holiness and righteousness, He left Hades. Just walked out! He went straight to paradise to become the redeemer, the reclaimer, the king.

The angels then realized why they collected all sin from all of time and piled it on to Yeshua, to be nailed to the cross then carried to Hades, where His righteous blood pouring out of His side cleansed the load of sin from Him. The sin slid off Him and He left the entire load of sin there and simply walked out of Hades, pure and righteous. Sin removed. Death defeated.

Yehovah then took Yeshua's blood and permanently wiped out the sins of the faithful as no Passover lamb could ever do. Their sin fell away like water off a duck's back. Nothing remained. Saints now stood sinless before Yehovah.

Next, Yehovah reached into the wound on Yeshua's side, took out a piece of His light and life, and placed it in each sinless, spotless, faithful person. Just like at creation when Yehovah reached into Adam to take a piece of him to create a new creature Eve, his mate. With the light and life of Yeshua placed into the faithful, the believers became new creatures. A creature, not just made by Yehovah, but made of Yehovah. A creature washed of sin by righteous blood, and a creature of His own kind. Spotless. Worthy. And able to walk out of paradise and out of the grasp of Lucifer. Out of the grasp of death.

The plan was completed. His intended chose Him. It was finished. Yehovah had His mate!

The dawn of realization hit Lucifer and his fallen ones like a bomb. Their screams deafened. They finally comprehended their conspired death of Yehovah-Man they thought was a win, was actually their biggest defeat. They just brought about their own defeat. For man, for the ones who chose Yehovah, death was defeated. The grave could not hold them. They would not join Lucifer and the fallen angels in eternal death.

Indeed, it was finished.

In paradise stood the righteous, the pure white faithful, the ones now of His kind. Yeshua gathered His new creatures to Him to take to heaven to await the day when they would put on physically immortal and incorruptible bodies.

The plan from before time and space had been implemented, His longing and desire fulfilled.

It interested Lani that Yehovah never shared the details of His plan with any creature within His creation. The corrupted angels looked on and thought mankind was mortal and so frail, it would be easy to obstruct Yehovah's plan for man to become His helpmate. They really thought they prevented Yehovah from having a mate. And all the while Yehovah planned for all of Lucifer's actions. Even in the fall of angels, the horde served a purpose and fulfilled their purpose without fail.

The angels marvelled at what just occurred. They saw a new creature formed within the old, decaying humans. These new creatures were something never seen in all of time or even before, Man-Yehovah, of Yehovah's kind. They finally saw Yehovah's stunningly beautiful mate. They thought it an inconsolably sad day, but Yehovah did the impossible. He gave of Himself to create a mate. After a silence of awe, they shouted and sang out their admiration and praise for such a glorious day. A day to be remembered throughout all of time. Yehovah-Man had His mate Man-Yehovah! It was a perfect mirror of Himself.

Lani looked at Lucifer. Rage and fury multiplied in his heart and mind. Lucifer was not in control of himself. He lost everything! He was appointed to destruction and Yehovah turned his scheme of Yeshua's death into a glorious victory. There was no longer only man, but now a new creature, Man-Yehovah born of Yehovah, and worthy to be His mate for eternity. Lucifer neared madness. He shrieked in pure frustration, committed to take out his fury and wrath on mankind. Man would pay for this victory. The fallen ones seethed in an infuriated, frenzied rage. They became even more vengeful on mankind in an attempt to keep as many of Yehovah's loved and precious humans from choosing Him. They intended to prevent man from becoming Man-Yehovah. They committed there and then to do all they could to hide the truth from mankind. The stakes had multiplied.

Lani viewed all of these scenes with Yehovah's hand heavy on her shoulder. Yehovah shared with her His longing and increasing desire for His helpmate before time and space began. And He exposed to her His increasing excitement and desire as He brought about His plan.

The moment He created man, He filled space with the tenderness of a very loving, attentive parent, caring for His prize in the incubator. All of this cosmos, this incubator, was for the primary purpose of Yehovah fulfilling His desire for an eternal mate, and man would be the desire of His heart. All of the creatures watching felt Yehovah's intense love and joy with His Beloved, mankind.

Lani pondered all she watched. She marvelled at Yehovah's willingness to put Himself into the form of man, and take every vile corruption of mankind onto Him, and then deliberately give Himself to an undeserved death. All of this He did for the object of His affection. When the fallen angels screamed in delight at Yeshua's imminent death, and the angels wept, Yehovah smiled, pleased with His accomplishment. Amazing.

In watching all this unfold in front of her, Lani realized before she ever drew a breath, in fact before the cosmos was created, Yehovah wildly desired to have her heart, to share the space of her mind and spirit, to make her a perfect, righteous, worthy creature, Man-Yehovah. In the long past, she had no idea she was more precious and valuable to Yehovah than anything else He possessed. Now she saw Yehovah passionately loved her so much that He gave the option of choice and then ensured it didn't matter how corrupted she became. He already had a plan in place to remove the corruption and replace it with His perfection, then love on her as His eternal helpmate. He really madly loved mankind and did so before time and space. Astonishing.

In His love for His Beloved, He made the heavens beautiful. He tended to every day's weather, deciding how hard the wind should blow and how much rain should fall. Daily He laid out a path for each and every strike of lightning. He kept the oceans inside their boundaries. Every day He painted the sky at sunrise and sunset for everyone across the earth. He ensured endless springs of water to rise up from the land. He cared for and fed the wild animals. He created enormous diversity and beauty throughout the earth for the enjoyment and inspiration of mankind. He directed the wild animals to be wild, and tamed the domestics to work on behalf of mankind. He created the laws of the universe, and directed the movement of the stars to declare His redemption plan.

Pulling Lani away from her thoughts, Yehovah said in a voice of thundering and crashing waves, "I will bring a thousand years of peaceful reign on earth while the fallen angels are bound. This will be the last opportunity for remaining mortal man to choose righteousness. During this time, I want you to show the nations the history and future of my love for mankind. I want mankind to see, know and understand my love before the fallen angels are loosed at the end, before they try to deceive the nations. My message is substantial, my love is immense, and how you present it needs to be as big as my love is immeasurable."

Lani's eyes went wide. *This was an enormous responsibility.* She swallowed. She began to feel overwhelmed and protested, "Yehovah-Adonai, who am I that I take the lead on such an important project? Lives are in the balance."

Yehovah answered, "My sweet Aha'La'anni love, you have followed my wishes in creating your series of sculptures, the love series. You follow my wishes with developing the Mayan, a spring of refreshing for my people.

"You are one with me. You know my mind and heart. Your existence is within me and I am joined in your heart, spirit and mind. We are eternally joined and a part of each other. Surrounded in my love I will lead you. My spirit will instruct you and inspire you. I gave you the creative abilities to ensure my heart is fully expressed. I will give you the team to bring about what is required."

Lani bowed in acknowledgement and felt an infusion of courage and trust move into her mind.

At the moment of her acknowledgement, the cherubim underneath the crystal platform of the throne flapped their wings and in a heartbeat they returned to the beach in front of her mansion. Lani said, "Thank you for sharing your intimate feelings about humans, and allowing me to see history from your perspective. I am so honoured to be given the responsibility of the Love Project. With your help I will ensure what I do brings you recognition, respect, praise and honour." As she began to move to the shore, Yehovah pulled her to Himself, holding her tight and said, "I love you, Aha'La'anni. I have loved you and longed for you since before time. I knew you before time. I delight in you and all you do. I take pleasure in sharing your thoughts, and I relish the time we spend together. I am in you, a part of you, and am with you always, my precious Beloved, Aha'Ahuva-ti."

Lani remembered standing on the beach, initially feeling the burden of this Love Project, but determined to stand in faith. Yehovah promised her all she would need to be successful. At the moment of her decision to stand in faith, Yehovah filled her mind with possibilities, courage and assurance. With His assurance she realized this became a very exciting project. She would finish her sculptures and begin to develop the Mayan. She knew she would meet her team through the Mayan. She would rest upon Yehovah for His timing, His inspiration and His team.

While the commission for the Love Project was huge, the project had barely started and couldn't be a part of her story. Maybe of future honour stories, but not this one. She had not brought any honour through this project yet, but seeing creation and Yehovah's plan for a mate of His own kind implemented from His perspective inspired her fifth sculpture. And that could be part of her story.

19 | The Mohar

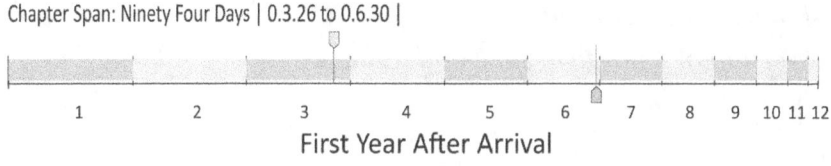

Chapter Span: Ninety Four Days | 0.3.26 to 0.6.30 |

1   2   3   4   5   6   7   8   9   10 11 12

First Year After Arrival

The weaver's poem: The Restoration

The lure of a far-off land.
Determined independence departs from the father,
Brokenhearted father, suffering grief and loss.
Youthful sin, inheritance lost,
A return to the father, in repentance and humility.
Welcomed in love and compassion,
Adorned as a prince.
Restoration to his first estate, his privileged position.

The weaver's poem: Living Water

At Jacob's well, a meeting of eternal consequence.
A life of loss, pain, grief, loneliness, and in sin,
An ordinary day, an extraordinary encounter.
"Please give me a drink,"

Opening the door to the offer of living water.
Desire and acceptance,
Eternal life and truth, the living water
Bubbling up from within.
Worship of Yehovah in spirit and truth.

The weaver's poem: The Mohar

A crown of cursed thorns, Eden's curse a mockery of His divinity.
Three spikes to complete our rescue from sin,
Blood for forgiveness,
Water for purification,
The final Passover lamb.
An empty tomb,
Vacant grave clothes,
Death and grave defeated.
Yehovah-Man DNA, holy and righteous DNA,
The second Adam's genes, implanted in man,
A new creature, Man-Yehovah.
It is finished, a mate of His own kind.

The Story Behind the Poems

Lani continued working on her sculptures, finishing the prodigal son and the woman at the well. It took many weeks, but she worked steadily. When she completed the prodigal, the unveiling brought well over a thousand people, and the woman at the well brought nearly 5,000. These unveilings had become a big event.

The morning after the unveiling of the fourth sculpture, Lani wandered along the line of sculptures, pondering all she had been given to honour her Beloved. She sat under the dome tree, looking at the huge lightstone that, as yet, had no visible purpose. It remained hidden.

Lani considered all her Beloved said. People could come and be re-minded of Yehovah's acts of love. A retreat where they spent intimate time with their Beloved, away from their business. And an oasis of refreshing.

She looked back at the sculptures. One of love and rescue. One of love despite the filth. One of love, welcoming reunion and restitution. One of love enough to offer a path to eternal life. When she looked down the line, it told a story – rescue, out of filth, reunion, eternal life. This was the story of the Love Project. The story of the intended, the betrothal, the acceptance and consummation.

They all illustrated His love for His intended. What lengths He went to in making a way for mankind to become a worthy mate. Who else would leave the comforts of God and become man to take all the sin of mankind to death? Who would willingly submit to being nailed to the cross if they could call on angels to slaughter everyone who conspired in His crucifix-ion? Who could or would will Himself to death, and give up His life for no fault of His own?

This moment in time, His willing death, really became the door mak-ing all of what Lani had now possible. This moment changed eternity for all the Ahuvati.

That's what this final piece must be! The vile earthly tools Yeho-vah-Yeshua turned to good. The tools He used to complete His mission and open the door.

Her idea took shape. Unlike the other sculptures which captured a moment in time of people, Lani intended this to be an artistic grouping of the symbols Lucifer intended for evil purpose, but used by Yehovah to fulfill His grandest purpose, a reconciliation with His intended. An exhibit.

She made a slab platform 7 ft. long by 3 ft. wide and 2 ft. high. She formed the edges with normal stone and whitewashed as was the way for sepulchres. She carved the centre of the platform into a level surface from layers of coloured stone to produce white light. Underneath the layers she placed the huge lightstone, so bright light shone white out of the platform.

Carved in lightstone she created the linens used to wrap His body.

She placed them as one of two objects lying on the platform lit from below. She shaped the linens to appear as though the body just rose up through the wrappings, leaving them still wound up, but empty. And she carved the linen used to wrap His head and placed it neatly folded at one end of the platform.

Lani then carved a crown of thorns out of red stone and artfully leaned it against the head of the platform.

Gilad planted some thorny myrrh bushes and giant aloe vera plants around one side and foot of the platform, the plants used in the embalming process.

Between the empty platform and the plantings she placed three other symbols of redemption. She carved a 10-ft. high cross out of blues and reds, and placed it between the foot of the platform and the plantings. She also carved a group of three 2-ft. high spikes out of light blues and placed it between the side and the plantings. Finally she carved a spear and leaned it against the cross.

It didn't take long to complete this final exhibit in the love series. Once completed Lani covered the entire exhibit, only to be revealed at the unveiling party. While she told a few select people the theme of the final one, she wanted the unveiling to be a surprise for everyone.

The day before the unveiling, Lani was busy. She expected a large crowd that evening and planned a special and memorable event.

People arrived late in the afternoon and by sunset about 20,000 people gathered. Lani welcomed everyone to the unveiling.

"Before I tell you about each of the sculptures, I want to tell a story of the first Adam and the second and final Adam.

"The first Adam longed for a mate, but creation was complete and Yehovah declared it was good. Yet Adam wanted a mate, so Yehovah put him to sleep, cut into his side and removed a part of Adam, his rib with his DNA by which Yehovah created Eve. Adam lived his life with a scar on his side as a witness to the fact that Eve was of Adam's kind, a worthy mate.

"The second and final Adam, Yeshua, followed this same pattern.

He wanted a mate. He gave up His life, a wound cut into his side and out poured His blood, His righteous DNA by which He would create a new creature, His mate. When we accepted Him as our Lord, He created Man-Yehovah within each of us. He still has the scar on His side as a witness we are of His kind and worthy to be His mate.

"The stories of the Bible tell of how He loved us and was the Light of the world. These sculptures depict the stories of His love with the heart of each sculpture made of lightstone. These sculptures have lightstone harvested from a wound in the side of a hill, symbolic of the Light He placed in us from the wound in His side.

"The sculptures in this love series are in sequence. They start with love and rescue, a love so pure it reached into the filth, love that welcomed into reunion and restitution, and love that offered a path to eternal life. This is our story of rescue out of filth, reunion and eternal life.

"I would like to start with this first sculpture I have entitled The Cherished. It is of the good shepherd when he found his loved lamb that was lost. In an hour I will introduce you to the second sculpture entitled, "Desperately Needed Hero." It is of the good Samaritan. At the third hour I will tell the story of The Restoration, the story of the prodigal son. At the fourth hour I will tell of The Living Water and the woman at the well. Lastly, at the fifth hour I will unveil the final sculpture in the love series entitled The Mohar."

Lani decided to recite her poems of the sculptures as an opening to each story starting with "The Cherished." She then told the story of the good shepherd. She arranged with Honani and her friends to sing a song after each story and left the choice of song up to Nan. For the good shepherd, Nan chose an old hymn "The King of Love My Shepherd Is." A group of singers and musicians joined with Nan and it turned out beautifully. All that knew the song sang along on the chorus, and Nan organized for H. W. Baker, the songwriter, to sing the second verse as a solo.

Afterward, Lani invited people to visit the refreshment tables and wander the gardens. She informed them that at the top of the hour she would start the next story.

She spent her spare time wandering the gardens and chatting with her visitors before she moved on to tell the Desperately Needed Hero story. Again, she opened with her poem The Desperately Needed Hero. When finished telling the story of the good Samaritan, Nan and her group sang "Amazing Grace." This time, Nan asked Eldad, Beloved of Yehovah, formerly John Newton, the songwriter, to sing the third verse. Eldad operated as a slave trader who cried out to Yehovah to rescue him from a fierce storm. He came to realize the filthy life he led when Yehovah saved his damaged, vile life. He wrote this well-loved song in 1779, after his encounter with Yehovah.

Again Lani took a break before telling the story of next sculpture. When ready, she stood in front of the sculpture and everyone quickly gathered. Again, she started with the poem "The Restoration" and then began her story.

"Here you see a broken young man in the arms of his father. Let me tell you about what brought this young man to collapse in his father's arms.

"He was the younger of two boys by ten years. Like Joseph, he was the apple of his father's eye. He grew up self-assured and full of confidence. He looked to his older brother as a friend, but his brother wanted nothing to do with this young upstart.

"The older brother felt his younger brother had stolen his father's attention. He spent years doing his father's bidding, but never felt he received his father's recognition, time, love and attention. Oh, his father divided the work fairly. But jealousy of the time and relationship his younger brother shared with his father simmered in his heart. This blackened his thoughts and he came to blame his brother for intentionally cutting him out of conversations. Everything this kid did seemed great in his father's eyes. He could do no wrong. One day in frustration and anger, he accused his brother of thinking himself perfect. The younger brother laughed and said, 'No, *you* think I am perfect,' and walked away. His anger and jealousy flamed and he immediately determined to never do anything that fa-

256

voured this kid. No, from then on he would only look out for himself. He wouldn't care who got hurt. And he hardened his heart.

"Undisturbed by the roiling storm in his older brother's mind, the young man grew up exceedingly successful at whatever he turned his hand to. He gained many friends, several among the caravan traders who loved to tell stories of exciting new lands. As he grew into a young man, the stories became discussions on opportunities in these far-off places. And the seed of an idea formed in his heart.

"Finally, he approached his father to ask for his inheritance. His father thought about his young son's proposal. He dearly loved this boy and was pleased at how he had grown into a sensible and successful young man. Despite knowing the destiny of the young man if he gave him his inheritance, the father agreed to the proposal without question and divided an equal amount between the two.

"Within days, the younger brother announced he would be leaving to turn his inheritance into great wealth. And off he went. It broke his father's heart to see his son leave his land and his protection, but he was a man and free to choose his path.

"The older brother laughed in delight at his brother's departure. He would now be the one his father would turn to. With his brother gone there would be no need to compete for his father's attention. He laughed at his brother's audacity to ask for and take his father's money and just leave. His brother was so selfish, doing nothing to support the family property and operations. This would be his opportunity to prove his value to this father. Unlike his brother, he would stay and contribute to the increase of family fortune. Unlike his brother, he would not take from the family fortune. No, he would only contribute. He would do his father's bidding, cost him nothing, demonstrate his worth, and shine a light on the failings of his younger brother. Yes, he was delighted with his brother's departure.

"As time passed, he spoke with the caravan traders to get news of his brother. At first, the stories of the big parties, the wild life, the people his brother knew and spent time with fuelled his jealousy. But over time, the stories told of his brother running out of money and his many friends falling away. He relished thinking about his brother's failure. It brought a mean smile to his face to think of his brother alone, moneyless and friend-less.

"One day came the news his brother was working as a servant, feeding swine. He laughed filled with glee at his brother's demise.

"The younger man moved to what he thought was going to be the land of opportunity. He indeed met lots of people, important people. He wanted to build a network to find the opportunity he would invest in, but it cost a lot to keep these people in his circle. He was swept up in the exciting lifestyle of spending, partying and womanizing, but sooner than expected, he ran out of money. And when the money was gone, so were his friends, and any hope of an opportunity to invest and build his wealth.

"He was alone and hungry. None of his friends could or would help him. Every day that passed brought him closer to starvation. In desperation he hired himself out to a farmer to feed the pigs. Starving, even the pig slop looked edible.

"Then it dawned on him. This was a poor farmer scratching out a living for his own family in a land of famine, and barely able to pay him a pittance. It was not enough to even feed himself. But at his father's house, the servants were fed for free, and in addition, were well paid.

"At that moment, he determined he would eat the pig slop to nourish himself to make the long journey back to his father's house. He would beg his father's forgiveness. He realized he broke his trust. In his youthful fear-lessness he thought he could do anything and it would be successful. He mistakenly thought he didn't need his father's steadying hand and practical wisdom.

"Then in his misery emotion washed over him as he realized he broke his father's heart. In all, he sinned against his father. He would beg forgive-ness and ask if he could work as a servant. At the very least, he wouldn't have to eat pig slop.

"It took several weeks of eating grass and slop before he felt strong enough to make the journey. It took several months, walking and begging for scraps from the caravans and farmers along the way, but finally he recognized the land of his youth and his gait quickened.

"He crested the hill that sheltered his family's home. As he started down he saw his father at the door. While still a long way off, his father looked for a time, then recognized his son. He almost fell to his knees. All the emotion he held at bay for so long burst forth unconstrained in a loud moan. His heart filled with love and compassion and he ran to meet his son, his beloved son.

"The household, alerted by the master's moans and shouts, came out in time to see their master running across the yard. Finally he reached his son, grabbed him to his chest and held him close. As he kissed him the young man collapsed to his knees and bowed his head. He confessed his sin and said he was not worthy to be called his son.

"The father yelled to the servants to bring his finest robe, his new sandals and his best ring for his son. And he told them to kill their fatted calf and prepare a feast, to start the celebration feast now. 'This son of mine was dead, but he has returned to life. He was lost, but now is found. So let the party begin.' Then the father bent down to his humbled son and kissed his head. And here you see the father restoring his son back to his place and standing in the family.

"Meanwhile, as the older brother returned from working in the field for lunch, he heard music coming from his father's house. When he got to the kitchen, he saw the staff dancing. He asked one of the servants what was going on, and they told him his brother was back. 'We are celebrating his safe return with a feast of the fatted calf.'

"The older brother filled with rage. *This kid turned his back on the family, squandered his inheritance. How dare he come back here and try to be part of the family again!*

"The more he thought about it, the angrier he became. He stayed and worked for his father all this time. He never made any demands on his father's wealth. In fact, he worked hard to contribute to growing it. And in return, his father never held a celebration feast in his honour. He never gave him a fatted calf so he and his friends could have a party. He determined he would have nothing to do with this celebration, and turned and walked out of the house.

"His father came out after him and begged the older brother to join him in celebrating the return of his younger son. The older brother complained, 'I slaved for you all these years. I never refused any request of yours. I always did as you asked. And in all that time you never gave me even a goat for a feast with my friends. Yet this son of yours blew all his money on prostitutes and you give him a feast fit for a king.'

"The father answered, 'My dear son, it is true you have always stayed with me and when your brother left, I divided my wealth between you two. Everything I have is yours. They were your calves and goats as much as they were mine. We have to celebrate this happy day, for your brother was dead and has come back to life. He was lost and is now found.' (paraphrased from Luke 15:11–32)

"While a disappointing ending with the older son, this sculpture captures the moment of joy of the father welcoming his lost son back into relationship. The son blew through what his father gave him, like Adam gave away the title deed to the earth and even our lives. But the son returned to the father to be saved from death, and the father offered restitution and relationship and an inheritance unimaginable. We too drew close to avoid death and the Father offered redemption, eternal marriage and paradise. You see the moment of love of a father no matter what the son has done."

As Lani stepped back Nan and her group sang "The Prodigal". When they finished the crowd broke into groups of friends, enjoyed the refreshments and wandered under the dome tree.

At the top of the next hour, Lani stepped up to the woman at the well sculpture to tell the story. She did some research on this story before carving it. The first three sculptures were based on parables, but this was a true story. Lani wanted to get this right, so she sought out the woman Yeshua met at the well. And Lani found her. Both the sculpture and the story were based on what this woman shared with her.

Lani started with the poem, "Living Water," then continued with her story.

"There was a beautiful young woman living in Samaria. She was born to a very loving, warm family. She loved to spend time with her father as he worked as a blacksmith. She was well known and loved by the townspeople from being in the workshop nearly every day. Her father adored her as his only child.

"One day a Roman centurion stopped by to replace a missing shoe on his horse. As her father was working to put the shoe on, the horse spooked and crushed him. He passed away in less than a day. This young girl was heartbroken and could not be consoled for days.

"Her heart ached over the loss of her daddy. Her mother made little time for her as she took on work as a servant to survive. As time passed, this girl gained the attention of all the boys in town because she grew into a very beautiful girl. The townspeople called her Susah, meaning young mare. She was given in marriage to a man when she was 12 years old. She agreed because her mother needed the money. He was several years older and she hoped to find the comforting love she experienced with her father.

"This man's first wife died before they had children, so he married this young girl Susah. It was not a marriage of love for him, but she hoped for at least respect. She became ill and he refused to pay for the cost of caring for her. Based on the Torah law, the priest compelled him to divorce her because he refused to care for her as his wife. He gave her a divorce, thinking she would die. She returned to her mother, divorced and quite ill, when she was 13.

"She recovered from her illness and soon the young men in town were interested in her again. Five months later she married a handsome young man just a few years older than she was. He loved her and valued her, and she fell deeply in love with him. They lived happily together and fell into a happy life within his family's home. But he was a bit of a hot-head and chafed at the yoke of Roman rule. His mouth and opinion thrust him into trouble with a small unit of Roman soldiers and he received a severe beating. He was brought back to his home to die. She had a few moments with him before he drew his last breath.

"Again, she suffered the loss of a loved and trusted man. All the pain and loss of her father came back, adding to this new loss, and she wept bitterly.

"An unmarried younger brother offered to marry her to fulfill his brother's marital obligations. Susah liked this boy, and by marrying him she would be able to stay in this home and family she had become comfortable with.

"With the older boy, she fell in love with an outgoing, gregarious and fun-loving young man, but his brother was quite the opposite. He was quiet, shy, smart, but rather sickly growing up.

"While she didn't come to love this boy as she had his brother, she was fond of him and quite happy to live her life with his family and care for him. They were content with each other and she enjoyed talking about things of Yehovah with him.

"After a couple of years his poor health took a turn for the worst. He was exhausted, profoundly weak, wouldn't eat and suffered with a fever. After a couple of days, diarrhea and vomiting set in. His skin, while pale, took on a dark grey colour.

"One of the foreign servants in town people turned to for medical help told her he would probably die within days – a prediction that turned out to be accurate.

"While Susah was not passionately in love with this boy, she came to deeply care about him. And here again she found herself facing another loss in her young life.

"After burying her third husband, she returned to her mother. She was now 15 and felt hollowed out inside. She was still a strikingly beautiful young woman, but felt emotionally numb. She cried out to Yehovah to heal her and provide a husband she could love and grow old with. Someone with whom she could have children and be blessed with grandchildren.

"While running errands for her mother, she caught the eye of the youngest son of one of the sheepherders. He was a vibrant, young, healthy man, tall, strong and handsome. He was a little shy, but had a spark of fun. Anytime she saw him, he had something to say that would lighten her day and bring a smile to her face.

"One day, his father came to visit her mother's house to ask her if she would marry his youngest son. Susah considered for the briefest moment. This man's son was healthy, kind, gentle and caring. He brought warmth to her frozen heart. She happily agreed, knowing Yehovah answered her prayers, and they married shortly after.

"Again, she moved in with his family. They were very gentle folk, often bringing the injured or needy lambs into their home. They were good, caring people and took to Susah right away. Her heart opened to all of them and she quickly came to love her new husband. Within months, they were expecting their first child. The entire family was excited, but her husband was particularly excited. She knew he would be a good father and would love and cherish his children.

"One night she awoke to great pain. Her husband ran to get his mother. By the time his mother came, she had lost her baby. Yet another loss in her life. She felt she let everyone down, but they rallied around her, ensuring she felt their continued love and support. They were a balm to her hurting heart.

"Susah counted her blessings and determined to not let this loss pull her down. She was surrounded by people who loved her and she married a husband who treasured her. They would try for another baby. Her husband continued to be a joy to her and soon she was pregnant again.

"In nine months she gave birth to a wonderfully big, strong baby boy. He looked just like his father. Life was truly good and she felt truly blessed.

"A year later they were blessed with a little baby girl and Susah felt her world was complete. Yes, it had been a sad life getting there, but her bitterness had turned to joy. She had a home, a good husband and beautiful children.

"One evening the men came home from the fields with a fever and aching muscles. By morning they were dizzy with headaches. Within days half the family had taken sick, some bleeding from their mouths, noses and eyes, others unconscious.

"In two weeks she was the only one alive. She lost her family, her husband, her children. She was in shock at the profound loss. Her grief was so deep, she couldn't even cry. She packed up and again returned to her mother's home.

"She would not speak of her pain, her grief, her loss. She simply laid it before Yehovah. She gave Him her broken heart. She would accept whatever He had planned for her. She would not expect anything other than food and shelter. Susah decided hers would be a life of loss and grief.

"Despite all this, it did not show on her face. She was still quite lovely and now carried a maturity about her. She was settled in herself, no longer looking for love, or children. She would be satisfied with food and a roof. This quiet settledness added to her attractiveness and she again caught the eye of a man who worked in a vineyard for a wealthy man.

"He often brought fruit, grapes and honey for both her and her mother, and they made dinner for him. It was a comfortable relationship for all three of them and Susah agreed to marry this man. But she would not hope for anything more than what she had today. Life taught her well that she could count on nothing for tomorrow.

"Her mother aged since the last time they lived together. She was tired and did not have the energy of her youth. Shortly after they were married her mother passed away in the night. It was a quiet and peaceful death. Susah was grateful it had not been painful or drawn out. While she loved her new husband, it was not the deep, needy, dependent love of her youth. She loved him when he was there and had no expectation for tomorrow.

"Shortly after her mother's passing, a couple of men from the vineyard brought her husband in. He had been out collecting honey when a bear attacked him. He lost a lot of blood and died while they were bringing him home.

"After burying her fifth husband, she found herself all alone. She had no mother to turn to. No family. No children. She experienced a flash of self-pity, but took a deep breath and carried on with her chores. Life would not defeat her.

"She remembered her third husband speaking to her of a promised Messiah. She would focus her thoughts on those conversations and what the priests taught.

"One of the vineyard workers stopped by often to check in on her and see how she was doing. They fell into a comfortable friendship. They would often eat dinner together and talk long into the evening. In time, he would stay over. Neither of them looked for marriage, or children. Just the comfort of their friendship was enough. Susah, if she was honest with herself, was afraid of getting married again and facing more loss. No gain, then no loss.

"One day, midday, she walked to Jacob's well to get water for the evening. She wanted to avoid the whispers of the other women. As she approached the well, she saw a Jewish man sitting on its edge. He was Jewish and she Samaritan. He would want to have nothing to do with her, so she went about her business of drawing up water when he said to her, 'Please give me a drink.'

"She was stunned as no Jew had ever spoken to her. She said, 'You are a Jew, and I am a Samaritan woman. Why are you asking me for a drink?'

"Yeshua replied, 'If you only knew the gift God has for you and who you are speaking to, you would ask me, and I would give you living water.'

"'But sir, you don't have a rope or a bucket, and this well is very deep,' Susah said. Then she thought for a moment. Living water. She never heard of such a thing. Water isn't alive, it's just water. 'Where would you get this living water?' she asked. 'And besides, do you think you're greater than our ancestor Jacob, who gave us this well? How can you offer better water than he and his sons and his animals enjoyed?'

"Yeshua replied, 'Anyone who drinks this water will soon become thirsty again. But those who drink the water I give will never be thirsty again. It becomes a fresh, bubbling spring within them, giving them eternal life.'

"Eternal life? Fresh bubbling spring from within her? That sounded pretty good. She could use something living, life, bubbling from within her after being emptied of life with all the loss and grief. 'Please sir, give me this water! Then I'll never be thirsty again, and I won't have to come here to get water.'

"Yeshua told her to go and get her husband. 'I don't have a husband,' Susah replied.

"Yeshua said, 'You're right! You don't have a husband — for you have had five husbands, and you aren't even married to the man you're living with now. You certainly spoke the truth!'

"This conversation had just taken a very personal turn. This Jew just pushed into territory she didn't want to discuss. And how did he know this about her? 'Sir,' Susah said, 'you must be a prophet. So tell me, why is it that you Jews insist that Jerusalem is the only place of worship, while we Samaritans claim it is here at Mount Gerizim, where our ancestors worshiped?' That was a good controversy, a good distraction, and a real opportunity to gain some understanding as to why there was such a division between her people and the Jews.

"Yeshua replied, 'Believe me, dear woman, the time is coming when it will no longer matter whether you worship the Father on this mountain or in Jerusalem. You Samaritans know very little about the one you worship, while we Jews know all about Him, for salvation comes through the Jews. But the time is coming — indeed it's here now — when true worshipers will worship the Father in spirit and in truth. The Father is looking for those who will worship Him that way. For God is Spirit, so those who worship Him must worship in spirit and in truth.'

"She thought this was indeed a prophet and he seemed to be talking about salvation for her people. She knew a little bit about the expected Messiah from her third husband. Susah said, 'I know the Messiah is coming – the one who is called Christ. When He comes, He will explain everything to us.'

"Then Yeshua told her, "I AM the Messiah!'

"Susah left her water jar beside the well and ran back to the village, telling everyone, 'Come and see a man who told me everything I ever did! Could he possibly be the Messiah?' So the people came streaming from the village to see Him.

"Many Samaritans from the village believed in Jesus because the woman had said, 'He told me everything I ever did!' When they came out to see Him, they begged him to stay in their village. So He stayed for a couple of days, long enough for many more to hear His message and believe. Then they said to the woman, 'Now we believe, not just because of what you told us, but because we have heard Him ourselves. Now we know that He is indeed the saviour of the world (dialogue paraphrased from John 4:1–42).'

"This is the moment at Jacob's well when Yeshua offered eternal life through Him to a Samaritan woman, and she believed. As a result her whole village believed. I would like to introduce you to Susah, now named Dalit."

The crowd cheered a welcome to this special guest saying, "Dalit, one who draws water, we welcome your eternal friendship."

When the noise died down, Nan and her group sang "Come, Thou Fount of Every Blessing."

Excitement rippled through the crowd because of Dalit. When Nan finished the final verse, many gathered around to talk with Dalit.

At the top of the fifth hour, Lani stepped in front of the fifth sculpture, still hidden. This would be the first time she showed anyone this sculpture and told its background.

She started. "We have finally come to the time to reveal the fifth and final sculpture of the love series. I named this one The Mohar. This is the term for the price paid for the bride." This caused a stir among the crowd.

She shared her poem, "The Mohar," then began her story.

"This sculpture is different from the other ones. They are all stories or parables that were told to explain His love for us. This sculpture is of the symbols of the mohar, the price He paid for His bride." Lani nodded to Gilad to remove the covering from the sculpture area. The crowd let out a gasp and began clapping.

Unlike the others, which were sculptures of people, this was an exhibit of an event or scene. On display was an empty tomb with brilliant light bursting forth, uninhabited death linens, a crown of thorns, a spear, the spikes and an empty cross in a setting with myrrh bushes and aloe behind. There were benches around where people could sit.

"Let me explain all that you see here. When Adam and Eve sinned, Yehovah turned to Adam and said, 'Since you listened to your wife and ate from the tree whose fruit I commanded you not to eat, the ground is cursed because of you. All your life you will struggle to scratch a living from it. It will grow thorns and thistles for you (Paraphrased Genesis 3:17–18).' Yehovah cursed the ground and as a result, thorns burst forth.

"Here you see the crown of thorns. Lucifer inspired the Romans to use the object of Yehovah's curse to mock His divinity, His kingship. How offensive to use the earthly result of sin. A crown of the results of sin for the sinless man. Not only had Yeshua given up His position of glory and honour to a position lower than the angels, He endured the degradation of being crowned with the results of His curse.

"Next, look over here and you see the nails, the three spikes used to nail Yeshua to the cross. Three symbolizes completeness. Jonah's three days in the whale, Yeshua prayed three times in the garden, He was placed on the cross at the third hour, there were three hours of darkness, He was three days in the grave and there are three in the trinity.

"Isaiah told us He was pierced for our rebellion, our sins and transgressions. Using three spikes, the number of completion, He ensured the full price was paid for our sin, once and for all. It was completed on the cross.

"Look over here. This is the spear that cut into His side. Out came blood and water, which indicated He was dead. The blood from His sacrifice was for forgiveness and payment for our sins, the water for regeneration and purification, washing them away. The source of our forgiveness, payment for sin, and our regeneration and purification poured out of His side. Just like when Yehovah reached into Adam's side to take a part of him to create a mate, so too from the side of Yeshua came the part of Him used to create His mate, the new creature Man-Yehovah. His blood and water from His side brought forth His mate.

"At the back you see the cross. The tree. His blood put onto the wood of the cross in preparation for Passover. The Passover, a remembrance of when the Hebrews placed blood of the lamb on their wooden door frames and the angel of death passed by. Yeshua was the fulfillment of the Passover feast. His blood is the final and complete requirement for the angel of death to pass over us.

"The cross lifted up was our escape, like Moses lifting his staff to provide a way of escape for the Hebrews leaving Egypt.

"Look at the empty tomb, the defeat of death and with it the grave. Yeshua is the way to eternal life, the truth and the light. Here you see an empty tomb with His light and life pouring out. There is no death here. He had been wrapped in these linens and simply arose, leaving the grave clothes still wound up as though He sat up through them and stepped away.

"Grave and death could not hold Him. The trappings of death could not encumber Him. The empty tomb and the grave clothes left behind point to His destruction of death.

"And last, look at the myrrh and aloe in the back, both spices used in the embalming process. You remember myrrh, the anointing and embalming oil gift given to Yeshua as a baby. Along with the gold that signified His kingship and frankincense representing His priesthood, the myrrh prefigured his death."

Indicating the entire display Lani said, "These remind us of the mohar He paid for us. He took and bore our sins on the cross. He gave up His life. He carried our sins to Hades where His righteous blood shed from His side caused the load of sin to fall away. Standing in purity, He announced His defeat of death and walked out of Hades, leaving the load of sin behind. He went to paradise to show those there that sin had been removed. Having chosen Him and awaiting Him in paradise, they stood gleaming white. He created a new creature worthy of becoming His mate of His own kind. What love is this that would pay that dear a price for a bride?

"I give you a memorial forever, The Mohar."

Lani stepped away as the crowd clapped and cheered for their redeemer. They sang "Christ the Lord is Risen Today" (Charles Wesley, 1739) then finished with Handel's Messiah (1741), led by Handel himself. Everyone was on their feet by then and singing with the group. Lani could not have been more pleased that such honour had been brought to her Beloved.

Asher organized a surprise for both Lani and all who gathered. He prepared a keepsake of the evening to give everyone. As the last strains of music faded, eh-bed handed out the memento, a carved cube with a lightstone inside. On each side was an etching of the sculptures, with the final sculpture etched on the top. Along the base of each side was the name of her place, the Mayan.

Asher created a special one for Lani with the priestly symbols of pomegranates and bells etched into the base along with the word Mayan.

Now that could well be her story. The lightstones from the wound in the side of the hill, the love series sculptures all pointing to Yehovah's love story. His desire before time began and the plan, now finished, to have a mate of His own kind. She would tell this story from her perspective.

Lani let this idea roll around in her mind.

Yes, this would be her honour story. Telling of the impact and development of others through the Mayan really would be telling their story. She felt settled about her decision.

She thought about the feast in a few hours. The anniversary of the arrival of the Ahuvati. She had some time still and decided to read the poem of her first day here.

20 | One Day, Last and First

Chapter Span: One Day | Before Arrival to 0.1.1 |

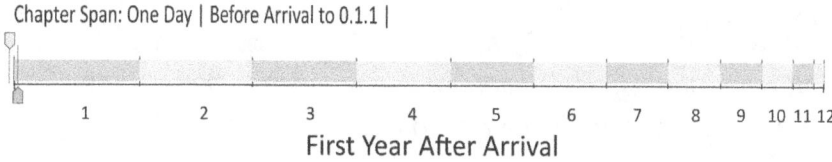

First Year After Arrival

The weaver's poem: Betrothed Becomes Wife

Longing, tired,
Waiting and watching,
Years, decades, centuries.

The blow of the shofar resonating around the world.
Come to me, my Love, my bride.

Blackness of old, filth, disease washed away.
White, radiant and luminous,
Incorruptible, immortal.

Come away, my Love.

Humans transformed.
A new name that speaks to the nature,
A new mission that fulfills desire and dream.

The ceremony,

Shared love words, commitment,
Shared precious jewels, new names.
Shared drink of the vine, blessings,
Celebration.

"It is finished!" a declaration for the intended to be betrothed.
It is consummated, the betrothed now His eternal mate.

Behold King Yeshua and His bride.

The Story Behind the Poem

The biggest event for Lani was the first time she saw her eternal love. In the long past, the MercyMe song "I Can Only Imagine" would always bring her to tears, but it was no preparation for the real event.

Remembering the day in her long past, she recalled she felt tired that day. It had been hard to get up, dressed and get to work. She longed for the promise of an end to all the heartache and grief, all the evil, all the hatred, the wars, the slaughters, all the struggle, loss, illness and death. Every day she wondered how much longer.

Every night she reviewed the news for signs the end was near. She knew in her head it had to be soon, but to actually be the day just didn't seem a reality. Anyway, to live thinking today was the day would just result in a powerful letdown – every day. She couldn't bear the emotional challenge of that. She thought about and longed for heaven, the promises, the arrival, but she could not imagine that day being THE day. Faith, things hoped for, but unseen.

She went through her daily activities as normal, but ensured she was ready to quickly shift gears should she hear any indication of the calling of her groom. She lived attuned to the point that she felt her ears always listened and monitored for the sound of the shofar and call. Once, while she listened to some tunes, she thought she heard something. She ripped out the earbuds and listened intently. Hopefully. Excitedly. But it was nothing.

The day, the *last* day of the long past, Lani came home after work and headed straight outside to play with the dogs, swimming in the pool. Lani's mom spent the afternoon throwing toys in for the girls to retrieve. All were happy to see Lani arrive. This was the best part of her day. She really did love summer and hated to see it coming to an end. It was already mid-September and the warm weather seemed to be holding. She sat down with her mom. Abbey came over to say hello in her exuberant way when she whirled around and turned to look up in the air above the corner of the property. Lani and her mom went quiet to watch. It always interested them, almost like a confirmation that God dispatched angels to guard their home.

Abbey watched intently, then quickly turned to the other corner of the property. She looked up and down, back and forth, unable to pick which corner to watch. The other dogs became quiet. Lani looked over at her mom. This was most unusual. Before either could speak they heard it loud and clear. The shofar! Lani could hardly breathe. Each blow resonated. This was no ordinary trumpet. The sound filled the air. She felt it in her lungs. Actually, she felt it down to her toes. Like the reverberance in your chest when lions roar. As the sound of the final blow faded, a voice boomed, "Come to me, my Love, my bride." Before drawing her next breath, they were gone. Lani, her mom, and her beloved dogs.

She felt a wave of warmth wash over her from head to toe, and something old, filthy, sick and diseased fell away. She knew she had just put on incorruptibility and immortality. She made a choice for righteousness, for Yehovah, and she was experiencing the fulfillment of His plan to have an eternal, righteous helpmate that chose Him. She was radiant, literally luminous. She was no longer clothed, yet covered. She left her clothes behind like Yeshua left his grave clothes.

Just above the earth, all who chose Yehovah gathered. All the people in the past who believed on Yeshua as their saviour, all the living who currently believed, and all animals and children that fell under the leadership of one who chose Yehovah. She noticed everyone clothed only in radiant righteousness. Lani lived her life putting up with clothes, but had little appreciation for anything confining or worse, scratchy. She wasn't too sure about the concept of floating around clouds in robes, but this radiant righteousness covering was fantastic. Such freedom! Like naked without any shame or embarrassment. And no wondering what to wear. And no washing.

"Away, my Love," and off they travelled at an unimaginable speed. In a breath, they arrived at a courtyard entry to the place prepared for them. Yehovah the Father was there. It felt as though the space could not contain Him. It was all overwhelming. There was intense holiness and righteousness emanating from the Father. And great love and joy from Yeshua. Contentment and satisfaction deeper and richer than any longed-for reunion Lani had ever had. This love and joy filled all lonely voids within her. Instantly she felt settled, as this was the place and person she was always meant to be. In her low times of the long past, Lani saturated her mind with a song that told her she was beautiful and intended for more than her earthly life offered. She realized the perfect fulfillment of her life in that moment.

God's righteousness and holiness blasted the courtyard with light. Yeshua's love and joy filled it with music and fragrance. Lani was beyond speech. She couldn't look up. She just wept. Overwhelmed, she fell to her knees and quietly wept. Silence surrounded her. She was aware of many, many others, on their knees and overwhelmed as well, but not a sound.

"My beautiful love. Aha'Ahuvati." Such tenderness, such deep love, a statement filled with longing. Lani looked up to see the face of her love, and knew He was much more than a redeemer. He intended to be her Boaz. He really did love her beyond measure. He paid a great price to have her as His helpmate. Forever.

"How long have I eagerly waited for you, my precious love. I have waited for you since before time and space. You are so beautiful." With a smile and open arms He said, "Aha'Ahuvati, let me hold you." And they all fell into His arms. All of them. Millions. All at once. He held them all, yet held Lani individually. She heard His heartbeat. This felt right, like this was what she unknowingly longed for her whole life, the missing piece that filled a big, deep hole. This was indeed what she was made for. She was exquisitely happy and whole.

Yeshua was present with each person individually. She could not have imagined the intimacy in His presence. There really was no explanation for how this could be. One perfect man, yet intimately present and close with millions at the same time.

This was not at all like on earth where He was constrained to being a man. On earth, people would press in just to touch the hem of His garment. Here He expressed Himself as fully God and fully man. While being Yeshua the perfect man, He was still Yehovah, and as such would always be omniscient and omnipresent. Now she got it! Lani remembered reading about James and John asking that they would be the ones seated on His right and on His left in glory. But that was just not how it worked here. As His eternal mate, they were all seated at His side, equally.

Inspired by the Ruach, everyone sighed, "You are Lord, my Beloved." Yehovah-Father announced, "This is my Beloved Son and His loved and cherished eternal mate. My plan is fulfilled. My desire is satisfied. I am well pleased." Angels and all sorts of creatures erupted into praise and celebration. Their joy was contagious, and all the people joined in. Exultation resounded through the heavens.

Lani remembered the nisuin (the elevation or consummation portion of the marriage). Funny, it was known as the elevation, and here they all were elevated physically to heaven. Lani would soon understand what this was about.

When the echoes of joy and praise finally faded, a canopy or chuppah descended and floated above the entire courtyard. The holy saints, who arose from their sleep in the graves and appeared to many in the holy city before going to heaven as the first fruits, joined the assembly. These were the witnesses to the nisuin! Together with the witnesses the Ahuvati recited seven blessings, circling around Yeshua.

When finished, creatures brought wine to every member of the bride.

Yeshua declared, "You are all beautiful. There is no spot on you. You have ravished my heart. You are perfumed with the fragrance of frankincense and fine oils. Let me see your face and hear your voice."

In delight, the Ahuvati all answered, "I belong to my Love and His desire is toward me. You are altogether handsome. You are my Beloved and my friend. Your head is adorned with crowns upon crowns. You are the king of kings, and the lord of lords, and yet you are my Beloved."

Yeshua replied, "My Kingdom has come, and as I promised I didn't drink of the fruit of the vine until today. Aha'Ahuvati, drink with Me in the commencement of our eternal union. I preserved the best wine for today."

Yeshua gave a standard blessing over the wine, and a blessing over their marriage. He finished saying, "To my Love, Aha'Ahuvati." And Lani took a deep drink of her wine. It was smooth, yet robust. It invaded her mouth and nose. The first taste was of peaches, then broke into a massive flavour of fruit and opulence, yet still elegant. It was flamboyant and yet refined, and became velvety and silky when swallowed. Exceptional! Like nothing she had ever tasted. She felt it dancing in her stomach as though alive.

They threw their glasses in the air, which dissipated into glowing embers and flew toward the Majestic City, taking on the flight of a large flock of birds. All the witnesses yelled, "Mazel tov!" (congratulations).

Angels beyond number watched the ceremony. The ones at the front stepped forward to the Ahuvati, carrying beautiful necklaces of gemstone Lani had never seen before. An angel handed one to her as Yeshua said, "Be sanctified to me with this stone taken from under the throne of Yehovah, the most precious of all stone in the cosmos. It has your new name and identification carved deep within. When I spoke the cosmos into existence, I engraved your names and identification within these thronestones. It was such before time. Wear these most precious stones as my token of eternal love and commitment to you. With your thronestone, you are permitted to the very throne of Yehovah."

Lani put hers on and turned to watch the ember birds disappear into the Majestic City. People followed them. They headed into the first festival meal to celebrate their marriage – anniversary zero – the first of countless marriage celebration feasts. This was not the marriage supper coming later, but a great feast to celebrate the first day of an eternal marriage. The Haga'at, the arrival or touch feast, was about to begin.

This was when Lani met her first and good friends Aymoon, Cheka, Honani and Kazhu. They walked, arms around each other, delighted in each other's company. As they approached the Majestic City, Cheka's mother, brother and sisters came over to hug and hold her. With no feeling of loss or jealousy on the part of the others, Cheka smiled back at the group and turned to join her family.

Lani was happy for her as she watched her family envelop her in their warmth. *I am well loved*, thought Lani.

Then Lani saw her mom's brothers and sisters, and hundreds of other people she never met before, and instantly she knew these people were her mother's ancestors. All the ancestors gathered together. Lani gave her three friends a hug of promise to reconnect and ran to join them. Lani, her mother, and her mother's mother held each other so very tightly. Lani felt their warmth and love, and tears welled up, but no, this was not a place for tears. She felt a brief realization of what a loss of relationship with Yehovah had occurred in the garden. But as quickly as that feeling pressed her heart, it passed. She suddenly saw eons of relationship ahead with these beautiful people. She knew she would spend this first feast in the company of her ancestors.

The Majestic City was more than majestic. It was alive with holiness. As they entered they could see the throne room. There was a rainbow encircling the throne made of jasper, emerald and sardine (blood-red stone). From the throne came lightning flashes, thunder and voices. Around the throne sat 24 elders clothed in brilliant white and wearing crowns of gold. The throne stood on a sea of pure crystal-like glass, as though the river of life formed the floor.

In the midst and around the throne were four creatures, covered in eyes front and back. The creatures were the same ones who transported Yehovah, the throne room floor, the throne and Lani through time and the cosmos. Each creature held its wings around and about the throne. The seraphim above continuously said, "Holy, holy, holy, Lord God Almighty, which was, and is, and is to come." She knew they looked at the seat of all righteousness.

The entire multitude of the redeemed bride stopped in awe. This was the source of holiness, might, righteousness, justice, peace, love, light and life. Yehovah-Father seated on the throne held a book sealed with seven seals. Among the creatures and the elders standing before the throne stood Yehovah-Yeshua, who appeared as the Lamb who gave up His life. The Lamb took the book, and the four creatures and the elders fell down to worship Him. Each creature carried a harp and a golden vial full of the prayers of the saints.

The elders sang, "You are worthy to take the scroll and break its seals and open it. For you gave yourself to death as a lamb to slaughter without resistance, and your blood has ransomed people for God from every tribe and language and people and nation. And you have caused them to become a Kingdom of priests for our God. And they will reign on the earth."

Then millions upon millions of angels joined in the song. "Worthy is the Lamb who was slaughtered – to receive power and riches and wisdom and strength and honour and glory and blessing."

Then the bride joined in with every creature in the air, land and sea singing, "Blessing and honour and glory and power belong to the One sitting on the throne and to the Lamb forever and ever." The four creatures said, "So be it," and everyone fell to their knees and worshiped the Lamb.

They all knew what would follow. Like when John the Revelator was taken to heaven to see the future (Revelation 4–19), the Yehovah-Ruach allowed them to see events to come, in the throne room. The seals would be broken open and four horses and riders dispatched, the souls under the altar would ask for revenge, followed by the breaking of the remaining seals. At the breaking of the seventh seal, there would be a silence throughout heaven for half an hour. Everyone, every creature, stood awestruck and brought to silence by what this final seal meant and what was about to happen. A huge amount of incense mixed with all the gathered and collected prayers of Yehovah's people.

These prayers were words of pleading made in Yehovah's own name from the heart of His Beloved and He preserved them in a place of honour. The creatures poured the prayers over the altar set afire as a final sacrifice that would incite Yehovah to let loose His offence and intolerance of unrighteousness. What was coming was not just Yehovah removing His hand of protection, resulting in bad things happening. The long past history was filled with examples of events occurring because Yehovah removed His hand of protection, and the corrupt angels stepped in to inspire evil in the hearts of man, combined with nature turning to chaos under the burden of housing sin. Kind of like a parent removing his hand of steady protection from the bike when his child is learning to ride.

No, what was coming was far worse.

Set afire, these prayers generated billows of smoke that rose up straight to Yehovah seated on His throne. The words poured out of the hearts of His Beloved now set on fire would accomplish two things. One, these prayers carried life because they were made in the name of Yeshua and made righteous by His defeat of death. With His Ahuvati safely removed, these living words, set on fire on the altar, would be righteous justification for Yehovah letting loose His wrath against those in unrighteousness who disrespected, dishonoured, hurt and killed His own Beloved.

And two, once burned, the prayers and reasons for them would be remembered no longer by those who had made them. The people would be able to say, "It is finished and the memory is gone like the smoke."

The burning of the living words brought Yehovah to wrath and anger. This had never been seen before and would never happen again. The depth and finality of this wrath left all watching speechless. Even the four creatures were silenced, knowing this would be a time on earth unlike anything that had ever happened before, or would ever happen again.

This was the silence for half an hour.

While this mixture burned, an angel took it from the altar and threw it to earth. This started unimagined hell on earth.

Following the half hour of reverential, awe-filled silence as the burned prayers of the saints roused God to justified anger, the seven angels blew their trumpets in sequence, releasing nature to explode in ever-worsening hell on earth as though releasing pent-up frustration from bearing the burden of sin for many centuries, millennia.

They heard a voice from the four corners of the altar speak to the sixth angel, "Release the four angels who are bound in the great Euphrates River."

When the seventh angel blew his trumpet, they all said, "The world became the Kingdom of our Lord and of His Christ, and He will reign forever and ever." The 24 elders had been sitting on their thrones before God, but fell with their faces to the ground and worshiped him. They said, "We give thanks to you, Lord God, the Almighty, the One who is and who always was, for now you have your Kingdom, your Beloved Ahuvati, who have begun to reign. The nations were filled with their own wrath, but now the time of your wrath has come. It is time to judge the dead and reward your servants the prophets, as well as your holy people, and all who fear your name, from the least to the greatest. It is time to destroy all who have caused destruction on the earth."

Then Lani saw the temple of Yehovah open up and she could see the original ark of His covenant inside. There erupted a great roar of noise, and lightning, thunder, an earthquake and a terrible hailstorm were all sent to earth.

Then Lani saw Yeshua seated on a white cloud, wearing a gold crown on His head and a sharp sickle in His hand. Another angel came from the temple and shouted to Yeshua, "Swing the sickle, for the time of harvest has come! The crop on earth is ripe!" Yeshua swung His sickle over the earth, and the whole earth crushed under the weight of Yehovah's wrath.

An angel came from the temple also carrying a sharp sickle. A third angel with the power to destroy with fire came from the altar. He shouted to the angel with the sharp sickle, "Swing your sickle now to gather the clusters of grapes from the vines of the earth, for they are ripe for judgment." So the angel swung his sickle over the earth and loaded the grapes into the great winepress of God's wrath and everyone knew blood was flowing over the earth.

Then Lani saw what seemed to be a glass sea mixed with fire. And all the people who died in spiritual victory during these horrors stood on this sea. They held instruments God gave them. Saved from eternal death they would serve in Yehovah's court for eternity. They sang:

"Great and marvellous are the things you do, Yehovah, the Almighty. Just and true are your ways, El Shaddai, king of the nations. Everyone honours and glorifies your name, for you alone are holy. All nations will come and worship before you, for your righteous deeds have been seen by all."

Then Lani saw Yehovah's tabernacle, the holiest place, thrown wide open in the temple. Seven angels emerged holding seven bowls holding seven plagues. The angels wore spotless white linen with gold sashes across their chests. Then one of the four creatures handed each of the seven angels a gold bowl filled with the wrath of Yehovah-El Shaddai. The temple filled with smoke from Yehovah-El Shaddai's glory and power. No one could enter the temple until the seven angels finished pouring out the seven plagues.

Lani heard a mighty voice from the temple say to the seven angels, "Go your ways and pour out on the earth the seven bowls containing Yehovah-El Shaddai's wrath."

One by one, these angels left the temple and poured out his bowl on the earth. Lani heard the third angel say, "You are just, O Holy One, who is and who always was, because you have sent these judgments. Since they shed the blood of your holy people and your prophets, you have given them blood to drink. It is their just reward."

A voice from the altar said, "Yes, O Lord God, the Almighty, your judgments are true and just."

The remaining angels poured out their bowls. Once the final bowl of plague emptied, a mighty shout came from the throne in the temple, saying, "It is finished!" resulting in great thunder, lightning and an earthquake on earth.

Because Yehovah-Ruach allowed them to see these events as a preview, they knew in the future, when they heard Yehovah announce, "It is finished!" they would ride with their Beloved to earth. They watched these scenes of the throne room and the temple like a video of what would come.

Lani found it interesting that Yehovah-Yeshua announced, "It is finished!" when He completed His part of the plan, and all who accepted His offer of salvation and marriage were saved, and here Yehovah would announce, "It is finished" when He completed His part of the plan and the remnant of the apple of His eye, the Jewish people, would be saved.

They headed further into the Majestic City to the gathering place. It was large, very large, yet so very intimate. An unknown material of delicate blues interwoven with gold formed handwoven tapestries that hung on the walls. They gently moved as though in a light breeze, yet no wind blew. Great tables laid out with gold cutlery, dishes of clear gold, and tablecloths of the same hues and tones as the tapestry stretched as far as she could see. The candelabras each carried eight candles, the number of perfection and completion.

Everyone found their way to their intended seat with much laughing and talking as people ran into others they knew. They shared a presence and sense of community and oneness as people greeted their table neighbours. Oh, Lani marvelled at how such a huge, mind-boggling crowd could be so cozy and companionable, everyone in such harmony.

Quietly, Yeshua moved to the centre of the huge room. A hush settled over everyone to hear Him speak. Not one person moved as no one wanted to make a sound.

Yeshua, smiling, slowly turned around looking over the crowd. Tears formed in His eyes. That shattered nearly everyone. The emotion of the moment overwhelmed many.

"My Love." His voice broke with the depth of emotion. With a deep breath, He carried on. "I have longed for you since before time began. I proposed, and you accepted. I watched you and watched over you, yearning for this day. You are so beautiful. I will never tire of you. My heart is so full, I can hardly speak.

"The time I spend with you is like lingering in a perfumed garden. It is intoxicating. I gave my all for the most precious gem in all the universe. And you, my precious Love, are a gem beyond measure. We will travel together through time and beyond.

"Raise your glass with me and drink to us. To my best friend, my wife, my bride, my mate. You are my joy, my Love, my light reflected. I love you forever with all my heart.

"Now come into our garden, our Garden of Eden, my Love. I will meet you and love you in the garden of our minds. Come taste the fruits of love for your love is sweeter than wine to me. You are a fragrant cologne. Join me in our garden. Open your mind and I will join with you."

For time not measured, Yeshua and his bride mentally explored their thoughts, leaping from one thought to the next. Lingering over the interesting ones, and dancing through meadows of pure joy and love. Lani never conceived of such pure love and to-the-core intimacy. She found it a thrilling, exhilarating experience. She knew she would never tire of her mental relationship with her lover.

As gently and quietly as He entered her mind, they returned to the physical world. The Haga'at, the arrival, the touch. She now understood the meaning of arrival and touch. They had consummated their love.

The doors were opened and guests waiting outside were invited in to join the bride and groom. The celebration began. Saints of the Old Testament streamed in. David, Joseph, Daniel, the greats drew deafening cheers.

When all the saints entered, the eh-bed entered with drinks, and realms of angels joined the crowd, celebrating this once-in-all-of-eternity wedding.

Adam rose and said, "I had my Eve drawn out from my side. My mate of my own kind at my side. I toast Yeshua who has His Eve from His side. Now, His mate of His own kind at His side for all eternity. To Yeshua and His bride."

Job stood and said, "I lost all that was precious to me, and Yehovah restored all that was stolen by the locusts. Yehovah-Yeshua lost Adam and Eve to the locusts, but He has restoration of multitudes. To Yeshua and His bride."

Abraham followed Job and said, "Yehovah promised me descendants as numerous as the stars in the sky and sand on the seashore. Before me I see Yeshua's bride as numerous as the stars in the sky. I am pleased to see the fulfillment of His promise and toast Yeshua, the seed of the woman and His redeemed bride. To Yeshua and His bride."

Moses stood and said, "Yehovah promised to redeem my people to a land flowing with milk and honey, the promised land. Before us we see another redemption. The bride has been redeemed and Yeshua and His bride have entered their promised land. May Yeshua and His bride enjoy it, their garden of intimacy, for all of eternity. To Yeshua and His bride in mental intimacy."

David then arose and said, "Yehovah promised a secure, strong Kingdom and an eternal royal throne through my descendant. Before me, the promise fulfilled. Behold, the King of Kings and Lord of Lords. And before Him, His eternal Kingdom come. To the king and His queen. To Yeshua and His bride."

Isaiah stood up and said, "As promised, from Israel's stump, Immanuel came. Yeshua, the holy seed, brought redemption through suffering and sacrifice. He gave His life to offer to His intended marriage. He proposed and His beautiful bride accepted. To Yeshua and His bride."

Solomon said, "I wrote the Song of Songs about the purity of love, sensuality and relationship reminiscent of life in the Garden of Eden. Adam and Eve lived in physical purity before sin corrupted. Now Yeshua and His bride enjoy their garden of mental intimacy. For all eternity, Yeshua and His mate will live their love in their garden. To Yeshua and His bride."

The last to toast, John the Baptist stood. "I lived at the cusp of the Kingdom. I was the messenger sent ahead of Yeshua to prepare the way for Him. I introduced the bride to their Messiah, their groom. I watched Yeshua gather the wheat into His barn. I am pleased to have been the best man. Actually, no one else wanted the job when they found out they would lose their head." This was so unexpected, it brought a roar of laughter. John was as blunt as ever. He finished, "To Yeshua and His bride."

The eh-bed brought in the first of a rich 12-course meal for the guests, bride and groom. Exuberant music and inevitably dancing followed each course.

After the first course the guests danced before the bride, singing praises of the Ahuvati and carrying all manner of silly items such as banners, signs, costumes, confetti and napkins. They called it the gladdening of the bride and Lani laughed at many of the characters dancing. The guests then invited the bride to dance with them, then Yeshua joined in.

Dancing erupted after each course. After the final one, only the bride and Yeshua danced together. The celebration closed with Yeshua and all the Ahuvati leaving the building. All beings in heaven and the saints of old lined the streets. As Yeshua and His bride appeared before the crowd, Yehovah in a thunderous voice announced, "Behold King Yeshua and His bride!" The crowd cheered and waved palms as Lani, along with all the Ahuvati and Yeshua, walked along. Lani felt like a true celebrity.

Ahuvati walked out emotionally overcome by the whole consummation and celebration. It seemed too much to take in. Then she heard a gentle whisper in her mind, "*I am the happiest groom in history. I am proud to have the most beautiful bride by my side. Stay close to me, my Love.*" Knowing her eternal love shared her mind forever, Lani smiled and settled comfortably in to the pomp and celebration.

A fantastic story, and certainly a fond memory. Lani looked up to the sky to note the sun lowering. As she headed back to her mansion, she made up her mind about her story. It would be the story of stones, of sculptures and unveilings.

21 | Honour Stories

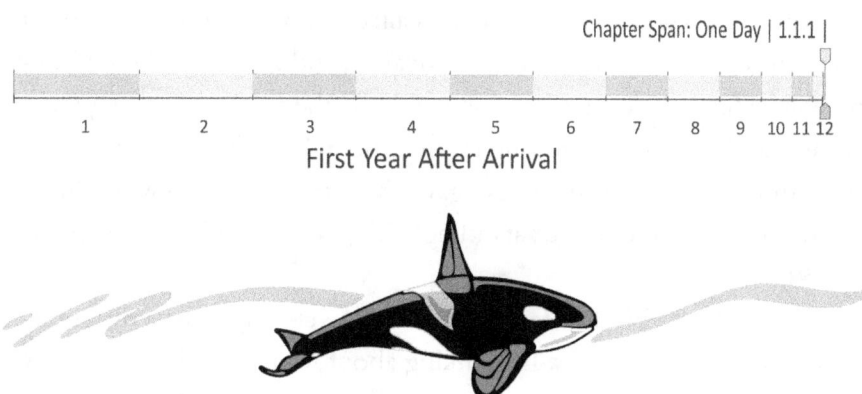

1　　2　　3　　4　　5　　6　　7　　8　　9　　10 11 12

First Year After Arrival

It was late afternoon and the time came to head into the Majestic City. Although Lani settled on the content of her honour story, when getting ready she reconsidered her decision. In fact, she changed her mind.

When rehearsing the story in her mind, she had an awesome idea so obvious, she wondered why she had not thought of it sooner. Lani knew it was the story, her honour story. She quickly pulled together the pieces and worked for the right flow. It reflected her creative nature. It wove together a big story. Yes, she was satisfied. The air filled with the scent of ocean, of creativity, and Lani knew she made the right decision.

It was time to gather with her friends and head to the feast. Lani called Boz down to the beach. Just as she was mounting him, she spotted Asher, Kaz and Honani circling above on their eders. As they made their way to the Majestic City, more and more friends joined them. Excitement buzzed in the air.

As they entered the feast room, everyone was greeting, laughing and talking all at once. There was rampant curiosity to find out what everyone would share, but no one divulged. When asked, most just laughed and indicated their lips were sealed. The secrecy added to the excitement.

Asher was the second to last of Lani's friends and acquaintances to speak. He opened with a quote from the Bible,

"And we know that God causes everything to work together for the good of those who love God and are called according to His purpose for them. For God knew His people in advance, and He chose them to become like His Son, so that His Son would be the firstborn among many brothers and sisters. And having chosen them, He called them to come to Him. And having called them, He gave them right standing with Himself. And having given them right standing, He gave them His glory (Romans 8:28-30).

"I might be a bit different than everyone else and take a different approach to my honour story. In thinking about what story I think deserves my highest respect and esteem by sharing with everyone, I found it was really hard to pick out just one.

"Instead, the story I would like to share is a story of everyone. A story of how Yehovah brought about good from evil, took the worst of our long past life and turned it to His good purpose here. Joseph's brothers in the Old Testament with evil in their hearts intended to harm him. But Yehovah used those circumstances and experience for good to empower Joseph to save the lives of many people. I would like to, with the permission of my friends, share several stories of how Yehovah took that which was meant for harm and turned to good.

"I will start with me. Traders ripped me from my family and home and sold me into slavery. Yehovah pressed on my heart to be a leader, but the ruler of the world, Lucifer, ensured I never received that opportunity. Lucifer's slave trader chose me, the chieftain's son, to steal and sell into slavery. Yehovah planted a desire for leadership in my heart and it remained a seed, unfulfilled in the long past. In fact, I led a very tough life in direct opposition to my birthright of leadership, and yet held onto Yehovah.

"On arrival here, Yehovah gave me the name Asher, meaning happy and blessed. I now live in abundant peace and joy, my reward for sticking it out through such difficult and unfair circumstances. My new name speaks to my inner reward.

"And Yehovah anointed me as a prince in His Kingdom. I now fulfill the desire He planted in my young heart. Praise Yehovah, He gave me a balm of joy and peace, and marked His goodness with a name of His nature. And Yehovah now gives me the place and circumstances to fulfill His purpose through my leadership."

Asher then moved to stand near Aymoon. Aymoon stood up and Asher wrapped his arm around him and said, "This is my friend Aymoon, the faithful. He lived in the first century in Northern Africa. He worked as the treasurer, a servant of Candace, the queen of Ethiopia. His supervisor read the writings of Isaiah for a year, then went to Jerusalem to learn more and to worship this God Yehovah. On his way back Philip told him the good news story of Yeshua. This man believed and Philip baptized him. When he returned to Ethiopia, he was a different man. Aymoon, in his early teens, learned of Yeshua from his supervisor and believed as well.

"He led a quiet, honest life in the service of his queen. He grew into a man of integrity. He read the writings of the apostles as well as the prophets of old. He paid close attention to the success, leadership and protection of Yehovah. He knew Daniel prayed to Yehovah every day and even as a youth, he committed to follow in his steps.

"When his supervisor died, the queen appointed him to oversee her money and doubled her wealth in his lifetime. He loved to read and study any writings on Yehovah, Israel, Yeshua and the apostles. He could not get enough reading material and studied late into every night. He shared what he learned with the young men who worked for him and soon had a large group sitting under his instruction. He was a leader and priest to his men. In all, a faithful, godly man.

"Yehovah pressed on his heart to study, to learn and to share. Aymoon, the faithful, now enjoys access to the best library in the universe and has immersed himself in learning. He already has a following and study group. True to his name, he was, is, and will continue to be a faithful ruler and priest. I listened to him speak of things he learned here, and he is truly blessed with a gift of understanding and teaching. Yehovah gave him the desire and access to more material than he could ever study."

Thousands stood and applauded Aymoon. Over the past year he touched and taught many people. Aymoon bowed, and turned to Yeshua and said, "In your honour, my Beloved." Everyone clapped and cheered, and a band of enthusiastic learners whistled. Aymoon continued to defer the honour to Yeshua.

Asher then moved to Cheka. "This is Cheka, full of laughter. She was born in Samaria while Yeshua walked the earth. She lived in the village around Jacob's Well. Cheka worked in the kitchen grinding barley for bread, churning milk for butter, making cheese, gathering fruit and growing vegetables, and going to the well to draw water for washing and drinking. Cheka grew up with Dalit, the woman at the well. She met Yeshua during the two days He spent in her town and came to believe He was the Messiah. Later she learned more under the teaching of Philip, Peter and John.

"The living water bubbled up through her and she filled with love, joy and peace. She longed to study the holy writings like the boys and teach like Philip, but that was not part of a woman's life.

"She quietly prayed. She made a home of joy and laughter for her husband and children. And she rested on Yehovah that He would one day fulfill the desires of her heart. Cheka, the one of laughter, continues to bring joy and laughter to everyone she meets here.

"Like Aymoon, Cheka spent many hours reading and studying and sharing. As many of you know, Cheka taught the mashqeh new recipes. I heard them laughing and learning together. Yehovah fulfilled her desire to learn and teach. Cheka loves working with the mashqeh and they adore her. Many of us are blessed with great cooks because of the recipes and the training work of Cheka."

Everyone cheered for Cheka. She was well known and loved. She brought fun wherever she went and people enjoyed being with her. But

Cheka was also impacting people through their stomachs. While the food was exquisite here, Cheka created recipes that brought it to a whole new level. Who doesn't love good food?

After hugging Cheka, she sat down and Asher moved to Kazhu. He stood and Asher said, "This is my friend Kazhu, the reliable. Born in China in the early 1650s, his parents died in a revolt and he became an orphan at the Chinese missionary orphanage.

"He was a bright and happy boy. He loved the stories the missionaries told from the Bible and re-enacted them with his friends, always playing the hero. Like many boys he quickly jumped in without thought. He grew up an earnest, keen, enthusiastic teen who often got into trouble. He made promises, but often failed to deliver.

"Because of regional unrest, the military came through the town to root out the dissidents. Despite the missionaries telling Kaz to stay off the streets, he was curious and oblivious to the danger. Several military men caught him secretly moving through the streets and questioned him. Their informant said he was from the Christian orphanage. The questions took a bad turn and Kaz denied his Christianity three times.

"They eventually let him go and he hid, ashamed of his behaviour. How could he possess so little substance, so little backbone? One of the missionaries found him and reminded him of the story of Peter the Rock's denial of his Lord three times, yet he became the leader of the young church.

"This experience tempered Kaz and he got serious about learning to live as a solid, reliable Christian man. He really saw himself in Peter. The way he would jump into action, but quickly lose faith and fail and then, as Kaz says, 'sink into the rough waves and water of circumstances.' He will tell you he struggled to reach Peter's status as a rock and a pillar, but circumstances and his lack of faith prevented him. He didn't understand the strength and courage Peter received at Pentecost.

"For his entire life he desired to be a man of faith, a man known to be reliable. One year ago Yehovah, in His grace, gave Kaz the strength he desired and the name as a testament to his faithfulness and reliability."

Kaz met so many people through his Entry Garden research, and many more asked him to visit to understand the meaning of their gardens. Everyone loved Kaz and only knew him as reliable. Lani certainly counted him a dependable, steady friend of good advice and the one who led the construction of the village and Sunrise. Everyone cheered loudly for Kaz.

Moving to Honani, Asher said, "This is my friend Nan, singer of songs, from Tahiti. Nan lived with a not very successful fisherman. They worshiped the cruel gods of the ocean, living in fear of the water. They had three children, but were doing so poorly, they sacrificed each child to the sharks to win their god's favour. Nan mourned for the first child, but with each subsequent sacrifice, her mourning turned to grief and filled her soul with a thick blackness. Inconsolable, she fell into a deep depression.

"Nan's husband came to know Henry Nott and learned about his God of love. He brought the stories home to Nan, but she remained unmoved. One day Henry himself shared the story of Job with them. Nan asked for Henry to tell the story again and listened intently. She asked Henry to confirm that his God restored all that was lost.

"Nan longed for more children, but just couldn't face throwing them to the sharks to appease her god. This God of love did not require that of His people and she accepted Yeshua as her saviour.

"Yehovah blessed Nan with five children and 22 grandchildren before she died of old age. Like Job, Yehovah restored what the locusts stole from her. Every morning Nan stood by the ocean to watch the sun rising over Lucifer's tools of destruction. She sang to her new saviour, thanking Him for His love and joy replacing the blackness in her heart and mind. She was tone deaf, but that did not matter. It was on her heart to sing, and through singing she found healing.

"One year ago, Nan received her new body with a voice as sweet as honey and pure as the living water. A voice with the power of storm waves and the joy of a gurgling mountain creek. Her desire to bring a beautiful sound before Her king is fulfilled and she is now on the worship project.

Many have enjoyed her concerts at Blue Rock."

Another wild and loud cheer and clapping arose from Nan's fans as Asher moved to Hanna. "This is my friend Hanna, the graceful. She was born to a poor family in a market town in Scotland in AD 435. From birth, her right arm was crippled and both legs were slightly malformed. The family simply couldn't afford a crippled child. At two years old they left her abandoned at the door of an abbey.

"One of the monks took her into his heart and she grew into a bright ray of sunshine in his life. All the monks loved and treasured her. She grew up self-assured in the shelter of the abbey. Her guardian educated her in the redemption story of Yeshua and she developed an innocent, simplistic, but solid faith in her Lord.

"Daily she headed into the forest to collect wood for the kitchen and would always collect a little extra for her guardian. Because of her misshapen limbs, this work took her all day requiring all her strength and energy. She watched the children in town running and dancing, and felt a deep longing in her heart to dance, to express her joy with legs that were strong and rhythmic.

"For a time Hanna turned away from Yehovah in a youthful rebellion, but in that rebellion she lost her wealth of joy and happiness. She soon came back to placing her love and trust in Him. And with grace He gladly welcomed her back into relationship.

"She died in her early teens and the abbey mourned the loss of her beautiful presence of joy.

"One year ago Hanna received her perfect body and has danced ever since. In the long past she desired to dance in joy for her Yeshua. She asked her guardian to tell her of when King David danced in the streets and thought she would love to lead people in dance worship. Hanna is now on a worship project with Nan, the desire of her young heart fulfilled."

Nan stood up and sang and Hanna danced. Happiness and joy erupted and everyone joined in, dancing and clapping.

Asher moved to Elia and when the crowd settled said, "This is my friend Elia, the one who rises. Elia was born in the late 1950s of a well-to-do family in Boston, America. He grew up in the country club set, all social drinkers. He worked in advertising, often lubricating his clients with alcoholic lunches and dinners. He slid into a lifestyle centred around drinking. He was either drunk or hungover. One night, after drinking heavily at the club, he insisted on driving his wife and young family home. He drove head on into an oncoming truck, killing his entire family and the driver of the truck.

"When released from the hospital, he attended Al-Anon meetings to deal with his addiction. He accepted Yeshua as his redeemer, but struggled emotionally with the loss of his family. Most days he lived under a heavy weight of guilt that would sweep over him in the morning and not leave him until he fell asleep. He understood Yehovah removed his sin, but because his family were dead, he could never have their forgiveness. He knew his wife died without redemption.

"He died before he was 30, the doctors said of cirrhosis.

"Elia, the one who rises, now has a healthy body and a renewed mind. Daily, he now rises to the heights of joy and happiness. At the Mayan, he rises to his place in leadership with an easiness and grace teaching many of us how to sail. Like me, his new name is a testament to Yehovah's love and provision, no matter how bad our circumstances. This is another life Lucifer intended to pull down, but Yehovah used the opportunity to meet Elia in the filth of death and loss and reclaim him."

When the cheers and whistles died down, Asher continued. "This is my friend Adi'el, a jewel. She was born of a prostitute in the Ganges delta of Bangladesh. She was never loved by her mother, and lived on the streets like her other abandoned siblings. She heard of the gospel when a missionary hired her to do the sweeping and garbage collection daily.

"Her culture viewed her as having no value, a waste of life. Growing up in those conditions, she believed she was worthless. She knew she was unloved by her mother and siblings, and had no idea who her father was. She desperately longed to be loved and that desperation drove her to hang around when the men would come to visit her mother. One man, a frequent visitor, took an unhealthy interest in her and paid her mother to have sex with this young girl.

"She listened to the missionary stories. When this evil man came to visit, Adi'el focused on the story of Daniel, where Yehovah stood with him when surrounded by evil and no harm came to him. Adi'el did as Daniel had done and prayed to her Lord and God every day. Yehovah answered her prayers and this man stopped showing up. Her mother said he died unexpectedly and was upset at the loss of income. Adi'el spent many times of prayer thanking Yehovah for standing with her.

"Adi really loved the stories of His love and would tell herself these stories when working. Her mind just couldn't comprehend that the Creator of the universe would have any more interest in her than the rest of the world. In her heart she clung to the stories of love and reminded herself of Yehovah's intervention on her behalf. Surely that was evidence of a great, loving God. She stepped out in faith and asked Yeshua to be her God, her king, her master, her All in All and He looked after her. And for a few years, she shone His light in the poverty and shacks of Bangladesh. Many children were redeemed because of her.

She often looked at photos in magazines she collected as garbage, particularly at the beautiful buildings, and wondered what it would be like to design such longstanding art.

She died in a typhoon in her fifteenth year.

"Her new name, meaning jewel, is an eternal confirmation of Yehovah's unending love for her. She is highly prized and loved now and for all of eternity. Yehovah turned her unwanted life to being the light that brought others to know Him. Her name also hints at the fulfillment of her childhood desire, to be an architect, creating ornamental structures of beauty like the Sunrise Studio and Art Gallery."

While people were cheering and clapping for Adi'el, Asher made his way to Keshet, his neighbour. Asher started. "Keshet, a rainbow, worked as a milkmaid in the service of a wealthy landowner. She married one of the young men looking after the horses. Keshet longed for children and lost two during pregnancy and one shortly after birth. She celebrated each pregnancy and loved her unborn child with her whole heart, and then became increasingly devastated at her loss.

"Keshet reminded Yehovah that in the Bible He remembered Hannah's plea for a child. Then one day her friend, one of the other milkmaids, died in childbirth. The young father, distraught at the loss of his wife, had no way to raise his new baby and asked if Keshet would adopt the child. Keshet, so grateful, named the little girl Samuela in remembrance of Yehovah's provision. She was indeed a gift from God, bringing much delight to her parents.

"One year ago, Keshet received her new name, meaning rainbow. The earthly rainbow was set in the sky by Yehovah as a reminder of His promise to never bring the worldwide devastation of a flood again. Keshet now has a name that reminds her and all of us that Yehovah keeps His promises and we will never face loss and death again."

Everyone thanked Yehovah for keeping His promise of redemption as Asher moved to Bayla. She stood and Asher hugged her to him. "Bayla was born a Native American Indian in the early days of white people coming to America. She was born with a facial deformity and was named Ugly. She grew up as the lowest person in the tribe. She spent most of her time with the youngest of children as they were too young to be cruel to her. When she came of age, she was not wanted by any of the young men in her tribe or any other. She was ashamed of her appearance, insecure and lonely.

"She finally married an old man who had been permanently and equally disfigured in a battle. This raised her to a position in the tribe with the other women and she was no longer an object of ridicule.

"When the white men came, they brought both stories of the Bible and the chicken pox. Bayla learned of Yeshua and believed in Him. Her husband died of chicken pox.

"Bayla, now a widow, had time to help raise the children of the tribe.

While teaching the girls to gather fruit and herbs, and how to cook, Bayla told the Bible stories to the children. The girls loved her and grew up knowing Yeshua, and passed this knowledge to their children.

"One year ago, Bayla received her new name, meaning beautiful. Bayla was given the desire of her heart, to have a restored appearance. She is now a stunningly beautiful woman. But more importantly, Yehovah named her beautiful for who she is, not how she now looks. Her name reminds her that she is as beautiful on the outside as she is on the inside." And everyone cheered and clapped for Bayla, the beautiful.

Asher moved to Shelomah to tell his last story. "Many know Shelomah, one of peace, who sings with Honani. Born in England in 1732, he was locked up in Bedlam Asylum with a falling down sickness early in his life. At first they confined him to a cell, but as he grew into a strong young man, they kept him chained to the floor. For entertainment purposes, Bedlam opened to visitors and people came in and taunted him, throwing things at him until he lost his temper. The frustration from the teasing and taunting brought on the head sickness. A steady flow of these visitors came looking for entertainment, offering him no reprieve. Shelomah longed for peace and quiet. Peace from the sickness that would sweep through his brain causing him to fall and shake. Peace from the taunts of people. Peace from Bedlam.

"One man, an old cobbler, had a son locked in Bedlam and would briefly stop to talk with Shelomah after visiting his son. When his son died, he continued to visit Shelomah and tell him about Yehovah. Shelomah came to believe in Yeshua and would call on Yehovah for His abundant peace in the times of torment. The cobbler taught him some songs he sang to soothe his heart and mind. It had the added benefit of entertaining the visitors and slowed down the taunting.

"Shelomah died in Bedlam, never seeing a day of freedom from being a spectacle. Despite the frustration and humiliation of his life, Yehovah gave him eternal peace. He is at peace now, and uses his beautiful voice to thank Yeshua for providing a way to everlasting health and peace. He now entertains through beautiful music and words. His concerts are un-matched."

Quoting Luke, Asher said, "A man prepared a great feast and sent out many invitations. He sent his servant to tell the guests, 'Come, the banquet is ready.' But they all began making excuses. The master was furious and said, 'Go quickly into the streets and alleys of the town and invite the poor, the crippled, the blind and the lame.' After the servant had done this, he reported, 'There is still room for more.' So his master said, 'Go out into the country lanes and behind the hedges and urge anyone you find to come, so that the house will be full. For none of those I first invited will get even the smallest taste of my banquet.' (Paraphrased from Luke 14:16–24).

"We are the poor, the crippled, the blind, the lame, the homeless and the unwanted. The nobodies. The master called and we accepted the clothes of the master to be worthy to attend. We were the earthly insignificants, yet Yehovah now has us leading His Kingdom."

Asher finished with, "These are just a few stories of how Yehovah planted in each of us the seeds of desire, but life in the long past the desires were left unfulfilled in an imperfect world. We were born to insignificant lives on earth. Yet Yehovah loved us, His creation, before time, regardless of our station in life. Regardless of our achievements or lack thereof. Every one of us has the testimony of a desire pressed on our heart, partly and often completely unfulfilled during our earthly life. Yehovah has now given us a name, nature, and opportunity to really fulfill that desire, to let the seed germinate and blossom.

"We all thank you, our Beloved, for giving us each a desire, a passion that will fulfill your plans, and a mission through which we can satisfy what you have put on each of our hearts.

"I thank you for the honour and mantle of leadership. I am humbled by your mission. I never could have imagined all of this during my earthly life, but am thankful you gave me the strength to hold onto you. I cannot thank you enough for carrying my sins to the cross, and defeating death and the grave on my behalf, for loving me when I was nothing to love. I offer nothing more than eternal gratitude and love, and for you, that is enough. Thank you, thank you, thank you. I am forever yours."

With that, the entire crowd erupted and sustained their cheers, clapping, yelling, praising and dancing. Thankfulness poured out for many minutes.

When it died down, Yeshua called on Remi'el for his story. Another huge eruption of cheers. Many people from the long past knew Remi'el from his prophesy updates that went out every week via the internet to the entire world. Twenty thousand would watch his message and he counted them his online church. These people and many more who met him over the last year cheered loudly.

Remi'el, mercy and compassion of Yehovah, stood before the crowd humbled. He covered his face with his hands and bowed his head, nodding slowly. The cheers only became louder. He sat back down, overcome with emotion.

Yeshua stood beside him, pulled him to standing and wrapped His arm around him. He looked Yeshua in the eyes, and indicating the cheering said, "Thank you. This is for you. This is because of you." Yeshua held him close and they hugged for a long moment.

The cheers finally quietened and Remi'el started. "I am truly honoured." He paused, gathering his emotions. "I was going to say, 'How can I follow Asher? What can I say after that!'" Everyone laughed. Remi'el drew in a deep breath and continued. "I would not be here without Yehovah intervening in my life, even before I was born.

"I was born of Egyptian and Lebanese parents who were prompted to move to America to escape oppression in 1961 when I was less than one year old. If not for life in America, I would not have learned about the path to heaven, of Yeshua our Messiah.

"Yeshua trusted me with a small church on the mainland, then moved me and my family to Hawaii to shepherd another small church. We started to devote half an hour every week to prophesy updates in 2006. We recorded and posted the videos to the Internet, but had no idea Yeshua would use this to reach thousands and thousands of people around the globe.

"He was so faithful, granting me and my wife the desire of our hearts. We were blessed with four beautiful children, all here with me today.

"I didn't know the impact those weekly videos would have, but Yehovah used them to bring many to Him." Turning to Yeshua he said, "I cannot thank you enough for all those saved that you credited to me. It was not me, it was all you. Your words, your message, your love, your mercy, your compassion.

"I am honoured to be the conduit to your mercy and compassion. I am more than honoured to have the name Yehovah's mercy and compassion. I am thrilled to live eternity as a testimony of that mercy and compassion. I am eternally honoured and humbled to now wear the mantle of Yehovah's shepherd in His Kingdom where there are so many He could have chosen.

"All that I have, all that I am, is yours. I will never tire of telling you I love you. I am privileged to lead your people, my Arab people. Thank you for letting me satisfy my desire to love on people and share your heart."

Again, the crowd went wild. Remi'el was a funny, sincere, lovable character. His personality drew many to him through his ministry in the long past. Even more so in this last year.

When the cheering died down, Yeshua then called on Lani to tell her honour story. Lani started. "How can I follow Remi'el, Yehovah's mercy and compassion?"

When the laughter faded, she continued. "Yehovah gave me the name Aha'La'anni, His weaver of stories of what was, what is, and is yet to come. Throughout this past year I captured my thoughts about significant events as poems. I carved these poems on stones of remembrance and placed them around my estate. Visitors came to call them weaver's poems. I selected and organized some for my honour story.

My Honour Story

This is the story of the Almighty Yehovah
Before time and space.
The unfolding story of romance,
The story of the eternal bride and groom,
The story of love.
Our story, my story,
My lover in my garden of my mind.

His Plan for a Cosmic Romance
Alone in vast nothingness
There arises a deep, longing desire for a bride, a mate of its own
kind.

His Secret Plan
Physical space, Yehovah's incubator.
Time, for creation and completion.
The creation of mankind, His intended.
The completion of His plan, resulting in His mate.

His Commitment
Constant attention, all evil turned for a good purpose.
Love, to squeeze His eternal spirit into physical form.
Humiliation, degradation and unwarranted death.

His Expectation
Triumph, physical victory over death and the grave.
Second Adam's DNA, Yehovah-Man's DNA, from His side.
Marriage proposal, the new covenant.
Acceptance, genetic conversion to a new creature.

His Success
Consummation with a mate of His own kind.

The Unfolding Pursuit of His Cherished

As was planned, His creation.
By Word, light.
By Word, life.
The cosmos.

By divine purpose, man.
His intended, and it was good.

As was known, a defection.
Angels, stepping out of their first estate
In jealousy,
purity corrupted,
beauty twisted to vile,
love poisoned by lechery,
light fouled by evil.
The intended left lost and ignorant.

As was planned, His redemption of His intended,
Devotion, His persistent desire despite his intended's betrayal.
Leave realms outside of time and space, Yehovah in human form,
A second Adam's rib, His DNA to create His own kind.
It is finished, a new covenant.
His proposal to His intended.

As was known, His intended's answer.
The mohar paid and a declaration, "It is finished!"
Sin left behind in Hades.
His offer and a choice to be made by the Intended.
Acceptance and commitment.
His betrothed.

As was planned, His desire fulfilled,
The final Adam's genes implanted, now a new creature,
A mate of His own kind.
Love gifts given, Paradise prepared,

Snatched away to His house.
Beings in eternal mental consummation,
A wife, a mate of His own kind.

The Story of the Bride
Seeds of desire planted in the young heart,
Life crushes,
Dreams unfulfilled.

Longing, tired,
Waiting and watching,
Years, decades, centuries.

The blow of the shofar resonating around the world,
Come to me, my Love, my bride.

Blackness of old filth, disease washed away.
White, radiant and luminous,
Incorruptible, immortal.

'Come away, my Love.'

Humans transformed,
A new name that speaks to the nature,
A new mission that fulfills desire and dream.

The ceremony.
Shared love words, commitment.
Shared precious jewels, new names.
Shared drink of the vine, blessings.
Celebrate.

'It is finished,' a way for the intended to be betrothed.
It is consummated, the betrothed now His eternal mate.
Behold King Yeshua and His bride

Morning, a New Day in Paradise

Evening is almost over.
The air becomes thick with silence
As the living water rises to water the land.
Looking east, standing on the edge of a new day,
Then the first brush of the colour palette on the horizon, giving announcement.
I stand in hope, quiet excitement, anticipation of what this new day promises.
Finally, the first ray of light bursts forth – a new day in paradise.
Light and life lighting across the expanse of the sky,
Diamonds dancing across the sea,
Uncontained excitement swells my heart beyond capacity.
With all my being I raise my voice to thank you, my Beloved.
I stand before you on the cusp of my destiny, my night long past.
Filled to overflowing, I sing my heart's thoughts to you.
Stars, angels, creatures, the sea and sand
All join to sing their tribute,
Praise echoes across eternity.
I dance under the sky painted in Yehovah's love.
May this offering fill your heart.

Eternal Remembrance of Love Before Paradise
Memorials
Formed of the land,
The Light, the heart, from a wound in the side.
Echoes of Adam,
Echoes from the cross.
The Cherished, The Rescue.
Found and rescued from the pit.
Cherished, rejoicing,
Embraced and kissed,
Together again.
Desperately needed hero, out of the filth

Love overcame.
Reclaimed from the filth,
Healed and housed.
The restoration, reunited.
A return to the father, in repentance and humility.
Welcomed in love and compassion,
Adorned as a prince.
Restoration to his first estate, his privileged position.
Living water, a path to eternity,
Desire and acceptance,
Eternal life and truth, the living water
Bubbling up from within.
Worship of Yehovah in spirit and truth.

Soul Sailing – Standing in Infinity
Leaving land behind, a freedom from anchors,
Sharp wind straining the sails, a path to unrestraint.
Rocking in the cadence, the joy of the ocean,
Sea spray mingled with sunshine on face, pure elation.
Enter into the vastness of sea, sky and air,
Endless blue, endless joy, endless Yehovah.
Cast away in time and space, vanished
In the breath of His nearness, awareness of His strength, His power.
Facing Yehovah in the enormity of His realms, without dimension,
I am small in the immensity, His unbounded presence.
I surrender my praise, my heart, my desires,
Magnified to fill the cosmos with the music and incense of offering.
I stand in infinity.

Lani sat down to enthusiastic cheers and clapping. Her story was the story of everyone. She lived up to her name and wove her story into the story of everyone. And intertwined their story into Yehovah's story. It was a story of what was and is. It was perfect.

The angels watching sang their praise for Yehovah.

When the noise settled down, Yehovah-Yeshua stood up to speak. The wild cheers, clapping and singing started up again. He bowed in acknowledgement and hushed the crowd to speak.

With eagerness, they strained to hear what their Beloved would have to say to them. "Thank you, my Beloved. You have honoured me greatly with your stories," and looking at Lani, "and your poems."

Yehovah-Yeshua warmly smiled and continued. "I've loved you before time and created you as my intended. I gave my life to make you my Beloved bride. I love you even more deeply for choosing me. You are beautiful, your heart overwhelms me."

Yehovah-Yeshua took in a deep breath and let out a sigh as though to clear His mind of His passion and focus on the commission. "It is now time for me to share what will come, my vision of what we will accomplish, and our mission on how we will achieve it."

22 | Life Calling

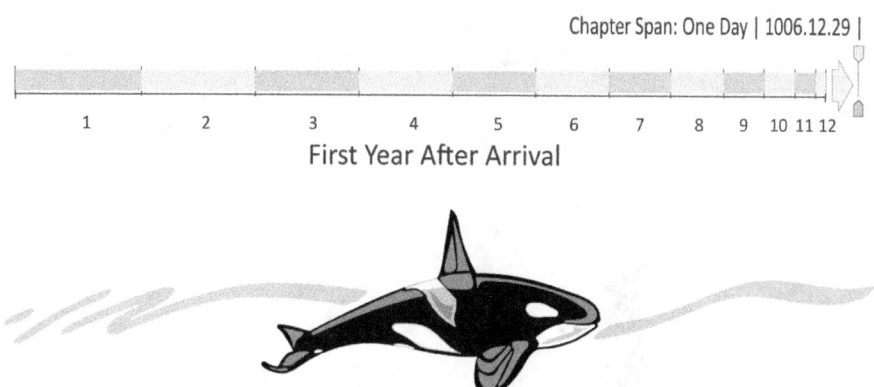

1   2   3   4   5   6   7   8   9   10 11 12

First Year After Arrival

A loud bark of excitement ruptured her thoughts and Lani was quickly brought out of her memories of a thousand years ago and back to real time, back to the here and now, back to daily life in paradise. She sat up to see Abbey charging down the beach toward her. She would be on her shortly with exuberant puppy kisses. And then she noticed Celebration approaching in the water. Life and her animals called her.

She still enjoyed the memories of her first anniversary and the day so long ago she spent here remembering and thinking. The honour stories on that anniversary came from everyone's heart. And the vision shared by Yehovah-Yeshua had been astounding. It laid out the thousand years to follow. The celebration had been a jubilant, emotional one.

Many anniversary celebrations passed since that first one, and Lani wove a great story for each one.

She would be heading off to this year's celebration shortly, but in the meantime would spend some time with Abbey and Celebration. They both danced and circled in anticipation of some playtime. They wouldn't leave her alone with her thoughts and memories any longer.

Lani got up from the warm sand, petted Abbey and said, "Okay, let's go swimming," and slipped into the warm ocean waters. Abbey didn't need to be invited twice. She bounded in and paddled out to Celebration. Lani gave her full attention to the laughing, swimming, water dancing and play. She gave herself to the joy of the day.

Memories of the rest of the story would have to wait for another time.

The End

What is Next

Prequel to Memory of Memories Coming Soon

The Flawless Life, a short story of a significant moment in Lani's life before her time in heaven will be released in the latter half of 2015. See www.se-renitymclean.com/books for more information. I will be giving away free copies during the first week of release. Sign up now for your copy when it comes available. Use the Stay In Touch panel on the right to sign up now.

Watch For Book Two

Lani's story continues in *The Omega Ages*, which will pick up from where *Memory of Memories* left off. Yehovah-Yeshua will share the Father's vision and mission for King Yeshua and His bride. It is the story of the preparation, development and implementation of the love project, and you will read about life during the 1,000 years of peace on earth under King Yeshua's reign.

Expect The Omega Ages to be released in 2016. If you would like to receive a pre-release bonus chapter visit www.serenitymclean.com/books for more information. Use the Stay In Touch panel on the right to sign up.

Message From Serenity

Thank you for reading my fictional and foggy view of what heaven will be like for those who choose to be the mate of Yehovah. What an amazing, exciting choice!

I want to stress this is just my imaginings. So much remains unknown. Contained in this book is just one possibility of what could be. I hope your imagination has been fired up and images of your piece of heaven now expand your thoughts of the afterlife.

Bonus Content

If you enjoyed the story, you can view posts with bonus content on my website, including a discussions on the book and additional stories of:

- The Stone Turtle
- The Backstory of the Creation Garden
- Water Tree Prophesy

at www.serenitymclean.com/bonus-content/. Use the password soulsailing to access.

Character Profiles

Adi'el, jewel of God (Adi)

Owns property in the hills of coloured stone. Helped Lani collect stone.

Long Past Background

Born of a prostitute in Bangladesh. Unloved. Raped. Prayed Yehovah would stand with her as He had done with Daniel in the lion's den. Died young in a typhoon.

Desire

Architect and designer.

First Year

Lani figures out the meaning of Adi's Entry Garden as the symbolic story of Daniel. Designs the Mayan village, and Sunrise Art Gallery and Studio for Lani.

Aha'La'anni, weaver of stories of what was, is, and is yet to come (Lani)

Main character of the book. Known as Lani, the creative or the weaver.

Long Past Background

Lived with mother and dogs at the time of reclamation. Spent many of her spare hours thinking of heaven. Longed for heaven.

Desire

To fulfill the prophesy of being a tree of shelter by waters of refreshing.

First Year

Developed the Mayan as a place of refreshing, provided opportunity for many to find their destiny, created and unveiled the series of love sculptures.

Asher, happy and blessed

Owns property in the hills of coloured stone.

Long Past Background

Son of an African tribal chief. Kidnapped and sold into slavery. Lost wife and children to yellow fever. Died of a beating.

Desire

Born to, then deprived of leadership. Inspired by Joseph, Asher hoped to rise above slavery, but life did not provide him the opportunity.

First Year

Selected the coloured stone for Lani's sculptures. Introduced Lani to Liora and the lightstones. First to spend time under the dome tree and leave remembrance stones. Prince and priest, a leader among the Ahuvati.

Aymoon, the faithful

Met Lani on the first day in the courtyard.

Long Past Background

A tall, handsome African male. He was the treasurer, a servant for the queen of Ethiopia. Worked for the man who met and was baptized by Philip. Studied the writings of Isaiah, the prophets, and apostles, and taught the young men under him.

Desire

To study, learn and share.

First Year

Takes Lani to the library. Shares the history of the eh-bed and the mockery Lucifer made of them. Teaches at Blue Rock.

Cheka, full of laughter

Met Lani on the first day in the courtyard.

Long Past Background

Lani's small and beautiful Samaritan friend, grew up with Dalit, the woman at the well. Met Yeshua during His three years of ministry. Learned under Philip, Peter and John.

Desire

To study and teach like the boys.

First Year

Teaches the mashqeh how to cook new recipes, creates unique Mayan recipes, brings joy and laughter to everyone.

Elia, one who rises

Met Lani on the beach, watching the eder fly up from the south.

Long Past Background

A drunkard member of the Bostonian country club set. Accidentally kills wife and children while driving drunk. Died young of cirrhosis.

Desire

To step up to his full purpose without regret and loss crippling him.

First Year

Rode the eder with Lani to Harmony Canyon. Teaches the eh-bed to captain the sailboats, and drive for waterskiing and wakeboarding. Lani's soul sailing buddy on the Surrendered.

Hanna, the graceful

Met Lani on the beach watching the eder fly up from the south.

Long Past Background

Born deformed in Scotland and given up by her family to an abbey. She strayed from her faith, but returned like the prodigal son to live in joy.

Desire

To dance in worship without the burden of deformity.

First Year

Rode the eder with Lani to Harmony Canyon. Has an Entry Garden of the prodigal son. Assigned to the worship project with Nan. Leads dance worship at concerts.

Honani, singer of songs (Nan)

Met Lani on the first day in the courtyard. Has an astounding singing voice.

Long Past Background

Polynesian. She sacrificed three children. Tone-deaf but once saved, sang to God every morning on the beach. Like Job she was given more children and many grandchildren.

Desire

To sing in a beautiful voice her praises.

First Year

Sings at Harmony Canyon and several sculpture unveilings. Opens Blue Rock Amphitheatre with several concerts. Organizes a worship sing-along. Assigned to the worship project.

Kazhu, the reliable (Kaz)

Met Lani on the first day in the courtyard.

Long Past Background

Very handsome Asian man born in China, raised in a Christian orphan mission. Much like Peter he denied his Christianity three times.

Desire

To be a man of faith, reliable, a rock like Peter.

First Year

Explains meaning of entry gardens. Leads and organizes all the construction for the Mayan village, and Sunrise Art Gallery and Studio.

Liora, light for me

Lives in the valley of the lightstones. Meets Lani through Asher.

Long Past Background

Born of Jewish parents that worshiped Molech. Was sacrificed as an infant.

Desire

Fulfill Yehovah's whispered promises.

First Year

First creative person to make use of Sunrise.

Remi'el, mercy or compassion of Yehovah

Met Lani at the First Gathering.

Long Past Background

Arab pastor in Hawaii. Records and publishes his messages on You-Tube. Lani and her mother always watched his videos and so knew of him, but never met.

Desire

To be found a good and faithful servant.

First Year

Begins teaching at Blue Rock and steps into his role of Yehovah's shepherd.

Shelomah, man of peace

Lani first hears Shelomah sing at Harmony Canyon with Nan, but didn't meet him until the First Gathering.

Long Past Background

Epileptic in Bedlam. Lived frustrated and humiliated by being put on show to the public who would taunt him to be entertained by watching his seizures.

Desire

Peace, freedom from torment.

First Year

Uses his beautiful voice to praise. Opens Blue Rock Amphitheatre with several concerts. Gives an enhanced holographic concert extravaganza called the Mayan Peace concert. Starts a choir.

Lani's Head Servants

Gilad, happy or good gardener – a ganan. Lani's head gardener.

Nectar, sweet and provider of nourishment – a mashqeh. Lani's cook.

Piper, leads with his pipe – a boqer. Lani's head herdsman.

Willow, slender, lithe, graceful – a naqod. Lani's head servant.

Minor Characters

Annikki, full of grace – helped to set up Blue Rock for enhanced holographic visuals and recordings. Provided training for the Jet Skis, boating and surfing.

Ario, air dancer – Lani's white horse.

Bayla, the beautiful – met Lani at the unveiling of the Good Samaritan sculpture and attended the First Gathering.

Bentley – Lani's big black horse of beautiful carriage.

Boz, swift and sure – Lani's male eder.

Celebration – the young orca Lani named, often swam with her.

Dalit, one who draws water – the woman at the well, formerly known as Susah, a young mare.

Eden, delight – helped to set up Blue Rock for enhanced holographic visuals and recordings. Provided training for Jet Skis, boating and surfing. Helped Adam create a digital art piece on Eden and heaven.

Eldad, beloved of Yehovah – formerly John Newton, the author of "Amazing Grace". Sang at the unveiling of the Mohar.

Eliana, my Lord responded – the white water rafting guide and trainer.

Elkanah, Yehovah has purchased – a messianic Jew Lani met at the first concert at Harmony Canyon.

Evron, bearing fruit – along with Gilam, figured out how to launch gliders and helped open Savannah Flying.

Gilam, joy of a country – along with Evron, figured out how to launch gliders and helped open Savannah Flying.

Jareo and Jalao – Lani's male and female lions.

Jarmo, lifted up by God – along with Lisi, the first to surf with the whales.

Keshet, rainbow of the gemstone hills – milkmaid orphan, desire for children. Raises Samuela.

Lisha, sweet, honest, truth – messianic Jew Lani met at the first concert at Harmony Canyon.

Lisi, promise of God – along with Jarmo, the first to surf with the whales.

Makani, lover of wind, steady and sure – Lani's female eder that flies her dog Abbey.

Matea, God's present – determined the rock face routes for climbing up Blue Cliff escarpment.

Sapphire – Lani's head female Ta'onka

Susah – The long past name of Dalit

Ta'onka – an elephant, only larger. The females are blue and the males are purpleskinned.

Yaara, sweet as honeysuckle – met Lani at the unveiling of the Good Samaritan sculpture and attended the First Gathering.

Glossary

Adonai – master, owner, sovereign ruler, exalted position.

Aha'Kaiya, my safe harbour – used by the mashqeh (the ones who prepare and serve food).

Aha'Mo'ee, my shelter – used by the boqer (herdsmen).

Aha'Qatsin, my chief – used by the ganan (gardeners).

Aha'Sarah, my princess – used by the naqod (principal servants).

Ahuvati, Beloved – what the reclaimed people have been transformed into. Aha'Ahuvati means my Beloved and is what Yehovah-Man calls His people, His spiritual mate. Ha'Ahuvati used by all to refer to Lani's race. It specifically states they are Yehovah's beloved mate.

Bene Ha'Elohim – fallen angels.

boqer – herdsmen.

eh-bed – a general term meaning servant.

eder – silently flying large birds with wings that transmit coloured light to the land below. Their call sounds like laughter. Lani has two called Boz and Makani.

Elohim – Yehovah's might, creative power, justice, rulership, sovereignty.

ganan – gardener.

Haga'at – arrival or touch and is the name of the anniversary feast.

hawyaw (Hayah) – Hebrew meaning to come to pass, become, be.

kiddushin – Hebrew meaning sanctified and set apart for a sacred purpose, to be the wife of a particular man.

LAT – low altitude transport.

Man-Yehovah – the new creature created within Christians, made to be a mate of Yehovah's own kind.

Mayan refers to Lani's property (mayan means oasis or spring of water).

mashqeh – cupbearer, refreshing, abundant provision.

Mayan – the name of Lani's property (mayan – oasis, spring of water).

Melchizedek – a title of respect that means king and priest in one being.

moed – Hebrew meaning appointed time, place, or meeting.

mohar – Hebrew meaning the price paid for a bride.

naqod – head servant.

nisuin – Hebrew meaning the elevation or consummation portion of the marriage.

qadosh – set apart for a special purpose.

Qatsin – chief.

Ruach (roo-akh) – the name of the Spirit aspect of Yehovah. It means air, breath, courage, exposed, heart, inspired, mind, points, Spirit, strength, thoughts, wind.

Tselem (zelem) – Hebrew meaning image.

Yashab (Yaw-shab) Hebrew word for consummate meaning abide, dwell, inhabit, enthrone, resident, seated, stay, wait.

Yeshua – Jewish pronunciation of Jesus, the human form of Yehovah.

Yehoshua – Yehovah is salvation.

Yehovah – the name of the God, the One who was, is, and will be. Used by people in relationship with God, those with whom He shares His heart. Spoken in love and respect. It also suggests His unerring morality. In the Bible where it says LORD (a title), the original Hebrew text stated His Name, YHVH pronounced Yehovah.

Yehovah-Man – Yeshua (Jesus), God in human form.

Ani shayakh le'ahuvati, ve'ahuvati shayekhet li – I belong to my Beloved, and my Beloved belongs to me.

About the Author

Serenity, born in Ontario, now lives in Western Canada. Like the main character Serenity spent many, many hours thinking about eternity and what it would be like.

She thought about writing a fictional book for awhile, but felt uninspired by any of her ideas. Then while sick in bed this story idea hit her out of the blue. It was so obvious, as the topic of the afterlife consumes her thoughts and reading.

As a "pantser" author (writing by the seat of her pants), she doesn't start with an outline, but simply writes the story. As the tale progressed, the life of the story, the storyline and characters took shape chapter by chapter. She met the characters chapter by chapter. In one chapter she thought one particular character would be Lani's best friend only to discover unexpected relations developed into close friendships in later chapters, quite the way life happens. You don't always know who will become your best friend.

You can read more about Serenity on her website www.serenitymclean.com.

The website shares Serenity's inspiration (music, images, links, readings and Bible verses) for each of her books. Sign up to be notified of new releases and access bonus content.

Visit her blog to read posts, including some from Abbey. Follow Serenity on Twitter as she tweets and exchanges thoughts about current events. Finally, connect with Serenity on her Facebook page.

Get in touch as she loves to talk about her books, current events and the prophetic timeline.

Blessings,

Serenity

Connect with Serenity:

Blog: serenitymclean.com/blog/

Twitter: @serenitymclean_ (note the underscore at the end)

Facebook: www.facebook.com/Serenityauthor

JD Farag

JD (Remi'el in the book) is actually a real person living in Kaneohe, Hawaii and is my online pastor. And yes, he really did change his name to JD, short for Jesus' Disciple. You can find him at www.youtube.com/user/alohabibleprophecy. He is a wonderfully honest and humble guy teaching on the entire Bible. He delivers an important message of hope in these days of global unrest and uncertainty. Each week he uploads videos from his Thursday Bible study, the Sunday service and the Prophesy Update to his YouTube channel (link above). All are great and well worth watching. If you are wondering *if* you are going to heaven, JD has a good news message for you.

The Good News of Salvation in Jesus Christ

The good news of salvation in Jesus Christ is also known as The Gospel, which means good news, your debt has been paid in full and you've been set free. However, in order for the good news to be good, there must also be bad news to make that good news good, thus we need the bad news first. So what's the bad news? Thankfully, the Bible is not silent concerning both the bad news and the good news.

The Bad News

Romans 3:10 As it is written: "There is no one righteous, not even one;

Romans 3:23 for all have sinned and fall short of the glory of God

Romans 5:12 Therefore, just as sin entered the world through one man, and death through sin, and in this way death came to all men, because all sinned-

Romans 6:23a For the wages of sin is death,

John 3:3 Jesus replied, "Very truly I tell you, no one can see the kingdom of God unless they are born again."

The Good News

Romans 6:23b ...but the gift of God is eternal life in Christ Jesus our Lord.

Romans 5:8 But God demonstrates his own love for us in this: While we were still sinners, Christ died for us.

Romans 10:9-10 ...if you confess with your mouth, "Jesus is Lord," and believe in your heart that God raised him from the dead, you will be saved. For it is with your heart that you believe and are justified, and it is with your mouth that you confess and are saved.

Romans 10:13 for, "Everyone who calls on the name of the Lord will be saved."

When you fully understand the bad news you'll want to hear the good news and call on the name of the Lord, confessing with your mouth that "Jesus is Lord," and believing in your heart that God raised Him from the dead. Then, if and when you do this, the Bible promises that you will be saved and have everlasting life.

John 3:16 For God so loved the world that He gave His only begotten Son, that whoever believes in Him should not perish but have everlasting life.

Here is an example of how you can call on the Lord and accept Jesus Christ's payment for your sin, which He paid for in full with His death on the cross and His resurrection from the dead:

"Dear Lord Jesus, I know I am a sinner. I believe in my heart that You died for my sins, and I confess with my mouth that you rose again from death. I accept you as my Lord and Savior. Thank You for saving me. Amen." Again, this is only an example of how you can call on the Lord and be saved. This is the most important decision you will ever make. When you make this decision, the Holy Spirit will indwell you and empower you to live a Holy life. Then, when He does, you will find that you no longer desire the things of your old life. Instead, you'll have a desire to read the Bible, which is the Word of God, and you'll also desire to go to church and fellowship with the people of God, this because you are now born again of the Spirit of God.

Thanks JD!
If you have accepted Jesus Christ's payment for your sins and now live with Him as your Lord and Saviour, both JD and I will see you in heaven! Remember no eye has seen, no ear has heard, nor has it entered into the imagination of any human the great things in store for those who belong to Him. Think big because it will be better than that!

Serenity